A PRINCE AND A SPY

A PRINCE
AND A SPY

RORY CLEMENTS

PEGASUS CRIME

NEW YORK LONDON

A PRINCE AND A SPY

Pegasus Crime is an imprint of
Pegasus Books, Ltd.
148 West 37th Street, 13th Floor
New York, NY 10018

ISBN: 978-1-64313-793-3

10 9 8 7 6 5 4 3 2 1

Printed in the United States of America
Distributed by Simon & Schuster
www.pegasusbooks.com

For George, with love

A PRINCE
AND A SPY

Chapter 1

Stockholm, 1942

Despite his reputation for wild living, the English prince had never been the most confident of men. He was nervous, his fingers and neck taut with apprehension and the burden of knowing the significance of this meeting. A meeting that must forever be kept secret.

He took his seat with the briefest of nods to his German cousin. No smile, for a smile might be seen as encouragement or collusion.

The German prince was less cautious, more sure of himself, and *did* offer a smile as he sat opposite his old friend. The two men had known and liked each other for many years but today there was to be no small talk, no comfortable conversation or warm, shared remembrances. Today they were enemies.

Their eyes met across the large table in a rather beautiful room with green silk walls and large paintings of long-dead royals from the days when Sweden was a great European power, and then they both looked away, like cats that cannot hold eye contact. The English prince studied the high ceiling and found himself counting the gilded crenellations on the cornice. He waited.

They were here in this room with only two others present – one aide for each man – with a single purpose: discovery.

What did the other man want? What could he offer?

Summer light streamed down on them from a tall window. Outside, the afternoon was hot, but here in this chamber in the heart of Drottningholm Palace, on the eastern shore of Lovön island in the forest-fringed Lake Mälar seven miles to the west of central Stockholm, there was a definite chill. The English prince shivered.

The flying boat that had brought him here was moored in a large lake several miles further west, well away from populated areas where it might draw attention. He and his closest aides had made the final leg of their gruelling and secret journey in an anonymous motor-launch.

No one from the Swedish royal family had been here to greet them; they could not be involved in this other than to allow the princes the use of this palace, a splendid eighteenth-century building said to have been inspired by Versailles but with its own distinctive Nordic flavour, with stucco exterior walls of smoky yellow.

Apart from the scraping of chairs, the only sound was birdsong, muffled and distant. The air was still, fresh and lightly perfumed by the wax polish administered to the table and chairbacks by maidservants that morning.

As the two princes settled in there was an awkward silence between them, such that one might wonder whether either man would ever break it. At last the German, Philipp von Hessen, spoke. 'We both want the same thing, Georgie – peace. Is that not so? Is that not the desire of the whole civilised world? Peace in Europe?'

'This is not about what *we* want, Philipp. The question is, what does your friend want?'

'My friend?'

'I wouldn't be here if I didn't know how close you have become to Hitler.' The English prince, easily the more handsome and imposing of the two cousins, chose his words with utmost care. His purpose could be so easily misunderstood, both here in this room and – if word of this meeting were ever to leak – in other places.

The German prince stiffened, almost imperceptibly. 'Of course, we know each other . . .'

'Some say you are his only true friend. His sounding board and his go-between.'

'You make it sound like an insult.'

'Little Otto's godfather, isn't he?'

Philipp confected another smile. 'I have many friends. I thought *you* were my friend, Georgie. That is why I agreed to meet you. All I can tell you is that the Führer is prepared to listen to what you have to say. I am his ears.' He spoke perfect English; he had after all been sent to school in the south of England three decades earlier and had been back and forth in the intervening years.

'But *you* requested this meeting, Phli.' Phli – or *Flea* – that was the nickname the extended family had used for Philipp since childhood. 'I assumed you had something to say, something to impart.' Prince George had not returned his royal cousin's smile. He could not afford ambiguity. His mind kept returning to the sensitivity surrounding this meeting; just one misplaced word, one misinterpreted expression might cause untold harm.

This was too delicate. There must be no suggestion that he had come to this place seeking any sort of accommodation with the Nazis. This was a recce mission, nothing more. There must be no misapprehension on that score.

'Georgie? Talk to me. Tell me what you want. What does your brother want, for pity's sake? You wouldn't have come unless you wanted something.'

Prince George, Duke of Kent, brother of the King of England, did not respond. He could have shaken his head and said 'that's not so,' but instead he just waited. He turned his head away; the grand fireplace in his line of vision had a gilt ormolu clock on the mantelpiece and he noted the time. How long should he allow this meeting to last? Ten minutes? Perhaps fifteen? Certainly no more than that. It would not do to seem keen to prolong the engagement.

Philipp and George were great-grandsons of Queen Victoria. In their scandalous, hedonistic youth, they had both exuded glamour and danger, but things were different now. There had been tales of women, of intimate relationships with men, of drugs and alcohol and scandalous parties. But for George those days were long gone. He might be diffident, but at least he had a maturity about him while his cousin, once beloved of poets and artists, still seemed not to have grown up. And there was something else that George noticed in his cousin – an air of tired desperation. The face that had once charmed men and women alike was pinched and diminished. Perhaps Hitler's charms were wearing thin; perhaps the aristocratic Philipp no longer felt secure among the lower-class thugs of the Third Reich.

'Then so be it, Georgie – I will *tell* you what you want as you seem so reluctant to say the words. You want to make an honourable peace with Germany. This week's events in northern France must have shown you that you have an empire to lose and nothing to gain by continuing this war. Your situation is hopeless. Damn it, you couldn't even hold on to Singapore. India will be next, then Australia – your colonies will fall like ninepins. So join us, Georgie – join us, save the British Empire and crush the bloody Bolsheviks.'

'Is that what Hitler wants, a joint effort against the Soviets? He needs England, does he?'

'You are twisting my words. Germany doesn't *need* England. But many of us have great affection for our old friends across the North Sea. We want to save you from unnecessary pain and destruction. We want you to keep your great empire. Imagine a federal Europe with German armies of the west and north returned to their pre-war stations, France and parts of the Low Countries back to their pre-war borders, all protected from the Asiatic hordes by a greater German Reich. Relations with Japan could be broken off with benefit to us all. We are natural allies – you know we are.'

'It sounds to me as though your friend is frantic to do a deal with us so that he can divert his western divisions to the East.'

A shaft of sunlight crossed over Philipp's eyes and he blinked rapidly. 'That is not so. He is conquering the world – you know he is. He is Attila, Tamburlaine, Alexander and Napoleon. No one can stop him.'

'Napoleon didn't fare so well in Russia.'

'Now you are being trivial. The advance on Stalingrad and the siege of Leningrad are just mopping-up operations.'

'Then why is he seeking an accommodation with England?'

'He has always loved your country. Read his book: it tells you everything you need to know about his aims. He wishes to share the spoils, nothing more. Has Germany not offered an olive branch already by cutting back on its bombing raids on your cities – even though provoked by your own raids?'

'That's not an olive branch, Phli, that's strategic necessity – Goering needs the Luftwaffe in the East.'

'Not so, Georgie – not so.'

'So it's an act of altruism by Adolf? Be nice to the poor little Brits?' Prince George smiled at last, then glanced again at the clock and laughed quietly as he rose from his chair at the table. 'Thank you, Phli, you have told me everything I wanted to know.'

'I have told you nothing!'

'Oh, I rather think you have. All except his terms – and you haven't even asked what Britain's terms might be. Your Luftwaffe has done much damage. It would have to be paid for. We wouldn't even agree a temporary ceasefire without the guarantee of substantial reparations.'

'Georgie, now you are making fun of me!'

'And you are trying to take me for a fool, Phli.'

'Georgie, Georgie, I beg you, don't throw away this chance. There will not be another. If you do not make peace, then he will crush you utterly – and neither of us can desire that. Please, let us meet again this evening. Perhaps over some supper and wine. Just the two of us.' He swept his left arm wide to indicate his proposed dismissal of their aides.

Prince George, Duke of Kent, hesitated. 'I don't know.'

'We can talk about old times. I want to know about your family – Marina, the children, the new baby. We have more in common than separates us, Georgie. Much more. It has to be worth preserving.'

'Just the two of us?'

'You and me. Like old times.'

Behind them, the eyes of their aides met. Philipp von Hessen did not notice.

At first Tom Wilde failed to recognise the young man. He looked older, wore a rather ragged military moustache and was in army uniform. Wilde smiled briefly and nodded, as you do when you're alone in a railway carriage and someone new comes in.

'Good evening,' Wilde said and returned to his newspaper.

The young man grunted, then slumped into a seat in the far corner by the window, delved into a khaki service bag and pulled out a tin of sweets. He lifted the lid and popped one in his mouth, then offered the tin to Wilde.

'Fruit drop, professor?'

Wilde looked up, astonished at being addressed by his title. He was about to ask how the officer knew him when he realised he was acquainted with the young soldier. 'Ah, it's you, Caze-rove – sorry, I didn't recognise you under the moustache. And thanks for the offer, but no to the sweet.'

'I imagine you'd prefer a Scotch. You always did, as I recall.'

'Do you have some then?'

'Afraid not.'

It was the last train of the day. The blackouts were secured and the train pulled out of Liverpool Street at a crawl. Wilde was surprised by Peter Cazerove's shabby appearance; he had been one of the more sharply dressed undergraduates, if not the most diligent.

'Changed a lot, have I, Professor Wilde?'

'Oh, you know, my mind was elsewhere, that's all. Still used to seeing you in your civvy bags and gown.'

'You look pretty much the same. Still at the old college, I suppose.'

'Indeed.' He wasn't going to tell this man that he was now engaged full-time working in Grosvenor Street for the Office of Strategic Services – or OSS – the newly formed American intelligence agency. This journey back to Cambridge was a rare break from a hectic schedule. He was longing to see Lydia and their two-year-old son Johnny for the first time in two months. He wanted Lydia badly. Even after six years together, the fire still burned. 'As I recall, Cazerove, you had plans to go back to your old school to teach.'

'That was always the idea. I did a year, then duty called.'

'Athelstans, wasn't it? War's buggering up a lot of careers.'

'Quite.'

'No time for sixteenth-century studies either, I suppose?'

'Oh, I read a little now and then.'

'I remember you were always rather interested in the French side of things. Henry of Navarre, Catherine of Medici, House of Guise . . .'

Cazerove smiled weakly. 'Debauchery, incest and poison, you mean?'

'Well, yes, they did indulge in quite a lot of that.'

It was clear they would have the carriage to themselves. The journey was certain to be long and gruelling at this time of night, the train stopping at every small out-of-the-way station en route, and so conversation was unavoidable, which was irritating. Wilde had had a long day of meetings, including a four-hour session with Lord Templeman and other senior MI5 and MI6 men on the practicalities of sharing information and ensuring the American and British secret services did not cross wires. 'You shall share our secrets,' Churchill had promised John Winant when he arrived as ambassador. Well, Templeman had been supremely accommodating; nothing would be too much trouble when it came to keeping their allies from across the pond in the loop. Wilde had listened with scepticism. He had had enough dealings with Britain's spies to know that they were about as trustworthy as a pride of lions babysitting infant wildebeest. But that was all in the past; they *had* to work together now, for the duration at least.

Here on this train, he was exhausted and wanted nothing but to travel home in silence, perhaps nod off for an hour and then, when he was home, drink a couple of whiskies with Lydia and retire with her to bed. Unfortunately the presence of Cazerove made silence impossible. Reluctantly he folded up his day-old copy of *The Times* and placed it on the seat at his side, looked up at his former student and prepared to make small talk. 'So tell me, how have you been keeping?'

'Do you really want to know?'

'Yes, of course, that's why I asked. Haven't seen you for, what is it, four years?'

Cazerove took another sweet from his tin. 'OK then, here goes. I'm the loneliest man in the world, professor. Broken. There. That just about sums it up.'

This wasn't what he expected to hear. For a moment, he was stunned into silence. 'I'm sorry to hear it,' he said at last.

'Well, you did ask.'

'Indeed, yes, I did.'

'So there you are.'

Wilde realised he was supposed to delve deeper. His former undergraduate badly wanted to get something off his chest. 'What is it, Cazerove? Girl trouble, perhaps? This wretched war? You're not alone, you know – these things get a lot of men down.' Wilde was embarrassed by his platitudes even as he uttered them, but what else was there to say? He was responding to an unanticipated outburst; usually people said they were fine, thank you, however badly things were going. 'Mustn't grumble, old man, we're all in the same boat.' That was the British way.

'Girl trouble, professor? Not in the way you mean it.'

Wilde tried to offer a sympathetic smile. But he was disturbed. He didn't like this encounter one bit and wondered where the conversation was going. Things happened on trains, and not all of them good.

'Do you want to talk about it? Not really my business, of course, but I'm a fairly good listener.'

Cazerove returned the smile, but it was still utterly humourless. He was, thought Wilde, a curious specimen. A strong, athletic face, quite handsome but certainly not in the movie-star mould. He wore a lieutenant's two pips, which was about right for his age – what, twenty-five or so? At Cambridge, he had not always been easy to teach because he had strong preconceived notions about history that were difficult to reconfigure. He was also a bit full of himself, as were so many of the scions of landed gentry that Wilde had encountered during his years in England; he certainly hadn't been one of the undergraduates that Wilde warmed to and nor did he expect him to achieve much. That wouldn't harm his prospects for a life of wealth and ease, however, because his family owned vast tracts of land in Norfolk, he recalled.

And as an old boy from Athelstans, he was most likely a member of the Athels. They tended to consider themselves the most elite and ancient of societies – both in Cambridge and elsewhere – and looked after each other. War or no war, the old boy network was here to stay.

That said, Cazerove had done enough to earn a 2:2.

'You'll hate me, professor,' the younger man said. 'You will loathe and despise me and spit on me. I was an arrogant and thoughtless young fool, conditioned to do the bidding of others, and I have paid a terrible price. Worse, my country has paid a terrible price . . .'

Once again, Wilde was caught off guard by the young man's vehemence. 'You're making it sound very dramatic.'

'I've just killed hundreds of men. Thousands, perhaps – I don't know the exact figure.'

Wilde couldn't help frowning. What had Cazerove just said? 'I'm sorry? You're losing me.'

'Killed in cold blood. Never stood a chance, poor blighters.'

'What?'

'Operation Jubilee. Lambs to the slaughter. The Germans were waiting for us.'

'You'd better start again, Cazerove. I'm not sure what you're saying.' A chill was shuddering down Wilde's spine, and he was beginning to think a slug of Scotch might be rather a good idea.

Cazerove was silent for a few moments. He was looking at Wilde, but his focus was elsewhere; his eyes were heavy.

'You know what I'm talking about, Mr Wilde.'

'Jubilee. That's the raid in northern France, isn't it? Didn't do badly, did we?' In fact, Wilde knew otherwise, but the population at large certainly didn't.

Cazerove snorted. 'You must know better than that. It was a bloody disaster. Hundreds of Allied troops killed, thousands injured or captured. Ships lost, a hundred planes shot out of the sky.'

'That's not what the BBC has been saying.'

'Well, they wouldn't, would they?'

'And you believe the Germans were waiting for us.' Wilde picked up his copy of *The Times*. 'Here,' he said, flicking through the paper, then stabbing his forefinger at an editorial column, 'page eight – it says quite clearly the enemy was taken by surprise.'

'That's bull, professor. Propaganda.'

'OK, so if I accept your version, Cazerove, perhaps you'll explain how you blame yourself for the debacle – if that's what it was. With all due respect, you seem to be a rather junior lieutenant. I imagine the decision to stage the raid was taken by men a great deal higher up the chain of command than you.'

'You don't know the half of it. It wasn't even the worst thing I've done.'

'Do you want to enlighten me?'

'You'll hear soon enough.'

'What? What will I hear?'

Cazerove shrugged, then slumped back into his corner and closed his eyes.

The train chugged on slowly into the night. Every now and then it waited an age at a darkened station platform, but no one seemed to get on or off. Wilde was rather glad that Cazerove had brought the conversation to an abrupt end, but he was also disturbed by what he had said. Sighing, he picked up his copy of *The Times* and turned back to the crossword. He had almost finished it and realised they must be approaching the end of the journey when some instinct made him glance across at Cazerove. Tears were flowing down his cheeks.

'Cazerove?'

He blinked furiously and wiped a sleeve across his eyes. 'Sorry.'

'I wish I could help.'

'No one can. I told them, professor. I told the Germans that we were coming. Date, time, numbers, battle plan, air deployment. The whole shooting match. That's why they were waiting – that's why our boys were shot to pieces.'

Wilde was aghast. 'Are you serious?'

'Deadly.'

'But how would you even have had such information?'

'Didn't I mention? I'm on attachment to the War Office.'

'Ah.' This was serious. 'Yes, I see. But if you inadvertently let some bit of information slip, I'm not the person you need to talk to. Go to your immediate superior, Cazerove. Face the music.'

'I followed *you*, Professor Wilde. I had no one else to talk to. You're American.'

'What's that got to do with it?'

'I haven't betrayed *you*.' Cazerove delved once more into his bag where his fruit drops were stowed. In the dim carriage light, Wilde saw him place a sweet on his tongue. He smiled strangely.

'Then tell me more.'

'That's the problem. I can't. I thought I could talk to you, but now that it comes to it, I simply can't. And northern France was just the beginning. Today was worse.'

'Today? What happened today?'

He gave a half-hearted shrug, as though he were almost past caring. 'If you don't know already, you'll discover soon enough . . . tomorrow.'

'We're almost in Cambridge. Where are you staying, Cazerove? Why don't you come home with me? Lydia will make up a bed for you – and we can talk in the morning when we've both had a good night's sleep. I know one or two people who may be able to advise you.'

Cazerove shook his head slowly and the corners of his lips creased into a smile of eternal sadness. 'An oath is sacred, isn't it? That's what the Athels always say. But which is more binding, professor – a vow of silence or a declaration of love?'

'They shouldn't come into conflict. But you'll really have to make yourself clearer, Cazerove. I'm afraid you're losing me again.'

'I'm sorry . . . there's so much worse to come.'

He bit down on the sweet, but it sounded more like crunching glass than the hard sugar of a fruit drop. For a few moments, he gazed on Wilde with a beatific expression, as though he were already in a higher place. 'I didn't want to die alone,' he whispered. His head fell forward.

'Cazerove?' Wilde suspected instantly what was happening.

The young officer collapsed sideways across the bench seat, a long groan of pain emerging from the depths of his tortured body, then a last exhalation of air from his lungs. Wilde moved towards him, trying to help. He cradled Cazerove's head, but there was nothing to be done. His lips were still set in that strange smile. His eyes bulged and bled cherry red.

A faint, bitter whiff of almonds caught Wilde's nostrils.

Chapter 2

Rupert Weir, police surgeon, examined the body, then stood back and gazed at it dispassionately. 'Prussic acid, almost certainly, but we'll have to get the forensics boys on the case to be sure.'

'It was very quick.'

'That's the point. That's why people take it. You'll need to give the police a full statement, Tom. Clearly suicide from what you say, but the method raises a few difficult questions. Where did he get a hydrogen cyanide pill? Can't buy them off the shelf at Jesse Boot's.'

Indeed, it had occurred to Wilde that poison capsules tended to be specially created for secret agents. The sort of thing the OSS would be handing out to its operatives behind enemy lines when it became fully operational in the near future. Useful for a quick exit when the unpleasant prospect of slow, agonising death at the hands of the Gestapo was the only alternative.

Weir yawned and loosened his tie. As always, winter or summer, he was wearing one of his signature tweed suits. 'Hell of a day. I'm wiped out, Tom.'

'Me too. All I want is home and bed.' He put a hand on his old friend's shoulder. 'And perhaps a small dram.'

'Good plan. By the way, do you have any information about poor Cazerove's next of kin?'

'Yes, I can help with that. His people are prosperous farmers, somewhere between Downham Market and Swaffham. The college will have details on file.'

Weir nodded towards the two policemen standing outside the carriage. 'The body's all yours, Sergeant Talbot. Get it to the mortuary at Addenbrooke's in the first instance, and I'll contact Scotland Yard about further tests.' He turned back to Wilde. 'By the way, the rest of the fruit drops in the tin seem like regular sweets, so he probably wasn't trying to poison you when he offered them to you. But I'll have them analysed anyway, just to be sure. Do you want to go to the nick and give a statement now?'

'I'd rather leave it until morning. Lydia will be waiting up for me.'

'Tomorrow morning will be fine, sir,' the sergeant said. 'I'll let them know you're coming in.'

'Thank you.'

'Come on then,' Weir said. 'Let's get you home.'

They walked down the platform with the sergeant, leaving the constable with the train guard to look after the body and organise its removal. Once more, Wilde went over the story of his journey with Cazerove, adding details as he remembered them.

As they passed the barrier, the concourse was empty save for a couple of members of staff. But then Wilde noticed a man standing outside the waiting room, which was closed for the night. He had his hands in his pockets and his dark, deep-set eyes had been following their movements. Something about him interested Wilde. 'One moment, Rupert,' he said and approached the man, who instantly made as if to back away. Wilde stayed him with a hand to his arm.

'Are you waiting for someone?' Wilde said.

The man was in his early twenties and he wasn't an impressive specimen, little more than five feet tall. He had the gaunt look of someone whose growth had been stunted by childhood malnutrition. Bow-legged like a jockey and with the pinched cheekbones of a rickets sufferer. He looked up at Wilde. 'Are you a copper?'

'No, why?'

'Well, your mate is, that's why.' He inclined his head towards the uniformed sergeant. 'Something happened, has it, mister?'

'A man died on the train. Were you waiting for him?'

'What man? How did he die?' The thin, reedy voice ratcheted up a couple of notches.

'You are answering my questions with questions of your own.'

'Well, I don't know who you sodding are, do I?'

'I'm Thomas Wilde, a professor here in Cambridge. Who are you?'

'You said a man died, who was it?'

'First *your* name.'

The young man hesitated, then mumbled a word. It sounded like 'Mortimer' to Wilde, but he wasn't sure he had heard correctly.

'Mortimer? Is that your name?'

'Call me what you sodding like.'

'Does the name Cazerove mean anything to you? Peter Cazerove?'

The young man shook his head, but his skin had turned a shade paler. His sharp, furtive eyes glanced past Wilde to where the large, tweed-clad form of Rupert Weir was coming their way. Without a word, the young man ducked down out of Wilde's reach and slid along the wall, then hurried towards the station exit. Wilde considered chasing him, but wasn't sure there was any point, so let him go.

'What was that, Tom?' Weir asked.

'I think he was waiting for Peter Cazerove. Taxi driver, perhaps?' He turned to Sergeant Talbot. 'Have you seen that lad before? He said his name was Mortimer.'

Talbot shook his head. 'No. Not a member of the Cambridge criminal fraternity to my knowledge – but from the way he scarpered when he saw me approaching, I think it's fair to assume he doesn't like bobbies.'

'My thought too. Very odd. He seemed to have a vaguely West Country accent.'

'I'll ask the lads down at the station. Easy one to describe, that boy. Someone might know him.'

As they drove slowly from the railway station through the darkened streets of Cambridge, Wilde recalled what Cazerove had said to him and posed the question to Weir. 'Cazerove referred to something in the news, something worse than the disastrous French raid. Has there been some kind of big event today, Rupert? I've been up to my eyes in meetings, paperwork and operational planning, so I'm afraid I've rather blanked the outside world.'

'Big event, Tom? The world is ablaze with big events.' Rupert Weir sat comfortably in the driver's seat, his belly propped against the steering wheel as he manoeuvred the Wolseley through the centre of town. As a police surgeon, he divided his time between his work as family doctor and police work whenever they needed him to examine a corpse or wanted to determine whether someone had been driving drunk. The hours were long and he looked as tired as Wilde felt.

'Something out of the ordinary.'

'It's all out of the ordinary. I long for the return of ordinary.'

Wilde was dropped at Cornflowers, the old house he shared with Lydia Morris, the love of his life and mother of his son. He had offered Rupert Weir a nightcap, but the offer was declined. 'I need my bed, Tom. Let's talk tomorrow after you've called in at St Andrew's Street.'

Lydia was sleepy-eyed and clad in a dressing gown as she opened the door. Without a word, she sank into Wilde's arms. They kissed and his hands strayed inside the gown, finding warm flesh. Then he stood back. 'Look at you,' he said, 'more beautiful than ever.'

'Smooth-talking bastard.'

He laughed, then hauled his suitcase over the threshold and followed her through to the sitting room. It was a cool late August evening. A standard lamp glowed above the armchair where he knew she would have been curled up like a cat, reading a novel.

'A drink, my master?'

'Just the one, and then bed. How's the boy?'

'Johnny's fine. Sleeps through the night then talks non-stop. All day long he's been saying "Daddy come, Daddy come". He'll be all over you in the morning. Anyway, what kept you?'

As Lydia poured two whiskies, Wilde told her about the incident on the train and Cazerove's despair and guilt over the disastrous Dieppe raid and some other 'big event'.

'Peter Cazerove?' she said, frowning as she handed Wilde his glass. 'Did I ever meet him?'

'You did, but you probably won't recall it. I invited him home for supper, but there were half a dozen other undergraduates along too. It wasn't a very memorable evening and Cazerove was rather quiet, I think.'

'Perhaps I do vaguely remember him. A bit stiff but very dapper?'

'That sounds about right.'

'It's all coming back to me. Wasn't he a rather effete young man?'

'Not a word I'd use for him. Bumptious, maybe. A bit aloof. He was an Athel – and they're all a bit like that.'

'Oh yes, the Athels. Rather austere lot, a bit like Jesuits in that.'

'Yes, that probably sums them up. But he wasn't like that tonight.'

'Did you like him, Tom?'

'Shouldn't speak ill of the dead, but frankly, no, I didn't. But then I don't think I've ever liked any of the Athelstans crew. Unpleasantly cliquey – seem to think themselves a cut above the rest of us. As an American who loves England, your snobbish elitism is one of the things that always left me cold.'

'*My* snobbish elitism?'

'Well, not yours personally, but you know what I mean.'

'Do I? Oh dear.'

'All those bloody clubs in Pall Mall whose sole purpose is to keep out the plebs. The Apostles here in Cambridge with their silly secrecy – even though everyone knows who they are. And then there are the Athels, who look on the Apostles as upstarts.'

She laughed. 'Says the man from bloody Harrow!'

Wilde couldn't help laughing too. 'Are you suggesting I'm a snob?'

She kissed his cheek. 'You tell me.'

'Well, I hope not, but yes, there were some arrogant bastards there. Some were downright cruel – but I've told you this before, haven't I? It was survival of the fittest and so I became a boxer. If I hadn't, I might have gone under.'

'And on the subject of privilege and discrimination, what about this university that employs you? I believe they're still insisting that women are not clever enough to be granted degrees.'

'Quite. That, too.'

'Got it all off your chest now, have you, darling?'

'Sorry, it's been one hell of an evening.'

'Well then, sink your whisky. You know I've got nothing on under this dressing gown, don't you?'

'I had noticed . . . you're shameless, Miss Morris.'

'Then what are you going to do about it, Mr Wilde?'

Chapter 3

Wilde woke at 7 a.m. to the distant sound of the telephone ringing and dragged himself downstairs to the hall, but Lydia had beaten him to it.

'Hang on, he's here.' She held out the handset to him.

'Hello?'

'Ah, Professor Wilde, it's Terence Carstairs here. I have been asked to inform you, sir, that Mr Eaton will be with you in the next hour or so.'

'Eaton? Coming here?' Wilde could not disguise his lack of enthusiasm for the message.

'Indeed, sir.'

'Any vague clue as to the purpose of his visit?'

'I'm afraid I can't help you with that, sir. Good day, professor.'

The phone went dead. Wilde held the handset for a few moments longer, as though it might yet impart some information, then replaced it on the stand by the front door.

'What was that, Tom?'

'Philip Eaton's on his way.'

'Oh dear, that always means trouble. Well, come into the kitchen and say hello to your son. He's been screaming for you this past hour. I've had the devil of a job preventing him from going upstairs and jumping on your head.'

Johnny was in his high chair wolfing down a bowl of porridge. As soon as he saw his father, he bounced up and down and burst into a fit of giggles. Wilde plucked him from his wooden throne and gave him a kiss on the forehead and a hug. In return, he received a splodge of the boy's breakfast on his pyjama jacket.

Wilde laughed, gave him another kiss and plonked him back in his chair.

The room smelt of brewing coffee, and Lydia held up the pot. 'Well?'

'You have such a thing as real coffee?'

'Reserved for days such as this when my man comes home and performs his nuptial duties with aplomb.'

'Well, that's quite an endorsement. Thank you. Real coffee would be perfect.'

'I imagine you get the proper stuff all the time at Grosvenor Street.'

'Classified information, I'm afraid.'

'That's what the diplomatic pouch is for, isn't it – coffee and hooch from the Americas. Anyway, we have rationing here, so I've only got one egg and it's for Johnny.'

'As is only right and proper. I'll be very happy with toast and Marmite. A little butter, too, if we have such a luxury.'

'You are a very demanding man.'

'As I recall, you were quite demanding yourself last night.'

'Can we stop the dirty talk now? There are young ears in attendance.' She laughed and ruffled Wilde's hair, then kissed his cheek. 'Here,' she said, sliding a newspaper in front of him on the kitchen table. 'You might want to take a look at this.'

Wilde glanced at the front page and the hairs on his neck prickled. DUKE OF KENT KILLED IN CRASH ran the headline in large type. The story was dated just before midnight and carried an official statement:

The Air Ministry deeply regrets to announce that Air Commodore HRH the Duke of Kent was killed on active service in the afternoon when a

Sunderland flying boat crashed in the north of Scotland. His Royal Highness, who was attached to the Staff of the Inspector-General of the Royal Air Force, was proceeding to Iceland on duty. All the crew of the flying boat lost their lives.

'Good God.'

'I thought you might be interested.'

'This . . .' he began.

'. . . is a big event.'

'Could this really be what Cazerove was referring to, Lydia? Look here.' He indicated the strapline at the top of the page. 'It makes it clear the news wasn't announced until just before midnight. How would Cazerove have known?'

She shrugged and poured two coffees.

'I suppose the War Office would have been informed hours earlier,' he muttered, half to himself.

'I know no more than you, darling.'

Wilde grunted. 'It's difficult not to draw conclusions.'

Eaton turned up at ten past eight. He told Wilde he had been chauffeured up from London by a ministry driver and had barely slept. Wilde offered his sympathy then ushered both men indoors.

Lydia took the driver off to the kitchen to be fed tea and toast, leaving Wilde in the sitting room with Eaton. Wilde was concerned to see that the MI6 man did not seem to be moving at all well. His left leg had been shattered in a road incident more than three years earlier, and he had lost his left arm, but the last time the two men had met, at Christmas, his physical health had been improving.

'Eaton, how are you doing?'

'Don't worry about me, Wilde. Bit stiff from the drive, that's all. Cooped up in the passenger seat for two and a half hours.'

'Well, spread yourself out on the sofa. Now, tell me, what does MI6 want with a Cambridge professor of history this fine summer's day?'

Eaton lowered himself gingerly into the soft cushions and breathed a sigh of relief. 'Ah, that's better. God knows why car seats can't be made as comfortable as a decent sofa.'

'Well?'

'Oh, I think you must have a fair idea why I'm here, Wilde.'

'Events on the train from London last night, is that what you mean?'

'Of course.'

'Then how in God's name are you here so quickly?'

'Ah, yes, well, that was the poison capsule. The local plod panicked, called the Yard, who immediately involved Special Branch. From there it was a short hop to Five – and then I got a 2 a.m. call from Dagger Templeman, who recalled my connection to you. He asked me to nip up here to see what was going on. It's possible you have stumbled into something significant, Wilde.'

'I didn't *stumble* into anything. Cazerove sought me out. He wanted to tell me something – but in the end he couldn't bring himself to do it. Found it easier to die than break some "sacred oath". At least I think that's what he called it.' He noticed Eaton nodding as though he quite understood Cazerove's point of view. Such was the effect of the English public school system, Wilde supposed. Loyalty and duty above all else. 'Anyway,' he continued. 'You still haven't explained why you're here.'

'Oh, I just wanted to hear exactly what Cazerove said to you. Some clue as to why he killed himself.'

'I told the police everything.'

'I'd like it from the horse's mouth. In particular, did he mention any names?'

Wilde began pacing around the room, aware of Eaton's eyes following him. He stopped and met the MI6 man's gaze. 'There were no names.'

'Are you certain?'

'Absolutely. He told me he had been seconded to the War Office. I suppose that means he had access to secrets. Is that why you're worried?'

Eaton held up his hand, palm forward. 'Forgive me, Wilde, I'm here to listen not talk.'

Wilde snorted. 'Same old Eaton. Gather information, reveal nothing. Well, my friend, we're in the same business now – so if you want something from me, I'll want something back.'

'Damn it, Wilde. You still owe me, you know.'

Wilde was well aware of his unpaid debt to Eaton for getting an extremely vulnerable young woman to safety against all the rules, but this might not be the time to settle it. 'I'm not denying it,' he said. 'But last night I spent a very uncomfortable couple of hours with a former undergraduate who then ended it all with some sort of poison pill. Right in front of my very eyes. Forgive me if I'm feeling a little brittle this morning.'

Lydia arrived with fresh coffee and they heard wailing from Johnny in the background.

'Your boy, I suppose. What is he now, two?'

'Getting on for two and a half.'

'Who does he take after?'

'Oh, Lydia's good looks and my reckless stupidity. What do you want me to say? Anyway, stop changing the subject. Yes, I owe you a favour, but as you know I am now working for the OSS, so I have other loyalties and oaths of silence. However, I can see no good reason not to tell you everything that passed between Cazerove and me – and in return I think a little cooperation on your part is also called for. Fair enough?'

'Message received.'

'Here goes then.' Wilde started at the beginning and went through the story of the train journey yet again. 'And that's about it,' he said finally. 'If anything else occurs to me, I'll let you know. But I repeat, there were no names mentioned. So tell me – is there really anything in his astonishing claim that he tipped off the Germans about the Dieppe raid?'

'Absolute tosh. Cazerove would have known very little about the attack. Anyway, the Hun has been waiting for something of the sort for weeks now, so of course they were prepared. They didn't need information from a junior British officer.'

'But it was a disaster.'

'Yes, Wilde, it was an utter fuck-up. It was poorly planned and doomed to failure all along. Churchill and the chiefs of staff knew there was no chance of success, but they needed a show – a rehearsal for the day we embark on a full-scale invasion. Damned unfair on the poor bastards who laid their lives on the line in an unwinnable venture.'

Eaton's summation left a bitter taste, which Wilde attempted to wash away with a mouthful of coffee. It was weak, but at least it was coffee. 'So Cazerove's guilt . . .'

'The man was a fantasist.'

'That doesn't mean he was innocent.'

Eaton shrugged.

'Anyway,' Wilde said, knowing he was going to get nowhere with specific questions. 'Ask away. I'll tell you everything I know.'

'I told you, I just want to know exactly what was said. A young soldier killing himself with a poison pill has to be investigated. You can see that, can't you, Wilde?'

'What about the other thing – his insistence that something else was looming?'

'Most likely another fantasy. Cazerove had come through Dunkirk. One must accept that he could have been suffering shell shock.'

'Then why would he have been attached to the War Office? Unsound men aren't wanted there, are they?'

'He was a bright lad, good education. Perhaps his nerves were too shot for the front line, but his brain was big enough for office work. Apart from that, no comment.'

'Oh, don't be ridiculous, Eaton.' Wilde tried to meet the MI6 man's eyes again, but Eaton was now gazing into his coffee. Time to push his luck. 'This other thing's a hell of a business, isn't it?'

Eaton looked up. 'Other business?'

'The Duke of Kent crashing into a Scottish mountain.'

Eaton frowned. 'Why do you mention that, Wilde?'

'Oh, you know – intuition. Big event . . .'

Eaton shook his head and laughed. 'Now your imagination really is running away with you. The RAF chaps are absolutely clear that the Caithness crash was a tragic accident.'

'I'm sure you're right.' The thing was, Wilde had no idea what possible connection there could be between the suicide of a lowly army officer and a plane crash in the far north of Scotland. But Cazerove couldn't have been much clearer:

'This is just the beginning,' he had said. 'You'll discover soon enough . . . tomorrow.' Well, tomorrow had come, and one item of news would be on everyone's lips: the death of the King's youngest brother. The war in the Pacific and Germany's advance on Stalingrad would have to take second billing today.

'There'll be a court of inquiry, of course,' Eaton continued. 'But look, can we get back to Cazerove – do you have any idea why he might have picked on you to witness his dramatic exit?'

'He said it was because I was American, so he hadn't betrayed me.'

'Were you close when he was your pupil?'

'Honestly, I can't say I ever liked him much.'

'You said he mentioned a woman.'

'Well, yes, he did – obliquely. He asked which was more binding, a vow of silence or a declaration of love. I assumed he was talking about a particular woman, but he didn't name names. And when I asked if there was girl trouble, he said "not the way you mean it". Talking in riddles. Anyway, does it mean anything to you, Eaton?'

'No, I'm afraid not.'

Wilde raised an eyebrow. Eaton's reply had come too quickly, as though he had already primed himself for denial.

Chapter 4

The conversation went in circles. After an hour, Eaton said he had to go, but that he would be in touch. As they shook hands at the doorway, Wilde was surprised to see that the ministry driver was standing beside a Rolls Royce.

'I hope my taxes aren't paying for that,' he said.

'We had to borrow it in a hurry,' Eaton replied. 'No pool cars available. Despite the price tag, it's still not that comfortable when you have a smashed-up leg.'

Wilde waved him off, then walked down to St Andrew's Street to give a statement to police. The inspector in charge was an officer brought out of retirement because of staff shortages caused by so many young men opting to fight in the military rather than walk the beat.

'Nasty business,' the inspector said when Wilde had completed his statement.

'Has there been any word on the poison he used?'

'Not confirmed, but Dr Weir seems pretty sure it was cyanide. The body will be taken to the Scotland Yard forensic lab later today.'

'Well, at least it was a quick death.'

'Indeed.'

'Can I go now?'

'Of course, sir. Your statement seems to fit what we already know. Just be aware that there will be an inquest in the next few days, once the Met science boys produce their report. The coroner will almost certainly want you there.'

'You know where to find me.'

He stopped off at the college before going home, picked up his mail from the porters' lodge and went to pay his respects to the Master, Sir Archibald Spence, who seemed distracted by administrative duties. 'Can't stop to chat, I'm afraid, Wilde.'

'I understand, master.'

'But good to see you all the same.' He patted Wilde on the shoulder. 'The place is full of ministry men and American service personnel. I tell you this, though – I wish I hadn't taken your advice on the chapel glass.'

'Hasn't been damaged, has it?' Wilde recalled that he hadn't actually advised the Master against removing the chapel's stained glass for the duration. All he had done was suggest that Cambridge would not be high on the Luftwaffe's list of targets. He had been wrong on that score.

'No damage, thank the Lord,' Spence said. 'But it was damned nerve-racking when Goering's boys started dropping their iron eggs. Had a few sleepless nights, I can tell you, Wilde. Anyway, hopefully the worst of it is over now. London's a lot quieter, I believe.'

'Yes, it is.'

'And you've had to give up your air-raid duties, I'm told.'

'I'm afraid so.'

'Well, I'm sure you're doing good work elsewhere. Good man.'

Wilde took his leave of the Master and went up to his rooms overlooking the old court. He worked his way through his letters then pushed them aside and set off for home. More than anything, he wanted to spend these days of freedom with Lydia and Johnny.

As he entered Cornflowers, the phone rang. Lydia was looking at him, eyebrow raised.

'Could you get it, darling?' Wilde really didn't want to speak to anyone.

'Oh, it'll be for you.'

He sighed and picked up the phone. It was William Phillips, new London bureau chief of the fledgling Office of Strategic Services. Wilde had been helping the old boy get his feet under the table since his arrival from America last month, working as his main adviser on the internal politics of Great Britain.

'Enjoying your little break, Tom?'

'You don't know how funny that is, Bill.'

'Have you seen the news?'

'What in particular?'

'The plane crash in Scotland. Any thoughts?'

'Ah, yes, I did see that.'

'And?'

'Well, the RAF say it was an accident.' Where, he wondered, was this curious phone call heading?

'You believe that?'

'I suppose so. Why, shouldn't I? Have you heard something, Bill?'

'Oh, just wondering what you thought. You know the British a great deal better than I do.'

'I'm told it was a straightforward accident.'

'Who said that?'

'Philip Eaton.'

'I don't think I've met him.'

'Well, I'm sure you will in due course. He's MI6. Used to run their Iberian desk but he's been moved into quite a senior role. Anyway, he appeared on my doorstep this morning and we got to talking about the Duke's death.'

'And when he said it was an accident, did you believe him?'

'Why do you ask?'

'Because, as I just said, you know the British.'

'Well, they do have a tendency to keep things close to their chest. But whatever the cause of the crash, I'd say it has nothing to do with us. This is a clear-cut British affair. We have to keep our noses out. You know the rules, Bill, because you wrote them: strict demarcation.'

'That's not the way the President sees it. He wants to know what happened.'

Wilde didn't like to contradict his new boss, but in this case he had to lay it on the line. 'Honestly, Bill, I really think we have to leave this one to the host nation. Well outside our remit, wouldn't you say?'

'FDR liked the Duke. They were very good friends and he was godfather to the Duchess's new baby boy. Little Michael George Charles Franklin, born last month. Notice the Franklin in there?'

'Yes, I noticed – and I understand his interest, but that has to be as far as it goes.'

'You don't know Roosevelt like I do. When he inquires in that reassuring New England drawl what the hell happened, what he is saying is – get the hell out there and *find out* what the hell happened. He doesn't trust the British line one iota. And I see his point; they're too quick off the mark with their "tragic accident" claims. Why aren't they investigating properly? John Winant wants answers, too. The Duke was at Bristol to meet him when he arrived here as ambassador. Everyone liked the Duke – he was one of the good guys.'

Wilde sighed; he had a horrible feeling that there was no interest in his opinion, but he forged on regardless. 'Perhaps they are investigating but just don't want to put it in the papers.

Perhaps the tragic accident suggestion is for public consumption. The people wouldn't be happy thinking their royal family was vulnerable to enemy attack.' He knew he was wasting breath. This affair was not about to end with a telephone call. His precious break with Lydia and Johnny was about to be cut short.

'To hell with public opinion, FDR thinks the Duke was shot down and he wants the truth.'

'A targeted assassination or a lucky shot? I mean, why kill the Duke of Kent in particular?'

'You know, Tom, the King's brother was more than just a royal stooge. Damn it, he helped negotiate the lend-lease deal. And he successfully persuaded Salazar to keep Portugal out of the war. He was an important player. A very senior go-between.'

'Of course.'

'Which means he was a prime target. He had enemies. And the way FDR sees it, the Duke's enemies are *our* enemies, too.'

Lydia was looking at him. He shook his head helplessly in her direction and suppressed a groan.

Wilde was aware that William Phillips had always been close to Roosevelt. They were of an age – at sixty-four, Phillips was only a couple of years older than the President – and they came from the same social stratum. Both were Harvard men. If a message was transmitted from the White House via Phillips, then you could be pretty darn sure it was to be acted on. 'What do you want me to do, Bill?'

'I want you to find out who killed the Duke of Kent – and why.'

'So you want me to come back to London? You realise I've only been home twelve hours.'

Phillips's deep laughter rumbled down the line. 'No, Tom, I don't want you to come back to London. I want you to go to Scotland.'

Wilde let his boss's laughter subside; he didn't find Phillips's proposition at all amusing. No, *proposition* was the wrong word. Phillips hadn't made a suggestion, he'd given an order – one that came directly from the President of the United States. One that had to be acted on, whatever Wilde's misgivings.

The mission was nigh-on impossible, of course. He couldn't just turn up unannounced in a remote corner of the country and ask questions. There was a war on, for God's sake. People who pried into matters which didn't seem to concern them were likely to end up in an internment camp on the Isle of Man. Or worse, shot out of hand.

Bill Phillips was already ahead of him, anticipating and answering his objections. 'We have arranged accreditation for you.'

'How the hell did you manage that?'

'The embassy talked to 10 Downing Street. Papers will be biked up to you this afternoon and you will take the overnight to Oban. From there you will be flown to Invergordon. Apparently, that's the same journey the Duke took.'

'And Invergordon – that's a naval base, right?'

'Royal Navy and Royal Air Force. The Duke's flying boat left from RAF Invergordon. Instructions to cooperate have been phoned through to them. That doesn't mean the guys up there will like it or be friendly, but they're not in a position to say no. You will be met in Scotland by a civil servant and will be given every assistance.'

'Is that necessary? I'd rather do this alone.'

'That part of the coast is very sensitive – seen as exceptionally vulnerable to enemy attack, so there are a lot of military installations in the region. Anyone nosing around will immediately be suspect. So you'll be chaperoned as closely as a virgin debutante.'

'What excuse did the embassy give for my journey? They couldn't say that the President doesn't trust the British.'

'Of course not. You will be there as a mark of respect, to pay tribute and say a prayer at the site of the crash and to do anything you can to assist the army and the local people. You will be expected to talk to nearby residents and, on behalf of the President and people of the United States, to thank them for their efforts in doing all they could for our good friend the Duke and all the others on the plane.'

As a cover story, it was solid enough, he supposed, particularly as it had been concocted at speed by Phillips. All his experience as a diplomat, including his most recent role as ambassador to Italy, must have come into play for the smooth but hard-as-nails OSS chief.

'Then I don't really have an option, do I?'

'I'm afraid you don't. You know, Tom, in my month here in London I have been wined and dined and treated like royalty by the British secret services. But they don't fool me for a moment – and I tell you this, I will *not* allow the London office of the OSS to be walked over by the British intelligence services. They will try to foist their version of events on to you, but you won't let them. Good luck – and keep in touch.' The line went dead.

Wilde put down the phone and caught Lydia's withering look. He shrugged dismally.

'You've only just arrived and now you're going away,' she said.

'You heard all that?'

'Your face told me everything.'

'I'm sorry. Hopefully it will be just a couple of days. I'm not going to find anything, am I? And then I'll come home, my duty done.'

Lydia raised a sceptical eyebrow. 'How many years have I known you, Tom? Too many to fall for that line. You won't rest until you've discovered the truth. Now, come on, I've made you some lunch.'

'Thank you.' He wandered to the window and looked out on the street, trying to collect his thoughts. It was a pleasant summer day, little wind, cotton clouds in a blue sky. There were times he loved this town, other times he wondered what he was doing here. Across the road, near the postbox, a little man stood with his hands deep in his jacket pockets.

Wilde peered closer, trying to see the face half-shrouded by the brim of a hat. He seemed familiar. And then he realised: it was the bow-legged young man from Cambridge station, the one who had disappeared hurriedly when the police sergeant approached. The one who looked like he should be riding racehorses on Newmarket Heath. Wilde opened the door. The man was still there.

'Mr Mortimer, isn't it? Are you looking for me?' he called as he crossed the road.

The young man shrank back momentarily, but then held his ground, his eyes sullen and defiant. Wilde was almost upon him now. 'Who are you?' Wilde kept his hands in his trouser pockets. The boxer in him was always ready for a fight, but he wanted to look casual so he could talk to this young man, not scare him off.

'What happened to him?' Mortimer demanded flatly.

'You're answering questions with questions again, young man. I've already told you my name – and I told you Peter Cazerove died on the train. Now, what's your business in all this?'

The young man seemed to think for a moment, then shrugged. 'Did you kill Cazerove? I need to know how he died.'

'No, I didn't hurt him. There will be an inquest soon enough – so go along to that. Now, Mortimer, what was he to you? I'm very happy to talk to you, but you really will have to tell me who you are. I imagine you were there to pick him up – but why?'

'You had a visitor this morning. One-armed man. Who was it?'

Wilde had had enough. 'You've obviously been spying on me. Come on, I think the police would like a little chat with you.' Wilde reached out to grasp the young man's arm, but he stepped back again, out of reach.

'Don't touch me, mister, or I'll do for you. I'm going nowhere near any police. What I want to know from you is what happened on the train. What did he say to you?'

'Come into my house then. Have a cup of tea and we can talk about all this.'

The young man hesitated, then made a noise like a growl. His left hand inched up from his jacket pocket and Wilde caught a glint of metal.

'If that's a knife . . .'

The hand slid down again and the glint was gone. 'Sod you, mister. You'll be hearing from us.' He backed away, his face rat-like and glowering, then he scurried away, just as he had done at the railway station.

Chapter 5

A few hundred feet below him, sunlight reflected off the dark, still waters of the Cromarty Firth. As the plane descended in a great arc, Wilde watched the formless grey specks on the surface grow into the menacing, yet comforting, shapes of warships and flying boats, dispersed across the length and breadth of the inlet.

The journey here had been long, first by train with two changes, then from Oban on the west coast across to the east aboard this Sunderland flying boat. The plane wasn't built for comfort. Hard, jagged edges enveloped him as he gazed back down the dark, conical crawlway of the fuselage to the bright core at the rear – the turret where a gunner nursed four .303 Browning machine guns. On take-off the craft had rattled and juddered as though it were in its death throes, but in the air it was smooth and sweet, if a little lumbering in its attempts to gain height.

The pilot had invited him to the cockpit, where the discomfort and the thunderous roar of the four 1,200 horsepower engines were alleviated by glorious views of Ben Nevis, the Great Glen, Loch Ness and the Black Isle.

'We call these planes flying porcupines,' said the pilot, who had introduced himself as Flight Lieutenant Duncan.

'Why so?'

'Spiky guns sticking out fore, aft and midships. Perhaps "hedgehog" might be more apt for a British beast, but it's pretty effective both in attack and defence.'

'Prince George died in one of these, didn't he?'

'So I'm led to believe, sir. A great sadness to us all. As was the loss of our own Wingco Moseley.'

'Your wing commander?'

'Yes sir, he was Officer Commanding 228 Squadron, Oban.'

'I'm sorry to hear it. Please accept my condolences.'

'That's war, Mr Wilde.'

They were silent a few moments. At last Wilde had judged it appropriate to pose a question. 'What's your theory, flight lieutenant?'

'Cause of the Duke's crash? I believe there was fog along the Caithness coast. Much thicker than forecast.'

'Then why didn't they just stay over the sea until they had enough altitude?'

'It saves fuel if you can cut off the far north of Scotland, but I suppose they had some sort of problem. Anyway, not for me to speculate. It'll all come out in the inquiry, of course. Just another sad accident, I imagine. We've lost plenty over Scaraben and those treacherous little mountains. The place is littered with bits of aircraft.'

'The Duke came up the same route as me, I believe. Was it you that flew him over from Oban to Invergordon?'

'No, sir. I had met him on occasion, but I didn't see him on this trip. We all liked him, you know – one of us, he was. Proper flying man, and a fair pilot himself, from all accounts. He'll be sorely missed by everyone in the service.'

'You'd think the pilot would have taken extra care with such an important passenger.'

Flight Lieutenant Duncan bristled. 'Pilots take great care whoever they're flying. It's their lives on the line, too, you know.'

'Of course.'

'But we're only human. And so mistakes are made.'

'Human error is a possibility, you think?'

'Or mechanical failure. I really couldn't say. You'll probably learn more from the chaps at RAF Invergordon.'

'There is another alternative, of course – enemy action. A lone German fighter, or a bomb on board, perhaps?'

'I suppose stranger things have happened.'

'So there has been no messroom gossip at RAF Oban? No word has come down from the crash site?'

'Not to me, sir.'

Wilde realised he was getting nowhere. The pilot was affable enough, but he either knew nothing or was simply well trained to keep shtum.

And now the brief flight was over. They touched water, effortlessly, and the huge aircraft slowed and skimmed to a halt, rocking gently with the current and the light breeze. Wilde knew from his briefing that they were between the towns of Invergordon and its neighbour Alness, both turned into RAF and Royal Navy bases for the duration.

A small marine tender arrived to take him ashore while the crew and engineers unloaded and refuelled the aircraft. The sky was cloudless and the landscape was spectacular. Gulls wheeled and cried beneath a canopy of barrage balloons, held aloft to deter enemy bombers. On land, two anti-aircraft installations poked their long guns towards the heavens.

At the jetty, a solitary man was waiting for him. He was a shade over six feet but didn't look as tall, for he held his shoulders hunched like a bird. He wore civilian clothes – a grey suit, narrow tie and black shoes, but no hat – and the light wind was whipping his steel-grey hair.

Wilde climbed out of the boat and mounted the steps. The stranger smiled as he approached. 'Mr Wilde, you're here at last. I am Walter Quayle.'

The name meant nothing to Wilde, but he shook the man's hand. 'Pleased to meet you, Mr Quayle.' Somewhat irreverently, he found himself wanting to brush the snowfall of dandruff from the man's shoulders. 'Would you like to see my letter of accreditation?'

'Oh, don't bother with that. It's quite clear who you are. Anyway, you're probably wondering who I am. Let me explain, professor. I was sent up here late on Tuesday to coordinate matters concerning the Duke's death.'

'Sent by whom?'

'By Number 10 – I'm a civil servant, adviser to the Prime Minister on royal matters, among other things. I knew Georgie – the Duke of Kent – very well. We had been friends for many years.'

'Then I am sorry to hear of your loss.'

'I'll be honest with you, I'm devastated. You know Georgie was only thirty-nine. Poor Marina – the Duchess – won't get over it. Left with three small children, including a babe in arms.' He shook his head as though to clear his thoughts. 'But for the moment, we must all put our grief aside and play the professionals. Now then, I know you are here representing Mr Roosevelt and the American people, and it would be an honour to assist you in your mission.'

'Thank you.'

'But most of all, thank God you're here. I need a drinking companion. Come on, I hear the whisky's not too bad in this part of the world.'

'I think I need some food, too.'

'Local inn's the place. Easy walk from here and they do a pretty fair steak and kidney pud.'

They stood in the bar nursing double whiskies while they waited for their food to be served. 'Ah, that goes down well,' Quayle said. 'Nothing like a drop of good Scotch on its home territory.'

Wilde nodded in agreement, trying to gauge the man. At first glance he was remarkably well-dressed and rather elegant, silky enough to be a ministry man. But the dandruff, the yellow teeth and the soup-stained tie told a different story. Something didn't quite add up. He was a little taller than Wilde, save for the stoop, slender, about thirty years of age but prematurely grey. He had a ready smile and an open manner, but still Wilde wasn't convinced.

His drinking was interesting. Wilde liked a whisky as much as the next man, perhaps more so, but this fellow Quayle was in a different class. The double Scotch descended his gullet and then the order came in for the next, and the next.

'Do you smoke, Wilde?'

'No.'

'Nor me. I like to keep one vice in reserve. I think it was Marlowe who said "all they that love not tobacco and boys are fools". Well, I'll pass on the baccy.'

'I think it might have been said *about* Marlowe, actually – by one of Walsingham's spies.'

'Well, you'd know. Your period, I hear.'

Wilde nodded. It seemed Quayle had been given information about him. 'What else do you know about me?'

'That you're half-American and half-Irish. Is that right? I suppose that means you're half in, half out of the war . . .'

Wilde didn't pretend to be amused. He was more interested in finding out a little about Quayle in return, but for the
moment, he had more pressing matters to concern him. 'I want
to get up to Caithness as soon as possible,' he said. See the crash
site before it's cleared up, he thought.

'Of course. And you'll want to meet the survivor – but I'm
afraid it'll be a while before he's in any fit state to talk.'

Wilde was bewildered. 'Survivor? I thought everyone died.'

'Ah, so you haven't heard? Well, yes, not surprising if you've
been travelling non-stop since yesterday. The rear gunner's
alive. His name's Andy Jack. They didn't find him at first. He
was quite badly injured – got disorientated and lost, wandered
the mountainside all afternoon and evening until he bedded
down and slept in the bracken. Poor bastard had lost half his
clothes. He was barefoot and burnt. Yesterday he finally found
his way to civilisation, knocked on the door of a local croft, collapsed – and now he's in hospital.'

'Have you spoken to him?'

'I tried to, but the fellow's mighty confused and sedated. He's
suffering burns and various other injuries. I'll try again though,
and you can come with me if you like. First things first, however –
we should get you up to the crash site and show you around. It's
two or three hours by road, so we'll drive up in the morning.'

'Where are you staying?'

'This inn has rooms, so here seems the best bet. Rather more
comfortable than quarters at the RAF base.'

'My instinct is to keep on travelling north tonight. I take it
you have a car?'

'Wilde, old man, the roads are atrocious. Let's wait until daylight. You don't want to end up dead in a Scottish ditch like the
Duke.'

'Talking of whom, where are the bodies?'

'Well, Georgie's already on his way south by train. Your paths might have crossed. Anyway, one thing I did want to mention was that the people up in these parts are close-knit and a little suspicious of outsiders. They might well be wary of your accent because they might not recognise it as American. There is a lot of military activity in this area, you see, so they are continually being cautioned to beware of talking to strangers. As a consequence, they're ultra-sensitive and very protective. Quite rightly so. They are likely to think you're a spy even when you've shown them your papers.'

Wilde downed his whisky. 'In the meantime, if we're staying the night here, I want to call in on the RAF and hear what they have to say.'

'Good idea. They're a fine bunch. I'm sure they'll tell you everything you want to know.'

The commanding officer, a group captain, was away so they were received by a stand-in named Wing Commander Geoffrey Frayne, who might have been anything from twenty-five to thirty-five. They had been shown into his office in a rather luxurious manor house, which had been requisitioned as headquarters for the air base. The man was taut and wary, as though he wasn't at all pleased to see them. But he was savvy enough to realise he had no option, given the interest of the President of the United States and the stamp of approval from Downing Street.

'We'd like to go to the mess, talk to some of the men,' Wilde said after their introduction.

'I'd rather you didn't,' the wing commander said, brushing his wide, luxuriant moustache with the back of his hand. 'The men have lost some very good friends.'

'I understand that.' Wilde saw the hollowness in the officer's eyes; he was clearly shredded after three years of war. 'I would, of course, be extremely sensitive, bring my condolences from the President and thank them on his behalf for their efforts.'

'No, I really don't think so. If there's anything you want to know, I'll do my best to give you answers.'

Wilde turned to Quayle for guidance. He was puzzled by the wing commander's intransigence.

Quayle shrugged helplessly, then smiled at the RAF man. 'Mr Wilde is only doing what his president has asked, wing commander. Mr Roosevelt is extremely concerned about the crash. He was very close to the Duke and is devastated by his death.'

Frayne failed to suppress an exasperated sigh. 'What you have to realise is that this is an operational base in the middle of a damned grisly conflict. Kill or be killed, as the cliché goes. Only in this case it's not a bloody cliché, it's real life – every hour of every day, somewhere in the world one or more of our men is killed. Our surviving men lose friends a great deal too frequently and so they go to the mess to drown their sorrows and remind themselves they are still alive. Death is not a subject for the officers' mess.'

Wilde realised this was going nowhere. 'In which case, perhaps you would tell me *your* theory, wing commander – how *did* the crash happen?'

The officer looked resigned. He and his two visitors were all standing with whisky glasses in hand. Wilde noticed that Quayle's was already empty; he really was an impressive drinker.

Frayne exchanged glances with Quayle. Wilde had already deduced that they must have discussed him beforehand.

'Very well,' Frayne said at last. 'I'll tell you what I think, Professor Wilde, but it goes no further than this room.'

'I can't quite promise that, I'm afraid. I have to report to my own boss in London, and he'll talk to FDR. But that's all.'

'Then make it clear to them, that this is for their ears only.' He paused, emitted a low groan. 'It was pilot error. That's the brutal truth of it.'

'Really? I thought the pilot was among your very finest.'

'I hate to say it, because it sounds as if I'm being disloyal to a very good man – and perhaps I am – but the captain of the aircraft *was* responsible. His name was Flight Lieutenant Frank Goyen. I knew him well and it causes me great pain to point the finger at him.'

'Why are you so certain?'

'Everything suggests it. No hint of enemy action or sabotage, no suggestion of engine failure. Had to be human error. He had plenty of time to reach a safe altitude and, anyway, even if he hadn't, then he should have stayed over the sea.'

'What about a navigation error?'

'That's the only possible alternative – but this flying boat had the most up-to-date systems aboard: long-distance radar, brand-new compass. Navigating in fog should have posed no problems.

'And Goyen was the most senior man aboard the plane?'

'In theory, the Duke was the most senior man. He was an air commodore. But in operational terms, the senior officer was Wing Commander Moseley, Officer Commanding 228 Squadron, presently based at Oban. But the man in the number-one pilot's seat aboard Short Sunderland 4026 was Goyen – and so he was the captain of the flight, and is therefore to blame for any mishap. He flew too low, and turned too early. A few miles further north he would have been over the flatlands of Caithness and it would have been quite correct to turn inland to save fuel.'

'You mentioned the fog. Even with top-class instruments, surely a flier could be disoriented?' Wilde said.

'That is for the inquiry to decide. But there is no doubt in my mind that Frank Goyen – an otherwise fine pilot who was considered experienced enough to fly Sir Stafford Cripps to Moscow last year – made a disastrous error of judgement in this case. The board of inquiry will almost certainly concur.'

Wilde was puzzled. 'I take it Wing Commander Moseley was a pilot too?'

'Indeed, a very experienced man.'

'Then if he wasn't the pilot in this case, why was he aboard the plane?'

'That's an operational matter. I have no information on such things and even if I did, I couldn't release it.'

'But isn't that unusual for the senior man not to be in the captain's seat?'

'I can't comment.'

'Did you see the Duke on Tuesday, the day of his flight?'

Frayne hesitated.

Wilde pressed on. 'He flew out of here – surely you would have made it your business to welcome him and see him safely away?'

'Yes, of course. He lunched in the mess soon before departure. Look, Mr Wilde, this is beginning to sound very much like an interrogation . . .'

'Forgive me.'

Walter Quayle stepped forward. 'Let's leave it there, shall we?'

Wilde stiffened. He knew he was being given the run-around, and these men – the RAF chief and Walter Quayle – had a script and were sticking to it. His first instinct was to pull rank and demand answers, but he knew that would get him nowhere and would be reported back to the Air Ministry. It might be more productive to simply smile and keep them onside. 'You're right, Quayle. And we'll need an early start.'

He held out his hand to the RAF officer. 'Thank you so much for your help, wing commander. Perhaps I could call in on you once again on my way southwards.'

'Of course, Professor Wilde, you will be very welcome here at any time. Just clear it with my office by telephone. In the meantime, thank you for being so understanding.'

'Oh, just one thought before we go . . .'

'Yes?'

'I believe the Duke was a pilot. Is it possible he took the controls himself?'

Again the RAF officer hesitated, then chose his words with care. 'There is no reason to believe so.'

Chapter 6

Quayle had requisitioned a dilapidated Ford and an RAF driver named Corporal Boycott, who turned his mouth down at the sight of the car and assured them in a Yorkshire accent that the vehicle was unlikely to last the sixty-odd miles to Dunbeath.

'You're a driver,' Quayle said. 'You must know how to keep a car on the road.'

The corporal, who had told them proudly that he hailed from 'God's own county', took a deep draw on his cigarette, then blew out a cloud of smoke and winked. 'Don't you worry yourself, Mr Quayle, I'm a mechanical wizard, me. I'll get you there.'

'And you won't be puffing on that thing when you drive. Professor Wilde and I are non-smokers.'

Boycott took another drag. 'Can't live long without me smokes.'

'You'll do as you're damn well told.'

After rain in the early hours, the day was hazy but dry. As they bounced along a narrow road, pitted, muddy and winding, Wilde was constantly aware of military installations and army traffic. He and Quayle sat in the rear seat and discussed the air crash. Every few minutes, Quayle took out a large flask of whisky and offered it to his fellow passenger.

'A little early for me.'

'You haven't heard of the skalk? It's the tradition in these parts – to drink whisky before breakfast. Must observe local customs, professor.'

Wilde waved the flask away, and Quayle continued to drink.

'What about the others aboard the flight?' Wilde said. 'So far, I've only heard about the Duke, Goyen the pilot, Wing Commander Mosely and the sole survivor, rear gunner Andrew Jack. Who else died?'

Walter Quayle removed a notebook from his jacket pocket. 'I've got them all here. Pilot Officer Sidney Smith, Pilot Officer George Saunders, Flight Sergeant William Jones, Flight Sergeant Charles Lewis, Flight Sergeant Edward Hewerdine, Sergeant Edward Blacklock, Sergeant Roland Catt, Sergeant Leonard Sweett. That's the crew accounted for. The passengers were the Duke's private secretary Lieutenant John Crowther, his air equerry Pilot Officer Michael Strutt and his batman Leading Aircraftman John Holes. As I understand it, that's the full complement.'

'That makes fifteen. Fourteen dead, one survivor.'

'Indeed. Perfectly bloody.'

'Do you have more information about them?'

'Scraps. I can tell you that Saunders was down as navigator. And that five of the non-coms, including Andy Jack, were gunners. I'm sure more will come out about all of them in due course.'

'And the purpose of the flight? The newspaper report said the Duke was on his way to Iceland to visit air bases. But do you believe that? This sounds like an extremely high-profile group for such an unexceptional mission.'

Walter Quayle shrugged. 'Oh, you know, the royals always like an entourage.'

'But why fly from the east coast – wouldn't it have made more sense to fly from Oban in the west? Surely that would have saved fuel and been more direct?'

'As I understand it, the Duke wanted to visit Invergordon and Alness in his RAF inspection role. That would have been quite logical.'

Wilde wasn't convinced but he said nothing. He had to keep reminding himself that this was not supposed to be an investigation but a pilgrimage in honour of the President's friend.

Quayle frowned. 'So what's *your* theory, Wilde?'

'I don't have a theory, Quayle. Just wondering aloud because FDR will want to know what his friend was doing and why he died. And I'm the one he'll ask.' He left it there and remained silent for a few minutes, trying to work out where else the Duke could have been heading. The tale of the Iceland trip might be true. Or it might not. But then he began to wonder whether he was suspecting conspiracies where none existed. It would not have been the first time; that's what came of being an authority on the devious workings of the Elizabethan spy chief Francis Walsingham. One tended to see plots everywhere.

The road became worse – damaged by the hundreds of tracked vehicles that had passed this way in three years of war – and the ride was jarring. When they saw a hotel, the Cameron Arms, in the fishing village of Helmsdale, Corporal Boycott took it upon himself to pull in to the kerb outside the entrance. 'I'll leave you two gents to refresh yourselves,' he said. 'Got to find a garage for fuel and a tyre check. Only twelve miles to go, but these roads don't half take a toll.'

'You mean you're dying for a cigarette,' Quayle suggested.

'Now that you mention it, sir, that sounds like a pretty fair idea.'

'Go on, corporal – sod off. Be back in twenty minutes.'

At the front of the hotel, looking out on to a walled harbour full of fishing boats, Quayle and Wilde settled into two worn leather armchairs and ordered a pot of tea, the only available beverage at that time of day. When their order arrived, Wilde asked the waitress, a motherly woman of about fifty, where he could find a lavatory, then wandered off in search of it. On his way back, feeling a great deal fresher from washing his hands and splashing cold water on his face, he spotted the concierge – if that was the right word for the man at the desk in these untamed northerly climes – and approached him.

'Can I have a word?'

'Take your pick, there's a fair few in the dictionary.'

Wilde smiled, happy to play the fall guy to the man's attempt at wit. 'Well, it's about the plane crash. Everyone around here must feel it very deeply.'

'Is that so?'

'Well, yes, it's a tragic event. The King's brother, all those others who died . . .'

'Aye.'

'What are people saying in these parts? How did it happen?'

'How did it happen? The plane crashed, that's how it happened.'

Wilde sighed. The man was probably the waitress's husband and he felt a sudden rush of pity for her, having to live with such an obtuse man. 'I mean, *why* did it happen?'

'I know what you mean, feller. What I don't know is who you are, and why you think it's fine to go around asking such questions.'

Wilde put out his hand as a gesture of introduction. 'My name is Wilde. Professor Thomas Wilde. I'm American and

I'm here to pay my respects on behalf of the President. He was a good friend of the Duke, godfather to his new baby.'

The deskman ignored Wilde's offer of a handshake. 'Then you probably know a great deal more than I do, Mr Wilde.'

'This village must be quite close to the crash site, though.'

'Oh, you've got a little further to go, then you'll have to climb out of your fancy motor car and use Shanks's pony to get yourself across the moor.'

'Can I ask your name, sir? Are you the owner of this hotel?'

'That I am, and the name's Cameron, just like the hotel itself. Hamish Cameron.'

'Did you hear the crash?'

'Och no.'

'But maybe you heard the aircraft going overhead?'

'Well, we get a lot of planes around here, as you might imagine.'

'Did anyone see it?'

'No one could have seen it. Thick fog all day. Couldn't see ten feet in front of your nose. And fog will always deaden sound. Look, Mr Wilde, you might be better off talking to the folks up at Berriedale or Ramscraigs. It was a mile or two inland, from what I've been told, but those are the closest settlements.'

Wilde was standing at one side of the desk, while old Cameron sat in front of an open register on the other side. As they were speaking, a young woman, small and dark, came down the gloomy and narrow staircase and took her place in line behind Wilde. She was carrying a rather battered valise. Wilde turned and smiled at her. 'I beg your pardon, are you in a hurry?'

'I just need to settle up.'

'Of course, you go first. Don't mind me.' He turned back to Hamish Cameron. 'Thank you for your time.'

The woman nodded at Wilde by way of a thank you, then stepped forward. She leant across the desk, speaking quietly, but Wilde heard her. She was saying that she had lost her wallet and could she forward the money to the hotel later in the day.

'I'm sorry, miss, we don't extend credit,' Cameron said in a voice too loud for privacy.

'But I'll be met at the other end and I'll send the money back with Mr Morrison.' She was entreating the hotel keeper as though her life depended on it. She gave him a seductive smile that would win over any man, but not Hamish Cameron.

'Neither a borrower nor a lender be. You've stayed the night and you must pay.'

'But what can I do? My money's gone.'

'Then that's your problem and not mine.'

Wilde stepped forward. 'Forgive me, miss, I couldn't help hearing . . .'

She looked at him wide-eyed, either beseeching him or something else. Fear?

'I have plenty of money. How much is the bill?'

'Two pounds, two shillings and sixpence,' the deskman said.

Wilde removed his own wallet. 'Would you allow me the honour of paying, miss?'

'I'll pay you back, Mr . . .'

'Professor Wilde. And I don't want the money back. Help someone else when they need it.'

'I can't thank you enough.'

'Think nothing of it, miss . . .' He waited for her to supply her name, but she didn't oblige. He counted out the money and handed it over to Cameron. 'There you go.'

The young woman touched his arm and their eyes met briefly. She mouthed the words 'thank you' again, and then she was gone out through the front door.

Wilde shrugged. 'Well, there you go, Mr Cameron.'

'I have a business to run, not a charity.'

Wilde returned to the lounge and drank his tea. It was weak and milky, as though the tea leaves had already been used for half a dozen pots.

Through the window they saw the Ford pulling up. 'Time to go,' Quayle said.

They paid for the tea and strolled out to the car. Wilde was just clambering into the back beside Quayle, when he hesitated. 'One moment, Quayle, I just wanted a quick word with the man at the desk, see if he has rooms for this evening. We might need them, depending on the situation further north.'

'Shall I come with you?'

'No need, I'll only be a sec.'

He went back to Cameron and discovered that there were rooms available. 'Dinner's at six, no later. Mrs Cameron does the cooking herself. We have soup and fish this evening. Shall I book you gentlemen in?'

'I'll call you a little later. By the way, what was the young lady's name?'

Cameron frowned as though affronted by the question. 'That would be her business, Mr Wilde. I'm not after tittle-tattling.'

'Of course not, just curious. Thought she might need a lift somewhere – we have an extra seat in the car.'

'Well, you're too late because she's already gone with Morrison in his taxicab. And in the other direction. Maybe she'll even find some money to pay him. Who knows with a floozy like that?'

Wilde resisted giving the man a piece of his mind. 'Well, we may see you later.'

He nodded to the hotelier with a false smile that was not reciprocated and wandered back to the car. Hamish Cameron might not have given him the woman's name, but he knew it now anyway. He had seen her name in the register: Claire Hart.

The name meant nothing to him, but for some reason he was intrigued. From the few words he heard, he would say she was well spoken, as though the product of an expensive girls' school. Certainly no floozy. The other thing he could not help noticing was that she was quite extraordinarily good-looking, rather like an unpolished version of Vivien Leigh.

Chapter 7

As they carried on northwards on the short last leg, Wilde found his thoughts returning to the woman in the hotel. Somehow she didn't fit in this rugged part of the world. If he were walking through Belgravia and saw her, he might not have given her a second glance. But here, in this land of rocky coastlines, gun emplacements, windswept mountains and moors, she was out of place, which instantly aroused his interest.

It occurred to him that she might be a reporter covering the plane crash. And yet her accent was not Scottish, and surely the national newspapers would have sent journalists from their offices in Edinburgh or Glasgow or Inverness. Would it not also be a matter that the Ministry of Information might have a say in? Would they want reporters sniffing around in this region?

Wilde was aware of northern Scotland's strategic importance – even a limited invasion of German troops from Norway could isolate and threaten the fleet in Scapa Flow in the Orkneys and cripple Britain's airborne operations over the Atlantic. It would also divert British troops from other theatres of war. An elite German division would be able to bed down quickly in the Highlands and would take a great deal of winkling out. So best not to let them land in the first place, which was why this area was stiff with military outfits on land, air and sea; as Bill Phillips had pointed out, this was not a place to dig for information unless you had authority.

Half an hour later, the road descended into the hamlet of Berriedale, where the stream of the same name flowed into the sea, then on past the hamlets of Borgue and Ramscraigs on the coast, before turning inland along a narrow track to the small settlement of Braemore. The haze had dispersed and the day was warm and clear now. As Corporal Boycott parked the car, Wilde pulled out strong leather walking boots from his bag and changed into them. It had been raining during the night, and the paths were boggy.

'I take it you know how to get to the crash site, Quayle?'

'Yes, I paid a brief visit early yesterday, but it's not easy. Even without last night's rain, parts of these moors are a swamp all year round.'

They left the corporal with the car and trekked southwards and westwards across moorland. They saw men in uniform at various stages, but didn't bother to approach them. Scruffy sheep roamed the hills. They crested a rise and stopped for a breather, looking to the west with the North Sea at their backs.

'I thought it would be more mountainous,' Wilde said.

'It's rough enough – but this is pretty much the last of it.' Quayle picked off the peaks. He pointed to the south-west. 'That's Donald's Mount with the Scaraben range behind it, then that lovely tit of a mountain with the nipple on top is Maiden Pap. No secret as to how that got its name. And then, if I've got this correct, that ridge ahead of us is Eagle's Rock, which is no more than 800 feet at its highest. That's where the Sunderland hit.'

'That's a hill, not a mountain! How in God's name did they not clear that ridge?'

Quayle smiled grimly. 'Pilot error, old boy. Just like Wing Commander Frayne said. Come on, let's go and have a look at the wreckage.'

'Who owns this land?'

'It's the Langwell Estate, the old Duke of Portland's place. Over 50,000 acres of nothing much – unless you like grouse shooting, deer stalking and salmon fishing, all of which I loathe. Oh, and there are sheep, too, as you might have noticed.'

'Is he here now?'

'Portland? I'm not sure, but his son Lord Titchfield is certainly in residence up at Braemore, the estate's hunting lodge, close to where we parked. I believe they were fishing at the time of the crash and organised a search party.'

'Were they first on the scene?'

'No, that was a shepherd named James Gunn and some locals. Then the special constables from Dunbeath arrived – Willie Bethune and Jimmy Sutherland – and they realised that the Duke was among the dead.'

'And they knew that how?'

'His air commodore's insignia, and the dog tags attached to his wrist. Then along came old Dr Kennedy, the local physician, and he pronounced everyone dead. But, of course, that was before they realised Andy Jack was alive.'

'I'd like to talk to all those people.'

Quayle's brow knitted with puzzlement and scepticism. 'What exactly are you looking for, Wilde? Bombs? Enemy action? You've been reading too much Ashenden.'

'I'm not going to interrogate anyone. I just want to thank them and perhaps get some explanation – a reason for this senseless tragedy. Something I can tell Roosevelt.'

Quayle affected a weary sigh. 'No one saw a damned thing, Wilde. Thick fog, remember.'

'I know, I know . . . I'm clutching at straws.'

'I can see that, but I'm not really sure why.' Quayle hunched over further, dug his hands deeper into his trouser pockets and shook his head with a resigned air. 'All right, Wilde. You do whatever you need to do. But be careful.'

Was that a warning? Or a threat? Wilde gave him the benefit of the doubt. 'Caution will be my watchword.'

'Come on, we've still got a trek ahead of us.'

Wreckage was scattered over a wide area. Wilde estimated it at a full quarter mile or more of debris. Thousands of fragments of metal of all sizes covered the hillside, as well as softer materials – the canvas of seats, scraps of clothing and bags. The shredded interior and exterior of a plane almost identical to the one in which he had flown less than twenty-four hours earlier. It was a sight to make a man weep.

A piece of the fuselage caught his eye. It bore words stencilled in red: DO NOT CLOSE BOMB DOORS WHILE TROLLEYS ARE OUT.

The heather and sheep grass were scorched, but the fires had long since died out in the rain. Along the slope below the ridge, four blackened and bent propellers cast incongruous shapes like abstract sculptures. It was not high here – probably no more than 600 feet, Wilde estimated – and it seemed ridiculous to him that a sound and well-maintained aeroplane should have come to grief in such a place. Eagle's Rock wasn't a mountain, it was a slope. Why wasn't Short Sunderland 4026 flying at 3,000 feet or more by the time it reached here from the Cromarty Firth?

There were about two dozen men in military uniform and others in civilian countrywear, all picking about among the debris, searching the scarred land and gathering in the remains of the plane, loading smaller pieces on to carts. The bigger parts – the twisted wings and fuselage – would have to be dragged away by heavy vehicles, if they could be brought up here.

'They never stood a chance,' Quayle said.

'And yet you say one man survived.'

'That's because the rear gun turret broke away on impact, missed the worst of the explosion.'

'Are any of the men who found the wreckage here?' Wilde asked.

'No, this is a military operation now, clearing the site.'

'Is that necessary? Hell of a lot of work.'

'Oh yes, orders from on high, professor – they don't want souvenir hunters coming up here to collect bits of royal memorabilia.'

Wilde nodded. That made sense, of course. But an intelligence man might wonder if there were another reason for their diligence: what if there were something up here that they didn't want to fall into the wrong hands?

'But it's difficult. A tracked vehicle – tank or armoured car – might just about be able to traverse these bogs, but ordinary trucks would not be easy. They had to bring horses and carts up here to take the bodies down to the ambulances.' Quayle cupped his mouth and moved closer to Wilde's ear. 'And a little bit of information – you might hear that quite a lot of money was found up here. Well, that's true – there was some Icelandic currency littered around. Quite normal to take a stash on trips like this because you never know what's needed. But of course a discovery like that will set tongues wagging among the locals, and it will inevitably get distorted in the telling.'

'Where is it now, this money?'

'Safely gathered in.'

'Nothing to worry about then.' He stretched his arms and feigned a yawn.

'Indeed not. Tired, Wilde?'

'It's been a long journey. Do you mind if I walk a little on my own, Quayle? I'd like to gather my thoughts.'

'Commune with the Holy Spirit?'

Was Quayle mocking him? Wilde did not rise to the bait. 'I was asked by the President to pray for the dead.'

'You go ahead.' The Englishman pulled out his flask, which had been miraculously refilled, and sat down on a metal cylinder. 'Snorter to put a spring in your step?'

'Later, perhaps. You realise you're sitting on an unexploded depth charge, don't you, Quayle?'

Quayle looked down at the grey container full of high explosives. 'Why, so I am, old man. Why don't they make these damned things more comfortable?'

As Wilde walked, he picked up occasional pieces – the sad detritus of tragedy: a solitary shoe, scraps of clothing, a few coins, an opened bottle of whisky that had somehow survived the impact. He found a Bakelite ashtray, identifiable as such only by the stubbed ash in its core. He looked at each article in turn then either put it down where he had found it or handed it to one of the uniformed men.

The stench of the fire still lay heavily across the moor. Parts of the plane were half-buried in a foul black brew of mud, sodden moss and burnt furze. He found himself thinking about the men aboard and wondered whether they had even known they were about to crash. Perhaps in the dense fog none of them knew their fate. That was some sort of blessing.

He stood still, bowed his head and mouthed the words of the Lord's Prayer. Even though he was not a believer, it was somehow appropriate. Perhaps the childhood churchgoer was still there in some part; once a Roman Catholic, always a Roman Catholic. His mother would expect no less of him. Anyway, what else was one to do when confronted with such appalling and senseless loss of life?

'Need that tot yet?'

Wilde turned to face Quayle, who seemed to have followed him like a faithful hound.

'Yes, I think I do.'

'Man's finest medicine.' He handed him the flask, then squinted and bent down to pick something up. Something dark and tangled, which at first sight looked like a mechanic's rag.

'What have you found, Quayle?'

Quayle unscrunched it and held it by two corners. It was very light and gossamer thin, fluttering in the breeze like a butterfly wing. 'Flier's silk scarf, I think.'

'Can I see?'

Quayle handed the silk square to Wilde. He thought it quite exquisite – black and green with a faint leaf pattern. 'It's beautiful,' Wilde said. He held it to his face. Even with the stench of ashes in the air, he could still catch its fragrance.

'Perfumed is it, Wilde? Probably given to one of the pilots by a loved one to wear as a keepsake, to give him luck – and to remind of him of all those scented nights in her bed.' He chuckled before taking the scarf back, sniffing it, then thrusting it unceremoniously into his jacket pocket. 'Devilishly sad. I'll try to find out which one owned it and have it returned to the grieving widow or paramour, poor girl. Someone at Invergordon will know, I expect.'

Wilde's attention was already elsewhere. Along the ridge above the stream – perhaps 800 yards away and on higher ground, a solitary figure was standing watching them, with a dog at his side. From this distance, it was difficult to be sure, but the man seemed to be wearing rough country clothes and cap and was carrying a long stick or crook. Wilde guessed he was a shepherd; he certainly wasn't one of the official military men.

'That's Gregor McGregor,' Quayle said. 'The local police identified him to me as one of the shepherds up here, but they said we'd get nothing out of him – and they were right. I'm told he's been hanging around and watching for the past couple of days. Bloody nuisance, actually.'

'He must have been among the first at the crash site, surely? I'd like to know what he saw.'

'So would I. Despite what the local bobby said on the subject, I did try talking to the fellow but he really has got nothing to say for himself. Not quite sure he's mastered language yet – bit soft in the head.'

'I'd like to talk to him all the same.'

'Go ahead. Weave your magic, old man.'

Wilde strolled off. The going began to get steeper and he soon realised that the shepherd was further away than he had thought. As Wilde approached, his objective moved too, as elusive as the end of a rainbow. Wilde was about to put on a surge, but then the shepherd stopped and within a couple of minutes Wilde was standing in front of him.

'Hello,' he said. 'I imagine you work up here?'

The shepherd said nothing, and Wilde saw that he was very young. Perhaps no more than sixteen. His skin was fresh and freckled, his hair a dazzling ginger-red. But his light green eyes were distant; his dog, a collie, seemed the more alert of the two.

'You're McGregor, aren't you – Gregor McGregor?'

Again, nothing.

'Perhaps I can call you Gregor, and you can call me Tom. Did you see the plane crashing on Tuesday? Perhaps you heard it.'

The boy didn't reply, but Wilde could swear that there was a change in his expression, a barely perceptible knitting of the brows as though he were thinking.

'Gregor? It's OK, you can talk to me. Perhaps you think my voice is strange – well, that's because I'm American. But I am a friend.' Wilde bent forward to pat the dog's head and was rewarded with a wagging tail. 'He's lovely – what's his name?'

Still nothing.

'Do you live near here? Where's your home, Gregor?'

He realised this was going nowhere. Quayle had been right. Even if this young man had seen or heard anything, he didn't have the wherewithal to communicate it. He smiled at the boy. 'Never mind. I expect this has all been a great shock to you.'

Wilde bent down and patted the dog once more, then he nodded. 'Thank you for your time, Gregor.' He turned and set off down the hill. He had gone no more than ten yards when he heard the voice.

'Mother said I was lying.'

Wilde stopped and slowly turned back. 'Gregor?'

'She said I was lying. She said I always lie. But I didn't lie this time.'

'What did you tell her?'

'I told her about the lassie.'

Chapter 8

'What did you say?'

'Mother said I was lying.'

'The other thing – you said something about a lassie. You mean a girl?'

'Aye, a lassie. I found her up here, dead. I told Mother, but she told me I should keep my dirty mouth shut and not say anything to anyone. She said I was a foolish boy and a liar.'

'Can you show me the body?'

'No, it's gone. Been took away.'

'But it was among the plane wreckage, with the other bodies?'

'Aye, sort of.'

'I don't understand.'

The boy's light green eyes began blinking rapidly. 'If you tell Mother I spoke to you, I'll get a beating and no supper.'

'I won't tell her. Where does she live?'

A tinkle of laughter emerged from the boy's throat, as though Wilde had asked the stupidest question imaginable. 'Where do you think she lives, mister? Ramscraigs, of course, where she's always lived. Where else would she live?'

'Can you tell me a bit more about this girl – this lassie? What did she look like?'

'She looked like a lassie, of course.'

'What was she wearing?'

'Clothes.'

'A skirt? Trousers?'

'Just clothes. Big clothes, like she was in bed. And a pack on her back.'

'You mean a Mae West and parachute?'

'A big pack. She was dead.'

'What colour was her hair? Was it long or short, Gregor?'

'I don't know. She had a thing on her head and sort of glasses. You're asking all these questions. Mother said I should keep my stupid mouth shut.'

Wilde realised he was unsettling the boy. He crouched down and stroked the dog again. 'You've got a lovely dog. Does it have a name?'

'Kite.'

'Hello, Kite, you're a fine fellow, aren't you, eh? Does he bring the sheep in, Gregor?'

'I've got to go now. I shouldn't be talking to you. I'll get another hiding.'

'Look, it's OK to talk to me – really it is. Why don't I come with you? We could go to your house and I'll talk to your mother, tell her that you've been helping and that you're not lying. How does that sound?'

'No, no, no, no, no!' His distress was obvious; he was so agitated, Wilde wondered whether he might strike out. The boy turned and ran, then fell over a rock, but picked himself up and ran on, the dog following eagerly, ranging from side to side as the boy disappeared downhill in the direction of the little stream.

'What happened, Wilde? Did you get the boy to talk?' Quayle languidly ran a hand through his windswept grey locks.

'Yes, I did.'

'Gibberish, was it?'

'He said he found a dead girl.'

Quayle's brow tightened. 'Are you serious?'

'That's what he said.'

'Well, I told you he was a simpleton.'

'Is that impossible then – that there was a woman aboard the Sunderland?'

'Well, of course, nothing's impossible, but why would there have been a woman with the Duke? And why didn't the RAF release the fact if that was the case?'

'Perhaps they wanted to save royal blushes.'

'What are you suggesting, Wilde?'

'I'm not suggesting anything. Merely wondering.'

'Look, whatever you've heard about Georgie and his crazy days, that was all behind him years ago. He has been as straight as a die and perfectly respectable since Marina came along.'

'I have no reason to doubt you, but the McGregor boy insists there was a dead girl among the bodies.'

'Well, all I can say is that he's an idiot. He probably couldn't tell a woman from a sheep anyway. Utterly preposterous.'

'How long did it take for the first search party to find the wreck?'

'An hour and a half. Good God, man, you sound like the CID!'

Wilde ignored the reprimand. 'So if Gregor McGregor was already up here he might have found the crashed plane and the bodies first, but not known what to do.'

'Anything's possible, but that doesn't mean it happened. It certainly doesn't mean there was a girl on the plane. For pity's sake, Wilde . . .'

'Do these questions bother you, Quayle?'

'I'm just astonished that you would listen to a half-witted shepherd boy. I was told you were coming here to pay your respects, not to play Maigret. You're making yourself seem ridiculous.'

'Then I'll say no more.' He looked up and saw a speck moving across the sky, a golden eagle soaring, lonely and majestic against the eternity of space. Momentarily, it lifted his heart. It was worth coming up here for such a sight alone, but then the joy vanished and he felt the uncomfortable sensation once again that he was being hoodwinked in some way and for some unknown reason.

There was perhaps more to be done up here among these hills and bogs, but not at the moment. He wanted to get to civilisation to talk with the people who knew this area best.

They drove to a village a few miles up the coast from Dunbeath. With a population of only a few hundred people, it wasn't quite big enough to be called a town, but it was a vital herring port and it was close to the hospital where the survivor of the crash had been brought.

The hospital was temporarily housed in the school in the nearby community of Lybster, because the one in Wick had been taken over by the RAF and its patients transferred.

First, they needed lodgings. There were no hotels, but they were told at the little shop that Mrs Orde – Jimmy Orde's wife – had a couple of spare rooms now that the older boys had gone off to the army, and that she would most likely be pleased of a few shillings in return for bed and board. Corporal Boycott would find a bed at Widow Fraser's house, just to the north of the straggling village.

Jean Orde lived two doors away from the shop. Her house was larger than some of the other fishermen's cottages and she was, indeed, happy to welcome Wilde and Quayle for the night, including supper and breakfast. She was a cheerful mother of five children, with three of them – aged from ten to seventeen – still at home. She said she would be pleased to feed her guests, if they wished. She had some mutton and was making a large stew, which would come with mashed potatoes and carrots. Wilde and Quayle accepted the offer.

'Now then,' Quayle said when they were alone. 'First a quick drink and then we'll call in on the hospital and see whether young Andrew Jack is in any fit state to talk.'

'Let's go and see him first, then drink.'

'I hadn't taken you for a killjoy, professor.'

The man was beginning to irritate Wilde. 'I'm not here on holiday, Quayle. I am here as a representative of the President, and I take my responsibility seriously.'

Quayle shrugged. 'Suit yourself,' he said.

'I will. I'm going to find the hospital – you do what you want.'

Quayle conceded that he had lost the argument. 'Have it your own way, old man. As your chaperon, it will be my pleasure to come with you. Don't want you being taken advantage of by these handsome Scots laddies.'

The hospital was in a grey stone building, just about large enough for its purposes – village schoolhouse in peacetime, hospital in war. A nurse in a blue uniform with a white apron allowed them in on being shown their letters of accreditation.

'He's been rather busy today, I'm afraid, gentlemen, so he won't stand up to much chatting. A couple of air force men came this morning with some official-looking papers, then the young man's relatives arrived at lunchtime and stayed an hour or so.'

'How is he?' Wilde asked.

'Och, he's a lot better than he was, but he's still not a well man. Considerable pain and discomfort from burns. He's very tired and groggy from the morphine the doctor gave him for the pain in the night, so don't expect too much from him.'

'Thank you, nurse.'

'He's a very brave man. His clothes were on fire and he had to rip them off. I'm told he also tried to drag the bodies from the flames. Go easy on him.'

'We will.'

'He was in his underpants when he got to Helen Sutherland's cottage, you know, and his face and lips all swollen. He just collapsed, so she wrapped him in blankets and gave him hot milk and biscuits.'

Now he was on his back, blankets and sheets up to his chest, very still, his eyes closed. His hands were outside the bedclothes in front of him, covered in gauze. He was a dark-haired, good-looking man, but his face was singed and torn, either by the impact when his gun turret came adrift and was flung to the ground, by the flames from the wreckage, or by gorse and rocks as he stumbled helplessly across the hillsides.

'Flight Sergeant Jack?' Quayle said softly.

Slowly his eyes opened and took in the faces of his two visitors. 'Aye,' he said.

'I am Walter Quayle and this is Professor Thomas Wilde. You won't remember, but I visited you before. At the time you were sedated and in a deep sleep. Are you feeling well enough to answer a few questions?'

'I'm to say nothing to anyone.'

'Really? On whose orders?'

'My senior officers.'

'But we are here in an official capacity. I am representing 10 Downing Street and the royal family, and Professor Wilde is here on behalf of the President of the United States.'

'Aye, well . . . careless talk costs lives.'

Quayle smiled and took out his flask. 'Where do you come from, sergeant?'

'I suppose I can tell you that – Grangemouth, not far from Falkirk.'

'Then you'd like a drop of the water of life, wouldn't you, young man? We won't tell the nurse.'

The airman shook his head and winced as the pain struck again.

'Where does it hurt?' Wilde asked.

'Everywhere. My hands are burnt, my feet are raw from roaming barefoot and my spine feels as though it's been crushed by a piledriver. I'll tell you that much, but I'll say nothing about the flight or the crash.' He paused a couple of beats. 'Why am I alive? I don't understand it. All those other poor fellows.'

Wilde forged on with his questions. 'Do you think it was pilot error? That's what is being said.'

'B—' he began then shut his mouth.

'For a moment there, I thought you were about to say "bullshit", flight sergeant.' Wilde looked into the young airman's eyes and saw tears welling. As though ashamed, he turned away.

'I don't use profanities – and I'm going back to sleep now.'

'Of course,' Wilde said. 'Would it be OK to come and see you again in the morning, perhaps? You might be feeling a little less tired.'

'No, I've said all I'll say.' His voice was choked. 'Are they really all dead? My friends and the Duke?'

'He's been warned off,' Quayle said as they walked along the short corridor to the front entrance.

'Clearly – but by whom, and why?'

'The RAF, obviously on orders from Whitehall and the Palace.'

'Strange they didn't convey the message to you then, Quayle, seeing as you're their man.'

'You know, Wilde, I didn't ask for this assignment. I didn't ask to be your guide, so please, don't take that tone with me. It's not necessary – I'm just a man on the margins doing my best in difficult circumstances.'

'I know – but you must be able to see as clearly as me that someone is covering something up.'

'Well, think about it. Just as neither the royal family, nor Number 10 – nor even the RAF for that matter – wants souvenirs taken from the crash site, so neither do they want the survivor giving his version of events before he's called in to give evidence to the board of inquiry. I imagine the two RAF officers who visited earlier made him sign the Official Secrets Act, though how he managed with two bandaged hands is anyone's guess.'

Wilde nodded. He had thought the same thing.

'Above all,' Quayle continued, 'the King and Queen are very keen to downplay this whole episode. They are deliberately avoiding a big public funeral because they don't want the nation to get the impression that they think their loss is greater than anyone else's.'

'I understand that.'

'Come on, it really is time you had a drink. Let's get Mrs Orde's supper inside us, then try out the local nightlife.'

The local nightlife was a dimly lit fishermen's drinking den near the harbour. It reeked of smoke and beer and fish. Wilde had a few whiskies, but Quayle had a great deal more and bought rounds of drinks for the herring men who had arrived home safely with their catches.

Wilde wanted to talk to the drinkers in turn, but they were a taciturn lot, and even the distribution of free drinks didn't seem to loosen their tongues. None of them knew anything about the plane crash and nor did they have any theories, or so they said. And when Wilde tried to advance the conversation to the matter of the searchers and the constables involved in the aftermath, they eyed him with suspicion and turned away.

He was left alone by the beer-wet bar wondering where this was all going, if anywhere. Wondering, too, about the weird testimony of the shepherd boy. Perhaps the body he saw, all wrapped up for flying at altitude and likely damaged by the impact of the crash, had been a man, not a woman. The lad certainly wasn't bright, and anyone could make a mistake. A voice at his side broke into his thoughts.

'Och, don't worry about them, Yankee man. I'll talk to you.'

Wilde turned to face the newcomer. 'How do you know who I am?'

The man laughed. 'Everyone knows who you are, Mr Wilde. You can't come to a place like this and slide around unnoticed.'

'Who are you?'

'I'm Jimmy, Jeanie's feller.'

'Ah, you're Mr Orde?'

'To the taxman or the pastor, I'm Mr Orde. But to everyone else I'm Jimmy.'

'Then I'm Tom – and I have to thank you for providing lodgings for Mr Quayle and myself.'

'Glad of the extra money. Times are hard.'

Wilde already knew from talking to Jean Orde that Jimmy was the skipper of a small trawler. He now discovered that the boat had arrived in harbour later than expected, and that Jimmy had gone home for a bath and some supper. He was almost as tall as Wilde; he had a greying, salt-encrusted beard, a thick mass of uncombed hair and a black and red check shirt with rolled-up sleeves. He smelt rather fresher than some of his companions.

'Jeanie has been telling me all about you and the Quayle feller,' he said. 'It seems you have come a long way to very little effect.'

'Oh no, that's not true. I came to pay my respects to a friend of America and I have done that. On top of which, I am seeing some fine countryside.'

'Aye, it's a fair place in August. Come back in January and February and tell me what you think.'

'Have you always lived here, Jimmy?'

'Why would I leave?'

'Why indeed.' It was a rhetorical question. Wilde doubted very much that *he* would want to leave a place like this if he had been brought up here. He instinctively liked Orde. He was hard, but he wore his toughness lightly.

The Scotsman did his best to read his mind. 'You're thinking we're a mad bunch of savages, eh, Tom? Is that what you're thinking?'

'I wouldn't put it quite like that, but yes, I'm sure life isn't easy up here.'

'Well, if you think we're hard, then you should meet our womenfolk.'

'I've met your wife.'

'Then you must know what I mean. I tell you, Tom, you wouldn't want to cross her if you didn't want your balls fed to the dog. She'd crack skulls before taking nonsense from any man – and that includes me. I've got the scars to prove it.'

Wilde thought of the slender, attractive woman back at their lodgings with three children to care for and two elder ones to worry about, and wondered whether Jimmy Orde might be exaggerating. A picture of Lydia back home in the relative comfort of Cambridge formed in his head; she wouldn't take any nonsense either, but she might draw the line at cracking heads or castration. She'd find other ways of keeping the men in her life in line. He changed the subject. 'You know this coastline well?'

'You don't want to talk about the women, Tom?'

'I value my balls.' Wilde laughed. He was beginning to feel mellow. The smoke and the whisky, the low ceiling of this bar, the blackouts at the window, and the company of this good fellow all conspired to make him feel at ease, if not at home. He ordered more whisky and the barman simply handed over the bottle so that Wilde poured two large ones. They clinked glasses.

'Here's to the herring and the end of the war!' Orde boomed so that the whole bar could hear.

All eyes turned to him. 'The herring!'

Wilde grinned, then followed the example of his host and downed his drink in one, before pouring two more. 'Look, Jimmy,' he said, when the other drinkers returned to their own conversations, 'would I be out of order in asking you a few questions? I know you've all got to be on the lookout for German spies, but, well . . . I want to give as complete a picture as possible of events up here to my president.'

'Of course you do. And don't mind the rest of the fellers. They don't know you, that's all. But I know when to trust a man – so fire away.'

'Well, you must have seen RAF planes often enough. You must understand the routes they take and what can go wrong. Have there been many crashes close to here? Has anyone hit Eagle's Rock before?'

'Och, the poor Duke and his crew certainly weren't the first men to come a cropper around the Scarabens and Maiden Pap. I don't know about the exact location of this one, but it's a real sadness for me to have to say that there have been many. Far too many, and it's a terrible tragedy and a waste. You'll find a fair bit of wreckage lying around up on the hills and mountains. No bodies, though – we give them the respect that's their due and bring them down for proper burial.'

'So what causes these crashes usually?'

'It's got to be one of three things – inexperienced crew, bad weather or equipment failure. Has to be one of those three.'

'Or enemy action.'

'Ah yes, there's that too. But this is a long way from Germany or anywhere else on mainland Europe.'

'So if they weren't shot down and if there was no equipment failure, then that just leaves pilot error or bad weather.'

'Or a combination of the two. They often go together.'

'But this crew were experienced. They were among the top RAF men. So I don't understand why they didn't go higher or stay over the sea if the fog was that bad.'

Orde ran a hand through his thick mop of hair. 'This would had been the Tuesday, I'm told. About lunchtime or soon after?'

'Yes. Why?'

Orde shrugged, then knocked back his whisky. Wilde did likewise.

'Another?'

'Go on then.'

Wilde poured two more shots. 'Cheers,' he said.

'Your health, Tom.'

'So tell me, Jimmy, does the timing of the crash mean something to you?'

'Och, it's probably nothing.'

'Go on.'

He looked around the bar, as if to be sure he wasn't heard above the deafening din. 'All right then, there was something that puzzled me a little bit. But don't go shouting it about, will you?'

'I won't.'

'Well, we were just leaving harbour – perhaps four or five miles east and north of Lybster, heading for a herring ground away from the enemy submarines, we hoped. I was at the wheel and I heard the drone of a low-flying aircraft, but of course I couldn't see anything because of the fog that day. But you know how fog drifts and swirls, well, it did – and then, for the briefest of moments, I saw a spot of blue sky and a plane – a flying boat, I could swear. Flying low, no more than a few hundred feet maybe. And then, after a couple of seconds, I didn't see it any more, or give any more thought to it. No one else aboard mentioned anything.'

'You think it was the Duke's Sunderland?'

Jimmy looked at Wilde with a curious expression, as though wondering whether he had already said too much, or perhaps fearing that he might be thought a fool. Then he shook his head slowly. 'No, it couldn't have been. The Duke's plane would have

been flying due north and a little eastwards from the Cromarty
Firth before turning in towards the land . . .'

'But that wasn't the direction of the plane you saw?'

'I had the boat's compass before my eyes and I tell you the
plane was coming directly *from* the east.' He held up his empty
glass. 'Jesus, look, my glass is empty again. How in the name of
all that's holy did that happen?'

Chapter 9

Wilde was pouring Jimmy Orde another double when the fight began. A loud shout from outside, then a series of thuds and cracking of wood. The packed taproom fell silent, then as one they all moved towards the door and tumbled out into the warm night air. Something was happening and everyone wanted to see what it was.

Walter Quayle was lying curled up on the flagstones in an alley at the side of the drinking hole. A fair young man aged about seventeen, wearing a grey woollen hat close around his brow and ears, was kicking at him. Another man, older and weatherbeaten, perhaps the father, was on his knees punching at Quayle's head.

'Stop!' Wilde shouted. 'Get off him.' He pulled the younger man away, then tried to drag the older man off.

The man turned to him, fists raised. 'Aye, you're one of them, too, are you? Like to touch my boy, eh?' He lunged forward with a bonecruncher, but Wilde easily parried the blow.

He held up his palms for peace. 'I'm not going to fight you. I don't know what this is about, but let's call it a day before any more harm's done.'

The man punched again, but Wilde sidestepped it and the man fell forward, stumbling to his knees. All the other drinkers from the bar had made a circle around them and were watching with eager fascination.

Wilde gripped the older man's arm and helped him to his feet. 'That's enough,' he said. 'Are you OK?'

'No, we're not OK, mister!' It was the youth talking, the one with the woollen hat who had been doing the kicking. He was standing, shoulders back, like a dog at bay, but one that didn't really want to fight.

Wilde caught the barman's eye. 'Help him,' he said, pointing to Quayle, who wasn't moving. He turned back to the two assailants. 'Now what is this?'

'He's a bastard queer, is what he is,' the older one said. 'Tried it on with my boy Malcolm.'

'Aye, I just came out for a piss. Just pissing against the wall here and the bastard queer came and stood beside me, real close, took out his thing, but he wasn't pissing. Playing with himself, the dirty queer bastard. Then he reached across and touched me. That's when I smacked him one. Bastard queer.'

Jimmy Orde stepped forward and stood beside Wilde. 'All right, lads, we've had our fun for the day. Whatever happened out here, I don't want anyone getting their neck stretched for murder, let's all just cool off.' The barkeep and one of his customers were tending to Walter Quayle. 'How is he, Davy?'

'Not good. He's taken a hammering.'

'We need to get him to the hospital,' Wilde said.

'Aye,' Orde said. 'We'll get him there and call out the doctor.' He turned to the assailants. 'You two get home and pray yon man's not badly injured or worse.'

The fight had already gone out of them. Their aggressive stance had been replaced by slumping shoulders and downcast eyes. The father made a move and motioned with his head for his son to follow, then together they slunk off down the street.

An hour later, Quayle was in hospital. He had concussion, a suspected fractured rib and a broken nose. He had a room to himself. Wilde stayed with him for half an hour then said he would see him in the morning and went back to his lodging with Jimmy Orde and his wife.

'I'm sorry about that,' Orde said as they sipped cups of tea in his kitchen. 'You'll be going home with bad thoughts about our hospitality in these parts.'

'Not your fault, Jimmy. That sort of thing could happen anywhere.'

'Aye, well, all three of them could end up in prison – one for importuning an indecent act, the other two for assault.'

'But that's not going to happen, is it?'

'Not as far as I'm concerned, no. I'll say nothing to the constable and I doubt anyone else will either.'

With the drama all but over, Wilde had other matters on his mind. 'You mentioned something – the direction of travel of a Sunderland flying boat at about the time the Duke's plane crashed into Eagle's Rock.'

'Aye, so I did.'

'Do you want to tell me more about it?'

'There's no more to tell. I saw what I saw, but I couldn't tell you that it was the Duke's plane, if that's what you're thinking.'

'But you're certain that plane wasn't coming up the coast from Invergordon?'

'Impossible. It was coming out of the North Sea, from the direction of Scandinavia.'

Wilde liked this man. He liked his doubts and his honesty. 'Who have you told about the plane you saw?'

'No one, except you.'

'Why not?'

Orde shrugged. 'Who should I tell? Why would anyone be interested?'

'Because you don't believe the version of events you've read in the papers, do you, Jimmy? You don't believe the Duke of Kent was going anywhere – you think he was coming back from somewhere. So why keep it to yourself?'

He looked uncomfortable. 'There's a war on. Doesn't pay to be too nosy, does it? If the powers-that-be want to give out their own version of events, who is Jimmy Orde to gainsay them?'

'Perhaps the powers-that-be aren't being told the whole truth.'

'Now you're getting into tricky waters, Tom. Any herring man will tell you to stay away from the shallows and the rocks.'

Wilde didn't like it, but he understood Orde's point of view. 'You may be right, Jimmy.'

Orde was picking up the cups. 'I think we've both drunk enough and said enough, don't you, Tom? And so I'll bid you good night. There's a basin in your room with hot water, and Jeanie will have put a chamberpot under the bed. The privy's out the back.'

The cups rattled as Orde carried them out to the kitchen, leaving Wilde with questions which he would somehow have to answer himself: firstly, wherever the plane was coming from, why did it crash? And if it was coming back from a flight instead of embarking on one, then where had it been? And why was the government so keen to keep it secret, and keep the Americans – and, indeed, the British people – out of the loop?

As he squeezed himself into the narrow cot bed that must have once been a child's, there was another thing that bothered Wilde. Assuming that Orde was correct and that the plane was returning to Scotland, why was it flying so low, and in thick fog? If it was in trouble, then why didn't it simply come down on the sea? Flying boats didn't need runways; they could find safe harbour on almost any stretch of water if it was calm enough.

Chapter 10

In the morning, Wilde paid another short visit to Quayle. He was sitting up in bed in a room next door to the surviving tail gunner from the Sunderland. Quayle's chest was swathed in bandages and a large strip of plaster was taped across the centre of his face, covering his damaged nose. He also had a black eye. The nurse had told Wilde that he would need to stay in hospital for at least one more day, perhaps two.

Wilde shook his head. 'You're an idiot, Quayle.'

'Nice to see you, too, Wilde.'

'This isn't the back streets of Soho, you know. That boy could have ruined your career, you realise that? He could have had you charged in a court of law. But you're lucky – none of it will come out.'

'Oh, the boy wanted it – he just didn't know he wanted it.' Quayle laughed, then clutched his chest. 'Jesus, that hurts – my bloody rib.'

'I didn't even know I'd said anything funny.'

'Do you think I care a fig what some Scottish fisher boy might say about me? He was quite pretty, though, don't you think? In a coarse sort of way.'

'Was he? I don't really share your interest in boys.'

'I realised that as soon as I met you. You don't know what you're missing. Anyway, you're a bit stuck now. You won't be able to go anywhere without me to escort you.'

'If you say so.'

'You can't go off on your own – you know that. This whole area is under military control.'

'Then I'll sit in the Orde house and read my book until you're up and about.'

'You do that, Wilde.'

Wilde had no intention of obeying Quayle. He knew that Corporal Boycott would have orders not to drive him, so he asked Jimmy Orde to organise a car. 'I'll pay good money. I only want it for the day. Quarter of a tank of gas should see me right.'

'That's very irregular, Tom.'

'So are you, Jimmy.'

Orde laughed. 'It's a shame you live in bloody England. If you lived up here, I could teach you fishing and make a man out of you. In another life, we might have been brothers.'

'Make a man out of me? I'll take you on in the ring any day of your choosing.'

'Yes, I noticed you were a pugilist. Anyway, I'll get you that car.'

'Can I use your phone while you're gone?'

'Aye, of course.'

Wilde called Lydia. 'Has anyone been hanging around outside?' he asked.

'Not that I've noticed. Why?'

'Nothing. Just developing paranoia, that's all.'

'You've got *me* worried now.'

'Forget I said anything.'

'Where are you, Tom? When are you coming home?'

'Scotland – and soon, I hope. Are you both OK?'

'Actually, there was something . . .'

'Go on.'

'The phone . . . there was a click on the line when you called. I noticed it when I spoke to Edie last night.'

Orde brought back a small Morris 8, which belched black smoke from the exhaust. Wilde thanked him then drove himself to the scattered hamlet of Ramscraigs, on the coast a little south of Dunbeath. He asked at the first house he came to and was directed to the mean crofter's cottage that Gregor McGregor and his mother called home. A tiny woman, no more than four and a half feet tall, with the same red hair as her son, opened the door and gazed up at Wilde as though he was some undiscovered species. 'Yes?'

'You're Gregor's mother, I think.'

'He's not in,' she said, attempting to close the door even as she spoke.

Wilde's foot shot out and held the door open. 'It's *you* I wish to speak to, Mrs McGregor.' He towered over the woman. He estimated she must be in her late thirties or early forties, though it was difficult to tell. Her hair was thin, her face was webbed with blue veins and her hands were ravaged and claw-like. Wilde took her for a heavy drinker and smoker.

'I've nothing to say to you, whoever you are. Now get your foot out of my door and away with you.' Her voice was rasping.

'I want five minutes of your time, Mrs McGregor, nothing more.'

'I told you, mister, I've nothing to say. My boy's getting the sheep in for the dipping. And even if he was here, he'd not say a word to you.'

'Five minutes.' Wilde pulled out his wallet and held up a banknote. 'Ten bob for your time.'

She hesitated no more than a second before reaching out and snatching the note. Wilde took the opportunity of her lapsed concentration to push the door open.

'Do you mind?' he said, stepping into her tiny front hall without waiting for her permission. The house was very small, no more than two rooms on the ground floor and another two above. The ceiling was low, the walls were damp and stained, and the smell that hit him was of boiling cabbage, burnt fat, and rotting rubbish. He gagged. It seemed to him that there were no colours in the house: little light came through the filthy windows, only shades of grime and mould.

'Here, mister, I didn't say you could come in,' she said, stuffing the ten shillings into her apron pocket.

'As I said, I won't keep you more than a few minutes. It's about what Gregor saw up at Eagle's Rock. He told you he saw a dead woman.'

'Well, he tells me a lot of things, but I take no note of the numpty.'

'But what if he *did* see a woman? He should tell the police, shouldn't he? He told me that you told him not to tell anyone.'

'I don't want no more trouble than I've got, mister, and I certainly don't want no more police. I have enough to do with him as it is. The sheep have more brains . . .'

He looked at her closely; her pursed mouth had clamped shut like a vice after her tirade and she was standing ramrod stiff, as though terrified of something. 'He should say what he saw,' Wilde insisted. 'If the police don't believe him, that's their business – but it's his civic duty to say what he saw.'

She snorted with derision. 'Civic duty! Someone pissed in yer whisky, mister?'

'Mrs McGregor, I think you're hiding something from me.'

'Well, I'm not hiding the door, so you know where that is – and you can sling your hook. Go on, away with you, out of my house.'

'Five minutes of your time and I'll give you another ten bob.'

She was thinking, her cunning eyes flicking between Wilde and the door. Ten shillings was difficult to pass up. 'Who are you, mister? You're not English with that accent, that's for certain. German spy, are you?'

'I'm an American citizen and I'm here on behalf of President Roosevelt. He was a good friend of the Duke of Kent.'

'Then if you're American you'll have a lot more than ten shillings in your pocket, now won't you?'

'No. Ten shillings it is – or nothing. Your choice, Mrs McGregor.'

'Fifteen.'

'Of course, if you discover that you have something inter-esting to tell me, then of course I could pay fifteen shillings, maybe a little more. A pound, perhaps.'

'Well, I can tell you that Gregor is a lying, thieving numpty.'

'Thieving?'

She shifted awkwardly. 'Lying, I said – lying.'

'You said thieving, Mrs McGregor.'

'Well then, I spoke out of turn. Anyway, what's it to you?'

'I want to know what happened up on that hill two miles from here. He said he found a dead woman. He was quite spe-cific about that. And he said you told him he wasn't to mention it to anyone. But he did mention it – he told me. Now why would you want it kept secret?'

She was small, but she had strength in her wiry arms, and she pushed him towards the door with determination. He didn't resist; what would have been the point?

'Go on,' she said. 'Get away with you and keep your filthy Yankee money.' She stood on her step, arms crossed over her apron. 'And you know what you've done? You've earned the boy a beating, that's what.' She reached out and pulled a heavy cane from just inside the doorway. 'He'll have the hiding of his life, thanks to you.'

Wilde reached into his wallet once more and removed a pound note. He dropped it in front of her and watched it flutter to the ground at her feet. 'Here,' he said. 'Take the money, but don't beat the boy. If I hear any harm has come to him, I'll get the police on to you.' He spoke forcefully, though he had no idea whether the police would act on such a complaint. It was, however, the only threat that came to mind.

She was scrabbling on the ground, picking up the banknote, spitting on it, then dusting it down before pushing it into her pocket alongside the ten shillings. Without another word, she went back into her house and slammed the door closed.

Wilde walked back to the car then drove a little way north before turning inland along a narrow road that amounted to little more than a farm track. This was the road he and Quayle had taken the day before, but now he went a bit further, reaching a scattering of houses known as Braemore, part of the Duke of Portland's 50,000-acre estate. He asked a woman walking a pair of dogs for directions to Braemore Lodge and was pointed towards an area of woodland.

The house was large and made of stone. Quite grand, but not palatial; most notable perhaps for the dozen or so chimney stacks, which suggested warmth was valued over stateliness in these climes. He parked in the shade of some trees and approached the front door. An old gardener was standing next to a flower bed watching him, trowel in hand. Wilde nodded to him but got no acknowledgement, so he carried on to the main door and knocked twice. There was no reply.

'They're no here,' the old gardener called out.

Wilde walked over to him. 'Do you know where I can find them?'

'Who wants to know?'

Wilde introduced himself. 'I was hoping for a word with the Duke of Portland's son, Lord Titchfield. I believe he has been staying here.'

The gardener neither confirmed nor denied this, merely tilted his grey head to one side.

'Is there any way I can get a message to him? Is he out fishing or stalking?'

'Write a note and stick it through the letterbox.'

'I'd much rather talk to him in person. Do you think he might be down at the house in Berriedale? Langwell House, is it?'

The old gardener shrugged. 'Go to Berriedale and ask them.' He got down to his knees to continue his weeding.

'One more thing,' Wilde said. 'Did *you* go up to the site of the Duke of Kent's plane crash? Were you part of the search party?'

'What if I was? What's it to you? Reporter from the big city newspapers, are you?'

'No, I'm not a reporter.'

'Well, I've nothing to say either ways.'

Wilde felt the anger welling up. What was the matter with these people? Yes, there was a war on – but this defensiveness was becoming ridiculous. He sighed and turned away to walk the short distance to his car. He heard the growl of another vehicle approaching. An open-topped military car came into view and slowed to a halt beside his own little Morris. Two armed soldiers emerged, one an officer with a holstered service revolver, the other a private with a rifle.

'Thomas Wilde?' the officer said.

'That's me.'

'I'm Lieutenant Hague. We've had complaints about you.'

'Oh really?'

'You have been observed wandering around these parts asking questions. You have been taken for a spy.'

'Would you like to see my papers? I have full accreditation from the government.' He removed his documents from his jacket pocket and handed them over to the officer, who examined them closely then returned them.

'Thank you, Professor Wilde. That all seems in order. But it doesn't explain your present movements. Nor the fact that you are operating without your designated escort.'

'What movements? Is there a law against calling on people?'

'That very much depends.'

'Look, I want to find out exactly what happened up at Eagle's Rock so that I can report back to the President of the United States. You do realise, perhaps, that we are allies . . .'

The officer was a stern young man with a cut-glass accent and sharp, athletic cheekbones. He reminded Wilde of a particularly cruel monitor from his early days at Harrow. 'Your point is well made, professor. But you will desist from asking further questions. The local people have been warned to look out for enemy agents – and I'm afraid that is how you are seen.'

'I don't suppose Walter Quayle has anything to do with this?'

Lieutenant Hague stiffened. 'Mr Quayle did indeed suggest we look for you up here. It appears he was correct.'

'Well, you can go back to Mr Quayle and tell him that I will see him within the hour and if he is worried about my movements, he can tell me so himself. Good day to you, lieutenant.' Without another word, Wilde opened the door of the Morris.

He felt the hard stab of a gun muzzle in his lower back and arched his body. Turning, he pushed the private's rifle barrel aside, then fixed his gaze on the officer. 'Do you think this is wise, lieutenant? Threatening a representative of the President of the United States of America?'

'We'll be watching you, Wilde. One wrong move and your life won't be worth living.'

Wilde shrugged, climbed into the car, fired up the engine in a cloud of stinking black smoke and set off down the track towards Dunbeath.

A mile along the road, he stopped in a small layby and waited until the military vehicle with the two soldiers came up behind him. They slowed down and looked at him suspiciously. He wound down the window and smiled at them. 'Just soaking up the scenery before I return to the south of England. You can squeeze past, can't you?'

The officer gave him a murderous look.

Wilde smiled again, then wound up his window and waved to them as they moved on with what seemed to be a great deal of reluctance. When they had disappeared into the distance, he climbed out of the Morris. He had seen something – a flock of twenty sheep on a rise, perhaps half a mile to the south, and coming his way. The shepherd herding them had a shock of red hair. Wilde set off in his direction.

A few minutes later he was standing in front of Gregor McGregor and his collie. The lad wasn't meeting his eyes.

'Hello, boy,' Wilde said, patting the dog. He looked up at McGregor. 'Kite, that's his name, isn't it? Fine fellow.'

McGregor said nothing, merely looked somewhere into the middle distance with his strange green eyes.

'Gregor, I've been to see your mother.'

That got a response. The boy looked startled and his eyes flicked straight to Wilde's.

'She talked to me about you.'

'No, no, mister, no. I'll be beaten. I'll get no supper.'

'You'll be all right – I gave her some money.'

'No, no, she'll beat me.'

'You're scared of your mother, aren't you? She said you steal things.'

'She makes me. She makes me steal and then I have to give the money to her.'

'That's why your mother told you she didn't want you telling anyone about the body you saw – because you stole money from the body and gave it to her. Isn't that the truth, Gregor?'

'I can't say anything.'

'Do you want me to go back to your mother?'

'No, mister, please, no.'

'Then tell me what you did.'

He was silent again, shaking, his head down.

'Gregor?'

The boy groaned. A sound from a deep well of despair that must have lain within him all his life. 'All right, all right,' he said.

'The dead lassie had a purse and there was money in it, pound notes and some coins – a few shillings, a half crown and some pennies. I gave them to Mother. She snatched them from me.'

'Anything else – something more valuable, perhaps?'

McGregor was backing away. The dog had moved from its position controlling the sheep and was at its master's side, protective, growling at Wilde.

'What was it? Have you got it with you? Show me – or I'll tell your mother you've held something back from her, and you'll be beaten.'

Wilde could see that the boy was terrified. He felt rotten to be doing this to him, but he had no option. The boy knew something or had something, and then he saw what it was. Gingerly, the boy dug his hand into his back pocket and pulled out a dark blue rectangle of cardboard, perhaps six inches by four.

No, not just any old piece of blue cardboard: a British passport. The boy held it out between thumb and forefinger as though it were hot and might burn him. Wilde took it.

'Thank you, Gregor. Your mother doesn't know about this, does she?'

He shook his head.

'And you haven't told anyone else, have you?'

Again he shook his head.

'You found this on the body of the dead woman?'

'In her bag. She had a bag. I took it because I liked her picture. It's pretty.'

'And can you show me where the body is?'

'No. It's gone. Must have been taken away by the soldiers.'

Wilde opened the well-worn passport. He found a name, Harriet Hartwell, and a photograph of a young woman he had seen once before, very recently. The woman who called herself Claire Hart at the Cameron Arms in Helmsdale twenty-four hours earlier.

She had seemed very much alive.

Heinrich Müller leant back in his leather armchair, his gaze fixed on the prisoner's eyes. 'Are you not getting tired of this, Herr Posse?'

'Yes, I am tired.' His fingers trembled in his lap.

'It says here in your file that you are almost sixty. You are an old man. Would you not like to live out your last years in comfort?'

'Of course I would.'

'Of course I would, *sir.*'

'I am not going to call you that.' The words were defiant, but the voice was faint with dread.

The rubber truncheon slammed into the back of his neck. Posse's head jerked and he let out an agonised scream.

They were in a large, windowless room in the cellars of Prinz-Albrecht-Strasse, 8, Berlin. Headquarters of the Gestapo and the SS. The air was thick with the stench of cigarette smoke and sweat. Apart from Müller and the prisoner, there were three other officers present, one of whom had wielded the cosh. The other two lounged against the whitewashed wall, smirking and giggling.

Müller yawned ostentatiously. 'All I require is a few answers, Posse, then I can go home and you can return to your cell. So tell me, do you know a man named Streletz? Heinz Streletz.'

Joachim Posse couldn't talk. He was gasping for breath. An arm snaked around his neck. 'Answer the Gruppenführer, pig.' The grip tightened. Müller watched the prisoner's face turn purple and his eyes bulge. He made a gesture to his junior officer and Posse was released, his head thrown forward against the hard edge of the desk.

'Well, let me enlighten you, Herr Posse. Like you, Heinz Streletz is a leader of what remains of the traitorous Red Front. Like you he is a filthy Bolshevik. He is your friend and confederate, so of course you know him. All I require of you is his present whereabouts. Simple, yes?'

The prisoner still either would not or could not answer. His breathing was shallow, his head bleeding and slumped into his chest. Müller sighed. It was going to be a long session, but Joachim Posse was an important prisoner, important enough that the chief of the Gestapo himself was directing his *Verschärfte Vernehmung* – enhanced interrogation.

Müller's nose wrinkled and his lip curled involuntarily at the new smell that invaded his nostrils. The prisoner had soiled himself. The Gestapo chief tutted. 'Dear me, how embarrassing for you, Herr Posse.'

There was a sharp knock at the door. Müller nodded to one of his underlings, who proceeded to open it. His secretary, Gretchen, came in and walked straight to the desk, studiously ignoring the prisoner and the unpleasant miasma of the room. She threw out her arm in a Hitler salute and handed him a sheet of paper. 'This message has just arrived, Herr Gruppenführer. It is marked urgent.'

'Thank you, Gretchen. Wait for me in my office, if you would.'

'Yes, sir.' Like a well-drilled soldier, she turned on her heel and within moments was gone.

As Müller read the paper, his muscles tightened. He was accustomed to difficult situations, many of them unpleasant, like the present interrogation of Joachim Posse, but such things were all in a day's work and when he returned home at the end of his long day he slept like a baby.

But he would have no sleep tonight.

He scanned the paper again, scarcely able to believe what he was reading. God in heaven, how had this been allowed to happen? The message Gretchen had brought was from an agent in England, informing him of a possible defection. A member of an important German delegation had gone missing in the neutral territory of Sweden, and the British were involved. The enormity of the incident was instantly obvious.

The problem for Müller was that the missing man had been employed in his own department in a senior role and was in possession of vital and delicate secrets. It would be bad for Germany if this confidential information was communicated to the Allies, but it would be a great deal worse for Müller himself.

He read the paper a third time, then folded it carefully and slid it into his jacket pocket. As the son of a police officer and with much of his own life devoted to police work, the Gestapo chief knew how to deal with this. But it would be difficult – and his one fear was that he might already be too late. He was making for the door when he remembered the prisoner and turned to his lieutenant. 'Take him back to his cell, Huber.'

'He seems to be dead, Herr Gruppenführer. A heart attack, perhaps.'

Müller glanced at the collapsed figure of Joachim Posse. 'Then send his ashes to the widow, and bill her for cremation expenses.'

Chapter 11

Before leaving the moor between Braemore and Dunbeath, Wilde pressed the shepherd boy for more information. 'At least you can show me where you found the woman, even if she's no longer there,' he said. 'Will you do that for me, Gregor? I can give you more money for your mother . . .'

'No, mister, I've got to get these sheep in for the dipping.'

'Yesterday you told me the body was near all the other bodies and the wreckage of the plane? But how close exactly?'

'I was lying a bit. She was away from them, down by the burn.'

'The stream?'

'Aye, Berriedale Water.'

'How far from the plane?'

He looked bemused, as though he didn't understand the question.

'A hundred yards – two? Quarter mile?'

'Och, I don't know. By the burn below Eagle's Rock.'

Wilde opened the passport and showed Gregor the picture of the woman he now knew to be Harriet Hartwell. 'Was this the dead lassie you saw?'

'It looks like her, but the one I saw was all dressed up like it was winter.'

'And you were sure she was dead? Did you take her pulse?'

'I've seen plenty of dead sheep – and she was as dead as any of them. I turned her over on to her front because I didn't want the ravens taking her eyes like they do to the lambs. She was pretty, you see, the lassie. I didn't want them to get her eyes . . .'

'OK, Gregor. Well, if I were you I would say no more about this.' He handed the boy a few coins. 'Tell your mother you found this money. Don't tell her you met me. I truly hope you're not punished.'

'What about that?' He jutted his chin at the passport. 'That's mine, that is.'

'I'm keeping this. I've just paid you for it.'

Wilde turned and walked away. He had one more thing to do. The petrol gauge was low, but it wasn't far to Helmsdale, about fifteen miles, and he reckoned he would make it there and back if he drove steadily.

Hamish Cameron was at his desk in the lobby of his small hotel. 'Good day,' he said. 'So you're back. Will you be staying the night this time?'

'I'm afraid not, but I have a simple question for you. When I was last here, there was a woman checking out. She gave her name as Claire Hart. How long had she been here?'

Cameron looked Wilde straight in the eye. 'I don't recall giving you the name of any of my guests.'

'This is important, Mr Cameron. I just want to know when Miss Hart arrived, whether she was alone, and what state she was in.'

'You seem very insistent, Mr . . .'

'Wilde. Professor Thomas Wilde.'

'Do you mind telling me what this is all about?'

'I can't.'

'Then we're in the same boat, aren't we? You won't say anything, and nor will I. Now, do you mind leaving my hotel. I have the books to attend to.'

This was going nowhere. He tried looking at the register again, but Cameron's arms were folded over it. 'Very well, Mr Cameron. But you may be hearing from others about this matter.'

'And I shall treat them with the same respect I have shown you.'

Wilde went back to the car. He sat in the driver's seat, fuming. Then he remembered: someone called Morrison had taken the woman in his taxicab. He climbed out of the car again. A passer-by directed him to Morrison's house, but no one was in. He knocked at the house next door. An old man with a stick answered.

'It's Morrison you want, is it? He's no' here today.'

'Do you know where he is?'

'Och, he comes and goes. I can give him a message if you want.'

'Does he have a telephone?'

'Aye, he does. Is it a taxicab you're after, because McIver will help you if you can't find Morrison.'

'No, it's Morrison I want.'

'I can find you the number, if you like.'

'Thank you.'

It had been a wasted trip. He drove back to Jimmy Orde's house at a crawl and dropped off the car.

'The military have been here asking questions,' Orde said.

'Such as?'

'They wanted to know what I had been saying to you and where you were. I told them we talked about herring and that you had gone for a walk, as far as I knew.'

'But you didn't mention the plane you saw?'

'No, Tom. I know when to keep my mouth shut.'

'Well, I'm sorry you're involved in this, Jimmy.'

They shook hands warmly and Wilde gave the fisherman his Cambridge contact details in case he should hear any more about the death of the Duke or the flight of the Sunderland.

'Be careful, Tom,' Orde said.

Wilde frowned, surprised by the exhortation. 'Are you worried about me, Jimmy?'

'Aye, I am. I'd say you were the kind of fellow that rushes in where others might fear to tread.'

'A little like you then?'

Orde managed a grin, but it was tinged with some unspoken concern.

Wilde's last chore in Scotland was to visit Walter Quayle in hospital.

'You've been up to no good,' Quayle said. He was a lot more wide awake than he had been at the last visit, but he still looked in a bad way with all the bandaging, the damaged nose and the black eye, which seemed to have coloured up yellowy-orange since Wilde's previous visit.

'Well, I'm out of your hair now, Quayle. I'm catching the next train south. And there really was no need to set the bloody army on me. That young lieutenant could learn some manners.'

'And you could learn to stick to the agreed terms of your business here. Anyway, what exactly have you been up to? Anything to tell me?'

'You mean about the dead woman Gregor McGregor found?'

'God, you're not on that line again, are you? Is that what you've been doing – trying to find some evidence to suggest the Duke had his fancy piece aboard the plane? You're out of line, Wilde. This is not the way close allies behave.'

'But what if there *was* a woman?'

'Have you found something to suggest there might be?'

'No,' he lied, 'but what if there was? Wouldn't you want to find out who she was? Or maybe you already know, Quayle – is that it? The British Establishment closing ranks? Perhaps you're keeping something from your American friends?'

'This is getting utterly ridiculous, Wilde. I think you're right – it's time to get you south. Corporal Boycott will convey you to your train.'

'There was one more thing. Is there any possibility that the Sunderland was arriving back in Scotland rather than leaving? What if a fishing vessel saw it coming in low from the east? What would that mean?'

Even beneath his injuries, Wilde could see Quayle's languid features hardening. He fixed his visitor with a gaze of such intensity that Wilde had a sudden feeling that the man actually loathed him.

'Well?'

'Who the hell have you been talking to, Wilde? Is this something you heard from our host, Mr Orde? God preserve us from fishermen's tales . . .'

'You seem very touchy.'

'Oh, sod off, Wilde. I'm sick of the sight of you.'

Wilde returned to London by a series of trains. It took him the best part of thirty hours and he did not stop off in Cambridge; his conversations with Gregor McGregor and Jimmy Orde – and the passport he now held firmly concealed in his inside jacket pocket – had instilled a sense of dread and urgency in him. Something strange was happening, and he wasn't at all sure what it was.

From the station he made his way directly to a newspaper office in Fleet Street. It was late at night, and dark outside. Inside, the lobby was suffused in a dim light. The receptionist put a call through to the newsroom for him and within a couple of minutes he was joined by a shirt-sleeved man with sweat-stained armpits and loosened tie. The epitome of a hard-bitten newspaperman.

They immediately grinned at each other and shook hands warmly.

'Hello, Ron, good to see you.'

'And you, too, Tom – though God knows what you're doing here.'

'All will become clear. But first, how are you? Any word of Edward?'

The men were old friends with a mutual interest in motor-bikes and the singing of Bessie Smith. Ron Christie was night editor of a national newspaper and father to a remarkably fine scholar, Edward, who had come under Wilde's tutelage in his three years at Cambridge.

'I think he's probably in North Africa, but his exact location is classified, of course. And you? How's the youngster?'

'Johnny's well, Lydia too.'

'Good. Well, come on up and give me a clue why you're here.'

'I'm looking for a girl – a young woman,' Wilde said as they entered the lift.

'Lydia not enough for you any more?'

'Have you heard the name Harriet Hartwell, alias Claire Hart?'

'Should I have?'

'I don't know.'

'Well, is she famous – singer? Movie star? – or is she a criminal?'

'Again, I don't know.'

'Come on, Tom, let's get you to the library. You can delve around in our cuttings to your heart's content.'

Christie took Wilde up to the third floor. From somewhere far below, the building shuddered, like the thunder of a battle-ship's engines coming to life.

'The presses are starting to roll,' the newspaperman said.

'How late will you be working?'

'Three in the morning, probably. Later if something happens. You never know these days – exciting stuff emerging from the Russian front.'

'And Egypt?'

Christie sucked in air through his teeth. 'Can't even bear to think about what Edward's up to, Tom. Anyway, here we are.' He pushed open the library door and they approached a wooden counter. 'I'll introduce you to Arkwright the librarian and he'll help you find your mystery woman. If you ask him nicely, he'll show you down to the editorial floor when you're done. And then we can go for a drink – you look in dire need of a drink. And food, for that matter.'

Arkwright was ancient and moved through his library with the plodding resignation of a pit pony whose entire life had been spent without sunlight. Wilde stood on the other side of the counter, waiting. A few minutes later, the white-haired retainer returned with a shake of his head. 'No Harriet Hartwell,' he said.

'Any other Hartwells?'

'A few. I'll bring them to you and you can look through them, Mr Wilde.' Moments later he was slapping a dozen envelopes on the counter in front of Wilde.

'Thank you.'

Some of the envelopes were quite new, others old and torn and yellowed. All were packed with newspaper cuttings going back fifty or more years, detailing the doings of various people – both rich and poor, sporting and criminal – sharing very little except their surname. Still no sign of a Harriet. Perhaps the one in the passport was the daughter or wife of one of these men, but there was no way of knowing.

Arkwright shuffled back. 'Any joy, professor?'

'No, nothing.' He decided to take a gamble and removed the passport from his pocket, opening it to the photograph page. 'This is the young lady. You must see a lot of photographs, Mr Arkwright – I don't suppose you've ever seen her, have you?'

The librarian studied it closely. 'No, sir, it means nothing, I'm afraid. But I've had another idea. Our snappers are very poor spellers as a rule. Let me try some other names – Harwell without the "t", for instance. Can I borrow the passport for a few minutes?'

Wilde handed it over.

'This could take a little time. Would you like a cup of tea while you're waiting, sir? I've got a brew on.'

'That would be very nice, thank you.'

Wilde and Arkwright went through all the Harwells and several other permutations besides. A grainy photograph of an attractive woman named Charlotte Hartley seemed almost possible, but Wilde wasn't convinced.

An hour and a half later they found her. She was in a file named Harriet Harlow. It contained a single cutting from the society page of a rival Fleet Street publication, dated July 1942, just over a month ago. A group of half a dozen people were raising their glasses in some sort of nightclub. Harriet Hartwell was in the picture but the photographer had taken her name down incorrectly, just as Arkwright had suggested might be the case.

Nor was she the only person Wilde recognised in the picture. There were three famous people – the actress Mimi Lalique, the immensely rich Lord Templeman and the playwright Noël Coward. The caption placed them as denizens of the Dada Club in Soho, and said they were raising a toast to their old friend the Duke of Kent on the birth of his son Michael.

In the newspaper picture, Harriet Hartwell was laughing and carefree. The woman Wilde recalled from the Cameron Arms in Helmsdale had been haunted and hurried. Or was that just his imagination running free with the benefit of hindsight?

'Can I borrow this, Mr Arkwright?'

'You can take it down to the editorial floor, but you can't remove it from the building, I'm afraid.'

Five minutes later, Wilde was sliding into a chair alongside Christie on the backbench – the powerhouse of the newspaper, where the next edition was developed and perfected. The ashtrays were overflowing and the sub-editors – all men, not a woman in sight – were lounging around waiting for work.

'How did it go, Tom?'

'Pretty good. Your man Arkwright is a miracle worker.' He placed the cutting in front of his old friend. 'Does this mean anything to you?'

Christie studied the article. 'Ah, the Dada Club . . .'

'You've heard of it?'

'Of course. It's the haunt of the louche and lovely. Our dear departed Duke of Kent was a regular for many years until marriage, fatherhood and respectability were foisted on him by his unforgiving family. So your lady friend is one of that crew, is she?'

'Well, she's in the picture, although they've got her name wrong.'

'Interesting bunch. Coward's been a chum of the Duke for many years. I believe he was at the funeral service. Some mischievous gossip-mongers say their friendship went a little deeper than the Duke would like to have been made public.' He stabbed the cutting with a nicotine-stained finger. 'This is a rather snide little article actually.'

'Why do you say that?'

'Well, its true purpose is nothing to do with the birth of the Duke's third child – it's just a reminder of the poor Duke's debauched past. Cheap gossip columnist's trick. I don't like it. Come on, Tom, the edition's gone – let's get out of here and find some sustenance.'

'Can we go to the Dada Club?'

'I think it's probably a members-only joint, but no harm in trying. The world turns upside down in wartime. I'll order us a car. The office driver will know how to find the place.'

Chapter 12

It was midnight. The street lights were out, but there was an almost-full moon. All they could see was a pile of bombed-out rubble. 'Is that it?' Christie demanded, nodding towards two stacks of sandbags with a space between.

'Yes, sir, that's all that's left of the place up here,' the driver said. 'But then you go downstairs. The club's undergound – still intact, I believe.'

'Looks nothing more than a bloody hole in the wall.'

They went down a few steps and came across a closed metal door. Christie knocked and it opened immediately on to a dimly lit check-in desk. A young woman with an insane tangle of very big hair was holding the door open. 'Come in, come in,' she said urgently, a thin roll-up hanging from her bottom lip. 'You're letting all the smoke out – I'll die of fresh air!'

Wilde and Christie stepped into a narrow passageway that led towards another short flight of steps. From somewhere not far away, the welcoming strains of a tenor sax and a great deal of conversation assailed their senses.

'Now what can I do you gentlemen for?' the hat-check girl demanded. She was tall and angular and wore a glitzy but flimsy sequined dress. 'Haven't seen you lovely chaps before.'

'We're looking for a girl.'

'Well, I'm a girl – will I do? The name's Tallulah.'

'Nice to meet you, Tallulah, but we're actually looking for someone else.'

'Ah, a professional? Well, you've come to the wrong place. Tarts gather in the alley across the road. Only amateur boys and girls here. We do it for fun, not money.' She laughed loudly.

'Actually, a specific girl,' Wilde continued. 'Harriet Hartwell. Is she here?'

'Darling sweet Harriet? No, no, haven't seen her in a week or two, I'm afraid. But you know this is a members-only club, don't you? I can't really let you in – unless you're signed in as guests by someone.'

'Think of us as men lost in the desert,' Wilde said hopefully. 'If we don't get a drink soon, we're liable to die.'

She smiled broadly. Her dazzling necklace caught his eye and she noticed the glance. 'This, sweetie? Very expensive Baltic amber – a gift from my secret lover in exchange for the delicious things I do for him.'

'Well, you could do a delicious thing for us – allow us in for one little drink.'

'Is it an emergency?'

'I think it probably is.'

'Well, of course, if it's an emergency, that's another matter. Rules are only there to be broken. Come in – but don't forget to bribe the door girl . . .' She held out a bowl which already contained a few coins. Wilde tossed in half a crown.

Downstairs, the bar was full of noise and smoke; there was scarcely room to move. It was showy and welcoming, just the sort of place Wilde had always loved, and the slow music was fine, too. Smoky red light picked out a saxophonist and a drummer, hemmed in on a tiny stage in the far corner. No one was taking much notice of them.

The women all wore shimmering numbers that clearly had not required much hard-to-come-by fabric in their construction; some of the men wore Savile Row, but most wore officers' uniforms.

'Where do we start?' Christie said, cupping his hand to Wilde's ear to be heard above the din.

'With a double, I think. Ease ourselves in. Not the kind of place to start questioning people ostentatiously.'

'You know what, Tom? I think you'll work better alone, so I'm going to leave you to it. Anyway, I need to get back to the office to make sure nothing's come in from the Far East. It's getting pretty hot out there by all accounts.'

'One for the road?'

'No. But call me if you need anything. I'll be on the back-bench until at least three. Have you got somewhere to sleep tonight?'

'I'll be fine. Thanks for your help, Ron – I'll give you a call in the morning.'

Wilde stood at the bar nursing his Scotch and listening to the duo playing some hypnotic jazz. His eyes were becoming accustomed to the gloom and he noticed that the walls were covered in framed and signed photographs. Laurence Olivier, Jessie Matthews, Charlie Chaplin, Marlene Dietrich, Chips Channon, Evelyn Waugh, the ubiquitous Noël Coward, Lord Templeman again – and many others. It seemed like a roll call of the most celebrated names of the 1930s and 40s. There were other pictures, too. Groups of revellers from festive nights, rather like the one in the newspaper cutting.

Wilde edged around the room, weaving his way through the drinkers, trying to look at the pictures closely, hoping to find another shot of Harriet Hartwell. He found several of the Duke of Kent in his younger, more disreputable days, including one of him between a beautiful young woman and a handsome man, his arms cradling them both. The Duke had been good-looking with an easy-going sparkle in his eye; he clearly loved the good life.

There were no pictures of Harriet. Nothing to link her with the Duke. But Wilde did find something else: another picture of a group of party people, a picture that he almost passed with barely a glance, but then looked at with increasing interest and disbelief, trying to make out exactly what he was seeing. He squinted up close to be sure his eyes weren't deceiving him.

It was Peter Cazerove.

Cazerove was a little behind the others and no more than half his face was visible. Unlike the other drinkers and dancers, he wasn't smiling. He seemed out of place. But was it really him?

'I believe you're looking for dear Harriet . . .'

Wilde turned at the voice and came face to face with Mimi Lalique. He had only ever seen her on screen before. Close up, she seemed a lot older than he had imagined her to be. Well into her fifties, if not beyond. Her face was lined and her makeup was poorly applied. Somehow, in his imagination, he had preserved her in the aspic of her silver screen days from the 1920s.

'Ah, yes,' he said, gathering himself. 'Do you know where I might find her?'

'Darling, we all want to know where she is. By the way, I don't believe I know you.'

'Wilde. Tom Wilde.'

'Yes, a name is all very well, but *who are you?*'

'I'm an American citizen resident in England, a history professor at Cambridge University.'

'Well, Tom, that's all very interesting, but what is your interest in our precious girl?'

Wilde noted that Mimi Lalique did not deign to give her own name; she obviously just assumed everyone knew her.

'I have something that belongs to her and I would like to return it.'

'Well, if you give it to me, I'll make sure she gets it when I see her next.' Mimi's long-fingered, rather bony hand snaked out, her palm open to receive whatever it was Wilde might be offering.

'That's very kind of you, but I'd rather give it to her myself.'

The palm remained open a moment, then curled back into a little ball and retreated. 'So tell me, what is this thing you have?'

'I'm afraid I can't say.'

'How mysterious. I love a secret, Tom – do tell. I promise it will go no further.'

'I'm sorry, Miss Lalique.'

She laughed aloud. Her voice was croaky from years of smoking. 'Miss Lalique!'

'Did I say something funny?'

'You sound like someone on set. *Miss Lalique is ready for her close-up. Please ask Miss Lalique to grace us with the pleasure of her company.* I'm Mimi, darling. Just plain old Mimi. Now then,' she whispered, so close to his face that her foetid breath made him recoil, 'no more teasing Mimi. I want to know about your interest in dear Harriet – I want all your scandalous secrets. Are you in love with her? It's not a very exclusive club, you know.'

What could he say to her? He had seen a woman fleetingly in a hotel lobby in the far north of Scotland, had given her a little money to pay her bill and had then seen a picture in a passport, which led him on to a second picture in a Fleet Street newspaper library, and now a third, showing a young former undergraduate who had killed himself with a poison capsule just six days earlier. No, he wasn't going to tell this inquisitive stranger any of that.

He had wanted to find Harriet Hartwell out of professional curiosity. Now, a chance encounter and three pictures later, he wanted to find her out of an overwhelming sense of dread. Bad things had happened and he had a horrible premonition that something worse was on its way, something to transcend a tragic suicide and a sickening plane crash.

'Forgive me. I would love to tell you, Mimi, but I honestly can't. It would be betraying a trust.'

She sighed dramatically and planted a red lipstick kiss on his cheek. 'Have it your own way, you naughty man. But stay, won't you? Charge all your drinks to the house – and do come again. You'll always find a welcome at the Dada. Just say you're a friend of Mimi. And if you do find Harriet, treat her with care. She's not like other people.'

It was long after midnight by the time Wilde decided he'd had enough of being importuned by strangers of both sexes – none of whom seemed remotely interested in the whereabouts of Harriet Hartwell, but all too interested in his athletic body. At last, he stumbled out of the Dada with Tallulah's resistible offer of a bed for the night ringing in his ears.

The moon was concealed by cloud. He wandered through Covent Garden, then down towards the Strand, intending to find his way back to Fleet Street. He was exhausted and needed somewhere to sleep. If Ron Christie was still at work, he'd take up his offer; he didn't live far out – Dulwich, wasn't it? – and would provide a bed or sofa for the night.

A large building loomed out of the darkness. He could just make out the legend STRAND PALACE HOTEL. That would be better than taking advantage of Ron's friendship; it was worth a shot, he decided, and walked into the lobby. He was in luck – there were rooms to spare. The old concierge found a key in the boxes behind his desk and held it out.

'No luggage, sir?'

Wilde had left his bag at the newspaper; it would be easy enough to fetch in the morning. 'Nope, just me.'

'Will anyone be joining you, Mr Wilde?'

'No.'

'Would you *like* someone to join you, sir? I could arrange it for you. Very good rates.'

'No thanks. But I'd be glad of a toothbrush if you have such a thing.'

'I'm afraid not, sir. Let me show you to your room. You'll be on the second floor.'

'I'll find my own way up,' Wilde said. He tipped the man and made his way upstairs. The room was comfortable enough. He loosened his tie and collapsed on the bed, his mind racing, circling around everything that had happened these past few days, and all the while desperate for sleep. The Dada Club had seemed like a cul-de-sac, but it wasn't, was it? He knew it meant something.

He took Harriet Hartwell's passport out of his jacket pocket once more and flicked through it, looking for something he might have missed. It was all straightforward.

Profession: Secretary. Place and date of birth: Clade, Suffolk, 8th May, 1917. Residence: Kensington. Height: 5ft 3in. Colour of eyes: brown. Colour of hair: dark brown. And that was all the personal information. There were a few pre-war visa stamps, including Germany, France, Switzerland, Italy and Egypt, but no recent stamp.

Sleep wouldn't come despite his exhaustion. He went downstairs to the concierge and asked for the London telephone directory. He looked up Hartwell but couldn't find anyone of that name in Kensington. It was the only directory the hotel possessed. The clock on the wall said 1.30. Ron Christie might just be still at work.

Despite his advancing years, the concierge had a quick wit and he was happy to help, likely expecting that a decent tip would find its way into his hand. Within a couple of minutes, he had found the newspaper's number and put through a call.

Wilde leant on the counter, the phone to his right ear. 'Ron? I'm sorry to bother you again – I need another favour.'

'Fire away, it's very quiet here now. Just about to wrap up for the night. Where are you, by the way?'

'Strand Palace Hotel.'

'The resort of no return.'

'You've lost me.'

'Renowned as a bolt-hole for journalists who have missed the night train home, or who have other, more disreputable requirements of a hotel room.'

'Closer to the first in my case. Look, Ron, you must have a full set of telephone directories in your office. Would you see if you can find me the number and address of a Hartwell – any Hartwell – in Clade, Suffolk? That's our woman's place of birth.'

'Good thought. OK, this will take a couple of minutes. How did it go at the Dada Club?'

'I got on rather well with Mimi Lalique of all people. It seems she owns the joint.'

Christie laughed. 'You certainly mix with the great and the gorgeous.'

'You know, close up, she wasn't so beautiful – and I'm afraid her breath stank. But she was a riot. Bought me drinks and said I was always welcome.'

'Better not tell Lydia. One moment, Tom, I'll see if I can find the Hartwell address and number for you. Hang on.' A few moments later, he was back on the line. 'Ah, here we are. Address in Clade and phone number for a Reverend H. Hartwell. Have you got a pen?'

'Fire away, Ron.' Wilde took down the details. It was obviously too late at night to call a stranger; he would do so first thing in the morning. Even better, perhaps, he would go to the town of Clade and introduce himself.

He slept for a while, but he woke before dawn, convinced there was someone in the room. He opened his eyes, but could see nothing in the unremitting darkness. He listened, but the only sound was the occasional growl of a car somewhere outside on the Strand or along Waterloo Bridge. Sleep came again and he woke at seven thirty. After a breakfast of kippers, toast, a mere scraping of butter and very weak coffee, he called Lydia.

'Bill Phillips has been trying to get in touch with you.'

'What does he want?'

'Didn't say, but I heard that infernal click on the line again. What's going on, darling?'

'I'll explain all. Kisses for you and Johnny.'

He made one more phone call, to a taxi driver named Morrison in the little town of Helmsdale. The phone rang and rang; he was about to give up when a thin Scottish voice answered.

'Hello?'

'Mr Morrison?'

'Yes, that's me.'

'I'm sorry to call you out of the blue, Mr Morrison. My name is Professor Tom Wilde.'

'Ah yes, you must be the American who was looking for me. What time do you want your taxi? Is it for today?'

'No, it's not a taxi I'm after. I just wanted to ask you about one of your fares – a young woman you picked up at the Cameron Arms a couple of days ago.'

'Aye, what of it?'

'Name of Claire Hart, yes?'

'That's the one, Mr Wilde. I took the young lady to Perth. I recall I told her the train from Helmsdale would be a great deal cheaper and might even be quicker, but she was insistent, so I didn't argue. A fare's a fare when all's said and done, and that should have been a good one.'

'Can you remember where in Perth you dropped her?'

'Why, at the railway station.'

'Did you chat with her on your journey?'

'She didn't say a word. Just sat in the back with me in the front. I tried to ask her about herself and what she was doing, but she was as silent as the grave, so I let her be.'

'What was her appearance?'

'Well, Mr Wilde, I don't like to speak ill of people, but I thought her a little shabby, truth be told. I couldn't help noticing that her skirt was torn, her shoes were awful scuffed and she was wearing no stockings. But she was a good-looking lass. Aye, a real beauty.'

'Anything else you remember about her?'

'Oh aye – that's easy. She had no money, or so she said. Didn't mention it before she'd had the ride and got out of the taxi, but then she told me she'd lost her wallet and would have to send the money on to me. Now, Mr Wilde, I'm not a wealthy man and I can't afford to be left out of pocket, especially with petrol so hard to come by and thin rations even for a professional cabbie. So if by any chance you're a good friend of hers, perhaps you'd see me right because I'm two pounds ten and six short and nothing has arrived from her in the post yet, though she promised me she would send a postal order by day's end.'

'I'll make sure I remind her when I see her.'

'That would be much appreciated, Mr Wilde.'

He needed air and exercise, so he walked to Fleet Street to collect his bag, then on to Grosvenor Street. He arrived at the OSS's new bureau before Bill Phillips, and the secretary rewarded him with proper coffee, imported from South America.

'If you don't mind me saying, sir, you look a little the worse for wear,' she said as she handed him the cup.

'Thank you, June, that's very kind of you.'

'I didn't mean it in a bad way, sir. I was wondering if I could help, that's all. Maybe just brush down your coat. Perhaps find you a fresh razor blade.'

He had been travelling light and hadn't had a change except for a clean shirt since Caithness. He supposed she was right; things had started to slip. Not least his sense of where things were going; he was no longer quite sure what he was trying to do or what was expected of him. He put these doubts to Phillips when his boss arrived ten minutes later.

Phillips listened to the whole story in silence then, when Wilde had finished, he took a few moments to mull it over. 'OK,' he said at last. 'Well, it's possible the Brits are not being entirely upfront about the Duke's mission, the nature of the crash, or the true details of those aboard the flight. But FDR's interest in the matter notwithstanding, we have to be sensitive here. And if the Brits believe they have a reason for keeping a lid on this, then maybe that's their prerogative. Anyway, you've done your bit, Tom, for which I thank you. You know, if they've got something to hide then perhaps we, as their allies, should not be looking too deeply into it.'

'I thought that's exactly what the President wanted me to do, Bill.'

'The problem is, when you come down to it all you've got is the word of a simple shepherd boy and a trawlerman you met in a pub. Doesn't really add up to much, does it?'

'Hang on, there was nothing simple about Jimmy Orde. He knew exactly what he was talking about, and was troubled by it. I'd say he was pretty certain the Sunderland he saw flying *towards* Scotland was the one that crashed.'

'But you just have his word for it. Anyway, I didn't call *him* simple; that was the other fellow, the shepherd boy – and it was the way *you* described him.'

'Tell you what, I'll get an affidavit from Orde. Would that convince you?'

'I'd take a look at it. I'd even pass it on to FDR, but I can't see what good would come of it.'

A few hours earlier, Wilde had been utterly convinced that he had chanced upon something dark and hidden. So why now, in the sober light of day, was he listening to Bill Phillips's doubts, and beginning to have some of his own? He tried to shake himself out of his scepticism. There *was* something going on. *Had* to be. 'Look, Bill, I take your point. But wouldn't you like me to dig just a little deeper?'

'Not at the expense of embarrassing Churchill or the royals. Write a report for me and I'll have it encoded and wired to

FDR. If he's still not happy, then we'll take his steer on it. For the present I want you back here. I have pressing matters for you to attend to. More meetings. We need to get this operation up and running.'

Wilde nodded. He understood. He took out Harriet Hartwell's passport. 'Just let me do this one last thing. I'm pretty sure I have found her family up in Suffolk. It'll only take three or four hours for me to go up there, hand over the passport and perhaps discover what she or her family knows. I'll go no further until I've reported back to you. And I promise I'll do nothing to annoy the Brits.'

Phillips looked at his watch. It was a little after nine. 'OK, take a car from the embassy compound, but be back by three o'clock. The Baker Street boys are coming over to see how we can collaborate and ensure we don't cut across each other. I'd like you here.' The Baker Street boys were the chiefs of Britain's Special Operations Executive, the organisation charged with sending men and women into occupied Europe to gather information and create havoc wherever they could. Few in this country or anywhere else knew of the organisation's existence, yet they had been doing fine work these past two years. It was a good model for the sort of operations that America's own OSS would now be doing. Wilde looked forward to the meeting.

After he had completed this one last task.

Chapter 13

As he drove north-east out of London, he enjoyed the mellow countryside of East Anglia. It looked ridiculously peaceful in its ripe, late-summer apparel of harvested fields, heavy-laden trees, slow-moving rivers and gentle white clouds. Who could think there was a war on?

The going was smooth to the pretty little medieval town of Clade in Suffolk. Just before arriving, he slowed down to crane his neck and watch a squadron of Hurricanes rising from a nearby airfield and thundering eastward. He drove on into the centre of the town, just past the church. He had no map to guide him through its myriad streets, so he stopped and asked a shopper for Old Cottage.

She looked puzzled.

'The Hartwells' house,' Wilde continued.

'The Reverend Hartwell?'

'Yes.'

'Well, he doesn't actually live in the town, you know. He's out near the school.'

'Ah, which school would that be?'

The woman was well spoken, probably in her sixties. She was walking an old black bicycle with a basket full of groceries attached to the handlebars. 'I'm sorry, I didn't catch your name,' she said.

'Thomas Wilde. Professor Wilde.'

'I'm sure it's none of my business, but why exactly are you looking for the reverend?'

'I have something to return to him. It's a private matter.'

'I see, well, you'll probably find him there. He usually goes to the Lakes for the summer, but I imagine he's back to get ready for the new term.'

'The school?'

'Athelstans, of course.' She sounded exasperated. 'He teaches Latin and Greek. There's no other school here unless you include the elementary for the local boys and girls.'

'I'm sorry, I live in Cambridge and I've never been here before. Could you direct me to the school?'

She sighed, considering the request. 'Very well,' she said. 'You don't look like a German agent, whatever they look like. You carry on along this road. Two miles north of here, you'll see two rather grand and ancient gateposts. There's no sign on them, but that's the way into Athelstans. Opposite the gates, outside the wall, there is a narrow, unmade road. That's the way you go to Old Cottage. It's about half a mile along there.'

Wilde thanked her and wound up the window. He was still reeling. He had always known that Athelstans was in Suffolk, of course, just as one knew that Eton was in Berkshire, but that was as far as it went. So the Reverend H. Hartwell was a teacher at Peter Cazerove's old school. Might that explain the connection between him and Harriet Hartwell? Assuming there *was* a connection. It was only surmise after seeing the young man's photograph on the wall at the Dada Club.

He engaged first gear, and drove on out of town.

Wilde stood in front of Old Cottage, having parked the car fifty yards further back along the track. He looked at the building from end to end. It was on two levels, perhaps built at different times. The thatch was in need of attention but, that aside, it was breathtakingly beautiful, a straggling half-timbered building that must once have been the home of a well-to-do yeoman farmer. Wilde reckoned its age at 500 years or more, which meant it must have been standing here before anyone had even heard of the Tudors.

The gardens all around were a mad profusion of flowers, not well tended, which could have been the result of the owner of the property spending the summer months elsewhere. That said, the colours and the heady mix of fragrances were quite spectacular. This was a proper English country garden. It really was quite exquisite, the sort of house he would love if he and Lydia and Johnny were ever to escape the smoke of Cambridge and move out of town.

He knocked at the door and waited. He thought he heard a sound from within, but it was very faint. He waited half a minute then knocked again, slightly harder and louder. Still no one came.

Perhaps the occupant was at the far end of the house or around the back. Wilde followed the flagstone path towards the rear. He could see no one outside in the garden so he knocked on the back door. Again, no one came. And yet he was sure he had heard something inside. He tried the door handle and it was unlocked. He called out.

'Hello, anyone at home?'

From somewhere deep in the house he thought he heard another noise, muffled and strange. Almost human, but not quite. A cat or dog perhaps? He called out again, louder. 'Hello, Reverend Hartwell?' And louder still. 'Hello! Hello!'

Now there was certainly a sound from within. A scuffling, a minor crashing of wood, like a small table or chair falling over, then another noise, a little like a cupboard door or window being opened. Wilde was alarmed. It sounded like a fight and he could no longer afford to observe the niceties of waiting to be invited in. He entered the house and found himself in a small and rather pleasant kitchen with pans, utensils and bunches of herbs hanging from hooks. The floors were broad, dark-stained boards which were worn with time and might have been there as long as the house had stood. As he made his way through the low-ceilinged rooms and dark, narrow corridors, he felt as if he was in some sort of medieval time capsule. On another day, the thought might have occurred to him that the house should be classified as a museum or national monument but for the moment, he was filled only with dread and foreboding.

At the highest point of the house, in an ancient room that was being used as a bedroom, he found the source of the noise he had heard.

An elderly man was lying on the floor at the end of a single bed. He was bound and bleeding. It looked as though his throat had been cut, but he was still moving, still alive, his feet twitching, his mouth gurgling. Blood was pouring from the wound, pooling on the floor like a crimson halo around his old white-grey head. The pool grew and seeped through the spaces between the boards.

Wilde crouched at the man's side, pulling and tearing at a bedsheet, bunching it into a ball to try to stem the flow of gore. But he could see it was hopeless. The wound was deep and deadly, cut savagely with a single, powerful strike that had almost certainly severed both jugular and carotid.

The dying man's eyes were open but empty. His lips were moving as though he had something to say, but no words emerged, just a ghastly frothing and bubbling of the incessant blood.

The window was open. That must have been the sound he heard. That must be the way the assailant had fled, for someone did this to the old man. There was no blade visible, so it was reasonable to assume this wound was not self-inflicted.

Wilde felt utterly impotent. His hands and clothes were drenched with blood as he cradled the man's head, desperately trying to think how he could give him a little comfort in his final moments. If this was the Reverend Hartwell, then he was almost certainly Church of England. Wilde had been born and raised a Catholic, yet he could not remember the words to say and, not being a priest himself, he could not give extreme unction, but he had to say something.

'Bless you, reverend. The Lord is with you . . .' The pathetic emptiness of the words sickened him.

The man had gone limp in his arms. The flow of blood had decreased to a trickle. Wilde held him for a few more moments, then gently lowered his head to the floor. The light had completely gone from the man's eyes so Wilde closed them with his thumbs.

As though weighed down by an anchor of solid iron, he slowly pulled himself to his feet. He went to the window and looked out. Somewhere out there a murderer was making his getaway. But that was not Wilde's concern at this moment. His first duty was to call the police and ambulance, though there was nothing that medical science could do.

He despised his hypocrisy. Amidst the blood and horror, he had said those religious words to the man, but he believed none of them. They didn't even serve as a bromide, for the dying man would have heard nothing. Wilde hadn't believed since childhood and, if he was honest, he hadn't really believed then.

His visits to church and the confessional had only been performed at the behest of his mother.

As he moved about the house, he soon discovered that the telephone wires had been cut, so there was no way of calling for assistance. There was no hurry, for no one's life was at stake, yet he felt compelled to act at speed. He looked around the rooms as quickly as he could and soon confirmed that this was, indeed, the home of Harriet Hartwell. There were several photographs of her, including a couple with the dead man, who was clearly her father. In one of them he wore a clerical collar, and they stood together, Harriet aged about seventeen or eighteen, on the forecourt of a large building. The words at the bottom of the frame said simply, ATHELSTANS, SUMMER 1935.

On the bedside table near the body, there was a photograph from a former age of a rather lovely, though slightly serious-looking, young woman who must surely be Harriet's mother. The absence of any further pictures of her suggested she might have died when Harriet was a child.

It wasn't ideal, but he had no option but to go and find a police station or a telephone. Perhaps the school would be the best port of call. He opened the front door and was relieved to see a woman in Royal Mail uniform appear at the end of the path on a bicycle.

The look on her face changed in an instant from one of workaday nonchalance to a mask of sheer panic and terror. For the first time, he realised the sight he must present: covered in blood – hands, face, shirt, jacket. He put up his hands as though to say, 'Look, I am no threat to you,' but the postwoman's mouth opened in a silent scream. In a frenzy, she tried to make a 180-degree turn, almost falling from her bike in the process. Regaining her balance, she pedalled off back along the path at breakneck speed.

Wilde climbed into the embassy car. He looked at his hands, wiped them on his jacket. If he were to go to the police now, how would he explain his presence here in Clade? How would he explain his interest in meeting the Reverend Hartwell? How would he explain to the police that he had walked into a stranger's house uninvited because he had heard a noise?

And why would they not immediately conclude that he was the murderer?

The postwoman's reaction told him everything he needed to know. The local police would have no option; they would have to lock him up as their prime suspect until he could prove otherwise. And how long would that take?

He switched on the engine, but for a few moments he did not drive, trying to work this through in his mind. There were other things to think of – in particular, the fact that the real murderer was on the loose and almost certainly still in the vicinity. He switched off the engine. At the very least there was time to make a cursory search before the police arrived. He might not be armed, but against a man with a knife, he had to believe his skills in the ring would neutralise the threat.

Beneath the open window, a path of trodden-down flowers and nettles showed the way the assailant had gone. Wilde followed the trail through the wildflower garden. He came to an apple orchard at the end of the patch. No more than a dozen trees, all heavy with fruit, but behind them there was a low iron gate, which was swinging and creaking in the breeze. Surely, the fugitive must have gone this route?

On the other side, the land dipped away into a meadow. Twenty or more cows were grazing. At the other side of the pasture, there was a boundary of hornbeam, hawthorn and bramble with an opening that seemed to give on to a track of some sort. Wilde trudged across the field, ignored by the cattle. He was almost at the gap in the hedgerow when he heard the roar of an engine, and then caught a glimpse of a motorbike surging past, billowing smoke from its exhaust.

It was ridden by a young man, a man he had seen twice before. Mortimer.

Chapter 14

Wilde raced back to the car, engaged gear and roared away down the path to the main road. The motorbike had been on a farm track which would have joined the highway from his right. He was certain it would already be some distance away. He guessed it would be heading north and west, in the direction of Cambridge, as that was where he had seen Mortimer before. It was pure surmise, of course, but he had nothing else to go on.

He floored the accelerator. The car, a six-year-old Jaguar SS 1, had a top speed of about 75 mph, but that was unlikely to be enough against a motorbike at full speed on winding roads, unless the killer stopped or slowed down for any reason. Wilde at least had the element of surprise; the killer knew he had been disturbed in the house, but he didn't know he had been seen on the road.

Halfway to Cambridge, Wilde gave up the chase. He had not seen the motorbike and had no idea if he was even on the same road. He had to make some decisions, and he had to make them fast. He couldn't go to the police in Clade, nor could he be seen in public smeared in blood. On a deserted section of road, he took a track into woodland and stopped close to a stream. Leaving the engine running, he climbed out of the car and immersed himself in the cool, slow-running water. He washed his face and hands thoroughly and did his best to make his clothes appear less alarming by rinsing off what blood he could.

Forty minutes later, he was pulling up outside the sand-bagged police station in St Andrew's Street, Cambridge. He did not kill the engine, because he was still uncertain about his plan. He had thought that the best move would be to make contact with Sergeant Talbot, for he would recall the confrontation with the stranger on the station concourse and should also be able to give a description. He was more likely to believe Wilde's story than the police in Suffolk, and that would hopefully go some way to clearing his name.

The problem was there were still things that couldn't be said under any circumstances. His movements and inquiries in Scotland, London and Clade – and the reasons behind them – were matters for the OSS and the White House, not for the local constabulary. These matters had to be kept confidential unless he was given high-level clearance to disclose them.

The engine turned over, rattling the bonnet of the SS 1. His fingers reached for the ignition key to switch it off, but then he thought better of it; this would be a wrong move. He simply could not answer the questions they would be certain to put to him. There had to be a better way to deal with this.

Instead he drove out to Girton. Rupert Weir was at home finishing his lunch, and immediately invited him in, studiously ignoring his sodden, stained clothes.

'I'm afraid you've missed the food,' he said, 'but I'm sure Edie could rustle something up for you.'

'A cup of tea would go down well.'

Edie was just poking her head around the door. She smiled in welcome, then blanched at the sight of him. 'Oh dear, Tom, what have you been up to?'

'I'll explain all.'

'Never mind. Tell Rupert while I get the tea on.'

'Well,' Weir said when they were alone together, 'tell all.'

'I stumbled upon a murder, Rupert. An Athelstan teacher, name of Reverend Hartwell down in Suffolk, just outside Clade.'

'Good God.'

'Poor fellow had had his throat cut. He died in my arms. I've already washed myself in a river but, well, as you can see, cleaning my clothes wasn't so easy.'

'When did this murder happen?'

'Less than two hours ago.'

'Have you spoken to the police?'

'What do you think?'

'I don't think you have, old man, otherwise you wouldn't be here, would you?'

Wilde emitted a deep sigh. 'The truth is, I can't go to the police. I simply can't. I beg you to trust me, Rupert. There are security issues involved and I won't be able to answer the police questions, so they'll have to bang me up. I can't even explain how I knew about Hartwell or why I was there. As it is, the police must already think I'm the killer. A postwoman saw me covered in blood – and must have seen my car.' He shook his head helplessly. 'For what it's worth, though, I assure you I'm *not* the murderer.'

'You don't need to convince me. But what about your diplomatic passport – can't you use that?'

He had already thought about it, but he knew that the US embassy would be horrified and consider it a misuse of immunity. So would the State Department, and it was bound to end up there. Apart from anything else, it would make him look guilty. 'It wouldn't work. Not in this case.'

'So, are you going to give me any more information?'

'Not much. It's better you don't know for the moment. Wouldn't do your career as a police surgeon much good if you started lying on my behalf.'

'But why have you come here? Why not home?'

He threw wide his arms to show his grisly appearance. 'Look at me – I can't let Lydia and Johnny see me like this. Anyway, that's likely to be the first place the police will go.'

'Yes, I see that. So what now? What do you want from me?'

'Well, I need a change of clothes for a start.'

Weir patted his rotund, well-fed belly as it strained against his tweed waistcoat. 'Don't think I'll be able to help you there.'

'No.'

Wilde had started pacing the room, his eyes flicking towards the window like a hunted man. 'That aside, what I think I'd like to do is give you a very plain signed statement of what happened when I was at the house. But it will not explain why I was there and so of course it will contain glaring holes. But so be it; I have no option.'

'What do you want me to do with it?'

'Take it to the police on my behalf, say it was delivered in an envelope through your letterbox. The thing is, I know who the killer is. I saw him haring off on a motorbike. He was that young man who talked to me at Cambridge station after the Cazerove suicide. Remember, you and Sergeant Talbot saw him too? He told me then that his name was Mortimer. At least I think it was Mortimer – he mumbled it and it was probably false anyway. You must tell the police that they should be looking for him, not me. Tell them, too, that I will give them a full statement in person as soon as circumstances allow. My initial statement will contain a description of the man. But you can give your own take, as can Talbot. It's possible Mortimer came back this way from Clade and there must be a chance he is known in this area.'

'So, what are you going to do now?'

Wilde sighed. 'I'm a fugitive. I've got to drive back to London as fast as I can and get to Grosvenor Street before an alert goes out for the car I'm using – it's an embassy vehicle. But first I'd like to use your phone and make a very quick call to Lydia.'

'Help yourself. God, Tom, I'm sorry you've landed yourself with this nightmare.'

She answered the phone at the first ring.

'Lydia . . .'

'Tom, where are you? The police are here.'

'I thought they might be.'

'What on earth's going on, darling? They say there has been an incident near Clade. They won't tell me anything more.'

Edie arrived with a cup of tea. He mouthed a thank you.

'All I can tell you is that I am a witness to a murder. Unfortunately, the police might very well think I was the killer, which I wasn't. I can't explain anything at the moment – but whatever you hear, you know I'm innocent.'

'Of course, darling. You still haven't told me where you are.'

'I'm not going to tell you that right now, but you'll find out soon enough. The fact is, I've got to disappear for a while. I'll try to stay in touch by phone.'

'Is this anything to do with your trip to Scotland?'

'Forgive me, Lydia, I really can't tell you any more at the moment. But at least part of it will be conveyed to you by the end of the day.'

Another voice came on the line, a man's voice. 'Professor Wilde? Detective Sergeant Robinson here . . .'

Wilde hung up.

Within fifteen minutes he had drunk two cups of tea and had written a brief and highly abridged version of events at Old Cottage on half of one side of foolscap. He handed the paper to Rupert Weir and thanked him.

'What about the clothes, Tom? You're welcome to mine, of course – but, well, my girth is twice yours.'

Wilde smiled at his old friend. They both knew that none of Rupert Weir's clothes would fit him. 'I think I know what to do.'

'Good luck, Tom. And don't worry – we'll keep an eye on Lydia and Johnny for you.'

He drove to college and parked outside the ancient gateway. Passing the porters' lodge he was waylayed by Scobie, who raised an eyebrow at the state of his clothes.

'Ah, professor, you've had visitors.'

'Anyone I know?'

'The local constabulary, sir. Seems they're very keen to make contact with you.'

'Are they still here?'

'No, sir. I told them you hadn't been in college for some days. But they did ask me to contact them if I saw you.'

'Then you must do so.'

'All in good time, sir. I have a few tasks to perform for the next hour or so.'

'Thank you, Scobie. And forgive my appearance – there's a rational explanation.'

'Not my business, sir.'

His rooms had seemed bleak before, but now they felt like a sanctuary. He kept a change of clothes in the wardrobe by the single bed. Hurriedly, he undressed, rolled the blood-stained shirt, trousers, jacket and tie into a ball and thrust it all into the bottom of the wardrobe; he presumed the filthy clothes would be considered evidence and so would have to be produced at some later date.

Dressing quickly in fresh attire, he gave his shoes a cursory brush, took a look in the mirror and adjusted the new tie. Suddenly he felt a great deal better about the world, but the sensation did not last more than a minute. The truth was he was beleaguered and could think of only one option: get to London and enlist Bill Phillips and the ambassador on his behalf, though what they could do he had no idea. What he needed was some way to explain his movements that didn't cause problems for America or the President, and he would have to get Phillips's backing for that.

He didn't often wear a hat, but today seemed the right time to make an exception. He grabbed his sad old dark-brown fedora from the hatstand and pulled it low across his brow. At the gatehouse, he was hailed again by Scobie.

'Again, sir, none of my business, but I couldn't help noticing that a couple of bobbies have parked themselves by your car while you have been in your set.'

'Thank you, Scobie.'

'My pleasure, sir, as always.'

So that was it for the car. The postwoman must have got the number plate – or perhaps it was the woman in Clade who had given him directions. He recalled now that he had even given her his name; she'd remember that well enough as soon as she heard about the murder – and news always travelled fast in country towns. Small wonder that the police had made it to Cornflowers and the college at such speed.

That only left the train. He thrust his hands in his trouser pockets, lowered his head, and walked straight past the two policemen standing guard over the embassy car, tipping his hat to them nonchalantly, as though he had not a care in the world. They didn't display any signs of recognising him, so he continued on northwards at a steady pace.

In King's Parade, he was just about to turn right towards the market before backtracking through Petty Cury and St Andrew's Street and making his way to the railway station when he became aware of a car pulling up beside him. He paid it no heed, but he heard a voice, low and urgent.

'Get in, Mr Wilde. Quickly.' A woman's voice. A voice to send a shudder through his body.

He turned and found himself face to face with Claire Hart – the woman he now knew to be Harriet Hartwell. She was sitting in the driver's seat of a tiny two-seater – a cream-coloured open-top Austin Seven – and she was gripping the steering wheel with the intensity of Nuvolari at the start of a grand prix.

'For pity's sake, get in.'

Without a word, he walked around to the passenger door, pulled it open and slid into the seat beside her. The car was minuscule and his shoulder was almost wedged against hers. She immediately engaged gear and accelerated without much conviction. If this car had a top speed of fifty with the driver alone, it certainly had nothing like that with both of them aboard. It seemed to take forever for the car to get out of second gear and up to third.

'Miss Hartwell . . .'

'Don't talk. Not yet. Let's get out of Cambridge.'

They were five miles outside the town heading south on the London road before she spoke again, almost shouting against the wind that whipped around their heads. Wilde had had to remove his fedora or it would have blown away. 'I've seen you before,' she said. 'In that horrid little hotel in Scotland.'

'Yes. You called yourself Claire Hart.'

'I'm told you have something of mine.'

'Your passport.' He removed it from his pocket and handed it to her. 'There you go. All yours, Miss Hartwell.'

She looked at it briefly, then placed it on her lap without thanking him. She had her foot down hard and the car was going flat out, but it wasn't going to break any speed limits.

'Ah yes,' she said. 'And I owe you some money.'

'Don't worry about me – but Mr Morrison the taxi driver would like to be paid.'

'Yes, of course, I will see to that.'

In Scotland, when he first saw her, he had thought her extremely attractive but had also decided he would perhaps not notice her on the streets of Belgravia. Now, as he studied her in profile, he realised that if anything the reverse was true and that she was even more beautiful than he had thought.

She turned to him. 'You're studying me, Mr Wilde.'

'Forgive me.'

'You may very well hear things about me, but I can promise you that none of them are true. I am a serious woman – and I expect to be treated as such.'

'Of course.'

'I just wanted to make that clear in case you got any ideas.'

'Don't worry. I have a family.'

'That never stopped any man I've ever met.'

Wilde had had enough of this. 'I'm sorry, but I am not at all sure what any of this is about. I'm not at all sure who you are exactly – or indeed how you found me in Cambridge.'

'Well, that was easy enough. I saw you arriving at your college. I recognised you and waited while you went in – and then the police started nosing around your car. They seemed to be checking the number plate as though it meant something to them. And then, when you came out, you were obviously keen to avoid them – now why would that be?'

Her answer to the question of how she found him was unconvincing. As for the rest of it, he simply said, 'I had my reasons.' He couldn't tell her, could he? He couldn't tell her he had just witnessed the murder of her father. He returned to the question of their meeting. 'You still haven't really explained how you found me or how you knew my name. How did you even know that I had your passport?'

'A little bird told me you had something of mine and that you were looking for me.'

'Mimi Lalique?'

She shrugged.

He looked at her again and was pleased to see a tiny flaw: a little scar beneath her right eye. There would be other taints, too. There had to be, because there always were.

In the silence, he could not get away from her father. He was horribly aware that she probably did not know that he was dead. And what, if anything, did she know about Peter Cazerove?

After all that, there was another matter that had to be dealt with. Something larger in the wider world, hanging like a giant shadow over the whole business: the matter of a Sunderland flying boat crashing into a hillside in Scotland, killing the

King's brother. But not her, though. Assuming she had been on the plane, why had she been one of the only two who survived? Why was her survival being kept secret? Why had she even been aboard the plane?

Whatever secrets Wilde had to impart, he was certain she had far more.

Chapter 15

'I have a lot of questions for you, Miss Hartwell – but I'm afraid I also have something I must tell you. Something of an extremely distressing nature.' He was struggling to find the words – 'distressing' was wholly inadequate, and the noise of the car and the wind did not help. 'I think you should find a layby and stop the car. I can't make myself heard properly above this wind.'

'What? What have you got to tell me?'

'Please, I really think you should stop.'

'Is this about Peter?'

They were on a narrow stretch. She swerved into a farm track and brought the car to a juddering halt, kicking up a cloud of dust from the dry earth.

'Well? Is this about Peter? I know he's dead, if that's what you mean.'

That was something at least. One piece of bad news that he would not have to break to her. 'There is that, yes – but something else, too,' he said, still searching through the recesses of his vocabulary for the appropriate phraseology. How could he tell this young woman that her father was dead, hideously murdered, his throat slashed in his own bedroom?

'Come on, Mr Wilde, spit it out. And while we're about it, perhaps you'll give me some clue as to why you were up in Scotland – and why you tried to follow me to London.'

'Your father's dead.' There, he had said it. Plain and unvarnished – and horribly brutal.

She frowned, her lips curled in a disbelieving smile. 'I'm sorry? What did you just say?'

'Your father, the Reverend Hartwell, is dead. I was there with him at the end.'

'What utter nonsense. Daddy isn't dead.'

Wilde nodded his head slowly, firmly.

'He *can't* be dead.'

'I dearly wish it wasn't true, Miss Hartwell, but I'm afraid it is.'

'How? How is he dead? He wasn't sick – people don't just die.' She was angry now and yet unsure of herself. Trying to weigh up the possibility that this man might just be telling the ghastly truth.

'He was murdered. I'm so sorry.' He reached out to touch her arm, but she shook him away as though ridding herself of an irritating fly.

'How dare you say such a thing? No, I won't believe it. You're lying.'

'He was killed at his home near Clade. I was there earlier today.'

'Daddy murdered?'

'I'm really, truly sorry. I wish there was some easy way to tell you this.'

'Who by . . . how?'

'He was stabbed. I can describe the killer to you, because I saw him fleeing on a motorbike. I believe his name to be Mortimer, but I can't be certain of that. I have no idea about the motive. That's all I know.'

She recoiled, shying away from him even as she faced him full on, disbelief in her eyes. Disbelief, rage and something else. Fear?

'I'm sorry,' he said again, for want of a better word.

'If this is some kind of cruel and unpleasant joke, Mr Wilde, I don't think it's very funny.'

He so wanted to give her a comforting word, but there was none to be had. 'It's the truth. I wish it weren't but it is. I was brought up a Catholic and wanted to give him the last rites, but I didn't know the words, or even if I was entitled to, not being a priest. I don't really believe but I thought some sort of blessing or prayer might bring him some comfort in his last moments. There was nothing more I could do for him, you see . . . nothing that could save him.' He was gibbering now, irrelevant information pouring forth from his mouth for want of anything better to say.

'No, I refuse to believe you.'

But he knew she did.

'Damn you, why were you there? Why didn't you save him? Did you kill him?'

'No.'

'Then what are you hiding from? Why are you avoiding the police?'

'Because I couldn't explain to them why I was at your father's home. I was there because I was looking for you – your passport said you were from Clade. I found his name in the telephone book. Nothing more to it than that. I turned up at the house, the door was open – and I found your father. Someone – the killer – had escaped through the window and I saw him riding away on a motorbike.'

She clenched her eyes closed and howled. A long, unrelenting wail that carried across the field like the cry of a wild animal. He wanted to put an arm around her, comfort her, but her hands were curled into talons as though she would rip into his flesh. Suddenly her whole body slumped and she was silent, save for the whisper of her shallow breathing.

Tears were streaming down her face. 'Was he tortured?'

'I don't know.' It was the truth. There had been so much blood, he could only see the obvious injury – the deep gash to the throat. On reflection, though, he now realised there *were* other marks – something like burns on his face. If he was being tortured, it was possible the slash to the throat was a panic measure when the killer was disturbed by hearing Wilde's knocks at the door, his voice and his footsteps approaching. A killer's strike to finish off his prey once his usefulness was done.

'They were trying to find me,' she said. 'They would have tortured him to discover where I was. But he didn't know anything, so what could he tell them? Anyway, even if he had known where I was, he would have said nothing, whatever they threatened him with, whatever they did.'

Wilde nodded. The thought had occurred to him already that she might have been the killer's true target.

'Why, Miss Hartwell? Why would someone go to such lengths to find you?'

'To kill me, of course. To silence me. Poor Daddy. He died because of me. Poor Georgie and all the others – they all died because of me.'

'Georgie?'

She looked at him as though he were slow-witted. 'Prince George. The Duke of Kent to you. He was never the target – I was. Me and Rudi. Georgie and the others just happened to be there on the plane. Wrong place, wrong time.'

'Rudi?'

'Oh, never mind. None of it matters now.'

'But if what you say is true, you're still in grave danger, Miss Hartwell.'

'That's about the size of it, yes. Bit of an understatement actually.'

'Shouldn't you go to the police?'

She laughed, even as she was wiping the tears from her eyes. 'You have no idea what we're dealing with, do you, Mr Wilde?'

'The police will protect you.'

'And you really believe that? Who do you think is trying to kill me?'

'I have no idea. I simply can't imagine.'

'*Cui bono*, as Daddy would have said. Who stands to gain? All you need to know is that if I went to the police, I would be dead within a couple of hours.'

'Then why trust me? If you are being hunted, why let me into your car?'

'Because you had something of mine. But mostly because Mimi trusted you and so did Peter. He had spoken about you often. He said you were the only person in Cambridge he had any confidence in. And clearly you are somehow involved, for why else would you have been in Scotland – and why else would you have gone to the Dada Club?'

'I had no idea I had made such an impression on Peter Cazerove.'

'Well, you did – which must be why he came to you when he decided to kill himself. He wouldn't have wanted to die alone.'

So she knew that he had been in the carriage when Cazerove poisoned himself.

'I'm afraid your presence here with me in this car puts you right in the firing line, too,' she continued. 'So what are we going to do, Mr Wilde? No, what are *you* going to do? You can get out now if you want and walk back to Cambridge or wherever you want to go.' She leant over him, yanked the door handle and pushed it open. 'There you are. Off you go. Much safer for you. I wouldn't want to be in proximity to me if I were you.'

Wilde made no move. 'Drive to the American embassy in London. I'm an American citizen. Whatever danger you're facing, I can offer you protection there.'

She pulled the door shut. 'No, we're going to Mimi's.'

Chapter 16

Lord Templeman – Richard to his family, Dagger to his friends and colleagues – was at his desk in Cambridge, dismantling a German wireless transmitter that had been brought to him earlier in the day. An in-box to his left contained a pile of decrypted papers, but none of them were considered highest priority so he was putting off reading them, preferring the practical work of examining a piece of enemy technology. It wasn't really what he was employed to do; as head of V Branch, MI5, he was responsible for day-to-day liaison and coordination between the various sections of MI5 and MI6, a position which allowed him access across the secret services. The door opened with barely a sound and he looked up. Philip Eaton of MI6 stood there, leaning on his stick and assisted by Walter Quayle of MI5.

Templeman put down his thin screwdriver. 'Take a seat, gentlemen, make yourselves comfortable. We have a problem to solve. A series of problems, in fact.'

Both the newcomers were limping – Eaton from the damage to his left leg incurred three years earlier, Quayle from the kicking he had received in return for importuning a young fisherman on the coast of Caithness.

'You look a sight, Walter,' Templeman said. 'Been up to your old tricks with rough trade, I hear.'

'Forgive me, Dagger.'

Templeman touched his forehead. It was a habit he hated but could not lose, however hard he tried. He did it because he had a port-wine stain above his left eyebrow and some wag at school many years ago had said it looked like a dagger. 'Nice boy was he, Walter? Well, stick to your own class in future. Anything broken, apart from pride?'

'One rib – and my nose has shifted. The doctor has prescribed brandy – and it's time for my medication.'

'Help yourself.' Templeman nodded towards the sideboard where three decanters and half a dozen fine crystal glasses awaited. 'And then we must work out our next step. We have to find the girl quickly, alive or dead. Walter, where exactly are we on this? And Philip, where's our errant professor?'

'The police in Cambridgeshire, Suffolk and all neighbouring counties have Wilde's description. We're having the devil's own job keeping the prying eyes of the local press away from the house in Clade. I've had to put a Defence Notice in place, but that doesn't go down very well in a small town where everyone knew the Reverend Hartwell, and everyone is already aware that he came to a grisly end. They even know the name of the man the police want to talk to. For some unknown reason Wilde identified himself to a woman in the town centre.'

Templeman unfurled himself from his seat and suddenly his study did not seem so big; he was six feet seven inches tall and his enormous height seemed to take up an awful lot of space.

'Yes, I came across your American professor a few days ago at a meeting with their new OSS outfit. Bunch of bloody well-meaning amateurs, but there you go. They might catch on by the time the show's over, I suppose. Wilde was the only one of them who seemed to have any idea what he was doing. Bill Phillips seemed exactly what he is: a superannuated diplomat. Anyway, we need to find Tom Wilde. Obviously he didn't kill Harriet Hartwell's father, but if he was there he must know exactly what happened. But why was he there?' He focused his attention on Quayle. 'More important in the first instance, however, is the whereabouts of Harriet herself. Where is she?'

'She's vanished, Dagger. Not a sign of her since Scotland.'

'Are we sure the shepherd boy found her?'

'Well, I believed him – and so did Wilde – but I doubt anyone else in the region did. He has a reputation as a fantasist and a liar. No one would listen to him. Nor would I except for the fact that I already knew Harriet Hartwell was on the plane. The thing is, the boy was convinced she was dead.'

'Your gut feeling?'

'She must be alive. Bodies don't just vanish.'

'So where is she, Walter?'

He shrugged. 'Search me.'

'Well, let's assume she's alive. Sergeant Jack was able to survive the crash, so why not Harriet too? It would probably depend on where she was in the plane.'

'Of course,' Eaton put in, 'it might be that she survived initially, got lost looking for help and died of exposure and injuries elsewhere on the moor. Is that possible, Walter? You know the area better than we do.'

'Yes, that's possible,' Quayle said. 'It's a vast estate. In fact, she could still be wandering around.'

'But we all know Harriet,' Templeman concluded. 'My money's on her surviving – and I think she's long gone from the moors. Anyway, that's the presumption we're going to work on. And then we come to the big question: why hasn't she made contact?'

'Concussion?' Eaton ventured.

Templeman shook his head. 'I don't buy it. What really worries me is the secrets she has. We don't know what she's going to do with them. You know what I think, gentlemen? I think she's gone rogue – if that's the right word for the female of the species.'

Eaton nodded gravely. 'That has to be a worry, given her link to Cazerove.'

Templeman looked from Eaton to Quayle, and back again. 'So I say again, where is she? We need to apply science. Do some proper detective work. Check on all her known haunts, everyone she knows – both inside and outside the service. And, Philip, as for your American chum, we have to pick him up and shut him down. We know he got as far as Cambridge because of the embassy car. Is he still here? He'll know a lot of people in the town.'

'If he is, I'll find him,' Eaton said.

'The problem is we can't trust him, can't even take him into our confidence.'

'He owes me a favour, a very big favour.'

'But he's American, so his loyalties will lie in Washington, not here. And we know he has suspicions and that he has some-how deduced that the Sunderland was returning from some-where rather than leaving.' Templeman's voice had lowered to a growl, the closest he ever came to overt anger. He turned again to Quayle. 'I have to say, Walter, that I hold you respon-sible for this. You were supposed to hold the man's hand in Scotland and make sure he returned home none the wiser. You opened the lid, now you must slam it shut and hope nothing has got out. There must never be even the vaguest rumour of the Drottningholm meeting. Understood?'

'Understood,' Quayle repeated.

'Philip, you too?'

'Understood, Dagger.'

'Because otherwise I'll have your balls fried with garlic.'

Wilde and Harriet carried on towards London. She was a good, confident driver. There was much to talk about, but conversation was limited by the noise of the wind about their ears until they reached the outer suburbs of the capital and had to reduce speed.

'You still haven't told me who wants to kill you, Miss Hartwell.'

'The Athels.'

At another time and under different circumstances, Wilde might have laughed at such a preposterous reply, but he didn't. Her father had just been killed and she was on the run. Even if she was having paranoid delusions, she deserved the courtesy of being taken seriously. 'Why would they do that?' he asked.

'Do you know about the Athels?'

'I know roughly what they are. They are certainly not the only secret society one encounters in Cambridge, or anywhere else for that matter.'

'Well, they don't like the course of the war, Mr Wilde. They think England has taken a wrong turn and they want to do something about it. I'm afraid they believe I might stand in their way – and they would be right.'

'Can you tell me more?'

'No, I can't.'

'You seem to think the Athels have links with the police.'

'Good God, they're everywhere. As they have been for almost 150 years. They own England, they are the secret beating heart of the Establishment. The Old Etonians and the Harrovians might take the leading public roles, but behind the scenes it is the Athels who make the real decisions. When you fall foul of them they are ruthless. And I have fallen foul of them.'

'And the plane crash? Are you saying they caused that?'

'They had reason to.'

'But how did you survive?'

'I really don't know, Mr Wilde. But they must realise I'm alive, so they'll do something about it. And if they discover that you've tangled yourself up with me, they'll do for you, too. Perhaps they already know. Did you tell anyone that you had my passport?'

'No, but there is a shepherd boy in Scotland who might have done, for it was he who found you and stole your passport and money.'

'Then you are also in grave danger.'

If someone had made such a claim a few days ago, he would have dismissed it as a delusion. But there had been deaths, unexplained deaths.

'Your father taught at Athelstans. Was he an Athel?'

'He loved the school, but he loathed the Athels. Anyway, they would never have accepted him – he wasn't nearly wealthy enough.'

'Be careful where you tread, Mr Wilde. There are dog turds everywhere.'

They had arrived in Westminster, in a street of large houses, mostly residential. Wilde looked around and saw bombed-out buildings on both sides of the road and a great deal of rubble swept back on to the pavement, but he couldn't see any canine excrement. Harriet, meanwhile, was looking not at the pavement but at the cars and pedestrians, as though worrying that she might be observed. It was a reasonable fear after what had happened. Wilde followed her a few yards along the path.

She stopped outside a large white terraced house with one of its two ground-floor windows boarded up. It was wedged between another house and an expensive florist that had a fading sign on the door saying it was closed for the duration. She knocked at the rather grand black door of the white house and they waited in silence. After half a minute, the door opened. Mimi Lalique stood there in a garish oriental kimono, falling open at the lower extremity to reveal mottled bare legs. A cigarette holder with a dead cigarette hung from her elegant fingers. Two Pekingese dogs with long golden coats were at her heels, yapping.

'Come in, darlings, come in.'

Wilde tried to shake her hand, but instead she folded him into an embrace, which only set the dogs off on an even louder and more jealous round of snappy barks.

'You had a close call,' he said, indicating the destroyed houses a few yards away.

'Oh, I know, awful business. And now we can't get the window re-glazed. No one can get any glass! Just lucky the other one survived. To be honest, I've had just about enough of this frightful war.'

Wilde followed Harriet Hartwell and Mimi Lalique along the broad hallway, the dogs ranging around them, still yapping. A smell assailed his nostrils and he quickly noted a couple of small turds on the Persian carpet; ah, Miss Hartwell had been talking about the house itself, not the pavement.

They arrived in a large sitting room which stretched from front to rear of the house and probably occupied half of the

ground floor. It was furnished with expensive carpets and luxurious sofas and looked out on to a thirty-foot paved garden
terrace, then a wall and, overtopping it, the back of another
house.

'Now then, darlings, what's it to be? I think it's cocktail hour,
don't you? Let Mimi do the mixing.'

'Horse's neck,' Harriet said.

'A Scotch, neat, for me, Miss Lalique,' Wilde said.

'Oh, you're both so boring. I want to try things on you. Do
let me experiment. If they're any good, I can use them at the
Dada. If they're simply awful, we'll still end up tight, so no
harm done.'

'OK,' Wilde said reluctantly. 'But nothing sweet. A dry
martini, perhaps.'

'Have it your own way, you darling man.' She afforded Wilde
a smile and just for a moment she had that fresh girlish dazzle
that had won a million hearts in the silent movie era. 'And I'm
so pleased you two lovely people managed to find each other.
Well done, Harriet – what a detective you could be.' She gave
her a very obvious wink, as though they shared a secret.

When they had settled down with their drinks and the
dogs had shut up and curled around their reclining mistress,
Harriet said simply: 'Daddy's dead, Mimi. The bastards killed
him.' She threw back her cocktail in one and grimaced. 'God,
that drink's foul.'

'Henry, dead? Oh, darling, I'm so sorry.' She rose from the
sofa and knelt at Harriet's side, hugging her knees. 'I only
spoke with him two days ago. This is so sudden. Oh sweet,
sweet Henry . . .'

'Didn't you hear what I said, Mimi? He was killed. The filthy
bastards murdered him.'

'Murdered! Oh my God, how simply awful.'

'Professor Wilde was with him when he died.' She turned in his direction. 'You still haven't told me exactly what they did to him.'

And nor would he. Wilde remained silent and cast his eyes down towards his drink. He really didn't want to reveal the ugly truth of the deed. There was something particularly cruel and depraved about the slitting of a throat. A knife to the heart and the shock that went with it, that was one thing. Bad enough. But the very thought of a knife cutting mercilessly into the throat, the unstoppable rush of blood, the inability to speak or breathe and the certainty of impending death. No, that was too much.

'Wilde?'

'He was stabbed, that's all.'

'Stabbed? Stabbed where? The chest? More than one wound?'

'Just the one, but it cut an artery. It was quick. I'm sure it was quick.'

Mimi stroked Harriet's cheek with the back of her veiny hand. 'He's trying to spare you, darling. Better to remember Henry the way he was, the way we all loved him. You don't want a picture of him dying when you think of him, do you?'

'I tell you what I want, Mimi, I want to slaughter the swine who did this. I want to do it slowly and painfully and I want to look in his eyes while he's whimpering and dying.'

'I know, darling, I know. I loved Henry as much as you did. I loved him from the moment Maggie brought him home.' She smiled at Wilde. 'He was my brother-in-law, you see, and he was a dear, dear man. I should have married him myself after my sister died, but my head was turned by all those handsome glittery men in the world of motion pictures. All those princes of the royal blood . . .' She laughed huskily, her voice rough from many thousands of cigarettes. 'God, what a fool I was.'

Wilde nodded, but he was thinking that perhaps she hadn't made a mistake. He could not imagine Mimi Lalique as a schoolteacher's wife. Particularly not a reverend schoolteacher trying to cram Latin and Greek into young heads.

'But at least I always had my darling niece.' She hugged her again and kissed her tear-stained face with unadorned affection.

'The question is,' Harriet said when she was released from the embrace, 'what are we going to do now?'

Chapter 17

'I started as a makeup girl, Tom. Of course I wasn't Mimi Lalique back then, just plain Molly Locke, vicar's daughter from Taunton in Devon. But don't tell my adoring public that, will you? I don't want my bad reputation ruined by letting on that I was ever a goody-two-shoes churchgoer.'

'You have my word, I won't tell a soul.'

She was bending down, looking at him closely, too closely for his comfort. The smoke from her cigarette was making his eyes smart. He tried shifting away from her, but she edged nearer. 'Yes, I'm sure I could do something for you. A few tweaks and you could walk into your own home and your wife wouldn't recognise you.'

'Let me think about it, Mimi.'

'Oh dear, you men. It's only a bit of camouflage so the police don't recognise you. A bit of makeup won't take away your manhood, you know. Now, Georgie, he was never like that. In another life, I do truly believe he could have been a star of stage or silver screen.'

'I take it you knew the Duke of Kent well.'

'Of course, darling. He was, well, how shall I put it nicely – he was a close friend.'

'She means they were once lovers, Mr Wilde,' Harriet put in.

Mimi laughed, throwing back her head, baring her yellow teeth and emitting a thin stream of smoke which had been lodged somewhere in the depths of her lungs. 'Oh yes, we were like rabbits in a hutch. I like to think I taught Georgie everything he knew about women's bodies. He was a very quick learner – and it wasn't long before I was having to share him with Jessie and Kiki and one or two others. But I could never wholly lure him away from the boys. He was a man of diverse interests and many parts – indeed, many partners. But perhaps I shouldn't tell you that. Such a merry-go-round we had. Those were the days.'

Wilde allowed her to meander on about her glittering silent movie career and the wild parties that went with it. Finally, she rose when her dogs became restive. 'Must feed Bertie and Vicky,' she said and went off to find food for the animals, leaving Wilde alone with Harriet. He looked at his watch. It was seven in the evening. He had to get out of here and make his way to Grosvenor Square. He rose from the sofa and put down his empty glass. 'I'm going to the US embassy. Do you want to come with me, Miss Hartwell?'

'It's not safe.'

'I'm sorry you think that, but it will work for me. Can I just ask you something before I go?'

'I've told you everything I'm going to tell you.'

He pressed on. 'Your passport calls you a "secretary", but you're more than that, aren't you?'

'Am I?'

'I'm sure of it. What are you, Foreign Office? The Palace? MI6?'

'Take your pick, Mr Wilde.'

'Look, I know I've said it already, but I was absolutely horrified by the deaths of your father and Peter Cazerove.'

'Yes.' Her voice was flat.

'Peter was your lover, wasn't he?'

'We were more like brother and sister, actually. I think he would have liked it to be more, but honestly, he wasn't really my type. Anyway, our relationship – if that's what it was – had been going on forever, since school days. I was a day girl at a girls' school a few miles away, so I was around Athelstans at the end of the day and the boys were always trying to flirt with me. Peter was the only one who talked to me like an equal, though, and we were the best of friends. I rather think Daddy thought we would get married one day, and maybe we would have.'

'So you were allowed to consort with the Athelstan boys?' Wilde was thinking of his own years at Harrow. Apart from Matron and the occasional teacher's wife, no females were ever in evidence.

'Well, it was frowned on, but boys of that age . . . well, you'd have to chain them to a wall, wouldn't you? Anyway, we didn't care. Peter and I got away from the world together. There was an old, disused shed near the walled vegetable garden at Athelstans where we would meet. Just the two of us.'

'Sounds very naughty.'

'It had to be furtive. He would have been expelled if anyone found out, and Daddy would have been sacked. Actually, I wish he had been sacked. He didn't really fit in. I think he was only tolerated because of his long service and his kindliness. They saw him as a harmless old duffer.'

'And his younger days? He was there for many years, wasn't he?'

She shrugged. 'Perhaps he fitted in better at first. I think he admired their aesthetic ideals and elitism back then. It was as if he saw them as akin to the early Christian martyrs in their ferocious dedication to a cause. But he expressed his doubts to me in later years. He thought they were changing, becoming a little too hard and military, and a little less Christian.'

'And the Athels, Miss Hartwell. Do all old boys become Athels, or do you have to be selected?'

'Oh gosh, no, you had to be selected and it was considered a signal honour. Only the sons of the richest, cleverest and most reliable became Athels. They were very secretive. But of course Peter couldn't resist telling me a little about their history.'

'Was he considered reliable?'

'His family is ridiculously rich.'

Wilde recalled talk of their vast landholdings in Norfolk. Yes, of course they were rich.

'Anyway, as I understand it, the Athels were founded as a secret society in 1795 in the wake of the French Revolution and the guillotine terror, with one express aim: to ensure that no such upheavals should ever threaten the status quo in England. Not Great Britain or the United Kingdom, you understand, but England. They see themselves as the deep core of the Establishment. Peter told me that over the years they have moved subtly to save England from upheaval on several occasions – from Peterloo to the General Strike. Whenever revolution threatened, the Athels would intervene – but invisibly. The population at large, even Parliament, would never have any idea that they were being manipulated.'

'And Peter was convinced by all this?'

'He became quite enthusiastic about the Athels. In fact, he told me he was something called an Autarch – that's their word for a senior Athel among those still at the school. I think they did most of the recruiting. But it wasn't always like that for him. In the early years at Athelstans he had a simply ghastly time. He was bullied mercilessly by the older boys, particularly Smoake – Richard Smoake. Every evening, Peter found his bed soaked in urine, and worse. His food was adulterated on a regular basis. He was thrashed by masters and senior boys alike. But he withstood the onslaught and, I'm afraid, began to think like them. Smoake stopped beating him and took him under his wing. That was when things began to run less smoothly between us.'

'You didn't approve?'

'I never liked Smoake.' She shrugged again, but said nothing more. He took her meaning to be 'yes'.

'So Cazerove was a member of the Athels when he came up to Cambridge?'

'Well, of course. And you must have come across others in your years at the college. Then, after university or Sandhurst, they are fed off into the great offices of state, the military, the civil service, the police, the press, the diplomatic corps and the church. And they sit there, smooth and charming, like fat toads waiting for an irritating fly to pass within range of their long sticky tongues.'

'Not so very different from Eton, then?'

'I thought it corrupt and, to be honest, rather juvenile. But that didn't mean they weren't dangerous. Oh, Peter told me they would murder you in a moment and call it patriotism – and he laughed about it. He told me they were everywhere, Mr Wilde. Every part of the body of England – every limb, every vital organ – is caught in their cancerous tentacles.'

Wilde heard the dogs yapping along the corridor and assumed they were about to get their bowls of food. 'Before Mimi returns, there is the other matter – the rather crucial matter, in fact. Short Sunderland flight 4026. Why were you aboard?'

'I've said enough. More than enough.'

'You weren't going anywhere – you were coming back from somewhere. Sweden is the obvious place.'

'If you know so much, you tell me.'

'Don't play that game, Miss Hartwell. Here I am, I've thrown in my lot with you for better or worse – so I would very much like to know what you and the Duke were doing in Sweden. And I would very much like to know what caused the crash.'

She let out a long sigh. 'I will tell you just one thing, Wilde. One more thing. I need to talk to Churchill, but I can't, because they will kill me before I get anywhere near him.'

'Then come with me to the US embassy. The ambassador will call Downing Street and get through to Churchill, then you can arrange everything in whatever way you like.'

'You think his line isn't monitored? You think there are no Athels in Downing Street? They will do anything to stop me. *Anything.*'

'There must be some way of getting through, even if we have to involve President Roosevelt.'

'Why should I trust the Americans?'

'You seem to trust me – I'm American.'

'Peter told me I should trust you. And there's something else. I don't know if I should tell you, but I have to believe in someone. There is a man called Coburg – Rudi Coburg.'

'You mentioned someone called Rudi before.'

'Rudi was supposed to be on the plane. He is central to all this . . .'

She didn't finish. Mimi was returning, minus dogs. As she entered the room, there was a hammering at the front door, followed by a din of yapping from along the corridor. Wilde and the two women looked at each other.

Mimi went to the window at the front, the one that hadn't been boarded up. Her face was ashen as she turned back to them. 'There are two men – they've got handguns. I think it's time for you two to make yourself scarce,' she said. 'Follow me.'

'Where?' He had seen that there was no way out of the back.

'Upstairs, through the lofts. Don't worry. It's simple enough. Hurry now.'

There was a cracking of wood. Whoever was at the door wasn't waiting for it to be answered and was splintering it with a sledgehammer. But it was a strong door and didn't break easily. Harriet was out in the hallway ahead of Wilde, sprinting up the stairs, bag clutched in her right hand. Mimi came next but was much slower, her silk kimono flapping about her knees. At the top of the second flight of steps, she stopped, gasping from the exertion, and ushered Wilde past her. 'Go on, Tom, up the stepladder. Don't worry about me – they don't want me.'

From below they heard another crash – the inward collapse of the front door – and then men's loud voices and footsteps. Wilde glanced back down the stairwell and saw one of the men standing in the hallway, his gun raised.

'Stop or I shoot!'

Wilde didn't stop. He ducked back out of the line of fire.

Mimi was clasping her chest and he could tell she was in a bad way. He also knew that anyone who hammered down a locked door rather than wait for it to be answered would not be likely to treat a frail woman with great courtesy or kindness.

The dogs were at Mimi's heels, snarling and yapping. Wilde picked her up in his arms. She was as light and floppy as a sleeping child and did nothing to prevent him. 'Come on, Mimi, you're coming with us.' The two Pekingese were snapping at his ankles now but he resisted the temptation to kick them away. From the sound of thudding footfalls, their pursuers were little more than a flight behind them.

'Leave me, Tom.' She was panting, barely able to speak.

They were facing a retractable ladder leading up into a loft. 'Up there?'

'Yes.' Her voice was little more than a whispered rasp.

Somehow, awkwardly, he pushed her up the ladder, rung by rung, and into the dark space. She lay on her back, fighting for breath, her fingers pressing into her breast as though somehow she could soothe her racing heart and bring calm to her tar-clogged lungs. Now he was with her, dragging the ladder up behind him. He heard a shout. He kicked the hatch closed and slid the bolt.

It was gloomy but not pitch black. There were no windows but there was a semblance of light to his left. He picked Mimi up again and moved as quietly as he could in the direction of the light. From below he heard the yapping of dogs and angry voices.

What now? They were stranded up here. Trapped like animals gone to ground. This had been a bad idea, but he had had no option. All he could do was move towards the patch of light and try to find a hiding place. But where in God's name was Harriet Hartwell? He supposed she must have climbed the ladder ahead of him, but there was no sign of her.

'It's open,' Mimi said faintly. 'The whole terrace . . . no walls. You must go. Look after Harriet . . .'

Chapter 18

Naked flesh. It was always there at the forefront of his mind these days. Naked female flesh, pale and soft and pliable. Reclining in white sheets on pillows of down. And then, the others. Was it only a month since that night and the dinner? Here in this little cabin on a rocky outcrop, a thousand miles away, it seemed to Rudolf Coburg that the night and the flesh had been there, in his memory, all his life and beyond. So much desire and gratification, such foodstuffs in a time of hunger and war, such dazzling surroundings in a vast and beguiling hunting lodge, deep in conquered Poland, such wondrous wine from the cellars of Paris. And the girls, the flesh! Pure, Aryan, clean, willing and warm of heart. Chosen personally for each man by Heinrich Müller. The counterpoints of passion. Pleasure more exquisite than ever in a world consumed by pain.

The girls had been there, in their rooms, when they arrived by Junkers Ju 52 from Tempelhof. Each room had an overflowing bowl of fruit, two bottles of vintage champagne, a signed photograph of the Führer, and a naked girl in a large double bed with crisp linen sheets and a duvet filled with down. Coburg's girl was called Dagmar, and she was exceedingly sweet-natured and pretty with skin like gossamer. After their love-making she was gone with a kiss to his cheek and a beautiful smile and a promise to return whenever he desired.

Twenty men in twenty rooms. All senior members of the party and of the various branches of government, entertained lavishly by Müller, the new head of the Gestapo. In the evening, they had dined together in a salon of darkened oak and guttering candlelight with antlers on all the walls, and they had drunk toast after toast from fine crystal glassware. First, of course, to the Führer, but then also to Himmler and then, in more sombre mood, to Reinhard Heydrich, lately the victim of an assassin's bomb in Prague. And then, as one, they had thrown their priceless crystal glasses into the stone hearth.

Never had he drunk so much, never had he felt so mellow and, to be honest with himself, so intensely alive. It was as if he had drunk of nectar and feasted on ambrosia. If he had had a sword in his grasp, he would have happily taken on an army single-handed and would have expected to slay them all. But that had always been the point, hadn't it? It was clear now; they were all supposed to be intoxicated by the fine flesh and the liquor, their minds dulled, yet their spirits elevated to a plane none of them had ever experienced. To ease them into the night ahead, and to prepare them for it.

At the head of the long table, Müller had risen to his full height of five and a half feet and made a little speech. He said the Führer himself had suggested he bring them all here into the conquered territory to this ancient hunting lodge. He wanted them all to know that though they were office-bound in Berlin, they were every bit as important to the Third Reich's struggle as the young men on the front line. In many ways, even more important, for they were the men who organised the labour, the armaments, the munitions and provisions that kept the engine of great Germany running. They were the men who organised the trains and made the removal of populations a reality. He wanted them to know that administrators could be warriors, too.

It had been a warm summer's evening. After the last course – there had been ten in all, including the *pièce de résistance*, roast suckling boar – they had trooped out into the torchlit gardens, laughing and rejoicing at the impending end to the war and the birth of a new Teutonic empire that would stand for eternity.

Twenty servants in white livery appeared with silver salvers, one for each of the guests. On each platter, a fully loaded pearl-handled pistol was laid. 'Take your guns, gentlemen,' Müller intoned. 'The fun is about to begin.'

Floodlights burst into life, illuminating a series of targets thirty metres away across the lawns. Each target consisted of a crude drawing of a Jew, in the manner of a *Der Stürmer* carica-ture. Large noses, stubbly chins, sneering lips – drawings that said 'this man is about to cheat you and rob you blind and steal your children for infernal rites'.

'Now then,' Müller had said. 'We take it in turns. Whoever shoots the most Jews wins a prize – a golden dagger commis-sioned by the Führer himself. You, Herr Coburg, are you a good shot?'

'Not bad,' he had said. Shooting parties had been part of his childhood education; he had not been the best, but he wouldn't feel out of place on a partridge shoot at a country estate.

'Then you go first.'

And so they had all taken their turn, shooting at the pictures, laughing like schoolboys, cheering when one of the cartoon likenesses was hit full square in the face. They imbibed more drink – schnapps and brandy – between shots. They admired each other's shooting or mocked mercilessly those who, like Eichmann, couldn't manage a single hit.

Coburg didn't win, but he achieved four out of six.

The fleet of open-topped Mercedes cars came for them at one o'clock in the morning. No one asked where they were going, for that would have spoilt the magic. This whole evening, surely, was designed as a wonderful thank you for all the hard work they had put in behind the scenes in their ministries back in Berlin. A party for victory with a finale full of mystery. The night was cloudless and the moon was full. The breeze in their hair and the beauty of the night served to enhance the anticipation. What could possibly be in store for them? A brothel, perhaps? Beautiful women? More fun and games? This place, sixty miles north-east of Warsaw, was a land of forests and rivers and dreams.

The journey was only about twenty minutes, perhaps eight miles along rutted roads, finally running at the side of a railway track. He gazed drunkenly from the window; it was dark, but occasionally he was sure he saw a corpse at the side of the line. And the night air was changing. No longer was it fresh, but imbued with a miasma of decay. He avoided the eyes of his colleague beside him in the back seat of the open-topped car. He resisted the desire to hold a handkerchief to his nose.

At last they arrived at a charming little railway station, where a long train of twenty or more cattle wagons was already standing at the low, ramp-like platform as though waiting to be unloaded. At the rear of the train was the locomotive which had shunted the train to this place. His companions in the car had gone strangely silent. Coburg noted that the clock beside the waiting room was telling the wrong time. He looked again two minutes later and noted that the hands had still not moved. How could they? They were painted on, not real. Time stood still in this place. He noted, too, the name of the station, a place name that meant something to him.

A name he had seen in documents in the office of Referat IV B4 back in Berlin.

Now, here in this beautiful little cabin by the sea, almost a month later and a thousand miles to the north-west, the name meant everything, but back then there was still mystery and the shudder of impending darkness. It was the smell that came first.

As they climbed out of the cars, the whiff of decay hit them like a fist to the face. The all-encompassing stink of human waste and rotting flesh, made all the worse by the furnace heat of that summer's day and the still warm night.

A parade of a hundred or so uniformed men, some with rifles, others with whips and Rottweilers and Alsatians on short leashes, stood in a semi-circle like a welcoming committee. Even in his inebriation, Coburg recognised them as Trawniki *Hiwis* – Ukraininan and Latvian volunteer guards – and a few SS troops. One of them, an SS-Obersturmführer and clearly their leader, strode towards the guests, clicked his heels and gave the most extravagant Hitler salute that Coburg had ever seen.

And that was just the beginning. The show had not even begun. At a snap of the officer's fingers, searchlights broke the darkness, turning night into day.

What came next meant Coburg could no longer sleep, and doubted he would ever sleep again.

Chapter 19

Wilde couldn't leave Mimi. He had no idea who the men below might be. Were they officers of the state or rogue elements like the man who murdered Harriet's father? If a defenceless old man's throat had been slit without a qualm, what chance would Mimi Lalique have? He had to fear the worst.

There were no dividing walls between the lofts of the terrace of houses. Wilde carried her through to the far loft and stood on the shattered joists above a gaping hole, torn open by a massive bomb. Above them, a shaft of sunlight pierced through a hole in the roof where the Luftwaffe's unwanted gift had ripped through the tiles.

It was what lay below that concerned Wilde. All he could make out was a dark tangle of broken boards and brick. The bomb had coursed through the centre of the house, collapsing landings and damaging staircases. Had it exploded, there would have been nothing left of the building; as it was there was wreckage enough to make the place uninhabitable.

Had Harriet come this way, climbing down through the broken timbers and rubble to the ground floor? Alone, he was pretty sure he could find a way down, but carrying Mimi was another matter. He weighed up his choices, wondering for a brief moment whether he could leave her here and go to fetch help. He instantly discounted that as an option; she was suffering badly – a heart attack, perhaps? – and the sooner she reached proper medical assistance, the better her chance of survival. He had to get her to hospital.

Behind him, along the line of lofts, he heard the sound of hammering once more. The men were trying to break open the hatch.

He manipulated Mimi around to his back, one arm over his shoulder, her legs over his other shoulder. She felt even lighter now and he had a hand free. Unlike the retractable ladder at Mimi's house, the loft here had the remains of a proper staircase. Steep and narrow, but with a banister down the left side. Slowly, he descended to the remains of the upper landing. Mimi was silent, showing few signs of life. But every few seconds he felt sure he could sense faint breathing.

Flight by flight, step by step he made his way down. On the second floor, half of the staircase had been torn away and he had to edge his way with his back against the wall. A misstep or a collapsing stair would carry them both away.

At last, they made it to the debris-strewn ground floor. No sign of the bomb; he assumed it had been defused and removed many months ago. London had not suffered much bombing this past year. Motes of dust hung in the air, catching the low evening light that crept in through the gaps where windows had once been. Wilde placed Mimi on the floor for a few moments while he caught his breath. He took her wrist and felt for a pulse, then put his ear to her chest. She was alive, but in grave peril. He could do with Harriet's assistance, but she had vanished.

The front door was unlocked. He poked his head out tentatively, looking back along the street to Mimi's property, expecting to see the men who had broken in. But there was no one. The men could emerge at any moment, however, either from above or below; he had to take his chances right now.

He picked up Mimi again and placed her across his shoulders, paused a moment in the doorway, then took a deep breath and strode purposefully out on to the street as though he did this every day. Walking to the right, he didn't look back, taking the first turning. Now they were out of sight. He could breathe again.

His initial instinct was to knock on someone's door – *anyone's* door. Everyone around this exclusive part of Westminster would have a telephone. But a black cab was passing and he hailed it.

'Hospital. Take us to the nearest hospital.'

'Hop in, sir.' The driver began manoeuvring a U-turn even as Wilde was laying Mimi out on the bench seat. 'That'll be St Thomas' – or whatever's left of it after the bloody Hun's done their worst.'

They pulled up outside the emergency department within a few minutes. The old hospital was so badly damaged that Wilde was astonished that any part of it could still be functioning. Two nurses and a doctor immediately took control of the situation. Wilde gave them Mimi's name but the nurses didn't seem impressed; a patient was a patient, however famous.

'Will you wait, sir?' one of the nurses asked.

'Do you really need me? I'm not related to Miss Lalique.'

'I think it better we have someone on hand who is acquainted with her, just in case. Do you know whether she has any history of heart problems?'

'I honestly don't know.'

'Asthma? Lung condition?'

'All I can tell you is that she was going upstairs and began to have difficulty breathing. She was clutching her chest as though she had a great pain and she was clearly becoming very weak. She just about managed to talk to me, but then she seemed to lose consciousness. Her breathing and heart rate were very faint. I brought her here as fast as I could. I thought it quicker than waiting for an ambulance.'

'You did the right thing, sir. It would really help if you could wait here a little while longer, Mr . . .'

'Wilde,' he said and then wished he hadn't.

'We'll need whatever details you have. Address, next of kin. Your own telephone number.'

'And then I can go? You'll be able to get me at the American embassy.'

The nurse looked at her watch. 'Well, of course you're not being held prisoner, but if you could just stay half an hour?'

He didn't want to wait – he needed to get to safety – but he felt he didn't have much option. The nurse escorted him downstairs to the basement where the wards and operating theatre had been relocated, and offered him a seat. The hospital was much reduced, but was still performing a crucial role. The electric clock on the wall said seven o'clock. He didn't want to sit down.

After twenty-five minutes another nurse came and offered him a cup of tea. He declined the offer and asked how Mimi was.

'Difficult to say, sir.'

'She'll certainly be kept in overnight, though?'

'Yes, sir. She has had a heart attack.'

'That sounds bad.'

'The doctor has given her some morphine for the pain and to relax her. You did well to get her here so promptly. There's very little else to be done. Just wait and see, I'm afraid.'

'But nothing I can do?'

'Not really, sir.'

'Then I'm going to have to take my leave of you. If anything happens, if you need me, you have my phone number and I'll be a fifteen-minute taxi ride away.'

'Yes, of course, I understand.'

He had to get to the embassy in Grosvenor Square so that he could contact Bill Phillips and get advice on what to do next. He guessed he would be advised to call in the police and allow them to interview him on embassy premises in the presence of counsel, in which case he might have to answer 'no comment' when asked what he was trying to do in Clade. Or perhaps he could find some way to get the whole thing sorted out through diplomatic channels? He was also keen to discover the fate of Harriet Hartwell.

Outside, the evening was fresh and clear. The sky over Lambeth was darkening fast and there were no street lights. He needed a taxi again, but legend had it that cabbies didn't like to operate on this side of the river. He might improve his chances by walking north across Westminster Bridge.

He didn't see Philip Eaton until it was too late.

There were two other men with him, men who looked a great deal stronger than Eaton; they wore plain clothes but had the demeanour of junior secret service officers. To the layman, they probably looked pretty anonymous, but for someone accustomed to the intelligence world, there was no doubt what they were. Wilde's first instinct was that these must have been the ones who had broken into Mimi's house, which meant they were armed.

'Goddamn it, Wilde, you're a devil to find when you make yourself scarce,' Eaton said.

'Eaton.' His body was tensed for flight, weighing up his chances. He was strong enough, too, and reasonably fleet of foot. But he had no weapon.

'Look, be a good fellow and don't make a fuss. I'm afraid you're going to have to come with us. That's our car.' A black Rolls Royce stood at the kerb. Just like the one Eaton had used on his trip to Cambridge the day after Cazerove's suicide. What was going on here? MI6 definitely did not have Rolls Royces in its fleet.

'You can't touch me, Eaton. Diplomatic immunity.'

'Sorry, old boy, needs must.' He nodded to his two men. They moved in on Wilde as one. He didn't fight them; he knew it was pointless, so he allowed them to bundle him into the back of the car. One slid in alongside him while the other took the wheel, with Eaton at his side.

'I won't let you get away with this, Eaton. This is no way to treat your country's friends.'

'Friends don't go around slitting the throats of ageing school-teachers.'

'You know damn well that wasn't me.'

'Then you'll have nothing to fear from being interviewed, will you? You have plenty of questions to answer. Come on, we've got a fair drive ahead of us.'

'Where are we going?'

'All in good time. Firstly, though, I would very much like you to tell me where the girl is.'

'Girl? What girl?'

Eaton sighed. 'This is going to be a very long night.'

The car finally came to a halt just before eleven o'clock. Wilde knew exactly where he was: Cambridge. They were right outside the ancient building commonly known as Latimer Hall. It was one of the grandest residences in the town. Wilde recognised it immediately – and knew who owned the place and called it home.

'Why have you brought me here?'

'I take it you know where you are?'

'Of course. Latimer Hall. Templeman lives here.'

'Got it in one.'

'Yes, he always was filthy rich, wasn't he? And I suppose this is one of his cars. I wondered what a secret service bod was doing riding around in a Rolls Royce.'

'Come on, get out. You'll have plenty of time for talking in a short while.'

Wilde was thinking. Strange that he was here at the home of Lord Templeman, yet another denizen of the Dada Club.

Templeman was in his large book-lined study wearing striped pyjamas and a cotton dressing gown, an outfit that would not have looked out of place at a boys' boarding school when the pupils were huddled around drinking their cocoa and Horlicks before lights out. His desk looked like a hobbyist's workbench, the remains of the German wireless scattered among various other bits and pieces, including screwdrivers, pliers and a soldering iron.

'Ah, Professor Wilde again,' he said. 'Thank you so much for coming to talk to us. Do take a seat.'

Wilde did not bother to reply to the welcome, which was spoken without a trace of irony. Nor was there any suggestion of a handshake.

'Now then,' Templeman continued. 'Mr Eaton and I are rather hoping you might be able to clear up one or two things for us. The first is the whereabouts of Miss Harriet Hartwell.'

'The name means nothing to me.'

'Oh come, come. Are you saying you just chanced upon her home in Clade by accident? And how exactly did you come to know her aunt Miss Mimi Lalique?'

'I will happily answer all your questions if you would care to call on me at the American embassy. In the meantime, I demand you put a call through to Bill Phillips.'

'And get the poor chap out of bed? I really don't think so.'

'Those are my terms.'

'I'm being a bad host. Perhaps you'd like a glass of whisky.'

'No, I don't really want anything.'

'Mr Eaton tells me you have performed great services for this country, which I suppose we should call your adopted home, even though you retain American citizenship. Wouldn't you like to help us on this matter?'

'OK, I'll have the whisky. And I'm sure you are aware that I have been issued with a diplomatic passport since taking up my role with the OSS.'

Templeman approached the sideboard and poured a Scotch for Wilde and brandy for himself and Eaton. 'There you go,' he said, handing over the glass. 'Now look, I'm a civilised man and I believe you are one too so I'm going to go out on a limb here and explain what this is all about and why we need to find Miss Hartwell.'

'I'm all ears.' Wilde was sitting on an upholstered chair in front of the desk. However 'civilised' this might all be, he knew he was a prisoner. He sipped the whisky.

The two junior officers who had bundled him into the car were standing just inside the door. Templeman jutted his chin at them. 'Leave us for a minute or two if you would, please, gentlemen.' They gave him an obedient nod of the head and slipped out of the room, closing the door behind them.

'Now then, professor, what I am about to tell you is top secret, known only to the King, the Prime Minister and half a dozen other people. The reason I am reluctant to discuss the matter with you is that, as an American and a member of the OSS, you will almost certainly feel duty-bound to convey this information to President Roosevelt. Our fear is that he might misunderstand our actions and that the alliance between our nations will suffer. I'm not going to insult you by swearing you to secrecy, but I would ask you to consider the potential harm that might be caused if you do break this confidence. The damage would be immense at home, too.'

Eaton cleared his throat. He was standing on the other side of the desk, at Lord Templeman's side. 'I'm calling in the favour, Wilde. You know what I'm talking about. You must tell us where she is.'

'I don't know – because I have no idea who you're talking about.'

'Damn it, Wilde,' Eaton said, hammering his cane into the boards. 'We *have* to find her!'

The MI6 man's explosion was uncharacteristic, especially as Templeman was being so emollient. For a moment Wilde wondered whether he was about to be lashed by Eaton's stick. He didn't flinch. 'Whoever she is, wherever she is, perhaps she doesn't trust you,' he said evenly.

'Why has she gone missing? What is the connection with Peter Cazerove's suicide? Because there *is* a link, we know that.'

'And why do you think I might know where she is?'

'You arrived at St Thomas' with Miss Lalique. Since picking you up, I have sent an officer around to her house in Westminster. The place has been ransacked and a pair of Pekingese dogs were found sniffing around and shitting everywhere, seemingly abandoned. Perhaps you'd like to tell me what's been going on.'

Wilde wanted to laugh. 'Well, you should bloody know!' he said. 'It's your men who broke in!'

'It most certainly wasn't.'

'Then who was it?'

Eaton slumped down into a leather armchair, placing his cane on the floor and wincing as he stretched out his injured left leg. 'Obviously someone else is looking for her. Perhaps they've found her. That's my fear.' He was still angry.

Templeman sighed. 'Calm down, both of you. I know you and Wilde have history, Philip – but this is all unnecessary. I've said I'll explain what this is about and so I shall. Perhaps Professor Wilde will then be more forthcoming.'

Wilde guessed that Templeman had a revolver, either in his desk or in his dressing-gown pocket. Eaton often carried a Walther. There really was no way out of this place. 'Very well,' he said. 'Tell me your secret – but don't expect me to swear an oath to keep it.'

'But you will use your judgement, honed by years of fine work in academia, and weigh your actions carefully?'

'I can promise you that. But nothing more.'

Chapter 20

Lord Templeman had opened a silver cigar box. He offered it to Wilde and Eaton, who both declined.

'Let me tell you a bit about Miss Harriet Hartwell,' Templeman said when he had lit his cigar. 'She worked for the Duke of Kent as secretary, in its rather more commonplace meaning – very different to the role of his private secretary, John Crowther, who was also aboard the Sunderland but sadly died. Her tasks were a great deal more menial – taking a full shorthand note and keeping his diary, that sort of thing. Although she was less senior than Crowther, she *was* held in esteem by the Duke and he enjoyed her company.'

'You mean she shared his bed?'

'Good God, no – well, at least I don't think so,' Templeman said. He turned to Eaton. 'Philip?'

'Who knows?'

'But there was more to her than simply being a shorthand typist,' Templeman continued. 'What you may or may not have deduced, Wilde, is that she is also a secret agent, working for MI5. Now she's gone rogue and we are extremely worried, because we have no idea what she is going to do with the information she has. Why has she not reported in? Is she working for someone else? We have no idea – and nor do we know what she is planning. Most of all, we don't know where she is and so we have to find her, to debrief her and ensure all is in order.'

Wilde said nothing.

'Let's go back a bit,' Templeman continued, a cloud of aromatic smoke enveloping him. 'The official story about the Sunderland flight is not quite the whole truth, but you were already moving in that direction, I believe. In fact, it wasn't leaving for Iceland, but returning from Stockholm at the time of the crash. In Stockholm, the Duke of Kent had a secret meeting with his German cousin Prince Philipp von Hessen. Have you heard of him?'

'No.'

'He's closely related to the former kaiser and is one of the very senior members of what remains of the old German aristocracy. He also happens to be a rabid Nazi and one of Hitler's closest friends. This is not something that is generally known outside high-ranking Nazi circles.'

'I imagine they were talking peace then,' Wilde said. 'Some sort of shabby face-saving deal. Does Churchill know about it?'

'Yes, Churchill knew about the meeting, but you're getting ahead of yourself. And your instant conclusion is what worries me – for if word of the meeting got out we could expect exactly the same reaction from both the Kremlin and the White House, not to mention our allies throughout the empire. They would immediately think we were doing what you suggest – looking for a shabby deal. And they would then assume, wrongly, that we were unreliable allies. Hitler would be delighted, of course, because he would love to drive a wedge between us.'

'Then if you're not looking for a deal, why meet this Nazi aristocrat?'

'To listen, Professor Wilde. Simply to listen.'

'You'll have to explain.'

'We believe the German advance in the East may be stalling and that they have underestimated Stalin's reserves. We also believe that hostility is rising in the occupied lands to the West. While some in France and the Low Countries welcomed the Wehrmacht with open arms back in 1940, that goodwill has been squandered by the killing of hostages and reprisal executions on a huge scale. Secret reports tell us that hundreds of innocent people were massacred in a village called Lidice in revenge for the assassination of the monstrous Heydrich earlier this summer. But that is just the tip of the iceberg. Hostages are being slaughtered in towns and villages across France in retaliation for acts of sabotage by the resistance movement.' He paused for a pull on his Havana cigar.

'Barbaric, utterly barbaric,' Wilde said. 'But I still don't understand the Duke of Kent's role.'

'To listen. To find out whether the Germans are keen on a deal, which might indicate that they are becoming severely stretched,' Templeman continued his flow unabated. 'If they are stretched in the West, it means that they have to keep more divisions back – divisions that they would like to throw into the fray in Stalingrad, Moscow and Leningrad. The Duke's mission was to try to find out just how desperate Hitler is becoming. He never had any intention of negotiating a peace deal with von Hessen. We had to assume the meeting place had been bugged, so the Duke was coached to say nothing that could sound remotely like an interest in any truce or pact. Nothing that could be used against him or us. The damnable thing is that, with his death, we don't know what he learnt, for he was supposed to report back directly. The only other person in the room during the talks was Harriet Hartwell, taking a note in her head. She has an actor's ability to learn lines.'

Wilde finished off the whisky and grimaced. 'What is this?'

'Bit peaty for you?' Templeman said. 'Sixteen-year-old single malt from my estates north of the border.'

Something in the recesses of Wilde's brain dredged up a recollection of Templeman's sporting lands – what was it, 30,000 acres of shooting and fishing? But there were more pressing matters, and in truth he was beginning to see a certain logic to all of this, but there were holes, too, in Templeman's version of events. 'Why not just come clean with FDR and Stalin? If the British motive was explained to them, they'd go along with it.'

'Good God, Wilde – there's already enough paranoia in the Kremlin about Britain's role. Stalin would explode at the very suggestion of Anglo-German talks.'

'But FDR would understand.'

'Indeed he might. But secrets shared have a tendency to get out, especially on Pennsylvania Avenue. There are still Nazis and Soviet spies in Washington DC, professor – you must know that.'

'OK, I accept what you say – but there's more, isn't there? You don't believe the crash of the Sunderland was accidental, do you?'

'No,' Templeman said. 'Not for a moment.'

Eaton took up the story. 'There is another element to this – the curious behaviour of Miss Hartwell in Sweden. She had been instructed to stay with the Duke every inch of the way, but we received word during the mission that Miss Hartwell had disappeared. They were all staying at Drottningholm Palace, but she had simply vanished from her room. The initial worry was that she might have been abducted, but then she reappeared just before the flight home.'

'At Bromma airport?'

'No, of course not. They had used a flying boat so that the Duke could land on one of the lakes near Drottningholm, to the west of Stockholm, and avoid the airport, where his presence would most certainly have been noted. There are many agents of all hues in Sweden, all watching our movements.'

'So did the wayward Miss Hartwell say where she had been?'

'All we got was a message to say she had arrived and was aboard the Sunderland. After that there had to be radio silence.'

'And the crash?'

'There must be many possibilities but one is uppermost in our minds,' Templeman said. 'They would have flown as high as possible – perhaps 17,000 feet, ceiling height for a Sunderland. At that height, all on board would have needed oxygen to avoid hypoxia. It is not impossible that the oxygen tanks had been tampered with before taking off or that they were somehow sabotaged *during* the flight. If the pilots were drowsy it might explain why the plane seemed to come in on a gradually decreasing course and why they did not take action to avoid crashing, either by landing on the sea or gaining altitude.'

'How do you think she managed to survive?'

'I suppose she was just damn lucky, like Sergeant Jack . . .' Templeman had paused as if considering some other option.

'Or?' Wilde said.

'Well, the obvious – she parachuted out.'

'You mean she sabotaged the plane?'

'Well, someone did – and we have to consider all possibilities.'

'The shepherd boy didn't mention a parachute. Have the men up in Caithness found one?'

'Mr Quayle has told me that the boy is a simpleton. Anyway,' Templeman said, not quite answering the question, 'survive she did. But why didn't she come straight to us? Why has she gone AWOL – and what did she do during the lost hours in Sweden?'

'You mentioned some link to Cazerove.'

'Well, how could we *not* see a connection after what you told us of the conversation in the railway carriage? In fact, I believe you said as much to Mr Eaton at the time. Anyway, Wilde, we have now laid our cards on the table. State secrets have been entrusted to you. I think it's time for a little payback. Where in the name of God is the girl?'

'I really don't know,' he said. And yes, everything they told him made sense. Yet he knew they were hiding something. *Tell a little truth to conceal a bigger lie.*

'But you've met her?'

For a moment, Wilde came close to admitting that he had indeed met her. But something stopped him. The attack on Mimi's house, perhaps, or the murder of Harriet's father. Perhaps those deeds were the work of someone other than the British secret intelligence service, but until he was certain, he would maintain his silence. Not that he had much to offer anyway – details of the car, chapter and verse on their conversation, that was about it. He looked at his watch. It was late, a quarter past twelve, and he was weary. He wasn't sure how much more of this he could put up with.

'I think I need my bed.'

'Tired are we, professor? I'm with you on that. We've all had rather a long day, what with one thing and another.' Templeman spoke softly for such a tall man, but there was nothing gentle in his intent. He meant to get more information out of his prisoner, whatever it required.

'Well, yes,' Wilde said. 'It has been a long day.'

'Perhaps you'd care to tell us your version of events at Old Cottage in Clade by way of starters.'

'Oh, that's fair enough. I have made no secret of the fact that I was there, calling in on the Reverend Hartwell.'

'Why exactly?'

'Because I wanted to find Harriet. I had her passport, you see.' Had he really just said that? He smiled foolishly. 'The shepherd boy had it. I think he liked her picture.'

'So he *did* find her?'

'Well, you know that already.'

'Then where is the passport?'

'I gave it back to her, of course.'

'Then you have met her?'

'No, you're twisting my words.'

'Why didn't you think to hand the passport over to Mr Quayle or, indeed, one of the officers at the scene of the crash?'

'I was curious. I wanted to know what had happened.' His tongue was loose and he wondered whether he had had too much whisky, but he couldn't stop now. This all needed to come out in the open. 'But then, with help from a newspaper friend, I found out a little bit about Harriet Hartwell and from there it was relatively easy to find her father in Clade. The poor man had had his throat cut, you know. But I can tell you who did it – a young man who calls himself Mortimer. Small, thin, rather malnourished by the look of him.'

'You saw him killing the reverend?'

'I saw him riding away on a motorbike.'

'And then?'

'I made my way to Cambridge and avoided the police as best as I could. That was when Harriet found me. I think she must have been waiting for me in her car outside college. I'd met her aunt, Mimi Lalique, the night before, so she must have told Miss Hartwell about me.'

He wanted to bite his tongue. He had just confirmed that he had met Harriet. This was what came of tiredness . . .

'The car . . . perhaps you could describe it for me.'

'Oh, it was one of those little Austin Sevens. Cream-coloured, I'd call it. Open-topped. Bit of a death trap actually.' Had he said this? Had he really given these details to Templeman and Eaton? Why did his brain want to stop but his tongue and lips keep chattering away?

'Did you get a registration number?'

'Funnily enough, I did take a note of that – AYT 827. Why do you want to know?'

Templeman scribbled a note of the number on his desk pad. 'You're sure about that?'

'Absolutely certain. Horrible little car, barely crawled up to fifty.'

'And then she took you where?'

'To Mimi's in Westminster.'

'What did you talk about?'

'This and that, why she was running. Why I was running. I told her about her father's death – not the worst of the details, of course – and she told me about the Athels.'

Wilde's head seemed to be swimming from the whisky and exhaustion. Was it only this morning that he had woken up in a hotel on the Strand in London?

'What about the Athels?'

'She's scared of them. Peter Cazerove was one. They were lovers, you know, after a fashion. Have I said that already? I'm losing track. Anyway, he was an Athel. You must know all about them. Eaton – you'd have come across one or two at Trinity, I'm sure. Harriet Hartwell says they're everywhere – she thinks they want to kill her. That's why she's gone missing.' He couldn't stop talking. What was the matter with him? He was never like this.

'Tell us more, Wilde. Tell us more about Miss Hartwell and the Athels.'

'Nothing to tell. I need my bed, I'm talking too much.'

'As soon as you've told us where she is, you'll have your bed.'

'I don't know. She mentioned a name – Coburg – but then she was interrupted, so I know no more about him. Rudi Coburg, that was it.'

'And where is he?'

Wilde shrugged helplessly and laughed. This was all ridiculous; he just wanted his bed. Not like him to get sloshed on a couple of whiskies.

Eaton touched Lord Templeman's arm. 'I don't think he knows, Dagger. But we've got details of her car. I'll get things moving on that.'

'OK. And go back with the team to the Lalique house. Do another search of Harriet's own flat in Kensington. There must be clues to other mutual acquaintances. Someone will be sheltering her.'

'What about Wilde?'

'Leave him with me.'

Chapter 21

Wilde could not have stayed awake if he wanted to. The drug that had loosened his tongue now knocked him out. Even when he was awoken an hour before dawn, he could barely get off the bed on which he had been dumped fully clothed. His head was hammering, his mouth desert dry.

'Come on, Mr Wilde, time to get you out of here.' A voice was talking to him, but who and why? Was he having a dream? Somewhere deep in his brain, he realised he had been drugged, but he had no recollection of anything else. Had they had some conversation? He knew he was at Latimer Hall, the expansive Cambridge home of Lord Templeman, and that he had been brought here by Eaton and two agents, but nothing more.

'I have to sleep,' he said, curling up like a child, the very movement sending spasms of pain through his head and neck.

'No, you have to go. His Lordship's orders.'

Wilde groaned.

'Come on.' The man's hands were on him now, gently coaxing. 'Just get your shoes on, Mr Wilde, and off we go. You can go back to sleep later.'

He moved as ordered, but he was horribly unsteady, his head swirling. Suddenly a particle of consciousness cut through the vortex of confusion and he realised that, yes, this was a good idea. Get out of this place. He had been brought here as a prisoner and drugged for some reason. Best to get away while he had the chance. Go somewhere he could sleep for twenty-four hours.

Sitting on the edge of the bed, he took a few deep breaths. He looked up without recognition into the face of the man who had woken him. He was silver-haired and wore a morning suit. 'I'm sorry, I don't know you.'

'Barker, sir, His Lordship's valet.'

'Well, Barker, just give me a few moments. I don't suppose you have a glass of water.'

Barker went to a basin against the wall and filled a beaker. He handed it to Wilde, who drank it down greedily.

'Oh God, that's better.'

'Would you like me to help you with your shoes, sir?'

'Yes, that would be a good idea. Thank you.'

'My pleasure, sir. All part of the service.'

Two minutes later, he was standing up, his hand on the bedpost to steady himself. For a few moments, he felt faint and wondered whether he might pass out. Barker took his arm. 'Come on, sir, I'll help you. None of my business, of course, but it rather seems as though you took a surfeit of hard liquor, Professor Wilde.'

'Something like that.'

'I'd offer you coffee, but the driver is waiting and His Lordship is keen that you get away in short order.'

The car, another of Templeman's expensive models, was on the forecourt with the engine running and headlights blazing. The uniformed driver climbed out, doffed his peaked cap, opened the rear door and assisted Wilde to his seat.

Before closing the door, the valet leant in. 'His Lordship asked me to apologise on his behalf for the inconvenience and hopes you will understand.'

'Inconvenience?'

'That was his word, sir.'

Inconvenience wasn't the half of it. He was lifted off the streets of London, brought here against his will and then doped up to the eyeballs. He was trying to focus, to force himself into alertness, to remember what he had said and to work out exactly what was happening and what his next move should be. He wondered if this was what senility was like. A small voice within was telling him he should be furious – particularly with Eaton, with whom he had worked in the past – but for the moment all he could feel was relief that he was free of the place.

'Where are we going, driver?'

'I've had instructions, sir. Not far from here.'

Wilde slumped back and closed his eyes. He felt the shudder of the gear being engaged, and then blacked out again.

Rudolf Coburg knew they would be hunting him. He knew that his life depended on complete isolation. He splashed cold water on the hot stones and a burst of steam enveloped him and took his breath away. Never had he experienced such intense heat. He wasn't quite sure whether it counted as pleasure or pain, but Axel Anton had assured him it not only gave great health benefits, but was considered the height of luxury these days. 'The Finns are very keen, Herr Coburg,' he had said. 'They swear it has health benefits, and I believe they may well be right.'

At his side, he had a bottle of vodka, half empty. He had had more than enough of it, but still it was tempting. Everyone drank vodka to dull the pain – all the SS guards in the camp, all the train drivers, all the *Hiwis* who did the dirtiest work. Who would not want to slip away into oblivion after what they did and what they witnessed? Who could bear to live in this hideous world?

It was dawn, the beginning of another day of hiding. He had left open the window in the night and had been tormented by midges. God, this place. Anton had sung its praises as the perfect hide-out and a place to meditate on life.

When he couldn't sleep, which was every night, he tried reading one of the German-language books Anton had left him, but he couldn't concentrate. He read a paragraph, then read it again. And again. A whole page became a saga, and his mind's eye drifted to the endless sea and the snakes sunbathing on the grey rocks. The snakes were there in his waking daylight hours, and in his mind after dark.

'Don't worry,' Axel Anton had said cheerily. 'You'll be left alone here. Nobody comes because they don't like the snakes. You'll be safe.'

Yes, it was a lovely, peaceful little island. The cabin was splendidly appointed with a large picture window, a pleasant sitting room where he could read and a comfortable bedroom which in other days might have been the perfect place to sleep. At first Coburg had been impressed and hoped it would be therapeutic, but every day was worse than the last.

And then there was this separate hut, the sauna, with its benches, its woodstove and its invigorating scent of pine. Surely this would soothe him into sleep? But it didn't.

Today he would drink no vodka, but he would keep the bottle with him like a talisman, just in case, because he couldn't bear to have it out of his reach. Even so, it did not improve things. Vodka did not make the world less wretched. Once, in London, long before the war, he had seen *Macbeth*. 'Sleep no more! Macbeth does murder sleep.' He would sleep no more. Sleep had been murdered in Poland at that little railway siding near forest and farmland and a short drive from the hunting lodge with its fine food and wine and girls.

The SS-Obersturmführer had welcomed them all most correctly, like a good Nazi. His name was Eberl. Herr Dokteur Irmfried Eberl, which was a name never to be forgotten, a name that would shame the circles of hell. He had a greasy little moustache like Hitler's and he shook each of his guests by the hand.

In the fields nearby, fires were burning and there was singing and the occasional pistol shot among the *Hiwis*, but on the ramp that served as a platform there was only the stench of faecal waste, decay and some sort of gas, the long railway train and the sound of moaning, half-human, half-animal. There were, too, great piles of belongings – shoes and coats, dresses and skirts, hats and suitcases, and piles of banknotes, spectacles and jewels. Piles of everyday clothing and other effects, ten metres high. Enough to dwarf a house.

Müller had stepped forward. 'What you are about to see, gentlemen,' he began, 'is the supreme example of German efficiency, and it is a credit to all of you whose efforts in Berlin make it possible. Let me explain how it works: the journey here by train has already thinned the weeds. The strongest of those left alive will form our workforce until they, too, are pruned by disease and lack of calories. The remainder, waiting inside these cattle cars, are already too weak to resist, which makes our unpleasant task all the easier. You may find it difficult to watch at first but, in due course, you will come to realise that this is all for the Fatherland and one day you will be able to tell your grandchildren of the part you played in defending your race and advancing the Reich.'

Coburg had stood transfixed. Horrified.

Müller clapped his hands. 'Now, let the show begin, Herr Dokteur Eberl.'

The Obersturmführer barked an order. Coburg couldn't hear what it was, but it meant something to his squadron of SS guards – the Unterscharführers – because they moved along the ramp with their leashed dogs and their Ukrainian underlings, five men taking up position in front of each wagon door, all of which were still closed, with barbed wire at the vent. With them went a larger squadron of bent men who wore prison garb. Each wagon was marked with a number in chalk – 120, 150, 180. These, Coburg now realised, were the numbers of people packed in each wagon, herded into a space designed for a few steers or oxen. They were the same numbers that appeared later on the transport paperwork at Referat IV B4.

As one, the guards produced a key at the end of a chain attached to their belts, unlocked the wagon door, pulled it open with one hand and clutched a kerchief to their mouth with the other.

'*Raus! Raus! Raus! Schnell! Schnell! Schnell!*' Out! Out! Out! Hurry! Hurry! Hurry! The shouts went up even as the whips began to crack. At first there was no obvious movement, but then, a woman fell from the wagon nearest the party guests.

Coburg recoiled. His first instinct was to go and assist the woman. But no one moved, and she simply rolled out and lay beside the track. He could tell that she was already dead and that no assistance would help, even if it were to be offered.

Other corpses began to tumble out and then, tentatively, a few living men, women and children climbed down from their hellish wagons.

Coburg watched. He couldn't bear to watch, but nor could he look away. He didn't want to meet the eyes of the others here, the men who had been laughing and drinking with him all night. He didn't want to see their helpless horror and shame or, worse, their excitement or indifference.

The living continued to emerge until there were hundreds of them. They were almost outnumbered by the dead. They stood hunched, clutching their valises and string-tied packs. They held their children close to their breasts or held their hands tightly.

'Everyone out!' The dogs were unleashed and leapt up into the wagons, snapping at those too ill to move, ignoring the dead. Old men and women who couldn't move were savaged where they lay by the dogs' ravening jaws. Others staggered and stumbled away from the dogs, trying to fend them off with their forearms or suitcases, tumbling down on to the tracks, facing the lash or the bullet even before they could pull themselves to their feet. The dogs followed them down, biting, snarling, drooling. Later, Obersturmführer Eberl confided in his guests that the dogs received immaculate care and ate the same high-quality food as their handlers. 'I insist on it,' he said. 'Animal welfare standards must be maintained.'

The white glare from the floodlights was blinding. The condemned had been in darkness so long, they could not look up and either closed or shielded their eyes.

They were being forced to move now, driven by the Rottweilers and the whips and pistol shots towards an iron gateway, beyond which were long low barrackrooms. As they moved, their heads down, half-dead with fear and hunger and thirst, they passed the party guests without a glance.

Rudolf Coburg wanted to vomit. The expensive contents of his stomach churned in his gullet and he fought to keep it all down. But then Eichmann, two steps away from him, did throw up and Coburg could no longer hold it in.

'It's quite natural,' Müller said. 'Do not be ashamed. In hospitals nurses soon learn to get over their queasiness, and so will you. Come along now, I want you to see the system that is used here. The system you gentlemen, each in your own small way, have helped to create. You must all take credit for this, and you deserve every honour. If there were an Iron Cross for your work, I would recommend you all.'

The guests followed Müller and Eberl through the gate into the camp. The women and children were whipped to the barrackroom on the left, the men to the one on the right.

'They are undressing,' Eberl said. 'The men will emerge first because the women will stay in their barracks and have their hair cut short – a nice style for their walk along the road to Heaven – and the hair that is removed will be sent back to Germany for the benefit of the Reich. Padding, perhaps, for comfortable slippers for our heroic submariners. There are good professional hairdressers in there, a dozen or more. The officer is kind to the women, he says, "Hurry, dear ladies, hurry to the baths while the water is still warm." And so that takes a little longer, which is why the men go first.' He turned to his guests. 'Stand here and wait a few moments, gentlemen. Watch as they fold their arms about themselves to protect their modesty, even as they go to their deaths.'

And then these pathetic people began to come out from their barracks, naked, their flesh white. Flesh like the luscious flesh of Dagmar, but a whole world away.

It did not take long for Coburg to understand the purpose of their visit. The night had been an initiation rite. *You are now one of us, and you share our shame and guilt.* It was about incrimination and complicity, nothing else. *You have seen it with your own eyes, you know now where the trains go and what happens to their human cargo. We're all in it together, so don't even think of turning on us.*

Two hours, the show had lasted. Two hours in which children, women and men had been herded into the gas rooms. Two hours of horror in which innocent people had been murdered without reason.

He heard their screams and cries and, after half an hour, he saw their bodies dragged out with long metal hooks, searched intimately for concealed gold and gems, and flung into the pit. No longer was their flesh like Dagmar's. This flesh was flecked with faeces and vomit. Bones were broken and twisted, bodies contorted into hellish shapes, breasts torn and bloody from the death struggle.

Later, like an unthinking horse led by its reins, he was taken to the infirmary – the Lazarett with its red cross outside the door – and was ushered inside where there was nothing but another pit, half-full of corpses. He stood to one side with the other guests and watched as the lame and the sick, who could not walk unaided to the gas room, were carried here on stretchers to receive a bullet in the back of the neck.

At the end the honoured guests were all given more schnapps and each was handed a gift of a precious item of jewellery, collected from the dead. 'Something for your loved ones back home,' Eberl told them. 'That is the way to a pretty girl's heart.' Coburg, unseen, had trodden the diamond ring he was given into the mud.

He was ashamed now of everything. Ashamed of his unquestioning loyalty to the Nazis over the past twelve years, ashamed that he had fired bullets at pictures of Jews, ashamed of being rather pleased when the Nuremberg laws were brought in to restrict Jewish rights, ashamed of the ghettos and the transports which he had helped Eichmann organise, ashamed that he had been too stupid to understand that there was no new homeland in the East for the Jews. Only death.

Ashamed that he was an accomplice to mass murder.

No, the word 'ashamed' was not enough for the depravity of what he had witnessed. It was a stain on his very name. A stain that would not be washed clean, however many generations came after him.

Here now, in this wooden hut on this little island, he threw more water on the stones, then more, until the air was burning hot. He wanted the steam to burn away the stain, to cleanse him. But he knew that 10,000 scaldings would never make him clean again.

Chapter 22

Wilde was curled up on the stone step outside the front door. The milkman looked at him for a few moments, then stepped past him and rang the bell. Lydia answered within a few moments. At first she saw the milkman's irritating grin, then looked down with horror at Wilde.

'Look what the cat didn't quite bring in, Mrs Wilde,' the milkman said, pointing at Wilde's inert form.

Lydia hated it when the milkman called her Mrs Wilde, because he was quite aware that she was still Miss Morris, but on this occasion she ignored him. She was more concerned by the sight of Tom lying unconscious at her feet. She immediately knelt down beside him and put the back of her hand to his brow. Finding warmth, she breathed a sigh of relief.

'Alive, is he, missus?'

She ignored the milkman. 'Tom? Please wake up, Tom.'

He groaned.

Johnny was now at her side. 'Daddy, Daddy,' he said. 'Daddy sleep.'

'Let me give you a hand, Mrs Wilde,' the milkman said. 'Help you carry your old man inside? Looks like he had a few too many bevies last night.'

'I'll deal with it, thank you.' Her retort was curt, and she instantly regretted it. Whether or not she liked the confounded milkman, she had to deal with him every day.

He huffed. 'Suit yourself, missus.'

'I'm sorry,' she said. 'I didn't mean to be so short.'

'That's all right, Mrs Wilde. I'll be on my way – you get the professor to bed.'

Lydia put her hands under Wilde's armpits and tried to pull him up. He groaned again, then shook his head. 'God in heaven,' he said.

'Daddy hurting!'

'Tom, what on earth is going on? Why did you sleep here? Even if you've lost your key, I would have woken up and let you in.'

'Just give me a moment.' He was on his knees now, clasping the edge of the front door. Gradually he pulled himself up. 'Dear God, Lydia, I've got the hangover to end all hangovers.'

'You must have drunk a whole bottle of Scotch. You smell like a distillery.'

'One glass, that's all. It was doped.'

'By whom? Why?'

'Templeman. Lord bloody Templeman.'

'You're not making sense, Tom. Why would a man like Dagger Templeman drug you?'

'To make me talk, I think. Come on, let's get inside. Make some coffee and I'll try and tell you everything. Or what I can remember. At the moment it's all as fuzzy as hell.'

Coffee, weak though it was, helped him feel more human, but it did little to improve his memory. He was aware that he had been abducted from the street outside St Thomas' Hospital by Philip Eaton and two of his agents. He was aware, too, that he had been taken to Latimer Hall and held against his will and he suspected he had been questioned regarding the whereabouts of Harriet Hartwell. 'Beyond that I can remember almost nothing.'

'Well, perhaps it will all come back during the day, darling,' Lydia said. 'But don't you think you had better tell me where you have been – and who exactly your new friend is? I don't much like the sound of Harriet Hartwell.'

'She's all right, I think – a serious woman.' He realised he was parroting her own words to describe herself.

'Is she now? You might be interested to know that she phoned here last night and asked me to give you a message.'

Wilde was suddenly alert. 'Yes? Did she say where she was?'

'I really don't know. It was rather strange actually. She just said, "Tell him the shed." At least I think that's what it was. Does she know you have a partner and a child?'

'Did she leave a phone number?'

'No. I tried to question her, but she just cut the call dead. There had been a click on the line, as usual nowadays. Someone is listening in.'

'Templeman's men, I imagine.'

'I assume the shed means something to you?'

He nodded. 'Yes, I think it does.'

'Then what are you going to do, Tom? Don't you think you've had enough of this game? If you ask me, you need to do one of two things – either trot along to St Andrew's Street, talk to the police and clear your name, or get yourself to the embassy in London and do it through diplomatic channels. You can't just go chasing after this woman, a fugitive about whom you know bugger all. And I'm pretty sick of visits from the local police and others asking if I've heard from you.'

'I'll call Bill Phillips and get his take on it.'

'And you know what he'll say? Kill this nonsense stone dead. The last thing he'll want is any sort of rift between allies.'

First though, he wanted to talk to Jimmy Orde in Caithness. He wanted an affidavit of what he had seen – Sunderland 4026 arriving in Scotland, not leaving. He wanted it so that whatever came of this affair, he had something on paper to prove he wasn't merely chasing shadows.

Jean Orde answered the phone in her low, lilting brogue, but a little flatter than he remembered it. 'Hello, Mrs Orde speaking.'

'Jean, it's Tom Wilde.'

'Oh yes, hello, Tom.'

'Is Jimmy there? I'd like to have a quick word with him.'

There was a slight pause; he could almost hear the catching of emotion in her throat from 600 miles away.

'Is something the matter?'

'He's missing, Tom. The boat's missing.'

He went cold. 'How long? How long has it been missing?'

'They were due back yesterday evening. This has never happened before.'

'Is the weather bad?'

'No, it's been fine these past two days and nights. I'm scared, Tom. We all are, all the wives. All sorts of possibilities go through your mind, none of them good. Some say they've been . . . torpedoed.'

The final word was uttered so faintly that Wilde wondered for a moment whether it had been spoken. But that was merely wishful thinking, for he knew it had been said. He felt utterly helpless. He had met a man after his own heart in Jimmy Orde, and his wife Jean was every bit his match. He thought of their warm, welcoming house with the splendid food and the children running around and imagined it cold and full of fear.

'Would they have had a lifeboat aboard?'

'Aye, and the search has been on all night. But there's not a sign – and there was no mayday call. We're all in despair up here.'

'Perhaps the trawler is drifting through loss of power.'

'Aye, perhaps . . .'

'I'm so sorry, Jean. I can't imagine what this is like for you and the bairns, and the families of the other men.'

'It's what I've lived with every day since childhood. My uncle Alec was taken by the sea back in 1913, but that was God and nature doing their worst. This feels like man's doing.'

'Can I give you my number in case you hear anything?'

'Aye, I'll let you know – either way. Jimmy liked you and trusted you, Tom.'

Wilde didn't know what more to say. The stoicism of the woman was, in itself, enough to bring a man to tears. Lydia and Johnny were watching him in silence. Even the boy seemed to understand that this was no moment for childish prattle.

Slowly he replaced the receiver.

'I understand,' Lydia said. She had seen the darkness in his eyes, and she knew that any hope of his giving up on the strange, perambulating quest that was consuming him had just disappeared.

Chapter 23

He washed, shaved and ate breakfast at speed, then kissed them both and walked to the side of the house where the Rudge Special was parked.

Removing the tarpaulin, he wheeled the 500cc motorcycle down to the road, checked the oil and the petrol – his whole ration for the month intact – and fired her up. He knew Lydia and Johnny would be at the front window watching him, so he threw them a smile and a wave, then turned the throttle and hit the road out of Cambridge at high speed.

The roads were clear of all but military and farm traffic and he made good time, reaching Clade in an hour and a half. He realised it wouldn't be term time yet, so the school should be empty except for the permanent staff. More than anything, he was worried that he might be recognised if his photograph had been circulated among the local police or if he encountered the postwoman or the woman who had given him directions, so he kept his face concealed behind goggles and flying helmet.

He rode through the ancient gateposts – which had no gate or other security – up to the front of the old school. A couple of cars were parked to the right of the building. Stopping the bike, he stretched his legs and gazed up at the ancient edifice. It wasn't very large and nor was it imposing. Built of limestone in, he guessed, the eleventh or twelfth century, it had mullions and transoms on its windows and it had the look of a religious institution – priory or abbey.

So this was Athelstans. He had expected something larger and more dramatic, but of course the true grandeur lay in its alumni and its pre-eminent position in England's Establishment.

He doubted whether this place could hold more than 300 boys at a time. Perhaps fifty to sixty boys a year, depending on what year they started. He actually knew very little about the school but imagined that its diminutive size served to add to its sense of exclusivity. Gardens stretched off to the left of the building and, in the distance, he could see a long, high wall and orchards. Behind the wall, there would be a vegetable and fruit garden and probably, beyond that, there would be glasshouses and sheds. He guessed that the old disused shed that Harriet had mentioned as her trysting place with Cazerove would be somewhere around there.

A figure passed across a ground-floor window. Wilde twisted the throttle and put the Rudge into a tight circle, then steered it back along the drive, through the gateposts on to the road. Opposite him was the track up to the Hartwells' house. To the left was the way into Clade, to the right the road back to Cambridge and, not more than a hundred yards away, a patch of unfenced woodland, where he concealed the bike and set off on foot.

The outer wall around the school grounds was easy to scale and beyond it there was mostly more woodland. He understood his direction of travel now, and quickly made his way through the trees to the edge of the extensive gardens. There were several outhouses near the walled garden. Could one of those be the old gardening shed? The problem was, they were so near the other buildings that Harriet Hartwell and Peter Cazerove would not have had much in the way of privacy there.

Surely, the shed she referred to had to be further away?

Staying as concealed as he could, he eased his way through the woods trying to spy out a likely wooden building. Sometimes he stopped as gardeners or maintenance workers made their way across his field of vision. The issue was, he was not at all sure what he was looking for – something rickety and old, but that was all. And he was even less certain that Harriet would be there anyway.

At last he spotted it, on the far side of the games pitches beyond the cricket pavilion. Not obvious but visible. It looked like the sort of place they might have gone for their secret assignments.

Keeping a wary eye open for groundsmen and other workers, he arrived at the building. The door opened with a creak. Inside there was nothing but cobwebs, a pile of planks, an old broken cup. It was just the one room. There were scuffed footprints in the dust, but they could have been made any time in the past five years. He didn't have to look around long to realise that she had either been here and departed, or that she hadn't arrived yet.

The door creaked behind him and a figure blanked out the light. He turned. A man was standing in the doorway, one hand in the pocket of his faded boiler suit, another holding a long-handled hoe.

'Who are you?' the man said. 'What are you doing here?'

'I was looking for someone.'

'Oh yes? And who might that be?'

The obvious move was to attack. The man was white-haired, about sixty years old and strong. Wilde's fists could get him past most men, this one included, probably, but something held him back.

'A woman,' Wilde said.

The gardener grinned. 'Well, if you're looking for a woman, I take it you'll be Professor Thomas Wilde. You fit the description all right.' It was a statement of assumption rather than a question.

Wilde hesitated.

'Don't worry,' the gardener said. 'You're safe with me. I'll take you to her.'

'Who are you?'

'A friend. I'm Dolby.' He offered his hand and Wilde took it. 'How did you get here, prof? Car?'

'Motorbike.'

'Where is it?'

'Woodland, by the road.'

'Let's go to it. You go ahead, I'll follow you. Try not to be seen this time. You were a bit obvious, if you don't mind my saying so. Luckily there's not many of us about, what with the call-up. We've to do two men's work apiece, for the same money of course.'

Within five minutes, they were riding back north to the next hamlet, which didn't seem to have a name. Dolby was riding pillion. He patted Wilde on the shoulder, signalling him to stop, then looked around to check no one was following. 'Take the path on the left,' he said, his mouth close to Wilde's ear.

Wilde turned on to the track. It led to a rather modern house – late 1920s, early 1930s – at the edge of a field. A car was parked outside – a cream-coloured Austin Seven.

'Here we are,' Dolby said. 'Home sweet home.'

Heinrich Müller always watched Adolf Eichmann with amusement. He liked the way he twisted his arms and twitched the side of his mouth, the way his body tautened as he strove to ensure he did not put a foot wrong or say anything that might be misunderstood. His fastidiousness was especially interesting for no one was better than Müller at seeking out and exploiting men's weak points. Such were the requisite qualities of a secret policeman. As chief of the Gestapo, Müller had had to use these exceptional skills on many occasions. Sometimes all that was needed to make a man talk was to make him uncomfortable but, at other times, a couple of blows from a *schlag* at that special point behind the ear was called for. There was no finer way of inflicting intense pain or, if there was, the Gestapo and its compliant medical department hadn't yet discovered it. But the *schlag* – the rubber truncheon – would never be necessary with a man like Eichmann. He cringed like a puppy, so desperate was he to please his master.

Of course, Müller was every bit as dedicated to his work as Eichmann. The difference was that Eichmann believed all the Nazi shit.

Eichmann's life had to be just so because otherwise none of this historic mission would work; there had to be painstaking attention to detail. That had always been the way things were done in Department IVA4b of the Reich Security Main Office.

Thus if a subordinate made an error, he or she would suffer a dressing-down of seismic proportions – and Eichmann would make a mental note never to trust that person again. Two errors, and the Russian front or an educational stay in Sachsenhausen would beckon. Eichmann was unbending in such matters.

It was the same with his uniforms. They were pressed every day, his high boots shone like glass, his military cap was inspected for motes of dust morning and night. He expected no less of those who worked for him. That was the way things were done here in Eichmann's rather functional office within the Jewish department at 115/116 Kurfürstenstrasse, Berlin. If

Eichmann made a mistake . . . well, he never did make a mistake, did he? The filing cabinets full of every detail of his work gave testimony to that. Everything was recorded here.

And yet Eichmann the perfectionist had made a grievous error, which was why he was here, standing like a schoolboy and squirming.

'We have word,' Müller said. 'About your man Coburg.'

'He's not my man. He was transferred to the staff of Prince Philipp von Hessen.'

'Don't answer me back, Eichmann. He *was* your shitty man. And that is all that matters. Reichsführer Himmler is speechless with anger. He is inclined to apprise the Führer himself of your unimaginable carelessness. Have you any idea what that will mean to your career?'

Eichmann clicked his heels involuntarily. He blinked behind his clerk's glasses and his small mouth writhed like an earthworm. 'Of course, Herr Gruppenführer, but I can assure you . . .'

'I don't want your damned assurances, Eichmann – I want this dealt with. This Coburg of yours has been in touch with the British and now he has disappeared in Sweden. We have reason to believe he is in possession of sensitive confidential papers – from *your* office. Can you think what those might be?'

The blood drained from Eichmann's already pale brow. 'Missing papers? There are no missing papers, sir.'

'Are you calling me a liar?'

'No, of course not, Herr Gruppenführer. I will double-check all our records to see if anything is missing. But I cannot believe—'

'Damn you, Eichmann, I don't want your ridiculous assurances. I want to know what papers have gone! Do you understand me?'

Eichmann nodded and clicked his heels again. He was sweating profusely. Before Müller, he had answered to Heydrich, who had trained him in his own image. But now Heydrich was dead, victim of an assassin in Prague, and so Eichmann had to obey this man and he didn't know how to deal with him.

Müller knew that Eichmann feared him. He knew that he considered him a brutal, selfish careerist who didn't share the ideology of his predecessor or even have the interests of the race at heart. But so what? He watched Eichmann's tell-tale signs of imminent capitulation, the twisting of the neck to relieve the pricking of the tight, sweat-soaked collar.

'You have some idea, don't you, Eichmann? You think you know what is missing from your department?'

'No, sir. I have no idea.' But his sweat and discomfort told a different story. It said that he had a horrible idea what the papers might be.

'So tell me about your man Coburg. Was he a good worker?'

'I considered him an excellent worker. No one understood the transports and cargoes better. His filing was beyond reproach. Had he been an army man, he would have made a first-rate quartermaster. I would say he was an important part of my team and I was sorry to lose him.'

'Then why did you let him go?'

'I had instructions that he was to be transferred to Prince Philipp von Hessen at the Führer's headquarters. It was an order that came out of the blue, but one I was powerless to countermand.'

'This was quite soon after our little morale-boosting trip to Poland, yes?'

'Yes, sir.'

'And what was Coburg's reaction to the trip?'

A PRINCE AND A SPY | 222

'I had thought him invigorated by it, Herr Müller. It was good for him to see the fruits of his labours – the destination of the transports.'

'So I ask again, why did he leave your department so precipitously?'

Eichmann blinked furiously. 'In truth, I had been minded to argue against the move, but I knew that the prince had the Führer's ear, and I felt that I was in no position to say anything.'

'And the missing papers?'

'I know of no—'

Müller cut him short. 'Why do I have to learn this from our people in England, Eichmann? Why do *you* not know your papers are missing and report their loss to me?'

Eichmann was shaking. 'You have learnt something of this matter from England?'

'Where else would I have heard it? You didn't think to tell me that papers had disappeared.'

'Forgive me, if anything is missing, then I didn't know.'

'Then find out. I want to know exactly what they are.'

'It will be done, Herr Gruppenführer. What else do you wish me to do? I will do everything in my power. Is there any way I can help in the hunt for Coburg?'

'I don't want you to do anything. If you are a religious man and if you care for your health, you might like to say a prayer or two that my agents in Stockholm flush him out, but that is all.'

'May I ask, sir, how did Coburg get to Sweden?'

'He went as the prince's aide on Führer business. That is all you need to know.'

'Then surely the prince must be involved.'

'You may well be right. I am warming a bunk for him in Dachau even now.'

Müller was small and humourless, but every so often he affected a smile, because he had learnt that human beings sometimes did that. 'You look scared, Eichmann, and you smell disgusting. Change your cologne, man. Are you going soft? Your reaction to the gas vans at Chelmno disturbed me.'

'One learns to harden one's soul. It was the first time . . .'

'And the trenches in the forest at Minsk? You scuttled away like a rat.'

'I was late – it was all just about over.'

'What of our little outing to Treblinka? You didn't avert your eyes that time?'

'No.'

'But Coburg? I saw him avert his eyes.'

'He seemed OK. I didn't doubt him . . . not then.'

'This is difficult work, Eichmann. The Führer ordered the physical annihilation of the Jews not from malice, but because there was no alternative. Such decisions are never easy and only a great leader rises to the challenge. But our children will thank us one day, and their children, too, and they will raise statues and tributes in our honour. I said as much at Treblinka. No one is pretending that what we do is pleasant, but we must believe the whole world will be grateful to us when they are rid of this canker. This unpleasantness will be seen as a price worth paying for the Pax Germanica.'

Eichmann nodded. He understood all this, and as Sturmbannführer Höppner from the Central Resettlement Office in the Warthegau region had pointed out, it had to be more humane to give the Jews a quick death by gas than a slow one by starvation. Yet his body rebelled at the memory of what he had witnessed – the shooting of a baby in its mother's arms at Minsk, the child's brains spattered across his leather greatcoat.

Eichmann's left eye fluttered all the more, as if afflicted by a loosely wired nerve.

'For the present, however,' Müller continued. 'It will not help our cause if word of what we are doing at Treblinka and Chelmno and Sobibor and Belzec were to reach the wider world. Perhaps the history books in 200 years' time – but not now. That is why we are worried about your comrade Herr Coburg.'

'He is not my com—'

Müller clasped him by his upper arms. 'Ssh. Don't follow that line. All you need to know is that we will do whatever is necessary to keep our great enterprise from the eyes of the world. You understand, don't you, Eichmann?'

'Of course.'

'The world does not need to know what we do with our Jewish livestock.' Suddenly Müller affected his learnt smile again. 'Hey, don't worry, my friend.'

'But—'

'No buts. I don't want you to spend any more time on this than necessary. You have important work to do – trains to run, ghettos to fill, ghettos to empty, property to be sequestrated, infestations to be cleared and purified. All I need from you is the identity of the papers Coburg has taken. Do that for me now and you will be forgiven . . .'

He didn't need to say what the alternative might be.

'It is just possible . . .' Eichmann began tentatively.

'Ah, you see – I knew you would work it out.'

'It is just possible . . . the notes from Wannsee.'

'Ah yes, you took a full note of Reinhard's January conference.'

'I instructed Coburg to clean it up, to insert the usual euphemisms so that the minutes could be distributed among all those present as an aide-memoire for the roles they were to play in the . . . in the solution to the Jewish question.'

'And did he do that well?'

'Yes, Herr Müller. Coburg's work was exemplary. Words such as killing, gassing, shooting were replaced by the usual terms – firm or stern treatment, for example – so that you and Herr Heydrich, God rest his soul, had few alterations to make to the final version of the protocol. I gave Coburg a bottle of Margaux from my own cellar as a reward.'

'And the original notes?'

'I told him to destroy them.'

'Not file them?'

'In this instance, no. Though in other circumstances that would have been the procedure.'

'And you think he obeyed your order and destroyed them?'

'I wish I knew, Herr Müller. But I fear it is possible that he didn't. And now that I think of it, there is something else, too.'

'Yes?'

'In the bin by his desk a shredded map was found – torn up as if it was a first draft that he had discarded.'

'And what did this map show?'

'The railway lines in Poland and the camps, Herr Müller. Belzec, Chelmno, Sobibor, Treblinka . . .'

Chapter 24

Harriet Hartwell was in the kitchen wearing an apron, standing with her back to the range, on which a large pot seemed to be bubbling. In one hand she held a ladle, in the other a small pistol. As soon as she saw Wilde, the tension in her eyes eased and she slipped the gun into the apron pocket.

For a few moments he wondered whether he had really seen it, but no, his eyes were not deceiving him. 'You're armed.'

She shrugged. 'Did you think I would have picked you up in Cambridge if I weren't?'

'It never occurred to me.'

'That's because you don't know who you are dealing with.'

'And the ladle? Is that a weapon, too?'

'Dolby and I are old friends. I'm making his jam.'

'Somehow I hadn't imagined you in a domestic setting. Smells delicious. Strawberry?'

'Very perceptive. You could be a secret agent, Mr Wilde.' She stopped stirring the pot and raised a withering eyebrow. 'I can't just sit around doing nothing. Anyway, jam aside, I'm a great deal more interested in the condition of my aunt. What can you tell me?'

'Not much, I'm afraid. All I know is that she was alive when I got her to St Thomas' Hospital and they said she had suffered a heart attack. They couldn't tell me any more than that.'

'Perhaps we could telephone them.'

'The phone might be bugged.'

'Still, I need to know.'

'Is there a telephone here?'

'Astonishingly, yes, there is. Dolby is a modern man.'

Dolby was standing in the doorway. 'I'm going to leave you two, if you don't mind. It's going to take me the best part of twenty minutes to walk back to Athelstans. I'm likely to be missed. Help yourself to as much tea and bread as you want. But if you use the phone, I'd be glad if you could leave me a shilling.'

'Of course,' Harriet said. 'Thank you, Dolby. Thank you for everything.'

After Dolby had gone, Harriet removed the jam from the heat. On the table she had a dozen empty jars and she began to fill them from the pot. Wilde watched her work, fascinated at her precision and single-mindedness. When she had finished, and applied caps to each jar, she smiled at Wilde. 'Now, professor, let's make that telephone call – and then I will tell you everything, from start to finish.'

'You have a good friend there in Dolby.'

'He always looked after us, Peter and me. Made sure we weren't disturbed.'

'Does no one else know you are close to him? Might someone suspect that he is helping you?'

'I don't think so. Not unless you were followed.'

He shook his head.

'Well, you pour the tea – the pot's over there – and leave the hospital to me.'

He found two cups and some milk while she went through to the hall. He could hear her voice, but couldn't quite make out the words. He heard the click of the handset and then she reappeared.

'Well?'

'She's alive, thank God. They offered to call me back if they had any further news.'

'You didn't bite?'

'Do I look stupid, Tom? No, I didn't give them this number.'

'Well, tea's ready.' He handed her one of the cups.

'Now,' she said, 'I have a lot to tell you.'

Dolby's little parlour was a strange room, a bachelor's space with dull brown curtains tied back with string, bare wooden boards, a hearth strewn with ash and no ornaments save one photograph on the mantelpiece of a man from another rather more starch-collared age. Wilde assumed the man was Dolby's father.

They sipped their tea in silence for a minute. Through the window, Wilde could see nothing but farmland and trees. If they had to hide, this was a good place.

'Well,' Harriet said at last, 'you seem to have already worked out that I am not a run-of-the-mill secretary. And yes, I was on a mission to Stockholm with His Royal Highness the Duke of Kent – Georgie.'

'Can you tell me any more than that?'

'He was meeting his cousin, Prince Philipp von Hessen. It was of course a mission of the utmost secrecy. The words "top secret" don't come close to doing it justice.'

That was the name Templeman had mentioned. It was beginning to come back to him.

'Have you heard of him?'

'Vaguely,' he said. 'I'm afraid these German aristocrats mean nothing to me.'

'Well, this one is a big cheese Nazi. A very close friend of Hitler and Göring. Also quite close to Mussolini and the Italian mob. He works as a liaison between Berlin and Rome. On top of that, he also happens to be a very good friend of our own royal family.'

Of course, the duke had been talking peace with him. The whole drugged evening was coming back to him. God, what had he given away? Her car – he had told them about her car, including its number plate.

Harriet continued. 'The duke's mission was simply to find out how desperate Hitler was to do a deal. Get an idea of the morale in the Nazi HQ. But there was always the worry that Georgie – the Duke – wouldn't stick to the script.'

'Is that what happened?'

'I really don't know. I was with him at the first, formal meeting because I not only have a very good shorthand note but I also have a quite remarkable memory. Perfect, when I set my mind to it, like an actor learning lines. In school plays I could learn a large role in a fraction of the time it would take anyone else. In this case I took a full note in my head and then transcribed it on to paper at the end of the meeting. There was only one copy made, and I gave that personally to Georgie. So the only people who know what was said were the Duke, myself, Prince Philipp – and his own aide. That should have been the end of it, but then Georgie strayed from the script and agreed to meet his cousin later in the day, man to man, no aides. I don't know what was said, and now that Georgie is dead we may never know. But as far as I'm concerned that's all a side issue. Something far more important happened in Stockholm.'

'You went missing.'

She looked shocked. 'Who told you that?'

'Philip Eaton. Perhaps you know him?'

'Of course I know him. When did he tell you this?'

'Last night. He wanted to know your whereabouts.'

'I damn well bet he did. Why were you talking with him? I thought I could trust you.'

'Lord Templeman was there, too.'

'Are you serious?'

'You know him, don't you? From the Dada Club.' They had been together in the newspaper photograph.

'Of course I know Dagger.'

'They had me abducted and questioned me.'

She looked alarmed. 'What did you tell them?'

'I'm pretty sure I was doped, but it's starting to come back to me – and I have a horrible feeling I gave them details of your car. I'm sorry. Apart from that, there wasn't a great deal I could actually reveal because I didn't know where you were or what you were up to. But I'm sure it's *you* they are after.'

'I don't believe it. Dagger's not an Athel . . .'

'Well, he's trying to find you.'

'We'll have to ditch the car. But how do you know they didn't follow you to Clade?'

'Visibility was clear. Very little traffic – I'd have seen anything pursuing me.' He said the words, but now he wasn't certain.

'I think we need to get out of here.'

Wilde had just kicked the Rudge into life when he spotted the black car at the end of the track. It hadn't been there when he arrived with Dolby. He turned to Harriet, who was about to get on the pillion. The black car started to move; someone was hanging out of the passenger side window.

'See that? Is there another way out of here?'

They heard a *crack-crack*. Two puffs of debris flew from the brickwork at the side of the house, six feet from the bike.

'There's a track through the woods. It'll be rough, but no car will be able to follow us.'

'Where does it lead?'

She hit him with her fist. 'Just go!'

Wilde turned the bike, the rear wheel spinning away in the dusty path. He looked back and saw that the black car was accelerating up the track towards them, and he saw the pistol in the passenger's hand. As he twisted the throttle, he heard another *crack-crack*, two wisps of smoke leaping from the man's pistol. The Rudge was digging up dirt in the pathway as he accelerated towards the woods behind Dolby's house.

The track Harriet had picked was no track at all. He rode on instinct, ducking below overhanging branches, swerving past windfall logs, stopping at impassable undergrowth and re-tracing their path until he came to another way, driving deeper and deeper into the woods. He stopped and turned to her. 'I think we're lost,' he said.

'We're fine,' she said.

'So long as we're not circling back.'

'I thought men were supposed to have a good sense of direction.'

'You're very amusing, Miss Hartwell.'

'Well, now you know I am also armed, so don't forget it.'

Wilde carried on, taking half-path after half-path. They came to an edge of the wood. From the sun, he reckoned they had made their way south and west of Dolby's house, perhaps a mile and a half. There was no road; they were in farmland, at the corner of a field lying fallow. In the distance they saw a farmhouse and outbuildings.

'I think we should wait here until dark, then make our way to London,' Wilde said. 'We'll find a road beyond those buildings.'

He leant the Rudge against a tree and they settled down on the perimeter of the field, just inside the trees.

'You were telling me about Stockholm, Miss Hartwell.'

'Oh, for God's sake, my name's bloody Harriet. And by the way, was that your wife I spoke to last night? Does she trust you?'

'I thought we were talking about Stockholm.'

'Well?'

'Yes, she does, I think. I hope so anyway.'

'More fool her. I've seen the way you look at me – the same way all men look at me.'

Wilde shook his head. 'Can we get back to the subject of Stockholm now? How did it come about – the meeting between the two princes?'

'By way of a middleman, name of Axel Anton. Have you heard of him?'

'No. Who is he?'

'I'm pretty sure he's Swedish. Certainly Scandinavian. He's elusive. Usually he contacts us when he has something to offer. Getting in touch with him at other times is more difficult.'

'That doesn't really explain his role.'

'You've very demanding, Tom. OK, let's put it this way – I suppose you'd call him a fixer or a go-between, used by everyone, trusted by no one. He's in it for the money, but he has astonishing contacts. He can get a message from Whitehall to Berlin or vice versa without involving neutral embassies.'

'Why would you want to get messages to Berlin?'

'Well, on a day-to-day basis, we want to warn them to play nice. Let them know that whatever unpleasantness they choose to visit on our citizens or PoWs will be repaid in kind. That if they drop gas on our cities, we will drop gas on theirs. It's the reason no phosgene bombs have fallen on London. They just need a friendly reminder now and then of what awaits them if they don't observe the rules of the game.'

'So Axel Anton fixed up the Stockholm meeting – but at whose behest?'

'The Nazis. Churchill would never have allowed us to approach them. As far as he was concerned, this was nothing but a fact-finding mission.'

'Was Axel Anton there?'

'Yes, he was at Drottningholm – that's the King of Sweden's summer palace – but not at the actual talks. Anyway, forget about him for the moment. I was about to tell you why I went missing. There's the other man I mentioned – Rudi Coburg. I was about to tell you about him in Mimi's house when we were rudely interrupted by someone hammering down the door.'

'Go on.'

'Rudi was Prince Philipp's aide – my opposite number in the initial meeting.'

'And?'

'We knew each other from way back. For one year in the mid-thirties, he was a pupil at Athelstans – which is how I became acquainted with him. He was a chum of Peter Cazerove's.'

'Very convenient.'

She glared at him. 'Don't take that tone, Tom.'

'Forgive me – it's just that I'm not very keen on coincidences. It's my job as a historian.'

'Well, this isn't a bloody archive, so infer nothing. Just listen.'

'But he knew you would be there, yes? Too big a coincidence otherwise . . .'

'That's enough. All you need to know is that he got a message to my room to slip away and meet him. He had something to tell me – something extremely important. But first, let me tell you a little bit about him. Rudi used to be a ferocious Nazi. All *Blut und Boden* – blood and soil. To be honest, I rather went off him towards the end of his year at Athelstans because he was forever ranting about how wonderful Herr sodding Hitler was and how the Aryan race would rise again. Not that he was the only anti-Semite at the school! But anyway, I was rather pleased when his father had him taken away from Athelstans at the end of the year and plonked him into one of those Nazi schools. *Napolas* or *Ordensburgen*, I think they're called – training the future SS in arrogance and the finer points of cruelty.'

'You said he *used to* be a Nazi? That sounds as if he's changed his mind.'

'He says his eyes have been opened. He saw something so terrible that even he was shocked. And now he is desperate for the world to know about it.' She took a deep breath. 'Right, here goes. He told me that the Nazis have built abattoirs to slaughter the Jews – Rudi has seen one of them with his own eyes. Men, women and children are herded like cattle into sealed rooms where they are gassed with carbon monoxide, pumped from an infernal engine, and then their corpses are relieved of gold teeth and wedding rings before being tossed, naked, into enormous pits.'

Was he hearing this? The words were plain enough, but the vision they conveyed was outside his comprehension.

'Thousands upon thousands of them are being murdered in this way, deep in the forests of Poland, away from prying eyes. Production line murder.'

He was silent for a few moments, trying to compute this information. Was this some sort of metaphor? 'You don't mean this literally, do you? You mean he is rounding them up in ghettos and keeping them short of food, with devastating consequences?'

'No, I mean he is killing them, choking every last one of them to death with poison gas. Every woman, every child, every baby, every man.'

'That's preposterous!'

'Yes, it is. But it happens to be true.'

'No. I don't believe it. Human beings don't do things like that to each other.'

'Of course you don't believe it – no one decent could believe such a thing. I didn't believe it either, because it's totally insane and disgustingly obscene. But now I do believe it and I wake up in the morning in a cold sweat. I think of it by day and dream of it by night. I am cursed with this photographic memory, so I recall every single word Rudi told me and I recall the fear and horror in his eyes and in his voice, and I know that he was telling the absolute truth. He would have to be an Olivier to be acting. But he isn't – and anyway he doesn't have the imagination. Every word he told me was the truth – and he will tell you exactly the same things.'

Wilde shook his head again. 'No, Harriet, I can't buy this. It's anti-Nazi propaganda.'

'I wish it was, but it's not – and I will prove it to you. Or, rather, Rudi will.'

'Then he's here in England?'

'No, he's in Sweden. He wanted to come back on the flying boat with us. Georgie agreed, but he was advised against.'

'By whom?'

'His aides. Perhaps they were right. Anyway, Georgie said he would arrange a special flight for him once we were home. But of course he never made it home, so now it falls to me.

I am going to get Rudi Coburg to England, along with his evidence. He is an eyewitness to the greatest atrocity the world has ever known – perhaps the only witness who will ever have the chance to talk because all the others will be dead. What's more, he has physical evidence – official documents – to back him up. And those papers are vital, because without them the Nazis would laugh off his testimony – just as you are now. And the world wouldn't believe it.'

'How does he know all this?' Wilde demanded, still refusing to believe it but fearing deep in his heart that it might just be true. 'What is his evidence? You said he saw something.'

'He knows it because he was directly involved in it.'

'You'd better explain.'

She had been sitting against a tree. Now she got to her feet and began to pace about. Wilde watched her, entranced. The afternoon was dry and sunny, but he felt a chill in the air, the first intimation of summer's end and the long descent into autumn and winter.

Harriet stopped right in front of Wilde. He could not take his eyes off her. Beauty can fade with familiarity; hers just grew. And as it did, so did the contrast with the depravity of her message. He looked away, aware of what she had said earlier, about the way men looked at her.

She didn't seem to have noticed this time, because she continued telling him about Coburg. 'He worked in a senior capacity in the department that is organising the logistics of the slaughter. The RSHA Referat IV B4, to be precise – that's the office of Jewish affairs and evacuation in the Reich Main Security Office. It is run by a man named Adolf Eichmann, who is answerable to Heinrich Müller, the Gestapo chief, and then upwards to Himmler and Hitler himself. The department organises the trains in which these poor people are conveyed to their doom. Scores of trains, each one packed with thousands of innocent Jews, clattering day and night from the cities and towns of Poland and the other occupied territories, through the forests of Poland to lonely outposts which have but one purpose: slaughter. Total annihilation of a whole race.'

'And your friend Coburg was doing this?'

'Yes, and now he is in despair. He was always an anti-Semite and he wanted the Jews out of Germany, but he denies that he wanted them murdered. He insists he didn't know what they were doing when they organised these trains. He thought these places were transit camps before the Jews were reset-tled in the East. But now he has been there and he has seen one of the camps in operation – and so he knows the truth. These places – these slaughterhouses – are the end of the line. And he has the evidence: names, maps, official written orders . . . if the Nazis do one thing well, it's bureaucracy. They keep records of everything.'

'Good God.'

'I must be honest with you, Tom. I still don't like Rudi very much. And I certainly loathe his politics. But in a way, that makes his testimony all the more believable. That and the fact that having betrayed his masters he knows he is a dead man.'

'You say he is in Sweden – but where exactly?'

'He has been concealed on a small island, one of thou-sands, in the middle of nowhere. Only Axel Anton knows its precise location, and so I must contact him. But before I do so, I need to get to Churchill to organise a safe way to get Rudi to England, to testify to the world and hand over his evidence. With Georgie dead, there is no other way. No one else I can trust.'

'I still don't really understand why you're being hunted in this country and what the Athels could have to do with it all.'

She laughed without a trace of humour. 'The Athels want a deal with Hitler, don't you see? This is the way they protect themselves from the threat of revolution or conquest. It has been the same for almost 150 years. They weigh up the threats – Nazism or Communism – and see Stalin as the greater danger. And so to preserve themselves, they decide on a joint Anglo-German enterprise against the Bolsheviks. They have but one policy – preserve themselves.'

'No political allegiance then?'

'Maintain the status quo. Whatever it takes. Nothing else. And so they can't allow the Nazis' reputation to be damaged by Rudi's testimony. I suspect, too, that they will have been contacted by Berlin to do their dirty work. Rudi must die, so must I. And I fear, Tom, that you will now be added to their list.'

'And you think it is the Athels hunting you?'

'Of course.'

'And the plane crash – they thought Rudi Coburg was aboard and they were trying to kill him?'

'They wanted to kill both of us – all of us. That's why I need to get to Churchill. I trust no one else. I have made that mistake once already, you see.'

'Peter Cazerove?'

She nodded. 'I contacted him from Sweden. I confided in him. He betrayed me.'

Chapter 25

Heinrich Müller found Prince Philipp von Hessen in his immaculate quarters at the Wolfsschanze – the Wolf's Lair – in East Prussia from where Hitler directed the war. He knew he would not have long with him alone, because the Führer had demanded the presence of both of them at lunch.

'Herr Prince,' he said, not quite sure of the proper way to address a prince, 'it is very good of you to see me at such short notice.' Müller smiled, laughing inside – as if anyone but Hitler himself would refuse to meet the *generalleutnant* of the Gestapo at any moment of day or night.

'It is my pleasure as always, Herr Gruppenführer. How can I help you?'

'Well, I was hoping I could ask you a few questions. We have a problem, you understand . . .'

'This is about Rudi Coburg, I take it?'

'Indeed, sir. Indeed it is. As you know, he went missing whilst a member of your mission to Stockholm. It is my task to find him. I'm sure you will think this a foolish question, but I have to ask it anyway: do you perchance have any idea where he might be?'

The prince shook his head. His face was almost handsome, but not quite: vaguely Teutonic, but lacking strength, the moustache too insubstantial to add authority or gravitas, the features too pinched. 'No, Herr Müller, it was an unpleasant shock to me when he disappeared. Indeed, I initially feared he had been abducted by enemy agents.'

'Well, yes, of course that could have been a possibility given the nature of your meeting, but I am quite sure that that is not the case, for I have certain confidential information from agents of my own. The truth is, he is in the process of trying to defect. But I intend to stop him, if only I could find him.'

'If I knew where he was, of course I would tell you.'

'At first it seemed he might have died in the plane crash that killed your cousin, but now I know that was not so. It is my belief he is still in Sweden.'

'Then you should talk to Axel Anton, Herr Gruppenführer.'

As if he hadn't already set the ball rolling in that direction. 'Of course,' he said. 'But that is not so easily done. Perhaps you could help me.'

'There are always ways.'

'Indeed.' Müller reminded himself that this so-called prince was still close to Hitler, so he affected a smile and refrained from telling him what he thought of him. 'I am glad we are as one on this. But to get back to your own relation-ship with Herr Coburg. I have to tell you that he is in pos-session of secrets which he intends to impart to our enemies, so I am keen to get his movements in Berlin absolutely clear. It is my belief that you requested his transfer from the Reich Main Security Office to your own staff, as chief aide. Is that correct?'

Prince Philipp looked confused by the question. 'Yes, broadly speaking that is so.'

'And why exactly did you do that?'

'Because he asked me to, and he is – was – an old family friend.'

'Ah, this alters things. So it was Coburg himself who requested the transfer, not you?'

'In effect, yes. He requested it of me, and I in turn requested it of Adolf Eichmann on his behalf.'

'But he didn't tell Herr Eichmann that that was the case. He made out that *you* were behind the move.'

'As I said, it was Coburg who asked to join my staff. No, that is not quite correct – he *begged* me to get him transferred. He said he could not stand to work with Eichmann a moment longer. Did I do wrong in acceding to his request? Are you intimating that he had some darker motive – that his disappearance was planned in some way?'

Müller was watching the prince closely, blue-grey eyes boring into the prince's. Philipp's forehead was beaded with sweat. As chief of the Gestapo, Müller knew when someone was about to piss himself with fear, and this prince of the blood royal – greasy with aristocratic vanity – was very close to that moment. 'Time will tell, sir. But let us get on to other matters – in particular your own relationship with Rudolf Coburg. Clearly you have known him a long time. Tell me about him – his history. I would like to know all about his links to England and, indeed, to Sweden. Can you help me with all that?'

'Of course. I will tell you everything – whatever you wish to know. If Coburg is a traitor he deserves everything that is coming to him. I will happily pull the lever on the guillotine myself.'

'Well, let's not get ahead of ourselves. First we must find him. So, his background. At what age did you meet?

'I suppose I was in my mid-twenties and he was a small boy of five or six. I have always been like an uncle to him. Our parents were friends. You know his mother was English, I suppose?'

'Some sort of titled lady, I believe.'

'She was daughter of the Earl of Brandiston, a big landowner in the middle of England. She spent a lot of time in Germany before and during the Great War. In fact, she is still here – she considers herself German now and has always been a great supporter of the Party.'

Müller already knew all this. He knew a great deal about Coburg, but he wanted to hear it from this decadent prince's own lips. He knew a lot about both of them. They had both spent part of their childhoods in England and he had never trusted either man. The age gap between them was twenty years or so, but that didn't mean they couldn't be warm brothers – homosexual lovers. Most likely, they were. God alone knew why Hitler ever allowed this dissolute aristocrat near him. Well, that would not last too much longer if he, Müller, had his way. And he would. He would destroy Philipp von Hessen and, if he could just run him to ground, Coburg too. First, he had a few more questions.

'And Coburg was always an ambitious young man?'

'Yes, that was always very obvious. He was one of the youngest graduates of the Ordensburg Vogelsang and was about to go on to Heidelberg University, but the war changed things and he quickly secured an excellent post within the Auswärtiges Amt in Berlin. Like many within the foreign service, he was wealthy in his own right but seemed to wish to do great work for the Reich. I don't think promotion came quickly enough for him, though, and he was becoming frustrated, so he was delighted when Heydrich agreed that he be transferred to the RSHA. But clearly something happened between him and Herr Eichmann.'

'I understand, so let us now move on. Your meeting with the King of England's brother – was that conducted in good faith by our enemies? Because, you see, I have had my doubts ever since I heard of it.'

The prince shook his head vigorously. 'No, no, it was genuine. I am certain that Georgie – the Duke of Kent – would not have dealt with me falsely. Axel Anton had given us reason to understand that the British were interested in an honourable peace treaty. The Führer wished to hear what they had to say.'

'But what happened to the plane this duke flew back to Scotland? That crash was no accident. And we didn't destroy it – did we?'

'I am as puzzled as you, Herr Müller.'

The Gestapo man mulled this over. It pained him to wonder whether there might be other elements in Germany working on the case without his knowledge. The Abwehr, perhaps? Who knew with that devious, treacherous bastard Canaris? He moved back to the events at Drottningholm. 'Now then, Herr von Hessen, I want full details surrounding the disappearance of Rudolf Coburg. Take me through it, hour by hour, if you would. Who was in the English prince's delegation?'

'Well, there was the crew of the plane – but they did not come to the palace. He had a team of four, as did I. His private secretary Crowther, his equerry Strutt, his valet and a woman.'

'A woman! His mistress, no doubt. She does not appear in the British newspapers.'

'No, I noticed that. Perhaps she was the Duke's mistress and so her presence had to be hushed up. At Drottningholm, he used her as his personal assistant at the first meeting, just as I used Rudi Coburg. We were both allowed just one aide. No notes were to be taken, no recordings made.'

'How remarkable. And this woman, I'm sure she must have had a name.' He already knew it, of course, but it suited his purpose to keep this from von Hessen.

'Harriet Hartwell.'

'Was she pretty and young?'

'Well, yes, I would say she was.'

'And were checks made? One must assume she was attached to the British secret services.'

'Yes, I assumed that was possible – likely even.'

'Anyway, you were all staying in the palace as guests of the King of Sweden. What time was this first meeting between you and the British prince?'

'That was 3 p.m. The meeting lasted no more than a quarter of an hour, and then we agreed to meet in the evening alone, without aides. That meeting was more fruitful. It became clear to me that Georgie had some sympathy for the possibility of a peace deal, though he was reluctant to say it in so many words. That was understandable, I thought, for this was merely a tentative exploratory meeting. Though it was agreed there would be no recording devices, one can never be sure. I sincerely hoped it might lead to something more formal, a pact which would benefit both of our peoples.'

'All very laudable, I'm sure. And while you and what do you call him – Georgie – were having your little fireside chat over a glass of schnapps, what was Herr Coburg up to?'

'I thought he was either relaxing in his room or having a drink in one of the royal suites with the other members of our party. But when I emerged from the meeting, it became clear that they hadn't seen him – and so we checked his room and he wasn't there either.'

'Where did you think he might be?'

'I had no idea. All sorts of thoughts went through my mind. Initially I thought it was probably something innocent like a walk. Then I wondered if he was involved in a dalliance with a member of the palace staff?'

'Fucking a maidservant, eh?'

'These thoughts go through your mind.'

'But he wasn't.'

'No. And then it occurred to me that he had either been abducted . . .'

'Or had defected.'

Philipp von Hessen nodded.

'And this woman – Georgie's assistant – where was she at this time?'

The prince looked puzzled by the question. 'I have no idea. Our people kept apart other than at the meetings.'

'Because, my dear prince, there is an old French saying – *cherchez la femme*. You understand what I am saying, I hope? I already have information that she is the key to this. If anyone knows where Coburg is hiding, it is Harriet Hartwell.'

'Then she is alive?'

'Oh yes, she survived the crash. And I have information that she was a friend of Herr Coburg going back to school days in England.'

'Good God, I had no idea.'

'Did you not notice their eyes meeting across the table? A flicker of recognition, perhaps?'

'No, nothing. My thoughts were elsewhere. Entirely on the matter in hand with Georgie.'

'You know, Herr Prince, it is difficult not to wonder whether the whole Stockholm conference was a set-up designed for your aides to meet. Perhaps you and the royal duke were the bit-part players. Or maybe you knew this – maybe you were involved in the arrangement, Herr Prince?'

'That is an outrageous suggestion!'

'Really?' Müller watched closely as the Prince shrank into his body and his soul shrivelled. 'Now then,' the Gestapo chief continued after a few moments, 'I think we need to find our old friend Axel Anton. Because I am damned certain he will tell us what's going on, if the price is right. And you, Prince Philipp von Hessen, had better hope that we find him quickly – and that he leads us to Rudolf Coburg or, at least, the British woman. Otherwise . . .' He didn't finish the sentence.

'I really think I need to get into that school,' Wilde said.

Harriet looked at him as though he were mad. 'Why, Tom? Are you hoping to find a list of important Athels so we'll know who to avoid? They're not that stupid, you know – they don't leave incriminating lists lying around.' She sounded irritated.

'No,' he said, annoyed in his turn by her undisguised scorn. 'Of course not. To be honest, I don't know what I'm looking for – just that I want to know who and what I'm dealing with. The Athels, the school itself. The whole place reeks of a secret society.' The sort of place he loathed. 'Anyway, you're the one who thinks they're trying to kill you.'

'Well, it's pointless. You wouldn't find anything. But I agree with you that we've got to do something – and quickly. I have told you what I want to do, but I don't know how to do it.'

'Then let's go to the American embassy. Surely there aren't any American Athels to worry about? If anyone can arrange a meeting with Churchill, the Americans can.'

She shrugged. 'I don't know.'

'Well, without a better idea, it's a risk I'm going to have to take. You can come with me, or you can stay here. Your choice.'

She thought for two seconds. 'I'll come,' she said.

Chapter 26

Alone on this outcrop, one little island among thousands, Rudolf Coburg wondered whether he was losing his sanity. The fuel for the generator had run out and he had no candles left, so at night he was all alone in a pit of darkness with the snakes.

The island was called Huggorm, which also happened to be the Swedish word for adder, or viper. It was well named, for Huggorm was infested with adders. In the warmth of the day, he watched the snakes on the rocks by the sea, soaking up the sun, and his eyes followed them as they slithered slowly through the rough grass or slid silently into the waves that lapped at the shore.

He wasn't scared of them, but he was fascinated by them and began seeing them as individuals rather than an alien mass. From his early years, when other children shuddered, he had always rather liked snakes, admiring their sleek sinuousness and their dazzling, shimmering patterns.

That admiration had always been from afar, but these ones were different; he gave them names. The one he knew as Himmler was always on the higher rock. He was large, active and dominant. Höppner stayed closer to the shoreline, a little diffident, sidling away for some space and seclusion. Eberl moved with sudden speed and showed his sharp, pointy teeth and his split tongue. Eichmann was more slender and graceful but his eyes were narrow and blank. Though Coburg couldn't hear it, he somehow imagined an intermittent hiss on the lipless mouth. Kaltenbrunner was long and pitted and stayed close to Eichmann as though they were intimate companions. Wisliceny, fat and sly, remained slightly apart as though he wished to be their friend but knew he was not quite of their milieu.

Müller exuded power and you just knew that his venom would kill you, slowly and with extreme pain.

On the land between the cabin and the rocks lay the still one, the dead one, its scales shrivelled and empty. He called this one Heydrich. It might be dead, yet it remained malign.

And then, finally, there was the half-seen one. The one always lurking in the shadows. This one he dubbed Hitler. He had seen it only once, side on, and had looked away because this one he feared. He didn't see it, but he felt its presence and his instinct told him that it swam between islands, controlling its colonies. He knew, too, that its eyes alone could kill.

Sometimes he wondered whether he should seek it out and accept his death. Would that end the nightmares? If he could be certain that death would be the end of his dreams, then it would be a price worth paying and he would happily gather all the adders together into his bed and join them naked, let them writhe over him and feast on his flesh. If only that would stop the dreams, but something told him it wouldn't; that the dreams would be there for eternity.

His eyes drifted up from the adders, across the sea. A boat was approaching.

William Phillips, chief of the nascent London bureau of the Office of Strategic Studies, shook his head in dismay.

'Good God, Wilde, what in the name of all that's holy have you got yourself into? And why have you deposited that woman outside in my waiting room?'

'That is Harriet Hartwell. I told you about her, if you remember? You won't hear it on the wireless and you won't read it in the newspapers, but she was aboard the Duke of Kent's Sunderland flying boat when it crashed and she, like the rear gunner, survived.'

'And does she confirm your theories about the direction of travel of the Duke's flight?'

'She does.'

It was late in the evening and Phillips had been about to return home after a long day. Whatever the occasion, his demeanour was never less than gracious, but he was not happy. Wilde had expected nothing else because he was aware that Phillips was disappointed in him; there was important work to be done getting the OSS operational and these meanderings by Wilde had, in his eyes, become entirely pointless and, indeed, counter-productive.

Wilde's physical journey here had been long and winding. He and Harriet had waited until it was almost dusk before making a move across the field in the direction of the farm. The buildings were on the edge of a village and from there they took a series of back roads, occasionally getting lost and asking for directions as they made their way to London, all the while avoiding major thoroughfares where they were likely to encounter road-blocks or police patrols.

On the journey, he could not but be aware of her arms around his waist and her head resting against his back and shoulder. It was a warm, pleasurable sensation and he felt guilty for enjoying it, even though he had done nothing to encourage her and had no intention of straying. But perhaps the thought was there. Perhaps Harriet was right, that such instincts were there in all men, however much they might deny it.

Phillips tapped the base of his fountain pen on the desk, a habit he had when thinking. As a diplomat it was second nature for him to examine Wilde's story thoroughly and with precision, reserving judgement until he was persuaded on the correctness of a course of action. 'No one else agrees, Tom. All the military personnel and ministry officials say the flying boat was leaving Scotland for Iceland.'

'They say what they are told to say.'

Phillips smiled. 'Of course they do. Well trained, these Brits. They have to be efficient to run their dirty goddamned empire, I suppose. Well, I expect you want me to congratulate you on your investigative powers, Tom, but somehow I can't really see why I should – because I honestly don't know how any of this helps America.'

'It's not a matter of helping America, it's about doing what's right. And it's about Harriet Hartwell needing our help.'

'And give me a reason why we should accommodate her. Pretty thing, isn't she? I don't suppose that has anything to do with it.'

'Oh, come on, Bill, you know me better than that.'

'Do I? Then explain why I should help her.'

'Because we're on the same side.'

'No we're not, we're on Britain's side – and at the moment it sounds as if both you and Miss Hartwell are seen as the enemy!'

'That's not the case. You need to hear her story – from her lips, not mine. This is the untold story of Hitler's gang – and it needs to come out.'

Phillips sighed. 'Well, I'm not convinced, but bring her in and let's hear what she has to say for herself.'

Axel Anton moored his motorboat to iron rings driven into the rock wall at the side of the little bay, then clambered out and strode nonchalantly through the scattering adders. Coburg was standing waiting for him at the doorway to the cabin. Anton plonked down a basket of food and newspapers, then shook hands. 'At least you're not alone, Herr Coburg.'

'The snakes are OK, but I think I could quite happily live without them.'

'Must be just like old times back in the Party Chancellery, eh? Plenty of reptiles around there.'

'The thought had occurred to me. What news, Anton? Has there been any movement? Word on a flight to England?'

'Bad news, I'm afraid.' Anton grimaced. He was a plump man of fifty but might have been handsome in his younger days when he would have been a good deal more slender. But he still had a sparkle in his eyes, clear skin and fresh, open features. He had fair hair that flopped across his brow. In another life, he often thought as he gazed into the mirror, he might have been a film star. Wouldn't that have been something, to play a love scene with Zarah Leander, the Swedish siren?

As it was, his face *had* played an important role in making his fortune. People trusted him. That is to say, they put their trust in him even though they might know or suspect that he was likely to do them down. He realised that both sides – all sides – were aware of his double-dealing, but that didn't matter. Because he never betrayed the highest bidder. Once he had carried out whatever was required of him, however, all bets were off.

'Bad news?'

'Very bad.' Anton ran his fingers through his thick crop of hair; it was more rakish like that than neatly combed. 'The Duke of Kent's plane crashed on its return to Scotland. Only one survivor – the rear gunner.'

'That means Harriet is dead?'

'I'm afraid so, although her death has not been reported. I have brought you Swedish and English newspapers – you'll see that *The Times* of London and the *Svenska Dagbladet* have good reports. Food and drink, too, for another week.'

'You mean I'm stuck here another week?'

Anton shrugged. 'Of course not. I can take you off now if you desire. But I have no way of getting you out of the country as yet. The prices would be crazy.'

'You want more money?'

'Everything costs so much in war.'

'You have already brought me close to bankruptcy, Anton.'

'Nonsense, you are as rich as Midas. Anyway, don't complain. I got you out of Germany and into the company of Miss Hartwell, did I not? Can you even begin to imagine a more expensive and difficult operation than that?'

'I'm sorry. Yes, you have been a good friend.'

'Your *only* friend at the moment, Herr Coburg. And was it my fault that the Duke baulked at taking you on his flying boat? In fact, you should think yourself fortunate now that you were left behind!'

'I'm sorry, but I don't feel very fortunate.'

'Don't despair. I will find a way. Now then, you will notice that there are a couple of bottles of Italian grappa in the basket. What say I share a little glass with you before I take my leave?'

Coburg's eyes were elsewhere and Anton could see that he was in danger of falling apart.

'Come on, my good fellow. A little glass to cheer us both . . .'

'This island, though . . .'

'I know, I know. The snakes. I don't mind them. Stay clear of them and they'll stay clear of you.'

'They talk to me.'

'And what do they say?'

'I don't know. I don't understand them.' Suddenly, as though realising he was in company, his eyes awoke and fixed on those of his visitor. 'Look, Anton, would I not be as safe on the mainland somewhere?'

Anton's expression was pained. 'Oh, how I wish it were so, if only for your sake. But you wouldn't last twenty-four hours, dear friend. There are German agents everywhere and many collaborators. And I have worse news, I'm afraid – Heinrich Müller himself has taken charge of the search for you and has arrived in Stockholm.'

Pleasantries were exchanged, coffee was poured and seats were taken. 'Professor Wilde has told me some of your story, Miss Hartwell. Perhaps you'd like to fill me in with the rest.'

She didn't look happy. 'Do I really need to go through all this again?'

'I want to hear it from you. Unvarnished.'

The story came out slowly. It included her long-term work for the Duke of Kent at the Air Ministry and their close understanding and friendship. It did not, Wilde noted, include any acknowledgement of her other role as a member of the British secret services.

'And how was it that the trip to Stockholm came about? Who mooted it?' Phillips demanded.

'That was Axel Anton. He came over to London via Gib with a proposal for a top-secret meeting between the two cousins – Georgie and Prince Philipp von Hessen. There would be no agenda, no publicity. Just two old friends meeting for a chinwag on neutral territory. The Duke put it to his brother, the

King. He in turn put it to Churchill, who has no desire for peace but was intrigued to discover the state of morale in Germany.'

'And what of FDR?'

'It was thought better not to include him at this stage – word travels like wildfire around the Capitol.'

'But something happened at this Stockholm meeting? Rudi Coburg went missing.'

'Yes, he came to my room. He said he needed my help to get to England and told me the whole story of the Nazi crimes he had witnessed.'

'Go on, Miss Hartwell.'

She told him everything she had told Wilde, then her shoulders slumped with the emotional toll of her story. 'Of course, I had no way of getting him out of Sweden, not then. Georgie wanted to help, but after talking to his aides, it became clear Rudi couldn't be allowed on the flying boat. But I did have the means to wire an encrypted message through to Peter Cazerove in London. I hoped he might be able to help, to organise a separate flight – I couldn't think of anyone else. I trusted him.'

Phillips gave Wilde a meaningful look. 'Your friend from the train, Tom? Anyway, carry on, Miss Hartwell. What happened next?'

'Axel Anton had foreseen everything, of course, and already had a safe place prepared for Rudi. In the early hours he spirited him away to hide on one of the islands in the Stockholm Archipelago. He would never be found. Anton told me how to make contact when I had found a way to get Rudi to London or Washington. But of course I have no way of doing that on my own – which is why I need to contact Churchill. I don't know who else to trust, you see.'

'What of the documents Herr Coburg brought out of Germany?'

'They are still in his possession. He will protect them with his life.'

There were a few moments more silence, broken only by the tinkle of a cup as the OSS bureau chief finished his coffee. At last he spoke. 'One thing doesn't add up, I'm afraid, Miss Hartwell: the coincidence of you and your old friend Rudi Coburg just happening to be in the same room in a Swedish palace in the middle of a war.'

'I can't explain it. All I can think is that Axel Anton was somehow involved. He knows everyone who is anyone in Berlin and has important contacts in London.'

'And the crash of the Duke of Kent's plane?'

'I don't know. It is difficult not to think Peter Cazerove was involved, because he was an Athel.'

'Ah yes, Tom has told me about them.'

Wilde broke into the conversation. 'Your instant fear was that Peter Cazerove betrayed you?'

'Well, someone wanted us all dead. It had to be the Athels.'

'Can you remember anything of the crash?' Phillips demanded.

'No, I think I must have been asleep. My last memory is crawling along the gangway towards the rear of the plane, and then nothing more. Or perhaps that was a dream.'

'Could it have been lack of oxygen – hypoxia? Or some sort of gas?'

She shrugged. 'Again, I don't know. Either might make you drowsy. I woke up on a hillside. My parachute was still strapped on but unopened. Perhaps that and my thick clothing and the angle of the slope saved me. It was cold in the plane and I was wearing thick clothes and a Mae West life jacket. I must have looked like the Michelin man. When I regained consciousness I had a ferocious headache. It didn't take me long to realise that I was a marked woman.' She met Phillips's gaze full on. 'Anyway, that's my story. And I swear it's true.'

'What happened to the parachute and the Mae West?'

'I hid them in the lee of a large rock. Someone will find them one day. I just wanted to give myself a little extra time to get away. I made it to the road and hitched a lift to the hotel where Tom saw me. I was wiped out and had to sleep. I had nothing. My money and passport were gone. It pains me to say it, but I actually considered robbery to get some money – until you stepped in so chivalrously.'

'All right,' Phillips said. 'If I take all this at face value, I am left with a big question: what do you want to do now? Because the way I see it, you are at an impasse. The Churchill idea is a non-starter.'

'Why? Surely the US ambassador can make contact?'

Phillips was having none of it. 'Wrong way round, Miss Hartwell. You need your witness here in London, complete with his evidence of this Nazi atrocity. You're not going to persuade Churchill to do anything with your own, second-hand version. It's nothing but hearsay.'

'Then I need a plane to Stockholm. Or a submarine.'

'And who is going to give you one of those?'

'You?'

He smiled with a hint of condescension, like a parent rather pleased with a child's efforts and reluctant to disabuse them about the actual worth of some suggestion. Then he switched his gaze to Wilde. 'Tom, explain to her – this is all mad talk.'

'What if she's right?'

'OK, say every word is true. This is still – to use the English vernacular which I am learning fast – arse about tit. Coburg needs to find a way to London on his own account. Use the fixer, Axel Anton. Pay whatever it takes.'

A flicker of anger crossed her eyes. Wilde spotted it and noted that hardness he had seen before. 'He can't,' she said simply. 'Sweden is full of SD and Abwehr agents. He can't move without our help. He's in limbo.'

Phillips rubbed a hand across his forehead then ran his fingers through his thinning but rather elegant grey hair. 'I'm tired,' he said at last. 'I want to sleep on this. You two can make yourselves at home here. We have a couple of camp beds.'

'Please, Mr Phillips,' she said. 'Please help me. The world has to know the truth. Your soldiers need to know what they are fighting against – and why. And we *must* tell the Jews of Europe the fate that awaits them unless they rise up and fight. Better to die with a gun or knife in your hand than herded like cattle into a slaughter room.'

'Goodnight, Miss Hartwell.'

Chapter 27

Invisible enemies. Not for the first time, Wilde was trying to work out who they were fighting – who they were trying to avoid. The murder of Harriet's father made it plain that someone was prepared to go to any lengths to find her.

Lord Templeman and Philip Eaton had lifted Wilde off the street and had doped him, but that was a long way short of the merciless treatment meted out to the Reverend Hartwell.

So there were two distinct factions trying to get to Harriet Hartwell. Was it possible that one faction was trying to conceal Germany's secret shame in the backwoods of Poland and that the other was trying to hide the truth behind the Duke of Kent's flight to Sweden? They were thoughts worth considering.

In which case, Wilde had to protect himself – and Harriet. With invisible enemies, it was necessary to become invisible yourself.

The American embassy wasn't really equipped for housing guests. Visiting dignitaries from the States tended to stay at the ambassador's residence. But Phillips had allowed them the use of a couple of offices with camp beds in the OSS bureau and had made sure they had food and drink. Then he left them to their own devices, secure in the knowledge that the building was protected by US Marines.

'I'll see you folks at nine in the morning.'

Wilde spent a long time on the phone to Lydia. She wasn't happy. Perhaps it had something to do with her own feeling of being trapped with a small child and being powerless to intervene in the unfolding events.

'I'm sorry,' he said. 'This will all be sorted out soon.'

'I just want you home. Johnny wants you home. You seem to be involved in something that has absolutely nothing to do with you, or us.'

'I know what you're saying, but that's not entirely true. You'll understand when I see you next and have a chance to talk to you properly.'

'Tell me *now*, Tom. What's going on? Why aren't you here? Haven't you done your bit for the bloody war effort?'

'There are many thousands of people giving a lot more than I have, Lydia.'

'Oh, so now you're feeling guilty because you're alive?'

Perhaps I am, he thought. It was a sensation that had been with him all his adult life, since he heard of British school-friends going off to the trenches in the last war while he was tucked up safe in America. Lydia knew his feelings, but this was not the time to open old wounds. 'No,' he said simply, 'that's not it.'

'What is it, then? And what about this bloody woman? You haven't told me very much about her yet.'

So that was it. 'I'm not sure there's much to tell. I barely know her other than that her name is Harriet Hartwell and her life is in grave danger. Do you just want me to abandon her?'

A pause on the line.

'Lydia?'

'Well, yes, actually, I do think there are more important people in your life.'

'This really isn't like you.'

'Well, maybe it's because I've heard a thing or two about the perfectly gorgeous Miss Harriet Hartwell – and I don't much like what I've been told.'

Wilde was horrified. 'Who has been telling you things – and, more to the point, what have they been saying?'

'She has a reputation, Tom.'

'What do you mean? What reputation? Who have you been talking to?'

'Philip Eaton, of course. He came to see me, to try to make me persuade you to turn in your bloody girlfriend. You realise she's seen as a security threat, I suppose. She is in possession of a secret that could harm Britain and its alliances.'

'It's a great deal more complicated than that.'

'Oh, I somehow thought you might have another take on the matter.'

'Look, Eaton has his own agenda. But why would you believe him when he tries to defame a woman you've never met?'

'They call her the Whitehall bicycle. Did you know that? Apparently, she knows a few professional tricks . . .'

'I promise you, that is not the woman I've met.'

'What, she hasn't slipped her hand into your bags yet, Tom? Give her time. Is she with you right this minute?'

'You're demeaning yourself, Lydia.'

'Don't give me that. Everyone's at it like there's no tomorrow – because for many of us there *is* no tomorrow. So when you're away from me with bicycle woman I know what's on the table – and it's very likely to be your good friend Harriet, with her legs in the air.'

'I can't listen to this.'

'Am I embarrassing you? Is she there with you right now?'

'Not here in this room, no. Anyway, I'm not handing her over to Eaton or anyone else. Look, I'm going to hang up, Lydia, because I'm in danger of saying things that can't be unsaid. All

I want you to know is that I love you and I love Johnny and I wouldn't do anything to hurt either of you.'

'We'll see, won't we.'

She hung up.

Wilde was left staring at the phone for a few moments. Gently he replaced it. There was a knock on the door and then it opened. Harriet peered in. 'Can we talk?' she said.

He sighed helplessly. 'Come in. Did you hear any of that?'

'Any of what?'

'My phone call to Lydia. My wife.'

'Of course, you're married. Have to phone the little woman. But no, I wasn't listening. I don't eavesdrop.'

'Good, because it wasn't pretty. She's not enjoying my absence.'

'But if you're working here in London as a matter of course, and she's back in Cambridge, what's the difference?'

'The difference is that we were supposed to be having some time together and the Duke's death put paid to our plans. And if you must know, we're not actually married.'

'So you both want to keep your freedom, do you? Keep your options open?'

The words stung. It had never been his decision to avoid marriage. That was all Lydia's doing. 'Forget it,' he said. 'What did you want?' He instantly regretted the curtness of his response. Whatever the difficulties between him and Lydia, it involved no fault on Harriet's part.

'Have I done something wrong?' She was giving him an expectant look, as though she wanted something from him and he was somehow missing the point.

'You mean apart from involving me in a problem without a solution?' he said, then softened. 'I'm sorry, that was uncalled for.'

'I think you'll find you involved yourself when you decided to drive to my father's house in Clade. Anyway, we need to come up with a joint plan of campaign. Your friend Bill Phillips isn't going to help us, so we need to think of something else. I know what he said about Churchill wanting evidence, but what about the King? It was his brother who died, so he must want to find out the truth. Surely he has the power to persuade Churchill to help us get Rudi over from Sweden.'

'Well, let's go and knock on the door at Buckingham Palace.'

'You're not being very helpful.' She was barefoot, having removed her shoes and stockings. Her maroon summer skirt swished as she moved, her blouse was cream silk and loose. She seemed to move constantly, picking up things – a pencil, a notepad, a paperweight, anything – inspecting them and putting them back down again.

Wilde tried to ignore her. 'Well, I've had a damned awful day, preceded by a foul night.' He nodded towards the put-me-up bed that had been rustled up for him and was presently stretched out with a pile of blankets and a couple of single sheets by the wall beneath the window. 'I need sleep. Badly.'

'Tom, you're a Cambridge don. You must have contacts, someone who could get us to the King.'

'None that spring to mind,' he said.

'How did you find out my address in Suffolk?'

'A newspaper friend helped me.'

'Reporters have good contacts. Maybe your friend could help us get an audience with the King.'

'I very much doubt it.'

'Well, why don't you ask him anyway? Call him now.'

Wilde had no intention of calling Ron Christie. The idea that a newspaper journalist could somehow fix an audience with the King was laughable. Harriet Hartwell looked at Wilde strangely. 'You're an unusual man, Tom. I can't make you out. Don't you like me?'

The question took him off guard. 'I don't know what you mean.'

'I mean what I say. I'm asking you if you like me. Men usually do, but you seem unsure.'

'I have a partner at home and a small child.'

'So do most men of your age. It doesn't seem to make much difference.'

'Well, it does with me.'

'Really?'

'Yes, really.'

'Then as I said, professor, you're an unusual man.'

She smiled at him, sighed and shrugged, then kissed his cheek. 'Never mind,' she said. 'Sweet dreams.'

The swastika fluttered in the late-summer breeze high above the sixth floor of the German embassy in central Stockholm. Axel Anton strolled in through the front door, past the checks by the two uniformed guards, as though he owned the place. The receptionist recognised him and immediately put a call through to an office on the second floor.

Within moments a uniformed SS officer was at Anton's side. He bowed stiffly with a salute and click of the heels. 'If you would accompany me, Herr Anton. The Gruppenführer is waiting for you in the ambassador's office.'

It was early morning and Müller was on his second coffee. He wore a smart civilian suit and was sitting at the desk of the ambassador, who was elsewhere in the building.

'Gruppenführer!' Anton said, with an expansive bow. 'What a pleasure, dear sir.'

Müller laughed at him. 'Look at all this, Anton. This is Viktor zu Weid's office. The height of luxury for the junkers while our boys are dying in Russia. God, they know how to look after themselves, these filthy aristocrats. How I hate them all. The devil knows why Hitler puts up with them.'

'Many of them have supported the Party since early days, have they not?'

'Supported the Party? Looked after their own interests, you mean. I'd happily shoot every last one of them. Anyway, talking of shitty aristocrats, that's why I'm here and why I wanted to talk with you.'

Anton knew exactly why the Gestapo chief was here. 'It is my honour as always, Herr Gruppenführer. I came just as soon as I received your message, sir.'

'I'm looking for a man. An aristocrat.'

'Well, you're spoilt for choice here in Stockholm.'

'Don't be droll, Anton. I don't have time for such things.'

'Then you had better tell me the man's name – and if I can help, I will do all in my power to assist you.'

'Rudolf Coburg. Some sort of minor aristo, distant relative of the Saxe-Coburgs, I believe. I want him very, very badly. He is an enemy of the Reich and I have reason to believe he is hiding out here in Sweden.'

'I have heard of the man. It is possible I even met him at some embassy party or other in Berlin.'

'Oh, I'm *sure* you've met him, Anton. You know everyone. Anyway, he was part of Prince Philipp von Hessen's little jaunt to Drottningholm which you, of course, organised.'

'Were you privy to that curious event, sir?'

'Well, I am now that Coburg is missing.'

'Of course, of course ... well, yes, it is true that Coburg was among the prince's small retinue. He was rather taciturn. I knew I had seen him before, but it didn't register at the time. Quite a clever young man, but not very forthcoming.'

'Not so clever that he'll survive this.'

'And he is now missing? I had no idea. I will not, of course, ask why you want this man, but do you have any information at all about his whereabouts or whom he might be connected to in Sweden? It is my experience that most people who go into hiding have some sort of assistance.'

'I can tell you this: there was a woman from the English delegation at Drottningholm and I know for certain that she was involved in Coburg's disappearance, but it is our information that she is now back in England. Her name is Harriet Hartwell, but that is all I know.'

Axel Anton did not react to this information. He had believed she died in the plane crash, but maybe Müller knew something he didn't. 'And is it possible Coburg accompanied her to England?'

'No. It is certain that he didn't.'

'Well, I shall do my utmost to locate this heinous fellow, for I have no doubt that he must be an enemy of the Reich.'

'There would be something in it for you, of course.'

With an extravagant flourish of his arm, Anton waved away the very suggestion that money might be involved. 'I wouldn't dream of asking for money, Herr Müller.'

'No?'

'Certainly not.' He hunched his shoulders and juggled the palms of his hands up and down as though weighing a side of bacon. 'There would be overheads, of course. Cases such as this often involve the use of bribery, which can become expensive.'

'What sort of figure are we talking about, Anton?'

'Oh, I don't know. Ten . . . twenty thousand Reichsmarks at the very least, I suppose.'

'Let us say a hundred thousand and be done with it.'

'Well, such a generous figure would make my quest all the easier. Astonishing how silver and gold loosens tongues, Herr Gruppenführer.'

'This must be done at speed. The longer this man is at large, the more dangerous he becomes. He is in possession of secret papers.'

'Then I am your man.'

'When you have located him, you will not approach him. Instead you will come back to me and my agents will deal with the matter. Is that understood?'

'Precisely,' Anton said.

Müller gazed at Axel Anton without expression for a few moments. The very thought that he would give this man a hundred Reichsmarks, let alone a hundred thousand. Preposterous. Inside, he laughed; this game, this charade. As if he didn't know that it was Anton who had arranged Coburg's disappearance. Of course he knew where the dirty traitor was.

Wilde slept until Bill Phillips woke him up. 'I've got coffee for you, Tom. You sure must have needed that sleep.'

'What time is it?' Wilde was struggling to his feet.

'Eight. Your friend is already up and about. She's in my office, waiting. Come on, get to it. I've got a proposition for you.'

Wilde took the cup from Phillips, blew on it briefly, then drank it straight down. The coffee was strong and black and it burnt his throat, but he needed the hit.

'OK, Bill. Tell me.'

'Come to my office.'

Somehow she looked every bit as beautiful as she had before saying goodnight. How did she do it? It was a trick every woman would like to know, and plenty of men too. 'Good morning,' he said.

'Sleep well, professor? Were your dreams sweet?'

He nodded, saw that there was a coffee pot on the table and poured himself another.

'Right,' Phillips said, ignoring the tension between his two guests, 'let's get down to business. I have been talking to Donovan in Washington DC and Herschel Johnson in Stockholm. You've got them both interested. Donovan says that this is just the kind of thing the OSS was set up for. He's very enthusiastic. Herschel has a different perspective. He says there has been a sudden increase in German activity in Stockholm, particularly among known agents. On top of that, Heinrich Müller has been spotted at the German embassy.'

'You've lost me,' Wilde said. 'Who exactly is Heinrich Müller?'

'Head of the Gestapo. It's believed he has taken charge of the hunt for Rudolf Coburg. It's big news that such a senior guy would leave Germany.'

'Then we may be too late,' Wilde said.

Harriet shook her head. 'No, they'll never find him.'

'How can you be so sure?'

'Because he is too well hidden.'

'Anyway,' Phillips said, 'we're not going to hang around. William Donovan and Herschel Johnson are both absolutely as one on this – if Müller wants Coburg, then we want him more. And unlike Müller, we want him alive.'

'I'm glad you all see it the way I do,' Wilde said.

'Hey, anything that harms our enemy's reputation has to be good news.'

No, Wilde thought, it was more than just that. A lot more. This wasn't merely about the propaganda war; this was the essence of the real war. To hell with Hitler's reputation. If he was murdering innocent people by the thousand, something had to be done to stop him.

'So,' Phillips continued. 'Freshen up, have some breakfast, then you'll both be driven to a US airfield from where you will be flown to Stockholm. I want you to bring Mr Coburg back to Britain, to this office, along with his stash of documents.'

'Simple as that?'

'Simple as that.' He turned and smiled at Harriet. 'Are you OK with this, Miss Hartwell? It could be a dangerous assignment and it will be one hundred per cent American apart from yourself. But you are the one who knows how to find our man.'

'She could tell us,' Wilde said. 'Map it out.'

'No, it's not straightforward. I have to go.'

'I rather thought you'd say that,' Phillips said.

'But I don't need *him*.' She nodded towards Wilde. 'Just give me a plane and a pilot – I can do this myself.'

Phillips laughed. 'No chance, I'm afraid. Wilde goes too or it's no deal. This is our operation now.'

Chapter 28

The pain was overwhelming. From his ankle, it swept through his whole body and left him almost paralysed. He had been bitten by an adder, and even in his fever he was certain that Eichmann was the culprit. Eichmann, the slender one with the blank eyes and the silent hiss.

Coburg was drenched in sweat and was sure he was dying. His throat had swollen and he was struggling to breathe. The throbbing pain was relentless. It had happened soon after dawn, following a fitful grappa-fuelled sleep. He had woken groggy, in desperate need of a piss. Stepping barefoot from his pine bed, he had trodden on the snake and it had gone straight for his lower leg.

He kicked the vile animal away, then sat down on the edge of the bunk and vomited. He had never known such pain. His mouth began to foam. He felt the poison spreading through his veins and knew there was nothing he could do about it.

Now, three hours later, he lay prostrate awaiting the end. Without anti-venom serum, without medical assistance, there was no hope. In his delirium, even as he fought for breath, he was sure that he felt his heart rate slipping, felt that his body was swelling by the minute. His eyes were fixed to his bare ankle, which was blue-black and grossly swollen.

Perhaps it was all he deserved. Perhaps it was like this in the gas room: the panic, the pain, the sheer horror. All those trains he had helped Eichmann organise, the emptying of the Polish ghettos, sending men, women and children to the camps. Of course, he had known they weren't merely transit camps. There had been no onward journeys to organise.

Nor were they labour camps, otherwise there would have been continuous transports carrying the supplies of food and other necessities such places would need, as well as return trains for the goods they produced. But all that ever returned to Germany were the valuables, the hair and the clothing that had been removed – stolen – from the Jews.

He had always known they were death camps, but his mind could not comprehend such a thing, and so he had not admitted it to himself. Even so, what did it mean on paper or at the end of a telephone line? It was only when you saw the results close up that you could see what your actions meant. Only when you saw a baby's brains being dashed out on concrete that the chalked numbers on the freight cars turned from statistics into horror.

He had no excuse now. He could no longer evade the truth about himself. He was a murderer. God in heaven, what would his church-going mother think of him if she ever discovered what he had done? It was one thing to expel the Jews from her town, another to slaughter mothers and babies. No Christian could countenance that.

The drive to the airfield in Norfolk took almost four hours. For the first half, they rode in silence, but then Harriet turned to Wilde.

'Was Peter drunk when he was with you in the train?'

'I wondered that. To be honest, I don't know. He wasn't drinking when he was with me, just eating those infernal sweets . . .'

'Until the one that wasn't a sweet. Was it painless?'

'Pretty much, I think. Quick, anyway. I still don't really understand why he was so eaten up with guilt. Could he really have ordered the plane crash?'

'No. But he could have passed on information from Stockholm to someone who did have that power.'

'But which bit of information?' He lowered his voice; this wasn't something for the driver's ears. 'The meeting at Drottningholm? Or Coburg's story?'

'What do you think? They wanted me dead. Perhaps they thought Rudi was aboard. The Duke and all the rest were innocent bystanders – incidental victims – just as you're likely to be, Tom.'

'And you can be sure of that?'

She didn't answer. Wilde knew she was holding something back. The only sound was the roar of the engine. Suddenly she clutched his hand. He looked down at their entwined hands. His was large, a boxer's, hers small and delicate. 'Do you realise how much danger we're in, Tom? I don't think you do. Stockholm won't be easy. They know me, and they almost certainly know you. We have to avoid public places. That means no hotels – certainly not in Stockholm itself – and no embassies.'

He wanted to remove his hand from hers, but he didn't. 'Yes, you're right.'

'You really don't like me touching you, do you? You're afraid of your own nature.'

He didn't know what to say; he had been thinking just that.

They arrived at the airfield just after four in the afternoon. The sentry waved them through and directed them to a Nissen hut with a windsock blowing above its corrugated roof. The hut was a canteen and it had a cosy, lived-in feel to it. A basic kitchen had been set up at the far end where a middle-aged woman in a pinafore was clattering cups and plates. There were cooking smells and steam was blowing from a whistling kettle.

Their eyes instantly went to the only other occupant of the hut – a leather-jacketed pilot sitting with his feet on the table. He held up his hand and gestured them to come over.

'Hi, folks,' he said, sliding his feet down to the ground and standing up. He held out a hand. 'You must be Tom and Harriet, right?'

No formality here, Wilde noted. He nodded. 'Yes.'

'I'm Chas. Major Charles Oldman from nowheresville, Nebraska, to the men under my command, but plain Chas to you. I'm going to be your pilot today.'

He was a small, weathered man of about forty, with an all-American crew cut and a smile as wide as the Great Plains. He had the look of a working man who knew his job and did it well.

'Pleased to meet you, Chas.'

'Likewise. Now take a seat and make yourselves at home. Coffee's on its way, then we'll talk about what we're going to do with you folks.'

Strong American coffee was produced and food was offered. 'I recommend the frankfurters with mustard, beans and French fries,' Oldman said. 'I don't know when you're next going to eat and I doubt you do. But I tell you this, you're going to be damned cold at 25,000 feet, folks. And if you're hungry, you're going to feel even colder. I suggest you eat.'

'OK,' Wilde said without enthusiasm. Harriet shook her head.

Oldman waved to the cooking woman. 'Same again, Gertie. Times one.' He had a half-eaten plate of food in front of him and returned to it with gusto. A very full plate arrived soon after and was placed in front of Wilde. As he ate, he began to realise he was hungry after all. Then Harriet started stealing his chips until, at last, she ordered a meal for herself.

There were only a dozen planes in evidence around the airfield. Wilde asked Oldman about it. 'Tough one,' he said. 'Just between ourselves, my B-17s are over France today and I'm scared out of my mind for the boys. A lot of Hermann's Messerschmitts have gone east, but there are still enough left over there to make things damned brutal for us.'

Wilde pushed his empty plate away.

'Now, folks, this is not going to be easy,' Oldman continued. 'I have been ordered to help you and it is my pleasure so to do. I will be flying you in a borrowed British de Havilland Mosquito which we're trialling. It is extremely fast, it flies high, is spectacularly manoeuvrable and it has the range to get us there. There is no better way to get to Stockholm in a hurry.'

'Perfect,' Wilde said.

'But it is going to be tricky because the Mosquito is really just a two-seater light bomber, made of plywood and balsa. In normal circumstances, that means just pilot and navigator. No armaments, no room for gunners, nothing to slow us down.'

'But there are three of us even without a navigator,' Wilde said. 'Sorry, I'm stating the obvious.'

'Three we can manage because we won't be carrying bombs, so we can fit one passenger in the bomb bay. That means one of you is going to be hellishly uncomfortable and the other is going to have to do a bit of amateur navigating. What's it to be, folks?'

'Harriet?'

'Do you know how to navigate, Tom?'

'I can read a map.'

'That's not the same thing,' she retorted. 'Anyone can do that.'

Oldman grinned. 'To tell you the truth, I could do without a navigator most of the time anyway, except the navigators' union might object.' He paused and watched their faces. 'That was in the way of a gag, folks. There is no navigators' union.'

Wilde managed a laugh. 'I'm sorry, Chas, I think we've temporarily lost our senses of humour.'

Harriet had already made up her mind. 'You're the excess baggage on this trip, Tom – so you can have the bomb bay.'

He raised an eyebrow, then laughed out loud. 'Looks like the lady has outvoted me, Chas.'

'You're very generous. It gets very cold up there at high altitudes. But don't worry, we'll wrap you up as warm as a polar bear and you'll be fine. And we won't be attacked because Hermann's got nothing to touch us for speed. Of course, if I happen to see him down below I might just drop you on his head. If that's OK by you, Tom.'

'Should be a soft landing with all that whale blubber he keeps around his waist.' There was something else that Oldman didn't seem to have considered. 'I take it you'll be waiting for us in Sweden, Chas?'

'Those are my orders. However, you will be back with me within thirty-six hours, or I will come home without you.'

'Fair enough. The thing is, we intend to have another man with us. That's the whole purpose of our trip.'

'Yes, I was told that. And I don't want to hear who he is or any more about it. What that means, however, is that one of you may have to stay behind in Sweden for a while until I come back to collect you. Is that a problem?'

'We'll have to deal with it,' Harriet said.

'OK, well let's see how big your man is and take it from there.'

After eating and refreshing themselves in the bathrooms, Wilde was zipped into a vast quilted suit, then a lifejacket and parachute. Harriet borrowed a leather flying jacket and pulled on a pair of over-large trousers over her bunched-up skirt, with thick sheepskin mittens for her hands.

Oldman nodded at a shelf full of well-thumbed novels. 'Borrow a book and flashlight, Tom. Pulp fiction's the thing to pass the hours. You'll find a couple of Chandlers there.'

'Thanks.'

'OK, let's go. If we leave now, it'll be getting dark before we approach the Norwegian coast, which will suit us very well.'

Wilde had to be helped into the plane. He was so heavily wrapped up against the cold, he could hardly move. Somehow he manoeuvred himself underneath the open bomb doors, and was helped up into the space. Chas Oldman connected the oxygen supply to his mask and showed Wilde how to alter the intake of the precious gas as they rose to heights where it was necessary for survival. He then checked the intercom.

'I'll let you know when you need the oxygen, Tom. That's all you have to do. Apart from that, try to relax, read a bit, sleep if you can. You won't see a thing, but you'll hear the relentless buzzing of the engines and you can chat to us over the intercom if you're really bored. Other than that, see you in Stockholm.'

Harriet was standing just clear of the bomb doors. 'Thank you, Tom. You're a gentleman after all.'

'Don't say I don't do anything for you.'

Slowly, the doors were closed on him and he found him-self in pitch dark, packed in tight. He switched on his torch to take in his surroundings. The space was black and functional with clips for four bombs. He turned off the light and closed his eyes. His own breathing sounded preternaturally loud in the enclosed space. Then the engines roared into life and that was all he could hear.

It was never a pleasant sensation to be utterly in the hands of others. Wilde imagined himself a cat, caught in a cupboard. There was nothing to be done but wait, so he tried to relax every muscle. Very soon, the Mosquito bumped into life, taxiing along the runway, then quickly he sensed it soaring upwards at an astonishing rate.

'All right down there?' The American pilot's soothing voice crackled through the intercom.

'Fine. Pure luxury.'

'We're almost at 10,000 feet. Time to start on the oxygen.'

Wilde read a little of *The Big Sleep*, then switched off the torch and gave himself up to a kind of half-sleep. He awoke fully to a bumpy landing. The bomb doors opened and he looked down on to a dark patch of Sweden. He realised that it was evening. Unhooking himself from the oxygen and intercom, he eased himself down to the ground. Crawling out from under the plane, he found himself on a brilliantly lit landing strip. Harriet was standing, hands in the pockets of her leather flying jacket, looking at him wryly.

'Good flight, Tom?'

'Not bad, actually. You?'

'Wonderful. Chas is good company.'

Major Oldman climbed down from the cockpit just as a black car approached across the tarmac. 'Good luck with whatever you're trying to do,' Oldman said. 'This is a Swedish Royal Air Force base. All completely unofficial. No passport control, nothing. I think the Swedes are beginning to realise Germany is not going to win this war, so we're allowed in here so long as we're unarmed. Anyway, I'll be in the officers' mess while you go about your business. And remember, thirty-six hours – not a minute more.'

'Thank you, Chas,' Wilde said.

The car slowed to a halt and the driver emerged. He was a young man in a good suit, white shirt and striped tie. In his hand he held a hat. 'Professor Wilde? Miss Hartwell? I'm Bateman, Ted Bateman, from the US legation. I'm to be your driver for the duration of your visit.'

'Do you know why we're here?'

'No, sir. But I have arranged hotel rooms for you tonight in a small town twenty miles north of Stockholm. I'm told you'll be avoiding the city.'

'And Herschel Johnson suggested this?'

'I believe the suggestion came from Mr Phillips in London, sir. I was also told to tell you that you are under no obligation to accept my services as a driver, nor to use the rooms I booked.'

Wilde looked at Harriet. She nodded. 'OK, well that's roughly the right direction, so take us there. We'll decide our next move on the way.'

'Can I get your luggage, sir?'

'We don't have any.'

Suddenly Harriet was looking at her watch. 'No, it's only seven thirty – that's not too late. We should go directly to

Ekberg. You know it, Bateman? It's a small fishing town on the coast north of Stockholm.'

'Well, I can sure find it on my map, Miss Hartwell.'

'Take us there.'

Chapter 29

They arrived, and Wilde was incredulous. 'Are you serious about this?' he demanded.

'This is where I was told to come.'

'You can't be right. It doesn't make sense.'

'You may have forgotten, Tom – I have perfect recall.'

'But this is just a family home.' Wilde looked up at the modest house and could not believe that the place had anything to do with an international arms dealer and fixer. 'It seems strange . . . unprofessional.'

'Good camouflage then.'

The building was well away from the little town of Ekberg, about three miles inland. It was deep in the countryside of farmland and forest, down tracks, nowhere near any main roads. Wilde had questioned her about the place on the way here, but she hadn't answered, merely jutted her chin towards the back of the driver's head, as if to indicate that she didn't want him to hear their conversation.

Before turning off the highway, they had passed a curious variety of Heath Robinson vehicles – ordinary cars converted to wood-gas because of the petrol shortage in Sweden. No such problems for the US embassy staff. In the darkness, they saw houses with lights shining behind unblacked-out windows, a welcome change from the eternal gloom of night-time England.

By the time they arrived, the moon was high and bright silver. The wrought iron gates to the property had been left open and they drove straight through. 'Park here and wait, please, Mr Bateman. We won't be long.'

The driver pulled to a halt right in front of the house. Even by moonlight, Wilde could see that it was a traditional Swedish house, constructed of wood panelling painted a faded lemon yellow with light blue window frames. Pretty, but certainly not imposing or grand. Not the stately home or headquarters of a wealthy man.

Harriet climbed out and Wilde followed her. She knocked at the door, then stood back and waited. The door opened to reveal a small girl of eight or nine with the fairest hair Wilde had ever seen, all tied up in plaits. She smiled at Harriet, gave a little curtsy, said something in Swedish then disappeared back into the house, calling out, 'Mamma, mamma.'

A minute later, a woman of about thirty appeared. She looked just like an older version of the child, her hair almost as fair and her skin gorgeously tanned from the long summer. She was wearing a light blue summer dress and a yellow apron, so that she almost matched her charming house. Like her daughter, she curtsied and smiled at her guests.

'Kerstin Larson?' Harriet demanded.

'Yes, that's me,' the woman answered in well-accented English.

'I am Harriet Hartwell. I was given this address for Axel Anton.'

'Ah yes, of course – do come in.'

The Swedish woman shook Harriet by the hand, then ushered her through into her front room before turning her attention to Wilde. 'Come in,' she said. 'Come in, whoever you are.'

'Thank you.'

'Now how do we go about this?' Harriet asked. 'Is he here?'

'Oh, Lord no, I am merely his exchange. One little step in the exchange. Mr Axel is most elusive and lives between various hotels in various countries. But I will make my call and with luck that call will be passed on quite quickly. But one can't be sure with Mr Axel, just as one can never be certain which country he is in at any given moment, but that of course is not my business, so I make no inquiries. Anyway, I heard you would most probably be coming, Miss Harriet, so you and your friend must make yourselves at home and wait. Would your driver like to come in?'

'No, he'll stay in the car.'

'Well, perhaps I'll take him a glass of schnapps. And I hope you will have one too. It is from my own plums, and is delicious if I say so myself.'

'Thank you, that would go down well,' Wilde said.

'But first make the call,' Harriet insisted.

'Yes, yes. All in good time, Miss Harriet.'

'I'm sorry, but we're on a very tight schedule.'

'I understand. I will be back with you in five minutes.'

They stood in the front parlour. A large wall-clock ticked loudly. It was a friendly room with light, floral wallpaper, a pine table and a photograph on the wall of a handsome young man in uniform.

'Who told you about this place – Coburg or Anton himself?'

'It was Anton. I went with Rudi to meet him that night at Drottningholm. When it was clear that Rudi could not go on the flying boat, Axel Anton said he would keep him safe until I had found a way to get him to England. When I came back I was to contact him via Kerstin Larson at this house. Until then he would be in a safe place, alone on an island where no one would find him.'

'What island?'

'One of 24,000. Only he knows which one. That way Rudi cannot be found.'

'Tell me about Axel Anton.'

'What do you want to know?'

'What does he look like – what is his character? I know nothing about him.'

'How do you imagine him?'

'I see him as a mountain of a man in a vast fur coat, selling cannon to tyrants in exchange for diamonds.'

She laughed. 'No, he is not vast, and he would be good-looking if he weren't a little on the chubby side. Nor was he in fur when I saw him, but you wouldn't expect fur in August, would you? I might say he looks Scandinavian, but that wouldn't be true. A better word is Baltic – but which side of the sea, I could not say, so that could be one of many places.'

'Not Swedish?'

'Perhaps Swedish, perhaps north German, perhaps Russian or Danish. I don't know. Does it matter?'

'No.'

'He struck me as an engaging fellow – unfortunately he is just as engaging to our enemies. Anyway, if all goes well you'll meet him soon enough. Judge for yourself.'

Kerstin Larson came back into the room, this time carrying a tray with a bottle and three small glasses. 'So,' she said, 'I have made my phone call. My contacts will make their phone call and so on – I don't know how many, which means I can give very little away. You could threaten or torture me and I would never be able to tell you where Mr Axel is located and even if I gave you the phone number I called, the person on the other end would be able to tell you nothing. Anyway, now we wait and drink a little plum schnapps. I don't know how long. Can I give you some food, too, perhaps? There is plenty to go around.'

'No,' Harriet said bluntly.

'That's a very kind offer,' Wilde said, 'but I'm not hungry right now.'

From somewhere else in the house, a phone began ringing. 'Well, well,' Kerstin said. 'That was extremely quick.'

'Just answer it, please.'

'Of course. Too much talk. Mr Axel is always telling me I am too chatty. Silly of me. One moment, please.'

She disappeared again, then returned quickly with an even wider smile.

'Well?'

'Mr Axel will be here within forty minutes. Isn't that good news? So let me pour that schnapps now and then, in a flash, he will be here.'

Anton arrived exactly forty minutes later. They heard his car pulling up and Harriet immediately went to the window. Kerstin left the room to answer the door.

Wilde had noticed the tension in Harriet all the time she had been here, but now her body visibly relaxed. She turned to Wilde. 'It's him, thank God. We're OK.'

'What are we going to get from him?'

'He will take us to Coburg. And then, God willing, we will be on our way home. All plain sailing. I was scared, Tom – petrified something would go wrong.'

Wilde nodded, but said nothing. Experience in the boxing ring had taught him that even when a bout seemed won, you should always anticipate the sucker punch.

Through the open doorway to the hall, Wilde watched the man enter and was surprised by what he saw; he was rather overweight with smooth, well-groomed features. If you encountered him on the London Underground you might initially think him a bespoke tailor or perhaps a well-meaning and well-fed Anglican canon. And if you happened to smile at him, he was the sort of fellow who would be certain to smile back. Wilde wasn't at all sure he agreed with Harriet that he looked Baltic. To Wilde, the man could be from anywhere in the Western world.

But Anton's appearance was not the only thing that caught Wilde's eye. It was Pernilla's behaviour that he noted. The little girl who had greeted him and Harriet with a prim curtsy now slunk away behind the kitchen door.

Axel Anton kissed Kerstin Larson on both cheeks and held her a little too long. But perhaps that was all right, as she had told them they were distant relatives by marriage. And then, in English, he said, 'Now come, where is my little Pernilla? Won't you give your Uncle Axel a lovely hug?'

Pernilla did not move.

'She's a little shy today, Mr Axel,' Kerstin said. 'Forgive her.'

'But I have brought her sweets.' He removed a packet from his pocket and dangled it from his chubby fingers. This was too much for the girl. She edged forward into the hallway, gave her customary curtsy and reached up for the packet.

He immediately pulled it away. 'First a hug for Uncle Axel.' The girl submitted to his blandishment and allowed herself to be pulled into his arms. The man held her tight and patted her behind.

Wilde's eyes strayed to Kerstin and he was sure she was stifling a grimace.

Anton released the child and strode into the front room. 'Harriet Hartwell,' he said, arms wide again. 'What a joy to see you here, safe and sound!'

Kerstin, who was standing to the side of the newcomer, gave her beatific smile again, then said, 'I will leave you three to talk among yourselves. I must put Pernilla to bed.'

They waited until the door was closed, then Harriet introduced Wilde and the men shook hands.

'Bring me up to date,' Anton said to Harriet. 'I heard about the terrible plane crash, of course – and I feared you were dead. But the fact you are alive must reinforce my belief in the Almighty.'

'I have been betrayed, Axel. In England I have been hunted and I don't trust anyone. But I have placed my faith in Tom Wilde here because I calculated that as an American he has nothing to gain from harming me or Rudi.' She met Wilde's eyes for a moment. 'That's true, isn't it, Tom?'

'Yes, that's true.'

She reached out and clutched Axel Anton's hand. 'Can you take us to him tonight? The sooner we get him to Britain, the better our chances.'

'Well, the good news is that Rudi Coburg is in excellent health and perfectly safe. But there have been minor complications, so first we must talk.'

Wilde saw the tension return to her finely carved jawline and noted that her slender shoulders sagged once again.

'What do you mean, complications? Just take us there.'

'Sweden is swarming with German agents. Even the damned Gestapo devil Heinrich Müller is here. They will do everything in their power to find your friend. They want him dead.'

'But you said he is safe. Anyway, only you know where he is!'

'I'm worried. It's possible they are looking for me. For a while I even feared I was being tailed here. My Berlin contacts have sent me warnings. This is all becoming hideous. I loathe these Nazis as much as you.'

'Then the sooner we get Rudi away from here, the better for all concerned.'

He sucked in air between his teeth.

'Well?' she demanded.

'Miss Hartwell, you know I would never ask anything of Britain, but I have to tell you that my expenses are becoming terrifyingly high. I am not impoverished, but I do live by my contacts – and they all demand payment.'

'Bribes . . .'

'I wouldn't use such a word. But yes, that is basically the truth of the matter.'

'You want more money?'

Anton angled his head to one side as though considering an awkward and unpleasant problem, as though the very discussion of filthy lucre wounded his pride. 'No, of course not – well, not for me, anyway.'

'Rudi has already paid you a fortune. I know he has.'

He gave an exaggerated sigh. 'This is war, Harriet. In Germany and the occupied territories people will pay ridiculous sums for a cup of real coffee or a piece of fruit. But information is even more sought after – and the penalty for talking out of turn is often death. Those who I usually rely on for information and help are terrified – they fear they are being watched and listened to. And not only by the Gestapo, the SD and the Abwehr. But the Allies, too. Come on, Miss Hartwell, I know MI6 is on my case. And now the Americans have an outfit up and running – the Office of Strategic

Services. What a dull, rather academic name for a secret service. Have you heard of them, Mr Wilde?'

'Can't say I have.' He knew his denial had not fooled Axel Anton for one moment.

'Well, I am sure they are on the same side as you and me, but that doesn't necessarily make my life any easier. My problem is that things have become so hot I have to buy silence from people everywhere or I will be denounced. Without pay-offs I am a dead man.'

Wilde decided it was time to cut to the chase. 'What sort of figure are we talking about here?'

Anton threw up his hands. 'Mr Wilde, you make me sound like a prostitute haggling over the price of her services! I am hurt.'

'For which I apologise. But I repeat, if you need more money to pay off contacts and protect yourself, what's the price?'

'I hardly dare to say it, but I am thinking a figure in the region of a hundred and twenty thousand Reichsmarks. It is preposterous, I know, and I will quite understand if you just get up and walk out right now.'

'No amateur dramatics, Mr Anton. Just tell me, what's that in sterling or dollars?'

Anton shrugged. 'I don't know, there is no official rate since America joined the war, but I would say five RM to the dollar, so that would make $24,000. Or £6,000 in British money.'

'That's a lot of dough.'

'As I said, these things are incredibly expensive. This war . . . it has turned the world upside down. I am not sure those in the West understand quite how ruthless these Nazis can be. Anyone who defies them or stands in their way risks his or her life. They are murdering people wholesale.'

Wilde had a sudden desire to punch the man's lights out. Instead he turned to Harriet. 'I think we need to talk privately.'

'Yes.'

'Could you leave us for a few moments, Mr Anton?'

'Of course, sir. Take all the time you need. But remember, this is not me – this is for the people who must be paid off. You have no idea of the pressure I am under. Sweden may be an independent, neutral country, but she is at the mercy of her German neighbours.'

Chapter 30

'He's taking us for fools, Harriet.'

'I can see that, Tom, I'm not an idiot. Will the US embassy get the money for us?'

'Why would they?'

'Because they want to hear Rudi Coburg's testimony.'

'I think Anton's bluffing. The bastard needs his arm twisting.'

'Be careful, Tom. We've come all this way – don't blow this.'

'Well,' Anton said when he returned to the room. 'How do you wish to proceed?'

'First let me ask you a couple of questions. One, are you saying that you flatly refuse to take us to Coburg unless we give you a hundred and twenty thousand Reichsmarks or equivalent?'

'I am merely explaining the difficulties I have.'

'Yes or no?'

'No, I am not saying that – but it will take longer. If you want this settled quickly, then I must have the money so that I can be sure I am secure.'

'What is the hold-up? You know where Coburg is. Take us to him – we'll do the rest.'

'I wish it were that simple.'

Wilde moved closer to him and put an arm around his shoulders, his grip a little too tight to be entirely friendly. 'It is that simple. Tell me, Mr Anton, have you given any thought in recent days to the question of who might actually win this war?'

'Of course, I realise it is finely balanced.'

'You think that? You're deluding yourself. The Germans don't stand a chance. They blundered when they attacked the Soviet Union and they blundered again when they declared war on America. The British and Russians are *both* building planes and tanks faster than Germany. They have hugely superior industrial capacity, food reserves and, critically, manpower. Now add the US into the equation. Wars are won and lost on material, men and food. Germany loses on all counts.'

'In which case it will be a cause of great joy among the freedom-loving peoples of the world, among whom I count myself. Yes, Mr Wilde, I think you are probably right.'

'Then you'd better start thinking very carefully about your place in the new world order. For I promise you this: there will be little room for those who have profited at the expense of the Allies – and even less for those who have harmed us through double-dealing.'

Anton moved away from Wilde's arm. 'I understand all this, sir. I consider the Americans and British the best of my friends. You do not need to threaten me. All I am asking is a little help with my expenses. These sums I mention sound large in the confines of this little house, but they are small in the scheme of things and this money will undoubtedly enable me to help you in other ways in the future. Coburg would not even be at liberty were it not for my intervention.'

'For which I'm told you have been handsomely paid.' Wilde looked at Harriet questioningly. She nodded – go in for the kill. 'So, Mr Anton,' he continued, his eyes boring into the other man's soul, 'you get us to him quickly and safely or I will make it my own personal business to destroy you. And believe me, I have the power to do that.'

Anton looked momentarily shocked, then forced a laugh. 'And you think I should be more scared of you than of the Gestapo or SD? Or Stalin? I'm sorry, Mr Wilde, but you really don't frighten me. You have no idea of the sort of men who threaten my well-being. Heinrich Müller – he scares me. Maybe you'll meet him if you hang around long enough. But if you want to avoid such men and get back to England, then it is going to take a little of your government's money. I have no room for manoeuvre. Forgive me if I speak plain, but it is as straightforward as that.'

For a moment, Wilde wanted to kill the man, but then Harriet moved between them. 'Wait, both of you. Coburg will pay the extra. A hundred and twenty thousand Reichsmarks is nothing to him. Just take us to him, Mr Anton, and I know he will pay you.'

'The problem is, Rudi Coburg cannot access funds in his present predicament. His wealth is tied up in Germany. So I cannot deal in this way – I need the money first or there is nothing to stop you simply flying away.'

'You have my word,' Harriet said.

'No. That is not good enough. I will give you tonight to organise the money, then we will meet again tomorrow. Here, at eight in the morning.'

'Is that it?' Wilde said.

'That is it, Mr Wilde. We both want the same outcome, but nothing comes free in this world.' He nodded briskly to both of them. 'Goodnight to you both.'

He moved towards the door, opened it and strode out into the night. Within moments, they heard an engine firing up, then the sound of the car growling away along the rough country lane.

Wilde looked at her and saw dejection written on her face. It had all happened so fast and had finished so unsatisfactorily. Suddenly, he was furious with himself for not doing more, for not somehow forcing Anton to stay and help them. But short of kidnap and physical assault – torture – what could he have done?

Kerstin Larson returned to the room. 'Is everything all right, Mr Tom?' she said.

Wilde had already noted her almost perfect English and had wondered about her. What was her relationship to Anton? There was no obvious affection between them, which meant they had some sort of business arrangement, but maybe no more. It was possible she owed him no loyalty, which could, just possibly, act in their favour. He shook his head. 'No, everything is not all right, Mrs Larson. In fact, it's very bad.'

'What are you going to do now?'

He put the question to Harriet. 'Well, what *are* we going to do? You said this would be simple.' He looked at his watch. It was 10.30 p.m. Three hours had already slipped by, which meant there were thirty-three left. No way of searching a country the size of Sweden in thirty-three months, let alone thirty-three hours.

'We go to the hotel and we come back here in the morning,' she said.

Wilde was thinking fast. He had already calculated that there was nothing to gain in going to the hotel and kicking their heels. Yes, they needed sleep and food, but more importantly, they needed information. Their only feasible assistance was to be found here, in this quaint blue and yellow house. He turned his attention back to their hostess. 'Mrs Larson, you offered us food and you have been kind to us. Do you think we might take you up on that offer?'

'Yes, I still have food. I will eat with you.'

'And I know it's a great deal to ask, but would you by any chance have rooms here where we might stay the night until Mr Anton returns? We wouldn't want to miss him.'

She seemed uncertain.

'We could of course pay you hotel rates. Just name your price.'

'I have only the one spare room . . .'

Kerstin Larson's daughter Pernilla was already in bed when the three adults sat down to supper. Wilde had sent the driver away with instructions to wait by the phone at the US embassy so the car could be returned to this house at a moment's notice.

He did not bother to make any inquiries about funds to pay off Anton, because he knew what the answer would be. And even if the funds were miraculously made available, he did not think for a moment that that would be the end of it. When you agreed to pay a blackmailer, the price immediately went up; everyone knew that. So let Anton sweat – let him know that no money would be provided upfront. His only hope would be to tap Coburg for more, and then only when he was safely in the hands of Wilde and Harriet.

Kerstin had served up large bowlfuls of elk and potato stew with fresh brown bread to dip in the gravy. They all ate with relish, drank more of her plum schnapps and talked about the war and conditions in Sweden.

There was a chill in the air. Against the outside wall, a large iron wood-burning stove held pride of place, but it wouldn't be lit for a few weeks yet.

Kerstin spoke of the privileges of Swedish life thanks to its curious position, surrounded by war on all sides but allowed to remain at peace. 'I think we have better food than the rest of Europe, but no gasoline. I know we are fortunate, and when we hear the stories of horror from Norway and Denmark, we often feel guilty for our good fortune.'

'You shouldn't feel guilty for not being persecuted.'

'Of course, I understand that. But nonetheless, it is hard to feel good about ourselves.'

Wilde understood perfectly. He knew, too, that Sweden hadn't remained entirely apart or innocent; that it continued to sell raw materials to Germany to fuel its war machine and that it had allowed Wehrmacht trains to cross its territory carrying troops to northern Norway.

'Anyway,' Kerstin continued. 'We never know whether we might ourselves be invaded. Germany needs our natural resources. Stalin wants them, too. We are an obvious target for invasion.'

'Won't you tell us a little about yourself?' Wilde asked softly, changing the subject. 'Where is Pernilla's father?'

Suddenly her eyes were filled with sadness. 'That is Johan, my husband. He was a teacher in Ekberg – as was I until we married. But he couldn't stand idle when Finland was invaded by the Russians in '39, so he went off to fight in the Winter War, and died.'

'I'm sorry.'

'Yes. He was stupidly brave and I wish every day he had remained here and stayed alive.'

Wilde saw the tears welling up in her eyes, and noted echoes of Lydia. He heard her in Kerstin's words. Lydia hated him putting himself in harm's way. 'And how did you become acquainted with Mr Anton?'

She thought for a few moments. 'Well, I'm not supposed to talk about these things, but as I mentioned already he was Johan's distant cousin. After Johan died, Mr Axel came to me with condolences from Johan's side of the family. He stayed two days and decided he wanted to help me and Pernilla. "You can be my telephone exchange," he said. Those were his words – telephone exchange. He said he travelled widely on business and needed someone efficient and trustworthy to pass on messages, in return for which he would pay me a regular salary so that I would not have to go back to teaching until Pernilla was older. He said the work would not be taxing, but that I must never ask questions. I suspected it was an act of charity, and I was grateful. But sometimes I wonder . . .'

'What? What do you wonder?'

'Well, it has become complex since then. I am no longer the only link in the chain, which suggests to me he is involved in dangerous affairs and wishes to keep his whereabouts secret from certain people. Anyway, it must be obvious to you what sort of man he is. And so I wonder whether I, too, am somehow engaged in illicit activities by association. You are nice and kind, Mr Tom – but there are others who worry me. I don't like them being around Pernilla.' She winced. 'I think I have said too much.'

'Why you, though? Just because of Johan?'

'No, I realise now that it wasn't mere charity. It is also because of where I live. The isolation here suits him because he can visit me unseen. Also, my languages are useful – English and German and French. And Swedish, of course. It was easy for me to accept his offer because Pernilla and I needed the money.'

'You must have become quite close to him?'

She shook her head with a desolate smile. 'No, I wouldn't pretend to know him well. I doubt whether anyone does.'

'Is he married? Does he have a family of his own?'

'No, but I think I have said enough. More than enough. He really wouldn't like me talking to you like this.'

'I understand,' Wilde said. He wiped the last of the gravy on to his bread. 'Thank you, Kerstin, this is fine food. You still eat well in Sweden.'

Harriet had been eating in silence, watching and listening. Now she entered the conversation. 'Has anyone else been here recently?'

Kerstin shifted uncomfortably. Her eyes drifted to the dark, uncurtained window as though there might be someone out there, watching and listening.

Wilde followed up on the question. 'Kerstin, I can see you are a good person. But your husband's cousin has entangled you and Pernilla in worrying matters. Has he ever suggested you might be in danger?'

'He hasn't said that, but I am not stupid. As I intimated, some of the people who come here would not be my choice of friends.'

'Look, I'm going to take you into my confidence, Kerstin, because I think it is only right given the present circumstances. Harriet and I are here in Sweden on a mission to expose a terrible crime that is being committed by the Nazis. The lives of many thousands of innocent people may depend on our success or failure. We need to find someone, a German named Rudolf Coburg. Only Anton knows where he is hiding and he is holding us to ransom, demanding sums of money we simply don't have. That is why Harriet is asking whether anyone else has been here.'

'I'm sorry, I don't know, I don't really understand . . .'

'If the Nazis have offered Anton money, and if they get to Coburg before us, they will kill him and many more people will die as a result. So I have to ask you this: have any Germans been here?'

He knew from her evident discomfort and the flush in her tanned summer skin that they had hit the mark.

'Kerstin? Please, this is terribly important.'

She was pouring herself another schnapps, a large one. 'If I tell you anything, you won't talk to Mr Axel?'

'You have our word.'

'Because we need the money, we really need it. And more than that, I am scared of him. To look at his soft face and soft hands, you could not imagine him harming a fly, but I think there is a darker side . . .'

'Who came here, Kerstin?'

'Three men. All German. One was evidently a great deal senior to the other two.'

'Did they give you names?'

'Only the senior one. He said his name was Müller. I was to tell Mr Axel that Herr Müller wished to speak with him, and so I did just that.'

'How did Müller dress? Was he military?'

'No, no. He was in a civilian suit. On the surface he was very charming to me and Pernilla, but I saw through him. So did Pernilla. She is very astute, my daughter, very knowing. She sees things in people. She trusts you two. This man, this Müller, asked her to show him her toys, but she wouldn't.'

'So after you put the call through to Axel Anton, what happened?'

'Mr Axel called back very soon.'

'And did you hear anything they said?'

'No.'

'Are you sure?'

'Yes, I'm sure. I would never eavesdrop.'

'Did they meet here?'

'No, they made other arrangements.' She was twisting her hands nervously. 'Please, I live here alone with Pernilla, two cows, half a dozen chickens, a pig and a potato patch. We live a simple life but I help Johan's cousin so that we can live. I know what Mr Axel is and what he does. He is a very rich man, and is in possession of great power. And so, no, I would not listen in to his conversations.'

'Anton told me he has hidden Coburg on a small island in the Stockholm Archipelago,' Harriet said. 'One where no one ever goes. Which island do you think he might have been referring to, Kerstin?'

'There are more than 20,000 islands. How would I know which one he means?'

'He might have said something.'

'Well, he didn't. If I knew, I would tell you.'

'Would you?'

Wilde was shocked. Harriet's question dripped incredulity and something else. Disdain, perhaps? This was no way to talk to the Swedish woman, their hostess. He threw a hard look at her and shook his head. 'Take it easy.'

'Tom, she's holding something back! She knows something.'

'Leave her be, she is the innocent in all this.'

'I don't believe it.'

The tension around the plain wooden table was palpable. Kerstin seemed close to tears. Suddenly, she did, indeed, collapse sobbing, her head in her hands.

Harriet stepped towards her and put an arm around her. She knelt at her side and gently stroked her hair. 'It's all right, Kerstin,' she said. 'Let it out.'

Kerstin raised her head and huge, heaving sobs emerged. Her face was wet with tears. She turned her face into Harriet's bosom and wept like a child in its mother's arms.

All Wilde could do was look on, astonished.

Chapter 31

Ten minutes later, her tears had just about dried. Wilde had filled their glasses with yet more schnapps and decided he really had to introduce a calming element to the outpouring of emotion. 'I'm sorry,' he said. 'We are your guests – we should not have been pushing you so hard.'

The Swedish woman seemed about to start sobbing again. She was holding Harriet's hand and Wilde saw that the English-woman's face, too, was streaked with tears.

'This is not even your war,' Wilde continued. 'It is just that we have little time – and we are desperate. You are our only point of contact – we have no one else to turn to unless Anton changes his mind and helps us.'

'Oh God, what would Johan think of me!' It was not a question but a cry from the heart.

'I'm sure he would be proud of you for bringing his little girl up so beautifully.'

'No, he would hate me for betraying his ideals.'

'Surely that can't be so.'

'He hated the dictators and the invaders. He died fighting against cruelty – against pitiless men like Müller and Stalin.'

'Then help us,' Harriet said, pushing a lick of damp fair hair back from Kerstin's cheek.

She nodded. 'I know so little. I don't think it will be enough. You are both right, though. We Swedes cannot just stand by while the rest of the world burns. We must help where we can.'

'Tell us then,' Harriet coaxed. 'It may not be much, but you *do* know something – so tell us.'

'There is something in the back of my mind, from some time ago.'

'What sort of thing?'

She stiffened again, fear back in her eyes. 'If I tell you, you say nothing to Mr Axel? I'm not scared for me – but for Pernilla.'

'We promise,' Wilde said.

Kerstin breathed deeply for half a minute, trying to settle herself. Finally she spoke. 'I thought of it when you mentioned the island, you see. Last year it was – in May, I think. Mr Axel was in one of his more jovial moods, talking about Johan and saying what a sadness it was that he had died, for he felt sure they could have worked together for their mutual benefit. And then, from nowhere, he started telling me about a little island he had bought. I think he was boasting about it. He said he intended to go there alone sometimes to clear his mind and relax and that we would be welcome to use it too perhaps, but he was afraid that Pernilla would not like it. He said it was the sort of place no one else would ever dream of going, but he would build a little cabin there and even had plans for a Finnish hot room, a sauna.'

'Where is this island?'

'I'm sorry, I don't know. There are so many islands. But he told me its name: Huggorm. That is a strange name, which is why I remember it, for it means adder or viper in English.'

'Do you have a map of the islands, Kerstin?'

'No. I'm sorry, Mr Tom.'

'A map of Sweden?'

'No, again. Why would I need such a thing when I know my way around this area? As schoolteachers, we have an atlas of the world, of course – but I can't imagine it has the names of the Swedish islands.'

'Would you show it to me anyway, please?'

Kerstin fetched the old, well-thumbed atlas from her amply stocked bookshelf and handed it to Wilde. He opened it at the page showing Scandinavia. The only Swedish islands with names attached were the large ones, Gotland and Öland. He handed the book back with a rueful shrug.

'Perhaps you remember more about the island, Kerstin. Is it near here?'

'I don't know. He told me no more. To be honest, I didn't really give it much thought at the time. This was all a year and a half ago. Anyway, he's probably forgotten that he even mentioned it.'

'It's very important to us. Are you friendly with any of the boatmen or trawlermen in Ekberg? Surely they would know. Could you phone them, please?'

'No! Of course I couldn't phone them. It is late at night. Decent folk are asleep.'

Coburg had crawled from the hut down to the edge of the sea. He wasn't thinking. It was simply instinct that told him the sea was nearer the possibility of help. He was still desperately short of breath and shivering uncontrollably, but he allowed himself to hope that he might not die. With the onset of darkness, the adders had all moved away to the warmth of their nests, but he had no fear of them anyway. He was still too sick to feel anything except the pain that suffused every nerve in his dying body. He had never known that an adder bite could inflict such pain, and had certainly never thought of them as lethal.

He looked out to sea, desperate for sight of a boat in the sliver of light cast on the still waters by the moon. How long had Anton said he would be? A week? He had lost track of how many days ago that was. All he knew was that he could not survive long without medical assistance. He hadn't expected to see out the day. Yet here he was, in the cool of the night, still alive. He saw something in the water. Was his mind playing tricks again? His eyes followed it. No, two of them, swimming in his direction, side by side, winding lazily through the water: Hitler and Müller.

A half-memory was coming back. Something Anton had said, something he had to do if bitten, something he had to remember. But he couldn't recall what Anton had said, because he hadn't really been taking any notice. His mind had been elsewhere, in the camp of murder where it would always remain, festering like a pus-filled sore, until the day he himself died.

He could barely move, but he tried to look around, searching for something to remind him of what Anton had said.

Nothing emerged.

Wilde slept on the parlour floor in an old sleeping bag that Kerstin had found in her garden shed. It was musty, but it served its purpose. Harriet got the spare room with its single bed. In the night, he dreamt she was standing there beside him, looking down at his sleeping form. She was naked and her arms were by her side. Her body was small and slender, very like Lydia but a few years younger. In his dream, his eyes were open and he watched her in the thin moonlight that cut through the darkness. She moved her lips but no words emerged and then she turned away and was gone.

They both woke with first light and met in the little kitchen. Pernilla was sitting at the small table eating her breakfast of rollmops and bread. At their entrance, she immediately jumped up and curtsied to them both.

Kerstin was outside feeding the chickens. She saw her guests through the blue-framed window and came indoors.

'Did you sleep well, Miss Harriet? Mr Tom?'

'Yes, thank you,' Wilde lied.

Harriet just smiled and said, 'Good morning. Can you make some phone calls for us, please? We need to discover the location of that island.'

'Of course, but first some coffee.'

Wilde looked at Harriet reproachfully. Her moods were like quicksilver. Last night she had been surprisingly tender in comforting Kerstin, now she was very bad at camouflaging her extreme irritation and impatience. Had last night's kindness been nothing but an act?

He too felt ill at ease and wanted Kerstin to get on with the matter in hand, but he had calculated that they stood a better chance of securing her cooperation if they were pleasant and cheery. He was also concerned that she might have decided she was too loose-tongued last night and could now clam up and refuse to help them any more. He took out his wallet and handed some of the krona banknotes which Bill Phillips had supplied. 'Is that enough, Mrs Larson?'

She took two notes from his hand and pushed back the rest. 'Thank you, that is ample.'

'And yes, coffee would be very much appreciated.'

'It's ersatz, I'm afraid, but not too bad. I quite like it now. Imported foodstuffs are hard to come by, but we have plenty of home-grown potatoes, berries and livestock.'

'Ersatz will be fine. But tell me, have you anyone in mind who might have some idea about the location of Huggorm Island?'

'I do. There is an old retired fisherman named Skoog in Ekberg. Everyone calls him Skipper. He spends every day on the quay smoking his pipe, reminiscing about his seafaring days or playing chess with his friend. I always pass the time of day with him when I cycle by, so yes, I think I would call him a friend and he will be the one to help if anyone can.'

'Do you have a car?'

'Of course, but I haven't used it since last December because there is no fuel to be had. I keep it in the barn and cycle everywhere.'

'But the car has some fuel in it?'

'A little, yes. I keep it for emergencies.'

'Will the fisherman be at the quayside now?'

'I think so.'

'Then can we use your car?'

'We will take you, Pernilla and I. We can drop her off at school. But we will not go until after Mr Axel has been, and only then if he does not agree to accommodate your wishes.'

At eight o'clock, the telephone rang and Kerstin Larson picked it up, knowing it would be Axel Anton. She listened in silence under the watchful eyes of her guests from England. After a few moments, she said, 'OK, Mr Axel,' then directed a question at Wilde. 'He wishes to know whether you have secured the money, sir.'

'We're working on it,' Wilde said.

She repeated the words, then turned back to Wilde. 'Do you perhaps have some other figure in mind, because he might be open to negotiation? He says he would much rather deal with you than others.'

'What others?'

She repeated the question, then passed on the answer. 'Hypothetical others, he says.'

'Tell Mr Anton that if he takes us to the island, we are certain that Herr Coburg will be able to find the sum he requires. By the way, I had thought Anton was going to be here to meet us face to face.'

Kerstin repeated Wilde's answer word for word, then listened intently. She shook her head before holding the phone away. 'He says he was unhappy with your response last night. He is even more unhappy this morning. He says this is your last opportunity – do you have an offer to make?'

'Only what I just said. Our problem is that a sum like the one he is asking cannot be secured at great speed – and we are ourselves on a very tight schedule. Look, let me talk to him.' He reached out for the phone, but Kerstin held it at arm's length.

'He will only speak to me, sir. He is saying he cannot afford to do business with you.'

'Please, give me the phone. Let me speak to him.'

'He won't talk to you, sir.'

Wilde pulled the phone from her hand. 'Anton? This is Tom Wilde.'

There was a click. The line was dead.

At first the engine of the old 1920s Volvo flooded. It took Wilde ten minutes to get her going and then the four of them headed eastwards towards the picturesque community of Ekberg, which stood in a sheltered bay at the end of a short sea inlet. First they dropped Pernilla off to school and, yet again, she performed her little curtsy for the guests as she said goodbye and skipped along the path to the schoolhouse.

They parked outside a bakery and walked down to the quayside.

Kerstin pointed towards a man sitting on a bench. 'There he is, as always.'

Anders Skoog looked every inch the grizzled old seafarer. He had a white beard, a weathered blue shirt and clenched an ornate unlit pipe in his left hand. Kerstin approached him. 'Hello, Skipper, how are you today?'

'Ah, today you speak English, dear Kerstin.'

'Because I wish to introduce you to two English-speaking visitors.'

Wilde and Harriet were now at her side.

'This is Professor Tom Wilde, he is an American. And his friend is Miss Harriet Hartwell.'

With the introductions over, Anders Skoog fiddled in his pocket for a box of matches and attempted in vain to light his pipe. Wilde immediately saw the reason; there was no tobacco in it. The Swede looked beseechingly at him. 'Have you tobacco, sir? Perhaps a foul old cigarette I could break apart?'

'I'm sorry, we don't smoke. But I could give you some money.'

'Money? Yes, I'd like a little money. Perhaps we can trade? What can I offer you?'

'We're looking for an island called Huggorm. Kerstin said you were the best man to help us.'

'But I don't go to sea these days. My hips, professor, I can't move well.'

'Have you heard of Huggorm Island?'

'Like the snake? No, I haven't heard of it. But I know islands where you can find the huggorms. That's easy.'

'There's more than one such island?'

'Of course. But there is one tiny island which is well known for having many, many snakes. It is beyond Svartsö, towards the open sea. I don't know what it's called. There are too many islands in the archipelago to know one-hundredth of their names, even if they all *had* names, which I doubt. It could be called Huggorm, of course. Why not? But no one goes there. It is rocky and small and full of snakes, and all they do is sunbathe and swim. Not the best place for humans.'

'Is it far from here?'

'An hour or so by fast motorboat, but could be twice that in something slower. All depends on the boat speed.'

'Is there a boat here that could take us there?'

'You look a strong man, Professor Wilde. Would you help me?'

'Ask, and I'll do whatever you want.'

'Then I will take you.'

'How much will I pay you?'

The old man shrugged and raised his spidery eyebrows. 'Whatever you want.'

Chapter 32

At a private mooring in the south of the city, close to Stockholm Palace and the ferries, Heinrich Müller and his two Gestapo subordinates, Huber and Felberg, climbed into Axel Anton's motor cruiser, the *Solpalats*. The three Germans were all in civilian clothes and armed with concealed pistols.

The day was bright and clear. Endless blue skies and dead calm waters. Müller was feeling pleased with himself. This would all be over within a couple of hours and by the end of the day he would be back in Berlin. With luck, his absence would not even have been noted. Kaltenbrunner would have ensured that no awkward questions were asked at the Führer's headquarters. Both men agreed this should never have happened; Coburg's erratic behaviour should have been spotted a great deal earlier, either by Eichmann or, latterly, by Philipp von Hessen, and he should have been put away in a concentration camp.

Müller nodded at Axel Anton and wondered about him. It was in his nature to examine every human being he met, both their faces and their souls. Sometimes the face gave everything away; at other times it told you nothing about what lay hidden within. Anyway, who cared in Anton's case? The deal had been done and Müller would have his man. 'You have made a wise decision in accepting our offer, Herr Anton.'

'That was the easy bit, Herr Gruppenführer. The difficult bit was squeezing information out of various contacts.'

'We don't have to play that game now, Anton. We all know how you operate. Now, drive this boat fast and safe and get us to our friend as quickly as you can.'

'Don't worry, he's not going anywhere without my help. I would ask you one thing, though – please, no hard tactics while you are in Sweden, and certainly not while I am with you. You gave me your word on that – and I have to carry on living here long after you have gone. It would do neither of us any good to have the waters fouled.'

'Do you doubt my word? I am a German officer, Herr Anton.'

'Of course. I meant to cast no aspersions. I am just a little tense. I know how important this man is to you – and to your enemies. I just want to be sure everything goes smoothly. Now then, I have some bottles below in the cabin if you would like a little aquavit. Please, you and your men must settle down and enjoy the scenery.'

'Fuck your shitty Swedish scenery, Anton. This is not a pleasure cruise.'

Anders Skoog did not need to consult a map as he wove his way through hundreds of shallow waterways, around rock shoals and scores of islands, both big and small. They all seemed to have shores of stone, washed smooth over the millennia. Some had areas of woodland and vegetation and sandy beaches, others were sparse.

The bigger islands had cabins and a few were occupied by full-time residents as well as far greater numbers of holiday-makers from the city. Occasionally, they passed islands with shops and guest houses and restaurants.

Despite his preoccupation with what lay ahead, Wilde found himself mesmerised by the strange, labyrinthine beauty of the archipelago in the late-summer sun. But a pain gnawed at his gut, the fear that this might all be in vain, that Skoog might have imagined the wrong island, or that Anton had made other arrangements and had got to Coburg before them.

The boat, the *Arethusa*, was rather luxurious in a quiet way. Long decks of varnished oak, a well-appointed little cabin with two bunks. It belonged to Skoog's wealthy grandson, who was away working in Stockholm. 'Something in the government or public service – I never quite understand what,' Skoog said. 'But I keep an eye on this fine new boat for him at Ekberg and he is happy if I use it. You have found me on a good day, for my hips are not so bad, which means I can move a little and I am happy. We all win, yes?'

'I hope so,' Wilde had replied.

They had said goodbye to Kerstin at the quayside. Wilde had wanted to give her more money than she asked for the food and lodging, but she wouldn't accept it. 'I trust no problems will arise for you with Axel Anton,' he said. 'You don't have to worry about us causing you any problems. We won't reveal anything.'

'I don't care if you do. Talking to you and Miss Harriet made me realise I have been living a lie. I now understand that I should never have agreed to work for him. He is a war profiteer; he makes money from misery and death even if he doesn't pull the trigger himself. I was protecting him – keeping his clients and enemies at arm's length.'

'If he is as ruthless as you suggest, you may not be safe from him.'

'Don't worry, I have a plan to deal with that. My good friend Gustaf Lund is a policeman. He will be receiving a visit from me and I will leave a sealed letter in his possession detailing everything I know about Axel Anton. If Mr Axel should approach me, he will learn of this and understand that he cannot harm Pernilla or me without destroying himself.'

Wilde nodded. 'You've thought this through well.'

'Of course, I am a mother. Anyway, good luck to you and Miss Harriet with your mission – and make sure you win this war. I must confess there was a time when I rather hoped the Nazis would crush the Soviet Union after what they had done to my Johan and all our friends in Finland. How dare they attack an innocent, peace-loving nation like that! But when I saw what the Nazis did in Norway, shooting innocent hostages, I couldn't forgive them either. Now I hate them all – the Communists and the Nazis. They all treat the lives of others with contempt.'

She kissed Wilde on the cheeks and did likewise to Harriet, though with a slight hesitation, Wilde thought. Or was that just his imagination? He wondered again about the mercurial Harriet Hartwell; had Kerstin seen something that he had not?

Now they were an hour out in the archipelago and the islands were beginning to thin out as they approached the open waters of the Baltic. Wilde sat beside Anders Skoog, their eyes fixed on the horizon. He listened to the old man's stories of his younger days when he travelled the world on the wool clippers from London to Australia, by way of the Cape of Good Hope and back via the Pacific and Cape Horn. His tales were laced with the romance of the sea – and Wilde, an amateur yachtsman in his own younger days, soaked them up with pleasure.

'But the great days of sail came to an end,' Skoog said. 'And so I married my sweetheart and settled down in Ekberg to fish the Baltic in a small trawler. I would be doing so still had the arthritis not done for my hips. How old do you think I am, professor?'

'Oh, I don't know – sixty?'

'Ah, you flatter me! I am eighty-eight years old.'

Every so often, Wilde glanced at Harriet. She was sitting at the edge of the bow, her legs dangling over the side as she, too, scanned the horizon. She had been terse at best this morning, taciturn at worst.

'Soon be there, professor,' the Swede said. 'Another ten minutes maybe.'

'You haven't asked why we're going there, Skipper.'

'Not my business. I know when to ask questions and when to keep my trap shut.'

'We're hoping to pick someone up, a man named Rudolf Coburg. I won't tell you why he is there.'

Skoog didn't react. Then he raised his head into the salt breeze and jutted his chin towards a speck in the distance. 'There she is, the island of snakes. Let us hope it is the one you are looking for.'

'Indeed.'

Axel Anton cut the engine of the *Solpalats* to dead slow as he approached Huggorm. From this direction he couldn't see the whole island, just the little bay, the cabin and the sauna hut. There were few trees.

'Where is he?' Müller demanded.

'Probably lying in the cabin. Sleeping, maybe. Not much to do on Huggorm except sleep and think, Herr Gruppenführer.'

'And, God in heaven, are those really snakes there lying on the rocks?'

'That is why the island is called Huggorm – it is Swedish for adder.'

'They look like decadent sunworshippers on the beaches of Sylt. Why does no one kill them?'

'Because they do no harm – and they frighten away unwelcome guests. Come on, sir, I will tie up the boat and you can go ashore and fetch Coburg.'

'How big is this island?'

'About twenty hectares, I believe. And little vegetation, so there is nowhere to hide. I think the owners plan to plant more trees and build a jetty, but these things take time.' He wasn't about to tell Müller that he, Axel Anton, owned this island. 'For the moment it seems it is perfect for its present purpose – keeping your man hidden away. But not from us.' He chuckled. 'And you will see that it is too far to swim away to another island unless you were an Olympian . . . or an adder.' He laughed at his little joke. 'Anyway, the nearest islands are even smaller, so why would you wish to go to them? Herr Coburg is trapped here, have no fear.'

'Don't tell me what to do, Anton.'

'Forgive me, sir. I was just trying to put your mind at ease.'

'Well, don't. You talk too much as it is.'

The Gestapo chief had already drawn his pistol, a Luger. His junior officers followed suit. With the boat moored securely to the rings driven into the rock wall, Müller stepped lightly ashore onto the higher area, followed by Anton and the other two Gestapo men. All four of them strode towards the cabin.

'Open it,' Müller ordered, standing back, pistol raised.

Anton hesitated, then pushed open the door. Inside, the small hallway was dark. 'Coburg, are you there?' he said with false bonhomie. 'I have brought some friends to see you. Your little holiday is over.'

There was no answer. Anton stepped inside. His eyes quickly adjusted to the gloom. He pushed through into the large sitting room with its picture window, but there was no one there, then into the bedroom. Newspapers were scattered over the floor. Among them lay the shrivelled corpse of an adder. Anton's heart began to pump fast. This was not good. He tried the bathroom and the tiny kitchen. No sign of Coburg.

'Well?' Müller demanded, now inside the cabin at Anton's side.

'He is not here.'

'What do you mean?'

'Perhaps he is sitting or lying down on the other side of the island, sunning himself. Come, let's see – it's only a few minutes' walk, just over those higher rocks there. And beware the adders. They don't like to be trodden on.'

'What about this hut?'

'Ah yes, the sauna. Maybe he's trying that.'

Müller flung open the door of the sauna room. Still no Coburg. Without waiting for Anton, he gave a curt order to his subordinates. 'One of you go left, the other right. Find him.' He took the middle route, marching straight across the higher rocks and the scrubby growth, then down to a little sandy beach. He turned around to see Anton floundering in his wake.

'He's not here, Anton.'

'There must be a simple explanation . . .'

Müller was not a tall man; he was even shorter than Anton. Now he grasped him by the neck with one hand and wrenched him off his feet.

'You demand a hundred thousand Reichsmarks from me, you waste my time on a jaunt to a shitty little Swedish rock full of fucking snakes. And then nothing. What is this, Anton? You think you can play games with the Gestapo?'

'Please,' Anton gasped, his fingers clutching at the Gestapo chief's hand, trying to release himself.

Müller dropped him, then stamped the hard leather sole of his polished black shoe into his balls.

Anton screamed in pain and doubled up. But Müller wrenched him back to his feet.

'One of three things has happened, Anton: you have lied and Coburg was never here, or Coburg has swum away, or someone else has collected him.'

'He must have swum away. Or maybe he hailed a passing boat. It's just possible. Do you not think that might have happened?'

'Why would he do that if he was in hiding?'

'Perhaps he became scared. I don't know. I really wish I knew. I'm so sorry, Herr Gruppenführer. We'll find him. I'll make it up to you and of course I will not charge you the full amount we agreed.' Even as he was speaking through the pain, tears streaming from his eyes, he was blinking, sure he could see something across the water in the distance. Another boat. He pointed. 'Look, Herr Müller, look – a boat.'

'So what?'

'Travelling away from us. Don't you see? As if it had been here on Huggorm. He must be on that boat.'

Wilde and Harriet had waded ashore and found Coburg lying in the open, close to the rocky inlet where Skoog had anchored the boat. He was shivering and his skin was blue and cold to the touch, but his eyes were open and he seemed aware of their presence.

'What's happened to him?' Harriet said, horrified.

'I don't know? Snake bite? There are a lot of them around.'

'This is far worse than an adder bite.'

'Whatever the cause, the sooner we get him medical attention the better.'

Together, they had carried him to the boat and placed him gently on a bunk bed in the cabin. His left hand clutched the handle of a slim briefcase like a hawk's claw. It was also secured to his wrist by a knotted cord. Anders Skoog took one look at the sick man and pronounced his verdict. 'He's in shock, professor. I can see where he has been bitten by an adder – look how the ankle is black and blue and swollen – but this is not a normal reaction.'

They waited no longer. There was nothing they could do for him here. Now they were heading back to the mainland at speed. The only good news as far as Wilde was concerned was that the injured man was conscious and halfway lucid.

Coburg clutched at Harriet's hand. 'Thank God you came, Harriet, thank God. I thought I was going to die. My throat . . . it was so swollen . . . I couldn't breathe.'

'You're safe now, Rudi. We'll look after you.'

'I trod on Eichmann. I killed him, but he had already got me.'

Wilde intervened. 'OK, Herr Coburg, don't try to talk. You're going to be OK.'

'Harriet . . . you came for me.'

'I said I would, didn't I?'

'Thank you, thank you . . . I don't deserve it.'

Outside the *Arethusa*'s cabin, on the gleaming wooden deck, Skoog was at the wheel, his grandson's beautiful boat cutting majestically through the still waters. He was talking loudly, and they weren't quite sure whether he was addressing them or himself; their thoughts were elsewhere and they weren't really listening. 'I have been bitten by snakes myself,' he was saying.

'One time in Australia – now that was bad, unbelievably painful and I was sick for days. I tell you, they have some bad snakes there. But adders? Who would have thought an adder could cause such an injury? They are usually no worse than the sting of a bee. Nothing to concern anyone.'

Harriet was mopping Coburg's brow with water from a flask. Wilde watched her in nurse mode and for the second time in twenty-four hours was surprised to see how tender she was. She had spoken scathingly about the German, but there was doubtless some affection in her ministrations. This time it most certainly did not look like an act.

'It is too late for anti-venom serum,' Skoog continued. 'He needs medical care now. To get the fever down. And then bed rest, lots of bed rest. It could take many days or even weeks to get over an attack like this. But I think he will survive. If his breathing is better, then he is over the worst of it.'

Wilde accepted this prognosis with relief, but there was a 'what if?' in his mind. They were heading for the mainland as fast as Skoog could manage – but what if Anton or the other searchers, the man named Müller, for instance, were also looking for Coburg? Even if they were to get Coburg to hospital, how would they protect him there?

Even more alarming, how could they get him to the airfield in time for the flight on the Mosquito to England?

Heinrich Müller peered through the binoculars. The only person he could make out was an ancient man with white hair at the wheel. If anyone else was aboard the boat in the distance, they must be below decks.

Then another head popped out of the cabin. A taller man with windswept hair. It was not Coburg, he was certain of that.

Perhaps there were others inside the cabin. Yes, Coburg was surely there. He *had* to be there – for it was the only hope there was.

He smacked Axel Anton on the back of the head with the palm of his hand and the Swede let out a grunt of pain as his head jerked forward. 'Faster, Anton, faster!'

'I have it at full speed, sir. You don't need to hit me.'

'You think that was a hit? You'll find out what a hit is if you don't go faster. I want to see who's on that thing. I see two men, but even from this distance I can see that neither of them resembles Rudolf Coburg.'

Anton rubbed the nape of his neck. 'Don't worry, Herr Gruppenführer, we will not let them out of our sight. But there are many shallows in these waters. We have to take some care, for we cannot afford to go aground.'

'Are we making progress? Will we catch them?'

'They have a fast boat, sir. Whoever is at the wheel knows these waters.'

Müller turned to his Gestapo men. 'Either of you two ever drive a motorboat?'

'Yes, sir,' Huber said, clicking his heels. 'My family has a little cruising boat on Lake Constance.'

'Take the wheel, then, Huber. Just follow the line of the boat ahead – I think they know the shallows. Keep to their line and we should be safe.'

Anton didn't want to let go of the wheel. As Huber appeared at his side, he protested. 'No, this is my boat – and I know these islands.' He looked beseechingly at the Gestapo chief. 'Please, Herr Gruppenführer!'

Müller shrugged. 'You let me down, Anton. Anyway, I think we will go a little faster with less ballast.'

Anton froze in horror. The muzzle of the SS-Gruppenführer's Luger pistol was pressed hard against his chest. It was the last thing he saw. Müller pulled the trigger twice and two 7.65 parabellum bullets pumped into his heart. Anton crumpled, his dying sigh lost in the summer breeze.

Müller looked down at the body without emotion, then nodded to the second of his two junior officers. 'Felberg, throw this piece of shit overboard.'

Chapter 33

Coburg's left hand was still gripping the handle of his leather briefcase. They had found him like that, on the shoreline rocks, under a warm, late-summer sun. He was half-dead but he wasn't going to let go of the case. His fingers were long and bony and they held on to his precious possession as if even death would not part him from it.

Now, deep into the voyage back to the mainland, there was still no sign that he intended to ever release his grip.

'Are they in there, the papers?' Wilde asked Harriet when she stood back from her efforts to soothe his fever.

She nodded.

'I'd like to take a look at them.'

'There's no hurry.'

'Still, I've come all this way on the back of what you told me – I'd very much like to look at the evidence.'

'Go ahead then, if you can get them off him. He doesn't seem inclined to release his hold.'

In the end, Coburg simply didn't have the strength to resist and Wilde gently untied the cord and prised the briefcase from his talon-like fingers. The German's eyes were wide and imploring, but he said nothing.

'I need to look at this, Herr Coburg. Don't worry, your property is safe with me. We're on your side.' Wilde snapped open the case and slid out dozens of foolscap pages, efficiently pinned together into different sections with large paper clips.

Coburg nodded in resignation. 'They tell you everything,' he said in perfect, though accented, English. 'The whole story. Müller, Eichmann, Eberl . . .'

Wilde placed the papers on a small fixed table and began to go through them. The paper on top was a hand-drawn map of what used to be Poland but was now divided up into districts of occupation and given new names denoting their changed status as integral parts of the Reich – the General Government, Bialystock, Warthegau. Within these areas, camps were clearly indicated by a black cross and a tiny skull. The crosses were fiercely inscribed in black ink as though stabbed with a sharp-nibbed pen.

Beside each camp was a single word: Treblinka, Sobibor, Belzec, Chelmno, Majdanek, Janowska, Auschwitz. Harriet had mentioned some of these names, but otherwise they meant nothing to Wilde. Given what he already knew, however, their purpose was all too clear. The inked skulls, the crosses and the testimony he had heard second-hand from Harriet told him that these were the Nazi death factories.

The chart was also a spider's web of railway tracks from major cities and what appeared to be holding camps, each leading ineluctably to the end of the line.

He looked through the other pages; they were official documents with printed headings of the RSHA – the Reich Main Security Office – and the department involved, Referat IV B4. Each was stamped with the words *STRENG GEHEIM* – top secret. Wilde spoke enough German to get the gist. These were official orders regarding requisitions and deployments of railway carriages, locomotives, drivers and guards. To the innocent eye, their import was not immediately obvious, but Wilde had a pretty good idea what they referred to. The figures, too, were informative. Each carriage of each train had a number beside it. With a chill, he realised that the figure referred to the human consignment on a specific transport. These cattle cars all seemed to contain upwards of a hundred people, so a train forty carriages long might hold 4,000.

The details of these transports were for internal consumption only, and never supposed to see the light of day. They were there because, despite everything, the Nazis still adhered to the correct Teutonic way of doing things. Everything must be in order, everything must be properly recorded – even their own insane acts of cruelty.

Then came papers headed as draft minutes of a conference held in a villa at Wannsee near Berlin and dated 20th January of the present year. It was an area of Germany that Wilde knew. On page one was a list of attendees, which was headed by the late Reinhard Heydrich, chief of the Reich Main Security Office and thus overlord of both the Gestapo and the SD. Wilde did a quick calculation; this conference had taken place less than five months before Heydrich's assassination in Prague by two agents sent from England. Wilde scanned through the other names but only two caught his eye: Heinrich Müller and a man called Adolf Eichmann, which sounded like the name Coburg had mentioned.

'Is it possible we are being followed?' Skoog said from above.

The words broke Wilde's concentration. He turned and saw Skoog at the entrance to the cabin. He wasn't sure that he had heard the old seafarer's question correctly. 'What did you say, Skipper?'

'I merely wondered whether it was at all possible anyone might be following us. Only, I have noticed that there is always a boat half a league behind us, and it seems like it might be the same boat. It is travelling at a not dissimilar speed to ourselves, which is unusual in these waters, for we are going at a good rate.'

Wilde hurriedly shuffled the papers back into the briefcase; time enough to study those in detail at a later date. But even at first sight, he knew they told a devastating story. This trip from England had not been in vain. He handed the briefcase to Harriet. 'Did you hear what Skoog just said?'

'Yes.'

'I don't like the sound of it.' He joined the old man at the wheel and peered back along the sleek wooden deck to the distant craft which Skoog had indicated. 'How long has it been behind us?'

'At least ten minutes, perhaps all the way from Huggorm. I can't say for sure.'

'Is it gaining on us, do you think?'

'Certainly not by much. You can't race through some of these narrow channels otherwise you risk being grounded, and no one knows these waters better than me. So we are going fast enough to keep our distance, I think, and I am sure we will beat it to Ekberg harbour. Why? Are you worried, professor?'

Wilde borrowed Skoog's binoculars. He could see three men aboard the pursuing boat, three complete strangers. He handed the binculars back. 'Yes,' he said, 'there is someone else who would like to find our passenger. Someone who does not share our good intentions towards him.'

'Then I have a challenge – and I love a challenge. I'll lose them.'

The visibility was perfect, yet the *Solpalats* lost the *Arethusa*. 'Where is the boat, Huber? I can no longer see it.'

'I think it has changed direction, Herr Gruppenführer. Somewhere among those islands ahead of us.'

'Give me the chart,' Müller ordered the other Gestapo man, Felberg, who had been standing at Huber's side doing his best to navigate. The officer clicked his heels and obediently held the large nautical map out to his master. Müller took it without acknowledgement, then spread it on the deck and got down to his knees to study it. After a few moments scanning the chart, he turned back to Felberg. 'Where do you think we are now? Which way did they go?'

The junior officer pointed to one of the larger islands. 'We have passed this one, Vindo, and I believe the settlement we saw on the left was Boda.'

'There was a channel there on the left – a narrow strait,' Müller said. 'They could have gone there.'

'Yes, Herr Gruppenführer.' It did not do to contradict Heinrich Müller. 'That is quite possible.'

'But you're not sure?'

'The boat was out of our line of vision when it disappeared, sir.'

Müller turned his attention back to the man at the wheel. 'Huber, what do you think?'

The young officer chose his words with care. 'Your suggestion that they went down the channel may well be correct, Herr Gruppenführer, but I think I would have seen them. In truth I have a strong instinct that they would have turned to the right immediately after that channel and headed for all those small islands to the north. The chart shows them as an impossible labyrinth, sir, the ideal place for a good steersman to lose himself. I fear our chances of locating them among all those rocky outcrops are remote, and our chances of hitting shoals and becoming grounded are greater. If they are trying to lose us, that might be the option they would choose. That is what I would do in their place.'

'Good thinking, Huber.'

'But if I may say, sir, with respect, I have had another thought.'

'Go ahead.'

'If they are trying to lose us in the maze of islands, that does not mean they have changed their ultimate destination.'

'Go on, Huber.'

'Well, it might be possible that they have only recently concluded that they are being pursued – in which case we might be able to divine their true destination from their direction of travel until this point. That means we could arrive in port before them and await their arrival . . .'

'And their likely destination? What do you think?'

'The little harbour of Ekberg looks quite likely, sir.'

Müller peered at the map again and stabbed his small finger at the map. Ekberg. Of course, that was the place they had gone to meet the woman who put him in touch with Axel Anton. Yes, indeed, Huber was almost certainly correct.

'Good man, Huber. If this comes off, I am recommending you for promotion.'

'Thank you, sir.'

'If not, of course . . . well, I leave that to your imagination.' Müller winked at the steersman. 'Only joking, young man.'

Skoog had suggested taking Coburg straight into the heart of Stockholm, where there was a fine hospital, but Wilde and Harriet were unhappy at the prospect.

'Isn't there one nearer your home port, Skipper?'

'Well, there is one some way further up the coast. Would you like to go there?'

'I think it's safer,' Wilde said.

'OK, then. But that will take us an extra hour or more. I thought you were in a hurry. What about our local doctor's practice? That would save a lot of time – and he is a fine physician.'

Wilde glanced at Harriet. She nodded.

'Good,' Skoog said. 'Then that is much more simple.'

Huber steered the motorboat into the small harbour of Ekberg. This was easy for a man with his boat skills; his father had taught him well.

'You two, tie up,' Müller said. 'And then we wait and watch.'

The other boat arrived three-quarters of an hour later, with two men visible – one at the wheel and another at his side. They looked like the men he had seen before through binoculars. Müller was surprised it had taken them so long and had begun to think they had chosen the wrong destination. But once he saw the vessel, he was as certain as he could be that this was the boat they had been following. No sign of the Englishwoman and Coburg, though. Either they were in the cabin or he had been pursuing the wrong boat all the way from Huggorm. Damn that Anton. He very much desired to kill him again.

Wilde jumped ashore with the mooring rope and tied up firmly and expertly. Then he helped Skoog on to land. The old man was struggling now after spending so many hours at sea. Wilde took him slowly, step by painful step, to the bench where they had found him that morning.

'Are you going to be all right, Skipper Skoog?'

'Oh, don't you worry about me, professor.'

'I want to get you some tobacco for your pipe. Is there anywhere in the town that sells it?'

'No, you worry about yourself. You have things to do.'

Wilde shook the old man by the hand and thanked him profusely, then took his wallet and offered him his choice of banknotes. Skoog refused.

'We have to pay you, Skipper Skoog. That was agreed. At least for the diesel.'

'No, my grandson can pay for that – and you can repay me by continuing to do whatever it is you are trying to do to defeat the Nazis. And if that is *not* what you are trying to do, then I am no judge of character.'

There was something about the face of the younger man with the windswept hair. Müller had a strange feeling he had seen him before, but where? He certainly had never met him, he was sure of that. But there was a spark of recognition. How could that be? It didn't make sense. And if that *was* the boat that had picked up Coburg, what part had the man played in it?

This was the perfect moment. 'Come,' he said to his two men. 'Fit your silencers. You are going to board that vessel. Make caution your watchword: I promise you the Führer would not wish an international incident on Swedish soil, but if we can finish it now, all well and good. It is possible the woman is armed. We know her to be a British agent. That said, don't hesitate to use your weapons. Shoot instantly, shoot silently, shoot to kill.'

Müller held back. As chief of the Gestapo he was too well known in the world – and he could not be implicated in a shooting in broad daylight in a foreign land, especially not in a country whose ball bearing and iron exports were so vital to the German armaments industry. His two junior agents, however, were expendable. If caught, they would say nothing.

Huber and Felberg stepped off the *Solpalats* and strode along the quayside. Reaching the *Arethusa* they stopped, looked around for unwelcome others, then jumped aboard. Now their pistols were drawn, lengthened by slim silencers. Felberg took up position on deck, partly concealed by the wheel from prying eyes ashore, then nodded to Huber who immediately ducked down into the cabin, his pistol clutched in both hands for stability.

From the *Solpalats*, Müller watched the proceedings on the other boat intently, waiting for the muffled, almost inaudible, sound of gunfire that was certain to come.

There was nothing, not a whisper.

Huber emerged from the cabin of the *Arethusa*, shaking his head. 'Not here,' he mouthed.

Müller raised his right hand and snapped it back sharply. His two men hurriedly disembarked and returned to the *Solpalats* as ordered.

'There's no one there, Herr Gruppenführer,' Huber said.

'And you are certain it was the boat we were following?'

'Yes, sir. The old man at the wheel and the other man were the same – as was the boat itself.'

Müller agreed, but he was puzzled. Yes, it was always possible they had been following the wrong boat all along – except for one thing: the feeling deep in his gut that he knew the face of the younger of the two men from somewhere. But who was he?

From this distance, they could see the two men talking at the far end of the quay. The old man was sitting on a bench and had a pipe in his mouth. 'This is what we are going to do, gentlemen,' Müller said. 'Felberg, you are going to use all your expensive Gestapo training and expertise to follow the younger of those two men. Huber, go and get a car for us in case he drives away.'

'How do I get a car, sir?'

Müller handed him a bundle of notes. 'Borrow one, buy one, rent one.'

Huber looked bewildered. 'But what if no one will agree?'

The Gestapo chief smacked the side of the young man's head. 'You hot-wire one, *dummkopf.*'

Chapter 34

'Well, Miss Hartwell, the patient needs a great deal of rest and fluids, but I think you already knew that. He had a rare reaction to the adder bite – something I have heard of but have never seen before. Such reactions can be caused by many things, from insect stings to certain foods, such as shellfish. They are often fatal, so your friend has been fortunate, for he will survive.'

The doctor lived above his surgery less than two miles up the coast from Ekberg. It was a large, delightful house of dark red wooden panelling, backed by woodland and fronted by a lawn that sloped down to the sea, where he had a private jetty. Skoog knew Dr Hansen well and had taken Harriet and Coburg there directly, certain that he would be able to help them.

Wilde and the doctor carried Coburg ashore and laid him on a narrow bed in his clean white surgery. Wilde would have stayed, but Skoog asked him to return to the boat for the last part of the voyage into Ekberg harbour. 'Just to fix the moorings and help me ashore, you understand, Mr Wilde. It will be only a half-hour walk from the harbour up to this house.' Wilde felt he had no option but to agree after all the man had done for them.

Harriet was now in the physician's surgery, watching as Coburg was examined with professional thoroughness.

'Yes,' the doctor repeated. 'I believe your friend will be fine.'

'Can he stay here with you tonight, Dr Hansen?'

The doctor frowned. 'That is a most unusual request, Miss Hartwell.'

'This is a most unusual set of circumstances, doctor.'

'My professional advice is that he should go to hospital.' He sighed and allowed the young woman a smile. 'But just this once, maybe you're right. On balance I agree it were better he do no more travelling today, so yes, he can use my spare room. Where will *you* stay?'

'I'll be here with him. I won't sleep. Perhaps Mr Wilde can sleep in an armchair when he joins us. We won't require food – just a brief use of your telephone to summon our car. We have to leave early in the morning, you see.'

'And leave Mr Coburg with me? That won't work. He can stay here this one night, but tomorrow I will have him conveyed to hospital.'

'No, Dr Hansen, we must take him with us.' She hesitated just a few moments. 'Well, I suppose I will have to tell you – we are taking Mr Coburg to England. He is a man of great importance to the progress of the war. Everything is arranged.'

The doctor shook his head. 'No, that is impossible.'

'We must be at the airfield by seven-thirty in the morning, at the very latest.'

'But Miss Hartwell, this man cannot fly in his present condition. By the sound of it, you may have saved his life by your actions today. To put him on a long flight to England would almost certainly jeopardise all your good work.'

'It's a risk we'll have to take.'

Wilde sensed he was being followed and stopped outside the little shop that catered for all the townspeople's needs. He went inside and asked the woman behind the counter whether she had any pipe tobacco for sale.

She couldn't speak English, so he cupped his hand as though holding the bowl of a pipe and raised it to just in front of his lips and made a sucking sound. 'Ah!' she said, then muttered something in Swedish and pointed him towards a small glass cabinet which had a selection of half a dozen pipes. Wilde nodded, then made a show of putting tobacco into his imaginary pipe. She shook her head sadly, but held out a packet of cigarettes by way of compensation.

He bought two packets, reckoning Skoog could cannibalise them for his pipe, then stepped out of the shop and looked around. He was in no doubt now. There were only two men visible in the street and they both looked out of place, one well ahead of him, leaning nonchalantly against a wall, the other, much younger, standing with his hands in his pockets at a corner fifty yards to his rear. He couldn't be sure, but he had a strong feeling that they were the men he had seen through binoculars aboard the pursuing motorboat. A car turned into the road, its exhaust spluttering black smoke, and stopped. But the driver did not switch off the engine and nor did he get out of his seat.

Wilde was now certain these were the men from the boat. If they were following him, it was because they believed that he would lead them to Coburg.

So he couldn't go to the doctor's.

He put his right hand inside his jacket and gripped the Smith & Wesson revolver with which Bill Phillips had supplied him. It was slotted into a shoulder holster that fitted snugly at the left side of his chest. Briefly, he allowed his jacket to flap open; he wanted these three men to know that he, too, was armed, and that he would not be taken easily.

Heinrich Müller had achieved his exalted position within the Third Reich hierarchy through dogged hard work and pragmatism. He had been a latecomer to the Nazi party, only joining when it was made clear to him by Heydrich that he really didn't have any option if he was to achieve high office in the current regime.

It had not escaped the attention of his enemies in the party that he had actively worked against the Nazis before they achieved power, nor that he had once referred to Hitler as 'a jobless immigrant house painter.' Well, he was, wasn't he? Or had been.

But politics meant little or nothing to Müller. He was happy to work for anyone who held the reins, and to do that work to the very best of his considerable abilities. He would happily accept that he was a man of limited imagination, but he knew that he put in the hours long after others had gone home to their wives or mistresses. Holidays did not exist in his small, enclosed world, for he was the ultimate functionary, a man willing to do anything, however distasteful, in return for power and status. Even go to Sweden to execute a traitor, if necessary.

That pragmatism kicked in now with the realisation that he had a lot more to lose than gain if he were to use force against this man in this street. But nor could he let this man go, for he was the key to the whereabouts of Rudolf Coburg. And Coburg had to die, for the Reich could not allow him to live.

Wilde had to decide between the three men. He chose the younger one – the one standing with his hands in his pockets fifty yards behind him down the hill – and began to walk in his direction.

As he approached, the man's hand went nervously to his jacket pocket. His gaze swivelled between Wilde and the older man up the street. Wilde turned briefly and saw the older man shaking his head, almost imperceptibly. The younger man began to back away.

'*Möchten Sie etwas?*' Wilde said. Do you want something? He held his jacket open so that the holster and pistol were clearly visible. The watcher stumbled backwards, then turned and loped away. Wilde laughed, then turned his attention to the older man up the hill. That one was clearly the boss; he had a look about him. Probably Müller, given that a man of that name had arrived with two functionaries at Kerstin Larson's house. He certainly fitted her description. Wilde began to walk up the hill, but the older one – not that old, only forty or so, but older in relation to the other men – simply strolled off.

Wilde considered his options and made his way back down the hill to find Skoog. He was no longer at his bench, but was hobbling painfully towards the little quayside bar. Wilde caught him up. 'I need another favour, Skipper Skoog.'

'Name it, sir.'

'I need a telephone.'

'Something has happened? Never mind, don't explain. Come to my house – I have a telephone. It's only fifty metres from here.' He pointed at an isolated wood-clad house fronting the bay.

They walked slowly, Skoog holding on to Wilde's arm. As they neared the building, the American expressed his admiration for the property, particularly its location. 'You must have wonderful views.'

'Finest in all Ekberg. I have to be beside the sea, you understand. If I can't see it and smell it, I am in purgatory. The ocean is my lifeblood.'

A few minutes later, they were inside the old man's kitchen. The place reeked pleasantly of woodsmoke. Wilde handed him the cigarette packets. 'They didn't have pipe tobacco, but I thought these might be better than nothing.'

'You are too good to me, sir.' Skoog pointed at the phone. 'Help yourself, professor.'

'Could you call Dr Hansen for me? I need to speak to Harriet.'

The old man dialled a number, got through, spoke quickly in Swedish, then handed the phone to Wilde.

'Where are you, Tom?'

'Harriet, I have encountered unwelcome company. Three men – the ones from the boat, I am certain. I don't think I can get to you without bringing them along in my wake.'

'What do we do?'

'I'll call the embassy and tell them to send the car direct to you and take you both to the airfield. Then you send it back to me here. I'm in Skoog's house on the quayside. The doctor will give directions. I'll join you at the airfield.'

'Dr Hansen doesn't want Coburg to be moved. He particularly doesn't want him flown to England.'

'There's no option.'

'I told him that. He says he could die.'

'We're going to take the chance. We can't afford to wait.'

'All right, I'm with you. But not yet – do it in the morning. Hansen says I can stay here with Coburg. That way Coburg will at least get a few hours' rest and Hansen can give him a last once-over. He's been making sure he gets plenty of fluids and I've cleaned him up. I think he's making some progress.'

'OK, I'll make it 4.45 a.m. for you; that should give us both time to get to the plane. Oh, and don't forget the briefcase.'

'I won't.'

'We still haven't worked out how we're going to organise this flight, but if I'm not at the airfield in time, you and Coburg just go.'

Wilde was aware that the Germans knew where he was. How could they not know? Now, they would be waiting and watching, certain that one way or another he would lead them to Coburg.

Well, they could wait and watch. And if they thought they could use other means to extract information from him, they would have to think long and hard, for they now knew that he was armed.

He made the phone call to the US embassy and arranged for the pick-up. He requested a two-man team, and this was granted. 'And tell them to bring guns,' he said. 'Preferably a Thompson.' He put down the phone before they could argue the toss, and gratefully accepted a glass of cold beer from Skoog. Wilde sipped it and gasped with appreciation. It had been a long, gruelling day.

'You like salmon, professor? With dill potatoes? Let me cook it for you.'

'That's very kind of you, Skipper. Yes, I'd like that. Do you need any help? I can peel potatoes, even turn my hand to cooking if need be.'

'No, I can manage well enough. You keep an eye out for your German friends. But tell me, are we to be slaughtered in our beds tonight?'

'I'm not going to bed. Don't worry, if they try anything, they won't get past me.'

Skoog laughed. 'I wasn't worried. When you have sailed around the Horn aboard a three-masted barque in hundred-knot winds, a few Germans with guns are not very frightening.'

'No, I suppose not.'

Huber returned the car to the empty street where he had found it. In a small town like Ekberg, such a theft could not be concealed long. He found a better vehicle – faster, with a half-full tank of fuel – on the forecourt of a garage on the outskirts of town. Huber still had the Swedish krona notes and he went to the office to buy or rent it, but there was no one there; the place was locked and deserted. It seemed too good to be true but in the circumstances he could not give in to his doubts, so he hot-wired it and drove back down to the bay.

Müller wasn't happy to be using a stolen vehicle again, but he accepted the situation. 'Keep it hidden,' he said. 'We don't want any trouble with the locals. Return here after dark.'

The Gestapo chief was on the quayside at the front of the house where his quarry and the old man had gone. Felberg was at the back of the building, crouched out of sight behind a chicken coop, one hand on the gun in his pocket.

Müller was certain now that these were the men with the key to Coburg's whereabouts. The man in the street had been armed, so it had to be him. Ordinary Swedish citizens did not go around with guns secreted in shoulder holsters. And his memory of the face was returning. A face he had seen in a snatched photograph, filed away in the archives at Prinz-Albrecht-Strasse. Certainly, he had to be a British agent. All he needed was a name to go with the face. Why had his English contact not mentioned this man?

More important was the other question: where had they taken Coburg? There could be no doubt he had been on the *Arethusa*. But where was he now? Where could they have taken him in the lost forty minutes at sea? Müller was left with two options: force his way into this fisherman's house and prise the truth from those within. Or wait, watch and pursue.

One way or another, he very much wanted to kill the man with the gun. But first he needed to find Coburg. At midnight he made his decision.

Wilde meant to stay awake, but sleep overtook him. Skipper Skoog had hauled himself slowly off to bed in a ground-floor room at the rear of the house, leaving his guest in a chair facing the front door. The house had no curtains. He had the Smith & Wesson in his lap and he watched the door until his eyes became heavy and closed.

He woke to a flash of light. Torchlight at the window to the left of the door, delving into the darkness.

The beam crossed his eyes, moved on, then returned and held briefly on his face. In the glare, he saw the shadowy outline of a face in the darkness behind the glass, then there was just the light once more. Wilde flung himself from the wooden chair, the pistol now gripped in both hands, targeted at the window. The light caught him again, then snapped off to leave pitch darkness.

But Wilde had seen enough – the distinctive outline of a gun barrel behind the glass. Instinctively, he pulled the trigger of his own weapon.

The explosion of the shot reverberated around the room. Glass shattered outwards.

Wilde moved on hands and knees to the window, then stood up and peered into the darkness. '*Ich werde dich töten*,' he growled. I will kill you. He heard running footsteps, retreating from the house. He fired again, high, a warning shot. The intruder wouldn't fire back because they didn't want him dead. Not yet, anyway.

He heard a footfall behind him and swivelled around. It was Anders Skoog in his pyjamas, standing bent and looking close to collapse, hand steadying himself against an old dresser.

'What has happened, Mr Wilde?'

'We had a visitor, Skipper. He's gone now.'

'And my window?'

'I'm afraid I shot it out. I'll pay for the repair, of course.'

'I hope you haven't woken the town.'

'They'll think it's a car backfiring.'

'Maybe. Anyway, we had better secure the window. Come, Mr Wilde, help me pull the dresser across. That will stop anyone trying to get in.'

Wilde didn't fall asleep again and nor did Anders Skoog. They had coffee and talked more. The car came for him at 6.28 a.m. He clasped the old seafarer by his ancient hands and thanked him profusely. 'Thanks, Skipper. I have no doubt that your assistance will help the Allies' war effort.'

'Good. To hell with the Nazis. They are shits – a word I would never use in church, but fine for you. I learnt worse words than that aboard the wool clippers, words not fit for your soft academic ears, professor. Look after your girlfriend.'

Wilde laughed. 'I'm a married man with a young son, Skipper. Harriet Hartwell is not my girlfriend.'

Skoog raised his spidery eyebrows, his surprise evident, then smiled and patted Wilde on the shoulder. 'Take care, professor. Come back and see me when this filthy war is over.'

Wilde peered both ways down the road. Satisfied, he climbed in the embassy car. The driver was Ted Bateman again. He introduced his colleague, James Ryder, who was lounging in the back, Thompson submachine gun in his lap.

'You delivered Miss Hartwell and Coburg without incident?' Wilde said as Bateman engaged gear and pulled away from the kerb.

'Yes, sir. The guy didn't seem too well, but there were no problems. Major Oldman has taken responsibility for them. By the way, the embassy high-ups weren't too keen on us bringing the guns. You might get an earful when you're back in London.'

'Don't worry about that. Let's go.'

There was only one road from the quayside. Just past the last house, a car was parked at the side of the street – a different one to the smoke-belcher from the previous day. Even from a distance, Wilde knew what it was. The car had two occupants – the older German and one of the younger ones. Its engine was running.

'Pull up alongside that vehicle, Mr Bateman.'

'Are you sure, sir? My orders are to get you to the airfield directly.'

'This won't take a minute.'

Wilde climbed out of the passenger seat. Bateman immediately took one hand off the wheel and transferred it to the grip of his semi-automatic. Ryder behind him did likewise, firming up his grip on the Thompson. Wilde walked around to the passenger door of the other car.

The window slowly wound down.

'I imagine you're Müller,' Wilde said in German, leaning his elbows on the sill and meeting the man's wary eyes.

'And you are Thomas Wilde, supposedly a professor of history from Cambridge University. I couldn't place you at first, but then I recalled – I have seen your file. It is remarkably thick.'

'I suppose I should be flattered, but I have also heard a bit about you and none of it good, I'm afraid. Anyway, feel free to follow us.'

'We will.'

'It's probably only fair to mention, however, that you're too late. Coburg left these shores hours ago. He'll be having breakfast in London right now. And who knows what will happen then? Conversations with the Prime Minister and the President, newspaper articles, wireless talks. The world will be very interested in what he has to say. I'll make sure you get a mention.'

'And what will he say? He knows nothing. He is a nobody.'

'Then why is an SS-Gruppenführer so keen to kill him?'

'Because he is a traitor. Tell him that being in England or America will not save his life. Our reach is long and we have the will.'

Wilde couldn't resist a grin and a shrug of the shoulders. 'Maybe you will get him, but I doubt it. Anyway, in the meantime your vile regime will have been exposed in all its foulness to the world. Enjoy your trip back to Berlin, Müller. I hope your Führer is pleased with your work. Does he usually reward failure?'

He gave the SS general another smile. Müller stared at him without emotion for a few moments, then looked away and slowly wound up the window. Wilde walked back around to the other side of the car, removed his revolver and fired two bullets, one into Müller's front off-side tyre, the other into the rear off-side tyre. He re-holstered the weapon and climbed back into the embassy car.

'Drive, Mr Bateman.'

Chapter 35

The airfield was fenced off and had a sentry post, but the embassy car was quickly waved through after a cursory examination of papers, and motored at a steady speed along the track towards the administration buildings. Wilde thanked Bateman and Ryder for their work and made his way to the door to the main building.

In the near distance, to the left, he saw that the Mosquito was still there, parked well away from other warplanes. Wilde checked his watch and saw that it was 7.10.

He found Harriet and Major Chas Oldman as they emerged from the officers' mess. This was a Swedish Air Force base. The Americans were allowed to use it on a case-by-case basis, covertly. No bombs, no machine guns, no records kept.

'Tom, you've made it.'

He smiled at her. 'I rather thought you'd have gone by now.' He nodded to the USAF officer. 'Morning, Chas.'

'Good to see you, Tom. You've cut it fine.'

'I'd call it being punctual.'

'The major has an idea,' Harriet said.

'Tell me about it, but first – where's Coburg?'

'He's in the Swedish Air Force sick bay, catching a little more sleep. But this idea . . . Chas believes it might be possible to get all of us home in one go.'

'Really?'

'Were you comfortable on the way here, Tom?' the pilot asked.

'It wasn't as bad as I expected once I had got over the alarming prospect that you might use me to bomb a submarine.'

'Well, I'm going to see if I can fit you and Harriet in the bomb bay this time. She's short, you're long. Neither of you is any great girth or weight. You can play sardines.'

Wilde looked at Harriet. 'Are you up for this?'

'It would be quite cosy. And Rudi would be better off up in the cockpit with the major.'

'OK, let's give it a go.'

With a bit of manoeuvring under the open bomb bay doors, they managed to fit in. They weren't exactly huddled together, but their close proximity lent an intimacy that Wilde was pretty sure Lydia would not like to know about.

He tried to think about other things. In particular, the feeling that even if they got Rudolf Coburg to England safe and alive, their problems were a long way from solved.

For one thing, Wilde was still a wanted man, chief suspect in the murder of Harriet's father, the Reverend Hartwell. She, too, was being hunted by someone who wanted her dead. He had many questions, but first there was the grave matter of Rudolf Coburg to be dealt with. Decisions had to be made about how to let the world hear his shattering, barely credible testimony that the Nazis were annihilating a whole race of people.

Major Oldman's voice came through their headphones. 'Time to take in a little oxygen, folks, we're approaching 11,000 feet and rising. I want to go a lot higher over Norway. Are you keeping warm down there?'

'Getting colder by the minute,' Harriet said to her microphone.

'Well, you'll both be warmer if you just snuggle up like bears in a snowhole.'

'I think he's scared of me, Chas. Doing his best not to touch me.'

'Man's a strange thing, Miss Hartwell. He'll walk into a hail of bullets, yet cower before a woman's welcoming arms. Anyway, you two take care. And for your information, the patient is holding up well.'

Wilde switched on his torch. He could see that Harriet was laughing at him. He laughed back.

The intercom crackled to life again. 'Two ME109s welcoming us to Norwegian airspace,' Oldman said casually. 'Let's see what Hermann's boys have got. My money's on the Mosquito. You folks want to stake a few dollars?'

'I think our lives are probably stake enough,' Harriet said.

'You keep us alive and I'll buy you a beer,' Wilde said.

'That's good enough for me. Turn up the oxygen and enjoy the ride.'

Nothing happened. The Mosquito continued to rise to over 30,000 feet and hold its westward course at 400 mph. Five minutes later, Oldman returned to the intercom. 'The Luftwaffe has given up and gone home. Should be plain sailing from here on to Norfolk. We're over the North Sea now, so I'll take the speed down a few notches to conserve fuel.'

Wilde killed his intercom and indicated for Harriet to do the same. She complied.

'So we're agreed that our first move is to get him to Grosvenor Street. We have the papers translated and we get him to annotate copies to explain exactly what is happening and the significance. From my brief look, I can see there's a rock-solid paper trail from the Reich Main Security Office to the death camps, with numbers, transport details, the whole kit and kaboodle. We will also extract a full and precise affidavit from

Herr Coburg detailing everything and everyone he saw at the Treblinka camp, as well as a run-down on the workings of his department. Names of staff, operating methods – and where the orders come from.'

'We have to get Rudi proper treatment before interrogating him.'

'His recuperation could take weeks. We can't wait that long.'

'But at the very least he needs a couple of days before the questioning begins.'

'Tell you what, we'll play it by ear. But then what? You and I have to return to the real world at some stage. That isn't going to be easy.'

She sighed. 'Oh, for God's sake, Tom, put your bloody arms around me. I'm freezing to death! I promise I won't bite and I won't say a word to your beautiful wife – or whatever she is.'

The Mosquito landed early in the afternoon. Half an hour out, Oldman had radioed instructions through to the base and a large Cadillac was waiting for them with a driver. Coburg was able to take up most of the back seat with his head on Harriet's lap. He remained silent on the long drive to London, except once when he screamed and then emitted a series of agonised groans. His eyes opened. 'I'm sorry, I was dreaming. I can't stop the dreams.'

Bill Phillips was in his office when they arrived at OSS headquarters in Grosvenor Street. With him were a doctor and nurse, both American and both attached to the embassy. A room had been set aside as a makeshift ward, with a metal-framed bed. Coburg was immediately made comfortable there while the medical team took readings of his vital functions and conducted a thorough examination.

'Well, Tom,' Phillips said, 'you and Miss Hartwell can stay here as you did before, or you can both come back to my apartment with me. The offices will be securely guarded as always and, in the event of an air raid, Coburg will be stretchered down to the shelter. Are you happy with all that?'

'Harriet?'

'He's got here alive, so I suppose he'll survive. A good night's sleep will do us all good. We'll come with you, Mr Phillips. But first we have to find out about Mimi . . .'

And Wilde had a phone call of his own to make, to home.

The call to Lydia did not go well. At times the distance between them seemed unbridgeable and he wondered about his own part in their problems. Was every relationship in Britain as troubled as this, with men going off to war, leaving wives and children at home? Would any marriage survive this insane conflagration? Perhaps it was inevitable that conflict between nations would always be accompanied by conflict on the domestic front.

He had to confess that she had not had an easy time of it herself. She told him she had had a visitor named Walter Quayle. 'Ghastly man with dandruff all over his shoulders – and his fingernails were a disgrace.'

'Yes, I know Walter Quayle. What exactly did he want?'

'He said he had things to discuss with you. I told him you weren't here. But he was more than a bit pushy, demanding to know your whereabouts. I took him for a secret service type.'

'Yes, I'm sure he is. Calls himself a civil servant, but he has Five written all over him. He accompanied me to the crash site in Caithness, then got himself into a bit of bother. Ignore him, darling. Tell him to piss off if he bothers you again. He's nothing.'

'That's all very well for you to say, Tom, but *you* know what's going on – and Johnny and I are stuck in the bloody dark. People come looking for you, the police want to interview you about a murder and I don't even know if you're in the bloody country.'

'I'm sorry.'

'And your bloody girlfriend? Is she with you?'

'Harriet Hartwell is here,' he said stiffly. 'And I suggest you don't take a blind bit of notice of what Eaton or anyone else has to say about her.'

'It's when you start denying things that we get worried. That's what men never understand, you see.'

'Well, what do you want me to say then?'

'Nothing. I want you to come home. Any idea when that might be?'

'Not too long, I hope.'

'Tomorrow? Next week? When the war's over? Nineteen fifty? What does "not too long" even mean?'

That was how they left it.

In the evening, Bill Phillips fed his guests good food and good wine. There were just the three of them, attended by Bill's house-keeper, who had done the cooking. After the port, Bill left Wilde and Harriet alone, apologising that he had to go off to his study to work on some cables. On his way out, he stopped momentar-ily. 'Just a cautionary word for you both. Those papers Coburg brought? In themselves, they prove almost nothing and will be denounced as forgeries. They have to be accompanied by a con-vincing narrative from Coburg. Likewise, his statement must be not only powerful but must accord with the paperwork in every detail. I have been in the world of diplomacy and politics long enough to know that one misstep, however minor, will be seized on.'

'The story will hold up,' Harriet said.

'Good. Well, make yourselves at home and I will see you both at breakfast.'

Alone together, candlelight flickered between them on the polished mahogany table.

'Mimi asked after you,' she said.

'That's kind of her.'

'She is recuperating well but she will have to take it easy, for she could suffer another heart attack at any time. The doctors prescribed no more smoking, no more alcohol, no more late nights at the Dada Club.' Harriet raised a sceptical eyebrow. 'As if any of that's going to happen.'

'It would be uncharacteristic.'

'By the way, she was told that she had been carried to the hospital by a man named Wilde. I think she's taken a shine to you. Her knight errant.'

Wilde smiled at the thought. The great Mimi Lalique, star of silver screen, taking a shine to an obscure history professor; it sounded like the fantasy of millions of men through the past three decades. 'But I'm already taken.'

'And that's your tragedy, isn't it, Tom? Mimi told me I was to hook my claws into you and not let you go. She said you were far too good a catch to be wasted on some dowdy provincial housewife.'

'One day you will meet Lydia Morris and you will discover that she is neither dowdy nor provincial. Nor even a housewife for that matter.'

'And that's *my* tragedy.'

Wilde badly wanted to change the subject. There were times in a man's life, however happy he might be with what awaited him at home, that he was in danger of falling. 'Have you ever heard of a man named Walter Quayle?' he said.

Harriet frowned. 'Of course I have. Why?'

'He was assigned to me up in Caithness. Now he has been visiting my home in Cambridge.'

'Walter was Peter's mentor. He's an Athel, an extraordinary scholar who went on to Trinity. Just missed Senior Wrangler in maths, then switched to classics. Double first.'

'Are we talking about the same man?'

'You tell me. Walter's easy enough to spot – he's as queer as a barking cat and makes no bones about it.'

'And I suppose he's MI5?'

'Oh yes. Just the sort they love there.'

'I must say his academic brilliance escaped me in the wilds of Scotland.'

'But not his queerness, eh?'

'No, he didn't try to conceal that.'

She ran a hand through her lustrous hair. 'When I said he was Peter's mentor, there was actually rather more to it than that. It was Walter who put a stop to Smoake's bullying and took Peter under his wing. Peter never said anything to me, but I felt that Quayle had some sort of Svengali-like hold over him. I loathe Walter Quayle,' she added. 'Always have.'

In the night, Wilde lay awake in the utter blackness in a comfortable bed in Bill Phillips's Mayfair apartment, his mind churning with impossible thoughts. A nightmare, a vision, a rational explanation of things unseen? His mind was racing. Perhaps he was wrong; perhaps Walter Quayle wasn't *nothing*.

The link to Peter Cazerove – how had he missed that? More importantly, what did it mean?

Wilde switched on the bedside light and glanced at his watch: 3.35 a.m. He had an idea in his head, fully formed from a thousand splintered nuggets of information, none of which seemed to make sense on their own. So what was it – rational deduction or commonplace paranoia?

He was thinking of the three senior intelligence officers with whom he had been dealing these past days – Philip Eaton, Walter Quayle and Lord Templeman, Richard to his friends. He knew now that Eaton and Quayle had both been at Trinity and he had a strong feeling that Templeman had been there too. They were all of an age and had all made their way into different branches of the secret service.

What else was there between them?

Of course, it was perfectly reasonable to assume that they were all working together for the good of their country in a time of war. That wasn't a conspiracy, it was joint enterprise for a common good.

In which case, what exactly were they trying to do? And if Quayle was linked to Peter Cazerove, why had the younger man taken his own life, ravaged with guilt over actions that seemed to have bugger all to do with the common good?

But there were inconsistencies. Someone had tortured and murdered Harriet's father, someone had ordered a violent raid on Mimi Lalique's Westminster home. And Wilde had been subjected to a drug-induced interrogation.

Each one of these events had but one aim: to find Harriet Hartwell.

But there were sharp differences between the three incidents. First, the murder of the Reverend Hartwell – by all accounts an unworldly, mild-mannered clerical gentleman – had been savage in the extreme. Second, the raid on Mimi's house had been brutally efficient. By contrast, the doped interrogation of Wilde had been rather tame.

They didn't sound as if they had all been ordered by the same person.

Chapter 36

Coburg was fully conscious and sitting up in bed, but he was still weak. He had already been through his evidence in painstaking detail, pressed hard by Wilde.

If all their efforts to get Coburg out of Sweden were to bear fruit, they had to be certain of his story. It had to be watertight. 'OK, Coburg, tell me again, what exactly was the purpose of your visit to this camp at the village of Treblinka?'

'I've been through this, Mr Wilde.'

'So what? I want to hear it.'

Coburg slumped against the pillows, his head lolling to one side. He was weakening fast.

'Come on.'

The German seemed to be asleep, but then opened his eyes and took one long, deep breath as though stiffening his resolve. 'Well, sir,' he said, 'we were invited to a weekend party at a grand hunting lodge nearby – a house that at one time must have belonged to Polish nobility. This weekend was said to be a special reward for all our efforts in Berlin and it was all organised by Müller.'

'Müller?'

'Heinrich Müller, chief of the Gestapo and one of my bosses in the RSHA. He said we were as important to the war effort as those fighting on the Eastern frontline and that we deserved to be honoured as such. But as I soon found out, there was a hidden motive. It was to implicate us, make us truly part of the gang. Until then – until I saw those people being marched naked to their deaths – I had no idea what was happening.'

'How could you have not known, Coburg? You were personally responsible for sending trainloads of men, women and children to this camp. What did you think would happen to them once they arrived? Did you think they were to be put up in a luxurious hotel with feather beds and room service?' Wilde did nothing to disguise the scepticism or disgust he felt.

'No,' Coburg said quietly and with something akin to contrition in his voice, 'no, I didn't think that.'

'These were innocent men, women and children, were they not? People living quiet, blameless lives who were torn mercilessly from their homes by you and your Nazi bully-boy comrades.' Wilde's voice was staccato, brutal. It had to be so. If Coburg was to be believed by the world's politicians and press, he was going to have to withstand hard and searching interrogation.

'I thought their accommodation would be basic but humane. I had visited Dachau before the war and that was reasonably well run. By this summer, however, things were different. A war was on, there were food shortages and Germany needed workers. They would be forced to work for us and then eventually they would be re-settled further to the east.'

'So you thought they were to be used as slave labour?'

'Those are harsh words, but yes.'

'Would you call yourself a gullible man, Coburg?'

'It seems I was fooled, so yes, I must confess that I am gullible.'

'Who else was there at this delightful house party?'

'I have already given you the names.'

'Well, give them to me again.'

Harriet put a pale hand on Wilde's sleeve. 'Tom, don't push him too hard, he's still unwell.'

Coburg shook his head. 'It's all right, Harriet, I have to go through this. I understand. Well, of course there was Müller himself, Adolf Eichmann, my line manager at Referat IV B4 whom I have told you about.' He continued to name all those he remembered from the various departments within the RSHA and other ministries. 'There were also a few others, whose names I did not know.'

'And at the camp, who was there?'

'The commandant, Obersturmführer Eberl. I knew his name from the transport directives, but I had never met him before. I know from files that in civilian life he was a physician and then became involved in Aktion T4 in which the useless mouths – the feeble-minded and infirm – were gassed.'

Wilde felt bile rising up in his throat. 'That's what you called sick people – useless mouths?'

'Yes, again it sounds harsh. But with desperate food shortages, it was not seen as rational to provide food for those who could contribute nothing.'

You revolt me, Coburg. He did not say the words, but there would be others who would not hold back. 'Carry on.'

'You want to know more about Eberl? Well, I know he had been at another camp, Chelmno, but I have no knowledge of what went on there.'

'Was that, too, a death camp?

'Almost certainly. It fits in with what I know of Eberl. In Aktion T4 his job was to kill people by carbon monoxide, and that was what he later did at Treblinka, so one might assume he was involved in similar practices at Chelmno.'

'Describe him.'

Coburg thought a moment, then laughed. 'You know, it is funny. He has a little moustache like the Führer or Charlie

Chaplin. I think perhaps he thought it would help his career.'

'I don't think there's anything to laugh about,' Wilde said, his voice sharp.

'I'm sorry, forgive me.'

'If you laugh when you are talking to journalists or Western politicians or, later, when you give testimony in court, you will be thought cruelly insensitive or false and it will damage our case.'

'I understand.'

Harriet took Wilde by the arms. He was sitting on a wooden chair beside Coburg's bed in the OSS office. 'Tom, that's enough now. You've been at him for three hours. Let him have a break. Apart from anything else, I need a break. An hour or so to clear our heads. Can't we get some fresh air – perhaps visit Mimi? It would be a pleasant walk from here to the hospital.'

Wilde took a deep breath. He didn't want to let Coburg off the hook. He despised the man and wanted to torture him with words. But he took Harriet's point. He looked at his watch and saw it was noon. 'OK,' he said. 'Break now. You can have some lunch, Coburg, and we'll be back with you at 1.30. Later, I will require you to write a full account of your experiences, both within the RSHA and also at your weekend house party, which you will sign before a notary. I want you to write it both in English and German so that there is no confusion or incon-sistency in translation.'

'Yes, I will do that.'

'It will be checked by a translator, so make it accurate. Do not deviate from the truth in the slightest way. In the mean-time, some lunch will be brought to you.'

'Thank you. And, sir, may I ask you – am I safe here?'

'Yes.'

'But what will become of me? How will you protect me from the Athels?'

'Why do you think they would want to hurt you?' Wilde said.

'Because my testimony is damaging to Germany and the Athels see Hitler as a better option than Stalin. Ask Harriet here – she knows the way they think. The Nazis are more likely to maintain Europe's class structure, or so the Athels believe.'

'But why the Athels? Do you have some evidence?'

'Peter Cazerove. He was an Athel. Harriet trusted him. The question is, who did he tell? Because someone from England must have passed information on to Müller.'

Perhaps he was right, but that was not Wilde's most pressing problem. 'Think it through, Coburg, you're in danger whether you testify or not, so I can't promise you protection.'

'I am a dead man.'

'Well, this is war, and many people lay their lives on the line.'

'Yes, yes, of course. I understand.'

'Good. Well, I despise what you have done, Coburg. But you are doing the right thing now – so you may yet find redemption.'

'I pray it is so.'

Wilde and Harriet got up from their chairs and made for the door.

'Before you go, Mr Wilde . . .'

They turned back towards Coburg. 'Yes?' Wilde said.

'There was something else I wanted to say, something that has been troubling me, for I have been doubting myself, doubting that I truly saw what I saw. But in describing Eberl just now it all came back to me, and now I am certain.'

'Go on.'

'There was someone else, you see, someone else at the camp.'

'What do you mean?'

'Well, two people to be precise.'

'Guards?'

'No, no, they were visitors like us, but not from our house party. They arrived separately – a few minutes after us – and left before us. One of them was immensely tall, an SS officer. But it was the one at his side, just a little to the rear in fact, who caught my eye. He was wearing his greatcoat, which was a surprise seeing that it was a warm summer's evening, and he had his collar up and his cap firmly down across his brow. His face was in darkness, until one of the floodlights swivelled through an arc and lit up his face, just for a moment.'

'You recognised this man?'

Coburg nodded his head. 'Yes, it was Adolf Hitler, I am certain of it.'

They knew it was foolish to go outside, but they both needed proper fresh air. It felt to them as if they had been crawling through a sewer full of rats all morning. A walk, a little walk in the sunshine was a risk they had to take.

As they strolled through St James's Park, Tom Wilde and Harriet Hartwell were deep in their own thoughts. It was a warm, hazy, late-summer day. The park was not what it once was, what with bomb craters and the overgrown, untended lawns and beds, but at least the birds were still singing and the Luftwaffe had other things to do than bomb London with the frequency it had employed during the Blitz.

Wilde broke the silence. 'Do you believe him?'

'About Hitler? I'm not sure. Do you?'

'Well, I would guess Hitler's Eastern headquarters could be nearby. It's clear to us that his wolf's lair is somewhere in East Prussia, so it could be within an hour or two of Treblinka. Even quicker by air, perhaps. Close enough for a short visit.'

'Why, though?' she asked.

'To see whether his murderous orders were being carried out to the letter?'

'Perhaps he just likes seeing people being killed.'

'God, what a vile thought, but I wouldn't put it past him. It's just a damn shame Coburg didn't get closer to him, or talk to him or find some hard evidence that he was there, because that would put Hitler right at the heart of the murders. The thing is, Harriet, any extra bit of information about the Führer's presence would be gold dust to our cause.'

'I'll work on him, Tom. Let me take over this afternoon. It's astonishing what people can discover they remember when they're asked nicely by a pretty young woman. Information hidden deep in the recesses of the mind.'

'Is that something you do in your line of work, Miss Civil Service Secretary? Interrogate captured Germans? Lure them to their doom with sweet smiles and soft words?'

She didn't have time to answer. They were just passing the base of a huge anti-aircraft gun, its snout poking aloft, when the attack came.

A man with a knife was moving in from the side, his long blade glinting in the noonday sun. Wilde saw it early and reacted instantly. He pushed Harriet aside and, in the same fluid movement, aimed his right fist full-blooded to the side of the man's head. The blade was coming up but Wilde was already fending it off, his left forearm cracking into the man's wrist.

The punch to the head was too hard to withstand. It connected with undiluted force. The assailant buckled and his knees crumpled, but his hand still gripped the knife.

As the attacker fell, his knife hand went down, blade first into the hard earth, trying to steady himself. The heel of Wilde's left shoe followed the hand, crunching down on the knuckles and forcing the weapon to spin away. The man let out a sickening cry of pain as finger bones snapped. Wilde descended with both knees into the man's chest and saw his face for the first time. 'You!' He hit him again, in the side of the head, then reached out for the buried knife and held the sharp edge to his throat. 'I should do for you now.'

Wilde turned to Harriet, to tell her that this was the bastard who had killed her father.

But she wasn't there.

Yet again, she had vanished.

The captive was struggling. Wilde let the knife cut a fraction into the man's throat. 'Who sent you? Who's paying you to do this.'

'My hand, you've broken my hand.'

'That's nothing. I'll slit your throat, so you know how it feels. Shall I do that?'

'Fuck you.'

A constable was approaching, ambling along on his beat. He stopped suddenly, trying to compute what he was seeing. Instinct and training kicked in. He pushed his service whistle between his lips and blew – hard and long. Then he moved forward with authority. He had dealt with fights many times before. This one held no terrors for him.

The police officer was with Wilde now, truncheon raised to strike. 'I suggest you remove that weapon from the man's throat, sunshine.'

'This man is a murderer, officer. He has killed at least one other person and he tried to kill us. If I release him now, he will run.'

The officer wasn't large, but he was fearless. He obviously had no idea which was the more dangerous of the two men he was confronting. 'Drop the knife. You're both nicked.'

Wilde noticed the look of relief on the officer's face as two fellow officers came running towards them in answer to the whistle. He threw the knife away, well out of reach of Mortimer's undamaged hand.

'I have a United States diplomatic passport so you have no authority to hold me,' Wilde said. 'But I am willing, of my own volition, to help you with your inquiries.' The time had finally come when he had to use his immunity.

He was in an office on the third floor of Scotland Yard, in the presence of a uniformed inspector named Alfred Foat.

'Do you have the passport with you, Mr Wilde?'

'*Professor* Wilde.' He didn't normally insist on his title being used, but in this case when he was trying to establish his innocence and credentials as a man of reputation, it seemed appropriate. 'My passport is presently at the OSS offices. I am a professor of history at Cambridge University, but I have recently taken on a new role with the diplomatic mission in Grosvenor Street. You can confirm that with Ambassador Winant or Mr William Phillips.'

Foat had papers on his desk. He picked one up. 'There has been a warrant out for your arrest, accused of committing murder in Suffolk.'

'Has been?'

'It has been rescinded. It seems you are no longer a suspect. This present incident, however, is a different matter altogether.

The constable says you had a man pinned to the ground and were holding a knife to his throat.'

'That man attacked *me*. I overpowered him.'

'So you say.'

'I also say that the man I tackled is named Mortimer and that he should be your chief suspect in the murder of the Reverend Hartwell in his home at Clade, Suffolk.'

'Indeed, and what is your evidence for this assertion?'

'I was at Clade at the time of the murder – and I saw Mortimer escaping on a motorbike.' Wilde sighed deeply; this was utterly pointless. 'I'm afraid these are matters well beyond your remit, Inspector Foat. We're both wasting our time here.'

Foat ignored him. 'You've told me you were with someone else, a woman. Tell me, where is this lady friend of yours? The constable says he saw no woman.'

'She ran because she was scared. She was the knifeman's target. The murder victim in Suffolk was her father, the Reverend Hartwell.' Wilde stopped; he had had enough. 'Look, inspector, this is a matter for the secret intelligence service. Miss Hartwell is a British agent. All you need to do is keep the man Mortimer – if that is his true name – under lock and key on a charge of attempted murder or attempted grievous bodily harm, then call in Special Branch or MI5. They will take over from you.'

'The problem, you see, is that we have no evidence on which to hold Mr Ned Mortimer.'

'No evidence! He came at us with a knife.'

'He says *you* attacked *him*. His right hand is broken and he is presently being treated. The constable says he saw you holding a knife to Mr Mortimer's throat. Unless you can find evidence to corroborate your story, what am I to do?'

'Find evidence – and find it quickly. That's your job. Perhaps you'd like me to give you a couple of telephone numbers? There are others who know the full story.'

'That won't be necessary.'

'Then let me question Mortimer myself. I want to know who he's working for.'

'And that certainly won't be possible. This is a police matter.'

Wilde rose from the hardbacked chair that had been placed for him in front of the inspector's broad desk. 'Then if you don't mind, I will take my leave of you now.'

'No, you have to wait until your claim for diplomatic immunity is confirmed with the embassy.' The inspector offered Wilde a cigarette from a rather fine wooden box. Wilde declined. 'And there is another thing, Professor Wilde. We are expecting someone else with an interest in this affair . . .'

There was a sharp rap at the door.

'Ah,' the inspector said. 'That must be him now.'

Chapter 37

Walter Quayle slid in. Wilde noted the blue-yellow remnants of bruising on his face and he saw, too, that the shape of his nose had been substantially altered – flattened – by the young fisherman's punch.

'Thank you, inspector,' Quayle said. 'Perhaps you'd leave us alone for a while. I'll call you in if you're needed.'

'Yes, sir,' the police officer said with a crisp salute. Without another word he vacated his seat behind the desk, and Quayle took his place.

Once the door was closed behind the departing policeman, Quayle smiled wearily. 'Well, well, professor, this is a fine mess you've got yourself into.'

Wilde wanted to brush the dandruff from Quayle's shoulders. Was it his imagination, or did the Englishman stink of liquor and stale sweat? 'You don't look too good yourself, Quayle. Ribs healing OK, are they?'

'This isn't about me, Wilde. This is about murder, assisting a fugitive and various other matters. I have information about your recent movements – disturbing information. God in heaven, man, what are you up to? I thought you were on our side, for pity's sake.'

Wilde laughed at the man's temerity. 'I think you're the one who owes *me* some explanations, don't you?'

'I'm not sure I do. I treated you with great courtesy in Scotland. Took you everywhere you wished to go. But as it turned out, you had ideas of your own. To be frank, you lied when you said you were up there to pay tribute to the Duke on behalf of the American president and people.'

'And you lied about everything else, Quayle. Direction of the flight? Number of survivors?'

'Ah yes, where is the delightful Miss Hartwell? We still wish to talk to her.'

'Is that why you're here?' Wilde laughed again. 'I can tell you with all honesty that right at this moment I haven't the faintest idea where she is.'

'Then I have no more use for you.'

'So I can go?'

'Of course, Wilde. You're a free agent.'

'And the man I caught, Ned Mortimer – what will happen to him?'

'Oh, don't worry, we'll get plenty of evidence against him and he'll be put away for a very long time. Deserves to swing, if you ask me – but the lawyers will probably try to save his scrawny neck.'

'He must have been working for someone, surely?'

Quayle smiled. 'Of course – and we'll get it out of him. I'll keep you in the loop, Wilde, never fear. By the way, I thought you might like an update on our half-witted shepherd boy in Caithness.'

'You mean Gregor McGregor?'

'Indeed. Well, it seems he's had a bit of good news. I'm told he's been offered a job as apprentice stalker on a neighbouring estate, complete with accommodation. Who knows, it might be the making of the boy.'

'I'm glad.' Anything that got the poor lad away from his mother had to be a good thing. 'Thank you, Quayle. And before I go, I'll make a statement to the police about what I witnessed at Clade, to help the prosecution on its way.'

'That would be perfectly admirable.'

'There was another matter from Scotland, Quayle ... why didn't you mention your friendship with Peter Cazerove?'

Quayle looked puzzled. 'Why would I have?'

Wilde thought she might have run back to the OSS bureau, but she wasn't there. Phillips was, however, and he wasn't happy. 'Had the bloody British burning up the phone wires again, Tom. What in God's name have you been doing now? And what have you done with your lady friend?'

Wilde told the full story, then glanced up at the wall clock. He had been stuck at the police headquarters for four hours. 'You still haven't told me about communication with Churchill. Has he agreed to meet Coburg?'

'He's really not that keen, Tom. I'm sorry.'

'But he can be persuaded, yes? The combined skills of you, John Winant and FDR should see to that.'

Phillips looked embarrassed. 'I don't think it's going to happen. His office has made it clear he doesn't want to meet any Germans. They asked us to send him one sheet outlining Coburg's testimony, typed and double-spaced, not more than 300 words.'

'That's preposterous!'

'But that's the way it's going to be. So finish your interrogation, write up your 300 words, keeping every detail possible, and we'll take it from there.'

'What about the suggestion that Hitler was there, at the murder camp?'

'You need something solid to back it up. The problem is the Hitler thing makes it all less believable, not more. It sounds like the ravings of a desperate man – which does seem to sum up Coburg, I'm afraid.'

'Well, I believed him.'

'I know you did, Tom. I know – and history might prove you right. But it's a risk we can't take on such slender evidence.'

'OK, I'll push him.'

'I'm sure you're aware that Coburg can't stay here indefinitely. We have to find a better place for the bastard.'

'I'll put my mind to it. And by the way, I take it you managed to get me removed from the wanted list of the British police. Thank you.'

'It wasn't easy.'

For the rest of the afternoon, he continued his grilling of Coburg, particularly his assertion that he had seen Hitler at the death camp, but he got no further and turned his mind to writing his allotted 300 words, adding details of the accompanying documents to back up the German's statement.

For a lot of the time, Wilde's mind was elsewhere. He needed to find Harriet. Would she be with Dolby up at Clade? Somehow he doubted it, now that she had been traced there once already. Where then? Perhaps Mimi Lalique would know.

He handed the Churchill memo over to Phillips, then said, 'I'm heading out for the rest of the day.'

'Going home to Lydia.'

'Not just yet.'

His Rudge was parked in the embassy compound. Fuel supplies were freely available for diplomatic staff and he filled it to the lip, then rode out towards the hospital. Mimi wasn't there.

'She was released this afternoon,' the receptionist said.

'Did she say where she was going? Surely she couldn't go home alone?'

'She was with a young lady in a taxi. I'm afraid I can't tell you more than that.'

Wilde gave the receptionist one of his most engaging smiles. 'What was her name, this young lady?'

The woman consulted the register. 'Curtis, sir. Miss T. Curtis.'

'Can you remember what she looked like?'

'Why yes, sir, she was extremely tall.' She hesitated as though about to add something, but not certain whether it was the correct thing to do.

'And? Can you tell me any more?' Wilde was already sure they were not talking about Harriet; no one would describe her as tall.

'Well, it's not really for me to say, but if you really want my opinion I thought she was rather overdressed . . .'

'Tarty?'

The receptionist looked shocked. 'That's not a word I would use, Mr Wilde.' But then she smiled sheepishly. 'But yes.'

'Was there any clue as to their destination?'

'I'm sorry, sir, I've told you all I know.'

'Thank you. You've been most helpful.'

He rode to Westminster, to Mimi's home, but he wasn't surprised to discover that she wasn't there. The door was still hanging open, the lock broken. He wandered through the building and saw that it hadn't been touched since the raid. The smell of dog turds was less intense than it had been. The two Pekingese had gone, hopefully removed to a dog pound somewhere. God, what a damned mess. One way or another, he would have to get someone to come and clear the place up before Mimi came home.

For the present, he had another idea. It was dark and his watch told him it was eight in the evening. Wilde wanted a drink and he knew just the place to get it.

'Well, well, it's the professor!'

Tallulah held the Dada Club door wide for Wilde and let him into the lobby. It seemed there was even more rubble outside than the last time he was here.

'We've been bombed again,' the tall hat-check girl said, as if reading his mind. 'Nothing too serious, thank the Lord. Now then, you look in need of alcohol. You can see yourself down to the bar. Hardly anyone in yet, but you'll probably find a friendly face to help you pass the time. Someone for every taste in the Dada, darling.'

'Actually, I was looking for you. No, that's not quite true – I'm looking for Mimi.'

'Dear, darling Mimi. What an awful time she's had lately.'

'Is she here?'

Tallulah shook her head. 'I'm sorry, professor.'

'But you know where she is, don't you? You picked her up at the hospital.'

'Did I?'

He held up a five-pound note.

Tallulah laughed. 'Do you think I'd betray Mimi Lalique for a fiver? Or any other sum for that matter . . .'

'No,' he said. 'But I'm sure you know I'm her friend. Harriet's, too. Are they together somewhere, by any chance?'

'Gosh, you are the detective today, aren't you? I'm sorry, professor, I'm teasing you.' She cupped her hand and lowered her voice, speaking directly into his ear. 'Yes, of course I know where they are – and I'll take you to them. But not yet. Go and get yourself a drink. And you can put your money away. You saved Mimi's life and it's on the house. Chef will rustle you up some supper if you want.'

'I can't really hang about.'

'You'll have to because I'm in charge here tonight. Anyway, we're not going until whoever is following you is safely tucked up in bed. Have you got transport?'

'My motorbike.'

'Oh, good. I love a motorbike.'

Wilde realised he had no option but to wait. He was hungry, not having eaten since breakfast, and happily accepted the chef's offer of veal and mushroom in a cream sauce, with peas and rice on the side. Wilde wolfed it down gratefully, but sipped his Scotch slowly. Tallulah wouldn't tell him where she was taking him, but he had the feeling it would be a long night. Important to keep his wits about him.

He didn't try to engage anyone in conversation, but he watched the other customers with fascination. This was another world, where lavishly attired homosexuals, both male and female, consorted in open defiance of the laws of the land. In his experience, Cambridge was already quite progressive and easy-going in such matters, but rarely so flamboyant as some of the Dada's clientele.

There were others, too, army and navy officers looking for a warm female body for the night, using the persuasive – and frequently successful – plea that they were about to be posted and might be dead before the week's end, so the least a girl could do was give them a decent send-off. If the man was expected to lay down his body for England, why not the woman?

Some of the revellers were semi-famous film actors. Wilde had seen them in the movies, but he couldn't name them. The hours passed in a haze of people-watching.

'Come on, professor. Time to go.'

He turned to see Tallulah beckoning him. She had changed into a pair of corduroy trousers and had a man's leather jacket pulled tight about her long, bony frame. Clearly not the clothes she had worn when she collected Mimi from the hospital.

'Are you finished?'

'Terry behind the bar will see the stragglers out and lock up.'

'Where are we going?'

'Not far. Just do a few loops to make sure we're not followed, then I'll direct you.'

They knew there was every chance the club was being watched, but Wilde was confident he could lose anyone on the Rudge. He rode around Soho, Mayfair, Covent Garden and the City, through into Whitechapel. It was slow going in the unlit streets, windows all blacked out, but at least the sky was clear and there was a gibbous moon. When he saw narrow passageways or back alleys that cars could not possibly get through, he took them. Sometimes he waited at the far end of short lanes to see if any motorbikes came after them.

'Now then,' Tallulah shouted into his ear from the pillion seat, 'I think we're in the clear. Head south across Tower Bridge into Bermondsey, then Elephant and Castle.'

Wilde stopped and turned around. 'I've heard of these places, but I don't know them. Just shout left, right or straight ahead into my ear.'

'OK, darling. I suppose this is all a bit rough and slummy for a toff like you.'

Wilde couldn't help laughing and rode on, following her instructions as they wound their way through the poorer quarters of south London, past many bombed-out houses, piles of shrapnel and rubble, all the time going westward. They passed a large area of open common with yet more anti-aircraft guns and a barrage balloon base. The roads were largely deserted, and the whole area was hauntingly quiet, as though the world was waiting for something.

A tap on the shoulder. 'Here we are, professor.'

He pulled into the kerb and allowed the engine to keep running. They were outside a semi-detached Victorian house in a long, straight row of terraced and semi-detached properties that seemed to have escaped the bombing. They looked as though they had been built for middle-class city workers at the end of the last century, but now they had an air of poverty, neglect and decay, even without the war.

'Is this a good place to park? My registration number will be known. Any beat bobby will have it listed.'

'Oh, you don't have to worry about the police around here. They have far more to do catching looters, black-marketeers and would-be gangsters than fugitive professors. But you'll probably have your wheels nicked by the local lads – so why not park her out of sight down the side of the house?'

'Who lives here?' he asked as he switched off the engine and wheeled the bike across the pavement.

'I do. Come on in, darling.'

The house was no less tatty inside than out. Drab wallpaper, stained by tobacco smoke and areas of damp, welcomed them to the hallway. The staircase directly ahead had bare boards, no runner.

'Pretty, isn't it, prof?'

'I'm sure it has its charms.'

'I was bombed out of my flat in Soho. This was my nan's place. She left it to me in her will, God bless her. One day, when the bloody war's over, I'll do it up. Doesn't seem worth it until Hitler's gone the way of all flesh.'

'Of course.'

'Anyway, come into the kitchen. It's the only cosy room there is, I'm afraid.'

Wilde followed her to the back of the house.

She opened the kitchen door with a grin. 'Hey presto!'

Harriet was sitting at the kitchen table with a tumbler in front of her and brandy decanter at the side. 'Well, well,' she said.

'Harriet Hartwell, I presume.'

'Can't get rid of you, can I?'

'And Mimi?'

'In the front room,' Tallulah said. 'We brought a couple of mattresses down and made up a bed for her. Didn't think it was wise to make the poor darling struggle upstairs in her condition.'

'How is she?'

'Not well,' Tallulah continued. 'Not well at all, but there was nothing more the quacks could do for her, so I thought I'd rather look after her myself. She's desperate to get her Pekingese back. The poor dear howls for the horrid little things. I suppose someone must be looking after them, perhaps a neighbour.'

Wilde turned to Harriet. 'I thought you'd phone me.'

'Oh, I knew you'd find me.'

'She insisted you'd show up at the Dada,' Tallulah said. 'Didn't trust your phone line.'

'Anyway, we can talk about all that later,' Harriet said, brisk as ever as she reached for the brandy and poured herself another shot. 'First I want to know what's happened. Has Phillips contacted Churchill?'

'I'm sorry, it's no go.' Wilde shrugged his disappointment. 'Not yet anyway. He says he won't meet a German.'

'What do you mean?'

'Just what I say. He said he'll read a 300-word testimony and that's it. And so that's what I've done. Ambassador Winant is getting it to him and we should have an answer tomorrow.' He glanced at his watch. 'Or later today, of course. Anyway, I wouldn't get your hopes up because I have grave doubts that it will be taken any further.'

'He'll look at the Nazi documents, though?'

Wilde shrugged. 'I can't say.'

'Tom, this is a disgrace. Has he even been told what Rudi saw? Does he know that Hitler was there?'

Wilde reached for the decanter himself. He hadn't drunk much at the Dada but suddenly he needed a livener.

'Tom? Answer me, for pity's sake.'

Wilde took a swig from the decanter. The Cognac burnt his throat and he gasped. 'OK, now don't fly off the handle, but Bill and I had a disagreement. He thinks that mention of Hitler being there wouldn't help our cause in the first instance. He says it makes the story less believable, more like the ravings of a desperate man. Those were his very words, I think.'

'That's outrageous.'

'Go easy on him. He's a diplomat. He knows the best way to frame reports, how to get things done.'

'Bullshit. We have to do something.'

'We have done something. We've brought Coburg to England. One way or another his testimony will come out. We just need a little patience.'

'Patience be damned. We're being blocked by someone close to Churchill.'

Chapter 38

Wilde was worried. 'How sure are you that you can't be traced back to this house?'

'Impossible,' Tallulah said.

'But you are linked to the club – and so is Mimi. They must know that. I've even seen Lord Templeman's photograph on the wall.'

There was a brief lull. Was it his imagination or did a knowing glance pass between Harriet and Tallulah? 'Did I say something?'

'Oh, it's nothing,' Tallulah said. 'Just a little in-joke. The thing is, you see, apart from Mimi no one at the Dada knows my real name – which happens to be Matilda Calderwood if you're even vaguely interested. Tilly Calderwood to my family. And the only address I ever used is now rubble. I still pick up my mail at the shop next door, and my ration book is still tied to that address. Don't worry, professor.'

'It's my job to worry. Worrying might just keep us alive. For the moment, I'm leaving you.'

'To do what?' Harriet did not seem happy.

'You want this story out there in the world? I'm going to do what I can.'

'Yes, but where are you going? Wherever it is, I'm coming with you.'

'You're still at risk. You have said yourself that the Athels are everywhere. They killed your father ... they tried to kill you.'

'And you, too, Tom. So we're both in danger. Well, I'm not hanging around here kicking my heels.'

Wilde was about to say something else, but Harriet was already putting on one of Tallulah's oversize jackets and it seemed pointless to argue.

The air in the newsroom was thick with the stench of tobacco smoke and sweat, and desks were covered with the detritus of the evening's efforts – early editions, discarded copy paper, over-flowing ashtrays and stained mugs. It had been a hard night for Ron Christie, but every night was like that these days. The Blitz might be history, but the war was balanced on a knife edge on all fronts. News came from every continent, and too much of it was bad.

As night editor, he had to take split-second decisions on the value of new copy long after the editor had gone off to some dinner party with the great and the good. In peacetime, the night editor's decisions were tough enough, but with the war-time scarcity of newsprint, it was a great deal more difficult, for the paper was down to four tightly packed broadsheet pages, including advertisements. For a story to get in, an important one might have to be dropped or, at the very least, cut to one or two short paragraphs.

But eventually the last edition was out. Normally he would slump back and enjoy the company of the late men over a glass or two of whisky or a cup of tea before making his way home to the warmth of the marital bed in Dulwich. Tonight, though, Tom Wilde was here again, in the company of a young woman, and he had parked them in the conference room to wait for him.

He stretched his arms and yawned, then said a few good-nights to the departing subs and joined his visitors. 'Sorry to keep you waiting, Tom. Bit of a panic on,' he said.

'Don't worry. And I'm sorry to be such a bloody nuisance again.'

'That's what friends are for, or so I'm told. Anyway, perhaps you'd introduce me.'

'Yes, this is Harriet Hartwell. Harriet, my old friend Ron Christie.'

They shook hands.

Christie narrowed his gaze. 'I recognise you, don't I? You're the girl in the picture at the Dada Club.'

'Got it in one, Ron,' Wilde said.

'Well, well, so you found her. Are you going to tell me what this is all about? You know you didn't even give me a clue when you were here before.'

'For the moment, there's a great deal I can't tell you.'

Before leaving the house, they had discussed in detail how they were going to play this. There would be no mention of the Duke of Kent or his flight to Sweden, and certainly no mention of the Stockholm meeting or Harriet's part in it. 'Whatever Templeman or Eaton may have told you about me, Tom, I can promise you I am not going to spill the beans about Georgie's mission. Believe it or not, I am a loyal Englishwoman.' And so the focus would be on Coburg and the story he had to tell, but without naming him at present. How much would have to come out about the way he came to England would be decided at a later date.

'That's not a very encouraging start,' Christie said.

'Please,' Harriet said. 'Just listen, then make up your mind. Many lives are at stake here.'

Wilde cut in. Once again, Harriet was not helping her cause by her imperious tone. 'What I can tell you is that we have a story that we want you to publish,' Wilde said.

'Well, the paper always likes a story. That's why we're here. Something to do with the Dada Club, is it?'

'No, it's a bit darker than that.' He exchanged glances with Harriet. 'I'll tell it.'

Christie listened without saying a word. When the testimony was complete, there was a full minute's silence. Then Christie said, simply, 'And the provenance of this story?'

'Trust me, Ron, it's true. This comes from a German who has defected and is now in Britain. He is a hunted man, though, and for the moment, I can't tell you exactly who he is – or where he is. I beg you to understand.'

Christie had been lounging against a noticeboard. Now he took a seat on the other side of the conference table, dug a crumpled cigarette packet from his shirt pocket, removed the last cigarette, and tossed the empty pack in the bin. Then he lit up. 'I'm sorry, it's my last one. Came in with two packets, now they're all gone.'

'I don't smoke,' Harriet said.

'Look,' Christie said, as calmly as always, 'do you not see the problem with this from a newspaper's point of view? If – and this is a big if – we were to publish a story like this, we would also have to publish its provenance. Without names, dates, pictures, the whole shebang, the story would be utterly worthless.'

'So tell me exactly what else you need from us so that we can discuss it and work out what's to be done.'

'I don't want anything from you. I'm only the night editor of this paper. You have to get a story like this past the editor himself and, in this case, the proprietor, too. They are the big cheeses. Then there are the Ministry of Information men. Decisions like this are not taken by the likes of me.'

'Are you saying this would have to get past the censors?'

'Of course, Tom – there's a war on. Don't be naïve.'

'But thousands – hundreds of thousands – of innocent people are being murdered every day,' Harriet said. 'Don't you understand?'

Christie saw the tears streaming down her cheeks. He thought of his own son out in Libya, putting his own life on the line to fight the wretched Nazi criminals, and his heart went out to her. 'Yes, of course I understand. And for what it's worth, I believe every word you two have told me. But it's not worth a light without the say-so of others a great deal more powerful than myself. You have to take this story to the government, perhaps even Churchill himself.'

He saw his two visitors looking at each other helplessly.

'This just brings us full circle, Ron,' Wilde said.

'I'm sorry, truly I am – but I'm trying to be honest with you. Look, Tom, Miss Hartwell, I'm not saying what you ask is impossible. I can certainly fix up a meeting between you and the editor, but he *will* demand every detail of how you got this story and he *will* want access to your source – and even then he will not make the decision alone.'

'Let us think about it,' Wilde said.

'What school did your editor go to?' Harriet's question came out of nowhere.

Christie's face betrayed his bewilderment. 'What an extraordinary question.'

'Well?'

'As a matter of fact I happen to know that Mack went to Athelstans, though God knows what that has to do with anything.'

'And you, Mr Christie?'

'I'm a grammar school boy.' He turned to Wilde. 'Tom, what is this?'

Wilde shrugged helplessly.

Harriet was already turning away. 'Oh, Tom, it's hopeless, don't you see? The Athels . . . they'll never let this happen.'

As they prepared to mount the Rudge in front of the dark Fleet Street building, Wilde found himself wanting to put an arm around her and comfort her, but knew it was a bad idea. Then, just as he stepped away from her, she fell into his arms, sobbing like a child. He stroked her hair and held her tight, just as a father might do with a distraught daughter.

'I have one more idea,' he said quietly. 'It's a long shot, but it has to be worth a try.'

Chapter 39

Wilde dropped her at the OSS bureau. He refused point-blank to tell her what he planned, and he was adamant that he would do it alone. 'It's too dangerous for you, Harriet. Look what happened when we let our guard down and walked together through St James's Park. Remember what they did to your father.'

'Then at least take me back to Tallulah and Mimi.'

'You really want to do that? Your very presence there puts them in mortal danger.'

'But the OSS office was being watched before – we were followed and attacked.'

'A mistake we won't make again,' he said. 'Anyway, I want you to stay here and work your magic on Coburg. See if he has any more recollections of Hitler – something that would really place him at the murder camp.'

Sullenly she accepted his judgement.

Now it was deep into the chilly hours before dawn and he was on the road west out of London.

He was too early for what he wanted to do, so he stopped in a layby and waited, huddling into his summer jacket. The nights were getting cooler and he wasn't dressed for this. At dawn he rode on until he found a workman's cafe and bought himself some breakfast. He took his time over it and drank several cups of tea. At nine, he paid the bill and rode on towards the large village of Iver, then turned northwards until he came to a gate at the end of a lane, where he was stopped by the raised hand of a liveried servant.

The house was called Coppins. He knew about the place from his discussions with Bill Phillips. Apparently, John

Winant had been here after the plane crash to pay his respects and offer his condolences. Wilde had no idea how he would be received, but what was the worst that could happen? If he was slung out without a hearing, then so be it. At least he would have tried.

'Can I help you?' the gateman said, eyeing him up and down with a complete absence of respect.

'Message for the Duchess,' Wilde said, exaggerating his American accent. 'From the United States embassy.'

'American, eh? That explains everything.'

Wilde had no idea what he meant. Some obscure prejudice, he supposed. He took out his diplomatic passport and presented it to the man.

The man looked at it with uncomprehending eyes, then handed it back. 'All right,' he said, 'give me the message. I'll make sure she gets it.'

'I have to hand it to her in person. Ambassador's orders.'

'Is that so?'

'Yes, sir. I'm told it's a wired message from President Roosevelt himself.'

The gateman hesitated, then shrugged. Everyone had heard of Roosevelt, because he was Britain's best friend these days. 'Better go on through then, hadn't you?'

Wilde rode slowly up the curving driveway, past pristine lawns and glorious cedars. Even in the midst of war, there were gardeners at work.

The house loomed out of a backdrop of woodland. It was wide-fronted with high chimneys and clearly had not been intended for a royal palace. It looked Victorian, a comfortable country house, perhaps originally the home of a well-to-do gentleman farmer. Now it was substantially improved and enlarged and was the home of the widowed Duchess of Kent and her three children and their staff.

This was the difficult bit.

A Daimler and an open-topped sports car were parked on the forecourt. Wilde drew up directly in front of the main door, switched off the engine of his motorbike and dismounted. He imagined there must be a tradesmen's entrance for delivery of telegrams and mail, but that wouldn't serve his purpose. A young footman approached him.

'Yes?'

'Message for Her Royal Highness.'

The footman held out a gloved hand to receive the letter.

Wilde went through the same series of replies that he had given at the gate.

'Wait here,' the footman said. Two minutes later he returned in the company of an older man whom Wilde took to be the butler, head of the household serving staff.

'I'm told you wish to see Her Royal Highness, Mr Wilde.'

'I have a personal message to give her.'

'I take it, sir, that as you are in possession of a diplomatic passport you are a man of some standing and not merely a courier?'

'That's correct.'

'What is your position with the diplomatic mission?'

'I will explain all to the Duchess in person.'

'But if you could at least tell me who you are and the nature of the message you wish to deliver, I will be better placed to see how Her Royal Highness wishes to proceed.'

'It is a personal message from the President of the United States. As I am sure you are aware, he is godfather to the Duchess's newborn son.'

'Still, a little further information would be appreciated.'

'I am not at liberty to say more.'

The butler knew when to cut his losses and gave a reluctant nod of acknowledgement, then disappeared back inside the house. Five minutes later he returned. 'Follow me if you would, Mr Wilde. Be aware that Her Royal Highness is still in deep mourning, so hand over your message then back out of the room. Be sure to bow on entry and leaving.'

'Of course.'

The Duchess of Kent, otherwise known as Princess Marina, was sitting at an escritoire close to the window with views across open lawns. The room was large and airy and extremely comfortable. When Wilde was introduced to her presence, she turned towards him, her gold fountain pen held like a cigarette holder between her delicate fingers. The butler bowed, then retreated to the open door, where he hovered.

Wilde bowed his head graciously. 'Your Royal Highness.'

'I believe you have a message for me.'

'Might we speak alone, ma'am?'

'Why do you not just hand me the note?'

'It is to be delivered verbally and is for your attention only.'

'How very odd.' She sighed, then nodded to the butler. 'Leave us, Jermyn. Remain outside the door if you would.'

The servant was obviously unsure about leaving his mistress alone in the presence of a stranger, but he knew his place. He bowed and stepped outside, closing the door behind him.

'Well now, Mr Wilde, where were we?'

Wilde was struck by the lack of expression in the woman's eyes. There was a distance there, perhaps unsurprising after the loss of a loved one, but there was something else, too; it seemed to him that she was examining him in the detached way a scientist might study a specimen from a formerly undiscovered species. Her English was good, but her accent was indeterminately European, the result of being born in Greece and spending many years there and elsewhere on the Continent. Even though she remained seated, he could tell from the way she held her shoulders back that she was slender and quite tall. She wore a perfectly tailored suit in widow's black, with just a single opal brooch at the lapel. She wasn't pretty, but she had presence.

'Mr Wilde?'

'Forgive me, ma'am, I am trying to work out the best way to explain myself.'

'I think straight talking is the best, don't you?'

'Yes, of course, and I so must immediately confess that I have gained access to you through a subterfuge. Before you have me removed, I beg you to listen – for what I have to say touches on the sad death of your husband.'

'Does that mean you are not from the American embassy – and that you do not have a message from Mr Roosevelt?'

'I do indeed work for the United States, but while I have diplomatic accreditation I am not actually part of the mission. I am attached instead to the Office of Strategic Studies in Grosvenor Street, America's new intelligence operation. You may not have heard of it.'

'Indeed, I have not. But please continue.'

She was still holding her pen but began screwing the lid on to close it. The room was both homely and lavish, with little gold and silver trinkets and boxes scattered tastefully on antique inlaid tables.

'I went to Scotland on behalf of the President. He had a great affection for you and your husband and was concerned that he wasn't being given the full story about the crash. I discovered things which have not been made public.'

'Such as?'

'The Sunderland was not leaving Invergordon for Iceland but returning to Scotland from Sweden. I also discovered that there was a second survivor of the crash.'

'Go on.'

'You don't sound surprised, Your Royal Highness.'

'I am listening to your message, Mr Wilde. Do not expect me to respond. You said something about a second survivor.'

'A Miss Harriet Hartwell, a civil servant and secretary.'

'Ah.'

'Perhaps you have heard of her?'

'Mr Wilde, I am not here to answer your questions.'

'Of course not, ma'am. Once again, forgive me. Well, in Stockholm, there was a meeting between your husband and Prince Philipp von Hessen. It is possible you know him, because I believe you have German relations. Certainly, I believe him to have been an old friend and cousin of the Duke.'

She waited; her expression did not change. She said nothing.

'This meeting was ostensibly to discuss the possibility of some sort of truce between Britain and Germany. But that was far from the case. Your husband was authorised only to listen to what the Germans had to say – as a way of determining the morale among the senior Nazis. To see how desperate they were to end the war with Great Britain. But there was something else, something seemingly unconnected: Miss Hartwell was contacted by a man named Rudolf Coburg, whom she knew back in the 1930s. In Stockholm he was a member of the German delegation and it was his intention to defect to Britain or America. He informed Miss Hartwell that he had evidence

of terrible atrocities being committed by the Nazi occupation force in Poland and he wanted to give his testimony to
the world. He begged her to help him get to Britain and claim
political asylum.'

'Stop there, Mr Wilde. This is all very painful for me.'

'Of course. Forgive me.'

'Because, you see, it is clear that you know exactly what you
are talking about. Everything you have told me I know to be
the truth.'

'You do?'

'Indeed. Do you imagine my husband would have kept me in
the dark about such matters?'

'But he could not have known about Coburg . . .'

'Of course he did. It was the reason he agreed to go. And it
was the reason that he took Miss Hartwell along.'

'But how could he have known?'

'Have you heard of a man named Axel Anton, Mr Wilde?'

'Yes, I have met him.'

'Apparently, he's not a nice man, but he has his uses, and
so there's your answer. I haven't met him myself but I know
that his idea was that my husband would bring Herr Coburg
back in the Sunderland with him. Of course, that was never on.
It would have been misunderstood, you see – misunderstood
by our friends. But at least the first part could be put in place:
the separation of Herr Coburg from the delegation by Miss
Hartwell so that he might be placed in hiding until a decision
was taken about his future.'

'Then Miss Hartwell knew about this before the trip?'

'I believe not. No one but Georgie and his brother knew
about Coburg. Oh and me, I'm afraid. Georgie could never
keep a secret from me.'

Wilde was silent for a few moments, his brow knitted in concentration. 'Could I ask you a question, Your Royal Highness? Does Churchill know about this?'

For a brief moment, a smile seemed to pass across the princess's sallow features. Then she picked up a small bell from her desk and tinkled it. Her butler immediately came back in and gave a bow. 'Ma'am?'

'I'd like some coffee please, Jermyn.' She turned to her visitor. 'Would you care for some, Mr Wilde?'

'That would be greatly appreciated. Thank you.'

After the butler had gone, Marina began to walk slowly around the room. Wilde watched her. He had asked her a question and she hadn't answered, and so he felt it right to wait.

At last she stopped. 'Where is Herr Coburg now? For that matter, where is Miss Hartwell? You say she is alive, yes?'

'She is alive, as is Rudi Coburg.'

'But you don't wish to tell me where they are?'

'I'd rather not for the moment. Their lives are in danger.'

'Do you believe the crash of the Sunderland was an accident?'

'I have my doubts. Do you?'

She smiled wanly again, but this time the smile remained. 'Everyone is losing loved ones in this war, Mr Wilde. Accident or enemy action, the outcome is the same – my three children have lost a father. And so I won't dwell on it.'

'I asked you whether Churchill knew all this.'

'Yes, I heard you. And you will have noticed that I chose not to answer. You must remember that the King is head of state in this country.'

'So the King knew what his brother was doing?'

'Well, Georgie would not have undertaken such a mission without the knowledge and approval of the sovereign. I think it will always be difficult to be the brother of a king, don't you? Well, be that as it may, my husband was always utterly devoted to his King and country.'

Wilde took it as a no, that the Duke of Kent had *not* informed Churchill of his plans. Whether the King had done so was another matter.

The butler returned with the coffee and poured cups for his mistress and Wilde, then exited the room again.

'Now then, Mr Wilde,' Marina said, stirring milk and sugar into her coffee. 'It is clear to me that you haven't come here merely to disclose these matters to me, interesting though they are. You have come because you want something from me. What might that be?'

'I want Mr Churchill to meet Herr Coburg, to listen to his testimony. At the moment, he is declining to do so.'

'Do you blame him?'

'I see that it might be difficult to meet a German, yes. But this is different. I would hope you might be able to persuade him that the world needs to be told what is happening in Poland. Your husband died trying—'

She cut him short with a flicker of her fingers. 'Please, do not bring my husband into this. You do not need to tell me my duty to him.'

'I'm sorry.'

'Drink your coffee, Mr Wilde.'

'Will you help?'

'I will consider my options.' She tinkled her bell and the butler reappeared. 'Ah, Jermyn, Mr Wilde is just leaving.'

Chapter 40

They were in Phillips's office and the chief was losing patience. 'What are your plans now, Tom? We need to move on this.'

'But Bill, you know what I'm waiting for – word back from Churchill. I take it he's read my summation?'

The OSS chief shook his head. 'I don't know. He's a busy man.'

'So what do we do? Can we get Coburg to America?'

Phillips let out a long groan. 'Tom, Tom, Tom – for pity's sake, man! Why would America want him if Churchill doesn't?'

'Because he's the messenger from hell. The world must listen to him, and the only way for that to happen is for FDR or Churchill to give the say-so. How many times does that need repeating?' Even as he spoke, he knew he had gone too far.

'Don't take that tone with me. Coburg is a criminal who, by his own admission, has sent thousands of people to their deaths. Any jurisdiction in the world would have him hanged. And his protestations that he didn't know what he was doing won't sound too convincing to a lot of folks. They'll say that he is yellow, that he sees which way the wind is blowing and just wants to get out of Germany while the door's still open. And I'm not sure I'd disagree with them.'

Wilde also found it hard to disagree. He had taken over from Harriet in interrogating Coburg further and harder than he had done before, particularly regarding the Wannsee minutes. She simply sat at his side and listened, having got nowhere in her attempts to pry more information about the Hitler sighting out of him.

'This meeting or conference,' Wilde said. 'Heydrich was in charge, yes?'

'Indeed, but I believe it was at Reichsführer Himmler's command.'

'And you were there?'

'No, I was merely required to edit and copy the minutes to be sent to all who were present.'

'You were subordinate to Adolf Eichmann, right?'

'Yes.'

'So he was at the meeting, taking the minutes – and he chose you to work on them?'

'No, it was Heydrich who selected me.'

'Why?'

'I had Reinhard's trust. I suppose I was his golden boy.'

'Reinhard? That's a very familiar way to refer to one of the most senior men in the regime.'

'Indeed yes, it is not the way I would have spoken to him on official business, but you see he was a very good friend of my mother's – and she always referred to him as Reinhard. And I suppose because of that I became his favoured son. But then it was never the same for me after he was killed earlier this summer.'

'Your mother is English, so you are half-English?'

'Yes.'

'But your loyalties always lay with Germany?'

'I spent most of my childhood there, except for visits to cousins and a short period at an English school. My mother insisted on it, you see, to improve my language skills and learn the ways of an English gentleman. But then my father wanted me back home and I was sent to a Hitler Youth leadership school.'

'From what I have heard, you were a Hitler fanatic already. In fact, it sounds as though your family was Nazi to the core.'

'Yes, it pains me now to admit it, but we were. Even my church-going mother, who still lives in Germany.'

'So you must have had a thorough understanding of the Third Reich's racial policy – and therefore, in reading the original minutes you must have gained a very precise understanding of the purpose and outcome of the Wannsee meeting?'

'That is so.'

'And what was the purpose?'

'To organise a solution to the Jewish question.'

'You mean the murder of Europe's Jewish population.'

Coburg merely nodded.

'Answer the question.'

'Yes, that is so.'

'This conference was in January – so in editing the minutes you knew about the murders and the true reason for the transports you organised long before you saw the operation at Treblinka.'

'Yes, that also is so. But it is different when you see the reality . . .'

'In what way is it different?'

'Well, take your bomber crews. They kill innocent women and children, but they don't see the results of their actions. It was the same for me.'

Wilde gritted his teeth and struggled to refrain from pulverising the man's face. He wanted to say, *If you think there is an equivalence, then your mind is more diseased than I had imagined.* Instead he said, 'The bomber crews are waging war, trying to destroy important property and industry to disrupt the Nazi war machine. The death of innocents is, sadly, an unavoidable side-effect of such action. But your cause – the Nazi cause – had only one intention: murder. The destruction of a whole race. The deliberate slaughter of children. It was nothing to do with furthering Germany's war aims.'

Coburg was silent again for a few moments. 'Then I am guilty,' he said at last. 'And that is why I have chosen to walk away. I will take my punishment, whatever it is.'

Wilde had walked out of the room, leaving Harriet with the German, because he could no longer bear to look at the man's face or listen to his weasel words. Now he was with Phillips and they were both angry. 'Then what do you suggest we do with him, Bill?'

'No, Tom – what do *you* suggest? You brought him and the girl here. They're your responsibility.'

'And I'm not trying to avoid it. But I need a little help. Before I went to Sweden you got the approval of Herschel Johnson in Stockholm and William Donovan in DC. Can't they get through to Churchill or Roosevelt?'

Phillips sighed. 'Do you have any idea how much passes FDR's desk each day? The same goes for Winston. They're fighting this war on a hundred different fronts. Coburg will just have to wait in line.'

'While Jews die . . .'

Phillips glared at him for a few moments, then suddenly softened. 'Forgive me – you're right. I guess it's just that I don't like the Coburg bastard and now that he's up from his sickbed I can't stand having him around us. This place isn't a hospital, it's not a prison – and it sure isn't a safe house.'

'You're right, too – we have to move on this. Can we at least get a steer from Washington? Can't John Winant make some sort of progress?'

'I'll talk to him. In the meantime, I meant what I said about wanting Coburg out of here. This is an intelligence operation – not the sort of place a German should be hanging out.'

They left at dusk with Wilde acting as outrider on the Rudge and Harriet driving an embassy car. Coburg was stretched out on the bench seat in the rear of the car. It was a route Wilde knew well: the road from London to Cambridge.

He felt ill at ease. Of all the places in England he would have chosen to take Coburg and Harriet, this was the last. And yet she insisted this was their best hope; this was where she had been hiding when she made her way down from Scotland.

Are you sure? He had asked the question in Grosvenor Street and again when they took possession of the embassy car. Now, they were committed to the plan and here, on the open road, he knew they were at their most vulnerable since the flight from Sweden. He wasn't convinced it would be any less dangerous when they arrived at their destination and found themselves cooped up in the home of a former Church of England bishop; nowhere could be as secure as the OSS bureau with its permanent armed guard.

Before leaving, Coburg had spoken only once more. 'The English side of my family,' he said. 'Perhaps I should contact them. It is possible they would give me asylum.'

'Do you still know them?'

'Only from childhood. But they would certainly remember my mother.'

'Forget it,' Wilde said. What he didn't bother to say was that there was absolutely no chance that Coburg, a man employed by the most senior men in the Nazi regime, was going to be allowed to roam the land free. He could remain in American hands or British hands, but those were his only options. If the British got hold of him, he would almost certainly end up in the London Cage, where he would undergo hard interrogation and internment for the duration. What the Americans would do was, as yet, undecided, but it was unlikely to be any more comfortable.

The bishop's home – Red Farm – was located in a couple of acres on the edge of a much larger estate. It had a variety of outbuildings, including a disused barn. All the windows of the house were blacked out as they drew into the short drive-way. Wilde put the bike on its stand and joined Harriet as she got out of the car and approached the front door. The building was a Georgian-fronted farmhouse in a village just south of Cambridge. The occupant was the Right Reverend Oscar Fry. 'He was Daddy's oldest friend,' Harriet had said. 'Oscar would do anything for me. He is the sweetest man you could imagine.'

The white-haired man who opened the door was exactly as Harriet described him. He was no more than five feet three inches tall and he wore heavy-rimmed bottle glasses that gave him an almost comical look, but his face beamed goodness. Wilde estimated him to be well into his seventies, perhaps eighty years of age. He stood with a stoop and peered up like a tortoise.

'Come in, come in one and all,' he said cheerily, shuffling down the steps and across the gravel to the car and motorbike to greet his guests. He looked at the large embassy car they had used. 'Ah, that's a shame,' he said to Harriet. 'I was rather hoping you'd arrive in my little Austin Seven. I miss the old dear.'

'I'm afraid it's stuck in Suffolk, Oscar,' she said. 'I'm so sorry.'

Wilde was alarmed. 'Are you saying the car came from here?'

'Of course,' Harriet said.

'But they have details of it. They'll know where it came from – this will be one of the first places they look. God in heaven, Harriet, why didn't you mention this before?'

Before she could answer, the former bishop stepped forward, an almost guilty smile on his beatific face. 'I don't really think there's any danger of that, Mr Wilde.'

'Our enemies have ways and means, sir.'

'Indeed, but they won't get very far in this case. The car used to belong to a young deacon in Ely, you see. He was about to scrap it after almost killing himself colliding with a tree. I took it off his hands for a fiver and have spent much of my retirement restoring her to her former glory. I'm ashamed to say I have neglected to register her in my name.'

'But your friend the deacon – they'll go to him, and he'll send them on to you.'

Oscar Fry shook his head sadly. 'He died a few months ago, killed by shrapnel in the first dreadful raid on Norwich.'

Wilde breathed a sigh of relief. There was a lingering doubt, but they were probably in the clear. And then he saw tears in the old bishop's eyes as the old man folded Harriet into his arms.

'Oscar?' she said.

'Oh, Harriet, here am I fretting about getting my silly little car home when you've lost your saintly father. My heart is broken, dear.'

Fry lived alone at the house. A housekeeper came in during the day to do his cooking and cleaning but he assured his new visitors that she was completely discreet and Wilde found himself believing the man. The emotion he displayed over the death of the Reverend Hartwell, his friend, could not be dissembled. This was genuine.

'Supper just needs heating up,' he said, wiping his eyes with his sleeve and trying to sound cheerful. 'Enid's wonderful beef casserole and dumplings with heaps of mashed potato. Not as much beef as one might like, of course – but there's a war on. Shall we say half an hour, after I've shown you your rooms and you've all had time to refresh yourselves?'

'Thank you, but I won't be staying for supper,' Wilde said. 'I would however be grateful if you would give me a tour of the house. I know you understand how important security is.'

'All has been explained by dear Harriet.'

'And you know that you, yourself, could be in danger?'

'So I believe. Well, I have always tried to live a godly life, so my fate – as always – is in His hands. What will be will be.'

'Keep the doors locked. Be sure you know who's outside before you open them. Say nothing about your guests if anyone phones.'

'Message received and understood, Mr Wilde.' He put a hand to his mouth as though he had misspoken. 'Oh, dear me, I'm sorry, that should of course be *Professor* Wilde – I know very well that you're a Cambridge don.'

'Part time at the moment.'

'I have admired your work from afar for quite a few years now, professor – your histories of Walsingham and Cecil are remarkable tomes. I have often wondered whether I might persuade you to come to dinner here, but then I couldn't quite summon up the nerve to approach you and ask, because I know what a busy man you must be. No time for a rather dotty superannuated cleric.'

'Never too busy for supper, Mr Fry. And I'm delighted to hear that you're interested in the late sixteenth century.'

'Oh, very much so. It was with horror that I read your descriptions of the appalling behaviour of Mr Topcliffe and the agonies of the Catholic martyrs. A shameful time for the English church, I'm afraid.'

It was a conversation Wilde would have loved to pursue, but not at this moment. It also explained to Wilde how Harriet must have found him when he emerged from college on the day of her father's murder: Bishop Fry had clearly passed on information gleaned from the biographical details on the fly-leaf of one of his books.

Tonight, he had other matters to consider. He was studying the house and it was anything but secure. It was a large, sprawling building which had been built over the skeleton of an earlier property, for though it had Georgian symmetry on the outside, inside it was a hotch-potch of styles with medieval beams in strange places and nooks and crannies and inglenooks in many of the rooms. There were five outside doors and eighteen windows, including ten on the ground floor. At least with the blackouts no one would be able to see in, but that hardly lessened the threat from a determined foe. Harriet was still armed, but he had no way of knowing how proficient she was with her pistol.

'Can you arrange it so Herr Coburg's room is close by Harriet's?' he asked the bishop.

'Of course. Leave it to me.'

'Thank you.'

He took Harriet aside. 'Keep the pistol loaded and keep it on your person at all times. Stay close to Coburg as much as you can.'

'You're going to see your common-law wife, I suppose.'

'I have to, otherwise there may not be much future for our common-law marriage. But I'll be back first thing in the morning.'

She smiled ruefully. 'Don't do anything I wouldn't do.'

Coburg was shown to his room. His movements were sullen and listless. He did what he was told but made no attempt at small talk. Wilde tried to explain the situation to him, but it was hard going. 'It is important you do not show your face outside this house – and that you obey Harriet Hartwell to the letter. Do you understand, Herr Coburg? You are not safe. None of us are, but we are doing our best to keep you alive.'

Coburg looked as grim as ever. His face was expressionless. 'The Athels,' he said, 'they will come for me here.'

Wilde wasn't sure whether it was a question or a statement. 'Not if you keep your head down and remain hidden,' he said.

'No, they will come for me. They will finish what the snakes started . . .'

Templeman's port-wine stain seemed to be throbbing. It wasn't large, but it was very prominent and conspicuous and he had always loathed it. In his mind it looked nothing like a dagger, more like a grubby parsnip or carrot, because that was what Uncle Erasmus had told him when he was eight years old, roaring with laughter as he did so. A year or two later, Templeman felt eternally grateful to the boy who suggested it looked like a blade. From being an object of pity he had suddenly become a figure of romance. He had allowed himself a smile when he heard a little while later that Uncle Erasmus had been trampled to death by a herd of cows.

Rising from his desk, he stretched his arms and tried to stifle a yawn. It had been a difficult day, both in London and back here at Latimer Hall in Cambridge, and he was tired and irritable. He fixed his eyes on Quayle. 'So they've left Grosvenor Street,' he said, his habitual easy manner replaced by an uncharacteristic briskness and anger. 'Where are they now, Walter?'

'Our bloody men lost them on the road north, not far from Cambridge,' he said. 'There was a roadblock near Duxford. Wilde was waved through. My men were held up. Cursed bad luck.'

'Perhaps they're going to Wilde's house. What do you think, Philip?'

Eaton shook his head. 'Wilde's cleverer than that, Dagger.'

'Is he really? Heading up here to Cambridge doesn't sound very clever. Yes, he must know a lot of people in and around the town, but it can't be beyond our wit to find out their names and check them out.'

'We'll find him,' Quayle said.

'Make it quick. By the way, Walter, what was that business with Wilde at Scotland Yard? The Met weren't at all happy.'

'Oh, that was nothing, some young thug trying to get the professor's wallet.'

'It sounded more serious than that.'

'I'm afraid the boys in blue overreacted, that's all.'

'Well, get on to what we know about Wilde's friends. I want them found tonight. Understood?'

Quayle nodded.

'Go on then, get on with it.'

After Walter Quayle had departed, Templeman poured a drink for Eaton. 'What have we got, Philip?' he said, handing him a brandy glass.

'Almost there, I think.'

'I'm worried. We've got to finish this – and finish it now.'

'I know.'

'Don't let me down.'

Chapter 41

Wilde had anticipated cold comfort at home. But Lydia simply put her arms around him and dragged him inside.

'Lydia?' he said when they finally disentangled. His face was wet with her tears. She was brushing his cheeks with the back of her hand.

'Oh God, Tom.'

'Lydia, I'm here now – I'm safe.'

'I can't live without you, you bastard. I thought I'd lost you. Why didn't I marry you when I had the chance? To hell with the war, I'm not letting you go again.'

'Lydia, darling, everything is OK. But I really can't stay more than a few hours. This is just a flying visit because I was nearby and I had to see you . . . I'm sorry.'

'No, you're not going. We need you. Johnny needs his father.'

'I'm sorry, I've got until dawn, that's it.'

'Then I've lost you?'

'No, of course not. What are you saying? Of course you haven't lost me.'

'What if I say you can't go?'

'Then I'll have to disobey you. Lives are at stake.'

'Your new friend's?'

'Lydia, please, don't be like that.'

'Well, she means more to you than we do. That's as plain as day. You've been chasing her around Scotland and England and God knows where else. Like a bloody dog, chasing the Whitehall bitch on heat or bicycle or whatever she is.'

Wilde guided her into the kitchen and made her sit down. He hunted around and found a whisky bottle, and shared the whisky between them in two tumblers. 'Now,' he said, 'first I want to know about Johnny. How is he? And then I want you to tell me more about the visit you had from Walter Quayle. Johnny first.'

'Oh, he's gorgeous, funny, a pain in the neck, not a great conversationalist. I miss adult conversation, Tom.'

'But healthy?'

'Yes. You can see him before you go – but don't wake him.'

'And Quayle?'

'That was a very strange visit. I didn't like Walter Quayle one little bit. And that had nothing to do with him being a queer, as you know, because I loved dear old Horace Dill with all my heart, and he was queen of queens. I could even put up with Quayle's dandruff and bad breath at a pinch, but it was his darkness – that was what made me shudder.'

Wilde picked up the tumbler and downed the whisky in one.

'You know that was the last of it. We'll be lucky to get any more before the end of the war.'

'Don't worry, I'll get some from the embassy,' he said absently. He was frowning, thinking of his time with Quayle on the road from Invergordon to Caithness and the crash site. He hadn't seen any darkness, had he? He had never warmed to the man – but *darkness*?

'What is it, Tom?'

'You said you saw darkness in Quayle. I didn't see that.' But Harriet had, hadn't she? She said she always loathed him from Athelstan days. Lydia's impression linked to Harriet's long-term knowledge of the man could not be a coincidence.

'I have more intuition than you. Perhaps it's a female thing. Anyway, it was there.'

'Oh no, I'm not doubting you. I trust your intuition implicitly. I was just wondering how I could have missed it. Tell me more. When did he come here?'

'End of the afternoon – a few hours before your late-night call. I was pissed off with you, if you recall.'

'He just turned up on the doorstep?'

'Yes. That's what happens when people visit, isn't it?'

'Didn't call first?'

'No.'

'And he asked you where I was?'

'Exactly. And I said you were almost certainly in London. Did I do wrong?'

'No, no, of course not. I *was* in London. Did he leave a contact number with you in case I turned up?'

She shook her head.

'But you were scared of him?'

'I don't think I said that. I was wary of him. I didn't feel an immediate threat. I just knew that I didn't like him and I showed him the door as quickly as I could.'

'And he just walked away?'

'He was driven away in a big black car. He had a driver, who was standing at the kerb. Squirt of a man. Looked like the runt of the litter. I didn't like the look of him either. He touched his forelock, held the rear door open for Quayle and then they were gone.' Her eyes met his. 'What is it, Tom? What have I said?'

'I've got to go.'

Somerset, 1930

Walter Quayle watched the boy for ten minutes, fascinated. The lad was kneeling on the stone pathway near the greenhouses, his face down. Every so often a tiny puff of smoke drifted up from the stone.

He recognised the boy as the gardener's ill-favoured son Ned. *The runt,* he was called by everyone indoors, including Quayle's parents and the servants. They all seemed to despise him as if he were vermin.

Quayle had no particular feelings about the boy. He wasn't attracted in a sexual way but nor was he repulsed. Anyway, most of the time Quayle was away at school so he had nothing to do with Ned. Now, he approached him and watched more closely and saw clearly what the younger boy was doing. He had a cheap magnifying glass and he was concentrating the sun's rays into a tiny speck of burning hot light, which he used to incinerate ants as they trundled across the path.

'That looks fun,' Quayle said.

The boy said nothing but Quayle heard something: a choking sob from the depths of the boy's throat. Then a single tear fell to the stone.

'What is it?'

'Nothing,' the boy said.

'Your name's Ned, isn't it? You're Mortimer's son,' Quayle said, knowing very well what he was and what they all called him, mostly to his face.

The boy nodded and more tears fell.

'Can I have a go at that?' Quayle asked.

The boy handed the magnifying glass to Quayle, who got down on his knees beside him and began picking off ants. It really was fun. After a dozen or so, he handed the glass back to the lad. 'Why are you crying?'

The boy turned his face towards him and Quayle saw that it was swollen, bruised and there was a smear of blood from a cut beneath his right eye.

'Who did that?'

'I fell over.'

'No, Ned, I want to know. Tell me – who did it?'

'My dad.'

'I'm sorry.'

The boy shrugged. His frame was so small. Watching him before, Quayle had noticed that his legs were bowed like a jockey's. But it was malnutrition that did that to a lower-class boy like Ned Mortimer, not riding horses. Anyone knew that.

'Do you want me to clean your face? I could take you in and get Nanny to have a look at you.'

The boy shook his head violently.

'Why not?'

'Dad would find out and hit me more. He'd hit me if he saw you talking to me.'

'Why did he hit you this time?'

'I took strawberries from the walled garden. Just a handful. He saw me eating them and hit me. But it was worth it; they were red and sweet.'

'Where is he now, your dad?'

'I dunno.'

Quayle was seventeen. He had one more year at Athelstans, then he'd be off to Cambridge for maths at Trinity. This might well be one of his last summers at home and he had brought his friend Richard Smoake with him. Today, Smoake had gone down to the lake with Quayle's sister. They seemed to have something going on. Meanwhile, the house was full of talk about possible financial ruin and European and Russian politics. Quayle already knew which way the wind was blowing. Only men like Mussolini could save the world.

He ruffled Ned Mortimer's hair. The boy shied away as though bitten. Quayle laughed. He reckoned Ned must be about ten, though he was about the size of a stunted seven-year-old. He left him to his ants. 'Cheer up, Ned, we'll see what we can do.'

'You can't do nothing.'

He caught up with Jonas Mortimer two hours later while he was drinking tea in the potting shed. 'Ah, Mortimer,' Quayle said, 'I was hoping to find you here. I know what an expert you are on all things horticultural and I was wondering if you could identify these flowers for me.'

Mortimer was not a big man, but he had strong, tanned arms and a hard, weathered face. He looked like someone who had spent their whole life outdoors doing demanding physical work. 'They're snapdragons, Master Walter. Otherwise known as antirrhinum.'

'Really? How ignorant of me not to know that. I so love flowers, don't you?'

'Aye, I suppose I do.'

'Perhaps you could teach me about them while I'm on holiday. I'd love to know what they're all called and how you grow them all.'

Mortimer looked uneasy. 'That's not really my place, young sir. Your mother and father might not like it.'

'Oh, don't worry about them. I could pay you, you know. Say a florin an hour for your time and expert knowledge? I'd so love to know a little of what you do before I head off into the big wide world next year.'

Mortimer's eyes bulged, as Quayle had known they would. Two shillings for an hour's work was a great deal of money for a man like him, especially when it would be extra on top of his usual wages.

'Do say yes, Mortimer.'

'Very well, Master Walter, we could give it a go – so long as you promise you won't tell no one.'

'It'll be our little secret.' He reached out and touched the gardener's forearm below his rolled-up sleeve. 'You have such strong muscles, Mortimer. They look lovely.'

'Just work,' Mortimer mumbled. 'Just hard work, that's all.'

Quayle smiled at him. In that touch he had discovered exactly what he needed to know. He had felt the electricity tingling in the man's body, the soft dark hairs on his skin standing up uninvited.

The seduction took only three days. It was in the second of their hourly sessions that he asked Mortimer if he could touch his chest and feel his muscles there, and it was half-way through the third hour that Mortimer could stand it no longer and touched the boy back. He put his hand on his trousers, above the fly. 'Do you do this in your bedroom, Master Walter?'

'What's that, Mortimer?' he asked, all innocent, but making no move to push the hand away.

'Touch yourself there, sir.'

'It feels very nice when you do it. Perhaps you'd show me what you mean.'

On the fourth session, they were watched by Quayle's friend Richard Smoake with his brand-new Leica and 135 mm telephoto lens.

The next day Quayle found young Ned killing ants on the path once more. 'What do you do when the sun's not shining?' he asked.

'I catch flies and drown them.'

'Did your father beat you last night?'

The boy looked surprised at the question. 'No,' he said, his brow knitted.

Quayle put an arm around Mortimer's thin, bony shoulders. 'Don't worry,' he said. 'He'll never beat you again.'

Cambridgeshire, 1942

Ned Mortimer had a pistol with silencer in the front of his belt, a knife secured into a sheath strapped to his leg and a sub-machine gun cradled in his arms. His right hand was bandaged, but his left trigger finger would do. The car engine had been killed and its lights were out. They were half a mile from Red Farm.

'We do this properly,' Quayle said, his bent, angular figure looming over the younger man. He had a service revolver, but he kept it holstered under his jacket. 'It's an outside chance, but we have to try to secure the papers before we kill him.' Even as he said it, he knew the odds were that the OSS would not have left the papers in Coburg's possession.

'And the others?'

'Hostages to fortune, Ned. Trading counters.'

'We could go in now.'

'No, we wait until we're certain they're asleep. The girl has a pistol, so does Wilde. He'll try to stay awake, but he will become drowsy. We move quietly and use silencers. The Sten is back-up. We don't want a shoot-out if it can be avoided. You have to have that clear, Ned.'

'Yes, Mr Quayle.'

'Good boy, Ned. You were always a good, obedient boy, weren't you? A fine servant to your master.' Quayle took out his whisky flask and tipped half of the contents down his throat before offering it to his man. Mortimer shook his head.

It had been a simple task to arrange the release of Mortimer from police custody. The words 'national interest' could always be brought out to excuse a multitude of sins, but it was in these dark days that they carried the greatest weight. Thanks to his senior position within MI5, Walter Quayle was not a man to be argued with by a time-serving police officer like Foat. 'Secret work,' Quayle had said, tapping the side of his damaged nose. 'I'm afraid Mr Wilde is not all he seems and so his testimony is to be taken with a pinch of salt. Mum's the word, eh?'

Foat had been impressed at being taken into the confidence of such an important secret officer. 'Of course, Mr Quayle, I totally understand.'

'Good man.'

Chapter 42

At night, in his half-sleep, Rudi Coburg descended into a demi-world of his own mind's making. It was a monochrome dream, punctuated only by splashes of red, but he knew it was real. He was on the platform at Treblinka surrounded on every side by serpents. Snakes, adders as far as his eyes could see. He had to get away, but if he climbed down from the ramp, he would be at their mercy, and they had no mercy. Twenty metres away, beyond the electrified perimeter fence, there was a forest of tall, dense trees; if only he could get there, into the branches, he might have some hope, somewhere to hide.

There were uncountable hundreds of the snakes now, perhaps thousands, writhing and spitting in the mud and dust. Their cacophonous hissing rose and rose in the night air, a crescendo of death overlaid with whipcracks, screams, gunshots and the baying of dogs.

The snakes came at night. Every night. In the daytime, he could live in a world without snakes, and converse with humans. If he kept his eyes open, he could make sense of his thoughts. Often they turned to his mother and the way things were in the old days, in the land of so much of his childhood. She was still there, in the grand manor house and estate in the countryside near the small rural backwater of Friedberg, where he had listened to her proud tales of their joint family trees and their tenuous connection to British royalty through the Saxe-Coburg cousins.

As a small child he had roamed those acres at will, deferred to by the family's servants. The only hard times were when his father was home; how he hated standing before him stiffly in the evening to recite Goethe. Rudi had shed no tear when he was killed by a cancer of the lung in the first month of the war. Mother was always warm and tender, though, and when she folded him in her arms, he was in heaven. His one desire was to please her and in that respect he had done well with his steady rise in the party and the promotions he received from Reinhard.

He knew, too, how delighted she had been when the Friedberg synagogue was torched in the Kristallnacht pogrom of November 1938, and even more so when the last of the town's Jews were deported to the Polish territories earlier this year. She was so proud that it was her own beloved son whose pen had signed the transport papers to take them to a place called Treblinka for resettlement.

But Mother didn't know what really happened there, for if she had been told the truth her religious sensibilities would have made her recoil in shame. He had to believe that of her; he had to believe that Mother would not be a party to murder.

Mother was too English for such crude brutality. Perhaps he was too. They both lacked the requisite hardness of the true Teuton.

Oh, yes, he knew the purpose of Treblinka before ever he saw it. So why did seeing it change everything? Was he merely squeamish, not a fit Member of the master race? Was the same true of Mother?

Tonight, still in his half-sleep, he crawled out from under the blankets and knelt on the bed, which was beneath the blacked-out sash window. In his dream, the bed was the Treblinka station house which he climbed so that he could look down on the snakes from a position of safety. But he could not get away from them.

The room was pitch black and his fingers clawed into the darkness, clutching at the blackout and dragging it down until the window was exposed. A little moonlight and starlight and the red glow of a distant bombing raid shone through the glass. Surely, he had found a way of escape. This window would take him away from the snakes. All he had to do was stand on the ledge and leap, and he would be past the filthy reptiles, over the barbed wire, and could dash for the safety of the trees.

The sash window was stiff and creaked as though it had not been opened in years, but his strength came from desperation and fear and at last it opened a few inches. The cool air of freedom blew in gently. He pushed up again and the window gave some more, allowing a gap just large enough for his head and shoulders. It would have to do, for there was no time to lose. He turned on his side and eased his right shoulder into the space, and then his head. He looked down into the world outside but couldn't see the snakes now; they were hiding in the shadows, waiting for him to falter.

Behind him the door was opening, and a thin yellow torchlight caught him in its beam.

'Rudi!'

It sounded to him like Harriet, but he knew it couldn't be her, for why would she be here at Treblinka station, on the waiting-room roof?

'Rudi, get back in!'

He pushed harder, desperate to get his torso and arms through the gap. The voice was clearly that of an impostor, a snake posing as Harriet to prevent him escaping. He was almost out now, but she had grasped him by the ankle and was trying to drag him back.

He kicked out at her, but her grip held.

'I could chance a shot.' Mortimer unscrewed the silencer one-handed and raised the pistol into his eyesight.

They were 200 metres away and they had a good line of vision to the ground-floor window. Quayle was in no doubt that Mortimer could take Coburg out with an enfilade spray from the submachine gun, but he doubted his chances with a side-arm, especially left-handed, and so he hesitated. If anything went wrong it would be their last chance. Nor would they be certain of getting to Harriet Hartwell or Wilde. They would never get into the house, which meant no chance of getting their hands on the RSHA documents.

'No,' he said. 'We know where he is now. We have time.' What on earth was Coburg trying to do? That was the question uppermost in Quayle's mind. He was clearly fleeing the house, but why? Was he being held against his will? Had the German had a change of heart, or was he being badly treated? Was there a chance of taking him alive, perhaps even returning him to Müller? It was a slender chance, but it was something that had to be considered. What would Müller say?

'There's something behind him, Mr Quayle.'

'Yes, I see. Someone's trying to pull him back.'

'Is it the woman or one of the men?'

'Hard to tell.'

With a last wrench, Coburg was back inside. Now he was awake and shivering, curled up on the bed, in that strange place between vivid dreaming and full consciousness, when you try to work out whether any of the things you dreamt actually happened.

'Don't attempt that again,' Harriet said as she closed the window and did her best to fix the blackout back into place. 'Or you'll do for us all.'

'I'm sorry.'

She switched on the bedside light and sat down on the covers beside him. She was exhausted; the struggle had been intense, but her determination got the better of his strength. 'We're trying to protect you. You need to stay alive. Do you understand?'

'Yes,' he said quietly.

'There's nothing to worry about, Rudi. No one knows we're here, but we have to be cautious. It's for your own good.'

'I know. I'm sorry.'

'Go back to sleep. I'm staying here in this room with you.' She removed the pistol from the pocket of her dressing gown and pushed its muzzle into his chest. 'This is to keep us safe, Rudi. But if you try another trick like that, it could just as well be used against you.'

'Forgive me, Harriet. Please. I was dreaming. I didn't know what I was doing.'

Wilde had seen light from the house. Some sort of struggle at the window of Coburg's room. He couldn't quite work out what he was seeing. His instinct was to move away from his place in the trees beside the barn, but he had sensed other movement outside the house, to his right, a thing he hadn't seen before in the two hours he had lain here silently watching.

There was something else. Whispering. At first, he thought it must be a night breeze in the leaves, but then he wasn't sure and wondered whether it might be voices. He gripped the butt of his Smith & Wesson and began to move, very slowly, in the direction of the noise.

He was thirty yards away when he heard the sounds again. This time he was certain. The whispering was real. Two men, talking low and urgently. One, he was sure, was Quayle. And the other? Could it be Mortimer? Had he somehow got away from his police cell?

Wilde weighed up his options and didn't like any of them. He couldn't just fire his pistol into the darkness. That was a recipe for murder, plain and simple, and he doubted a diplomatic passport would save his neck.

There was only one thing for it. He edged behind the broadest tree trunk. 'One move and you're dead,' he said. Not a shout or bellow, but a firm, commanding voice that would carry through the night air.

He instantly heard rustling, the click of metal.

'Throw out your arms – then stand up. You're surrounded,' Wilde said. 'Weapons are trained on you.'

He took his torch from his jacket. It threw a narrow yellow beam on to the patch of ground between the tree that sheltered him and the cover where he was certain Quayle and Mortimer were concealed.

The reaction was instant. A submachine gun rattled and a dozen bullets spat into the tree trunk and the undergrowth around him. He loosed off two shots of his own, then swivelled the torchlight across a wide arc, and caught them full in the beam. He fired two more shots, one for each man, then removed his shoes.

Quayle had pulled Mortimer away by the collar. If Wilde was out here, they had to take him down and get into the house. No hope of avoiding a firefight or choosing a time to suit them. This had to be done now.

Two shots hit the dust between them. Quayle instinctively dropped down. Mortimer swivelled and pulled the trigger of the Sten.

'Keep firing, Ned, short bursts. Conserve ammunition. The direction of the light.'

Mortimer was well trained and did as he was ordered, popping off two-second sprays into the night. His right hand was in pain but steady enough to cradle the muzzle while the left pulled the trigger. The sound was sharp and staccato; the empty cartridge cases flew to his right. Then the light went out and he no longer knew where he was firing.

They ducked around the side of the old farmhouse, backs to the wall, catching their breath. Quayle had now unholstered his own revolver. He didn't want to use it. Not yet.

'Fucking empty,' Mortimer cursed. He unclipped the magazine and slotted in a new one.

'Did you hit him?'

'I don't know.'

Inside the house, Harriet had flung herself to the floor beside the bed, dragging Coburg down with her. Why the hell wasn't Tom here? Was he still at home with that bloody common-law wife of his? Why hadn't he called at least? She thought she had heard his motorbike returning hours ago, but then nothing. She pushed Coburg under the bed with a barked whisper: 'Stay there.'

'But . . .'

'Not a sound or you die.'

Crawling across the floor, she made it to the door. The light in the corridor was on and the elderly bishop was tottering towards her in his slippers and nightgown.

'Harriet, what's going on?'

'Hide, Oscar. Find yourself somewhere to hide.'

'Oh dear, we don't have a cellar.'

'Go to your room. Make yourself as scarce as you can. Not a sound.'

'I'm going in, Ned. Guard my back.' Quayle twisted the handle of the front door; it was locked. He kicked the door but it didn't budge. 'Shoot out the lock.'

Mortimer put two shots into the lock with his revolver, then kicked again and the door flew open. Quayle edged in sideways. The hallway was at the entrance to a long corridor which stretched from left and right. Low-wattage bulbs gave them light.

'To the left, Ned. I saw movement. Cover me with a short burst, then stay back.'

Harriet had already heard the door crashing open and had seen them enter. She slid back into Coburg's room, certain that she, too, had been seen. Pistol at head height, she glanced out, saw two shadowy men at the end of the corridor and fired. Something to slow them down.

Her shot was met with a burst of submachine gun fire.

She was shaking but she knew she had only two hopes. Either keep them at bay in a gunfight or escape through the window. The first option seemed to have a vanishingly slim hope of success; she had no spare ammunition and only five shots left. The second option might be worse; how many other men were waiting outside?

Coburg emerged from beneath the bed. 'I'll go to them, Harriet,' he said. 'It's me they want.'

'You're going nowhere, Rudi.' She hadn't come this far to let her prize slip through her fingers.

'If I don't they'll kill us both.'

'Back under the bed.'

A rattle of gunfire splintered the door at her side. She crouched down, back to the wall, pistol gripped tight in both hands, ready to take at least one of them with her.

The gunfire deadened the soft sound of Wilde's approach, padding across the gravel on sock-clad feet. Mortimer had stepped back outside and was crouched low, scouring the driveway and the hedging at the front and sides. Wilde was concealed behind the embassy car, waiting his chance. He had a clear view of Mortimer, silhouetted against the open doorway.

They heard another shot from indoors. Mortimer instinctively turned to see what was happening. It was enough. Wilde moved forward. His quarry didn't hear him coming, didn't see him.

It took Wilde one shot. He lined the Smith & Wesson at the back of Ned Mortimer's head and the bullet drove into his skull. Mortimer fell forwards, dead even before he hit the stone doorstep.

Quayle was twisting and turning, distracted by the shot from outside. Along the corridor he saw Harriet emerging, an arm and half her face visible. She was ranging her pistol. Quayle dropped to one knee and fired at her, swivelling as he did so to the open doorway to ensure Mortimer was covering him.

Wilde was there, just six feet away.

Harriet's move had given Wilde the split second he needed. As Quayle turned his gun arm, Wilde fired. The bullet shattered Quayle's knuckles and the service revolver spun from his hand across the black and white tiled floor. Blood sprayed in an almost perfect arc, like a pink rainbow.

Quayle let out a cry of agony, clutched the remains of his hand to his chest, and dropped to his knees. Wilde placed the sole of his foot square in the centre of Quayle's back and pushed down hard, sending him sprawling across the floor, blood from his broken hand streaking the tiles. Quayle screamed again as he reached out with the torn remnants of his right hand to try to break his fall.

'Stay there, Quayle. One move and you'll go the way of your little friend.'

The injured man didn't need the warning. He curled up, moaning and whimpering.

Wilde ignored him and picked up the discarded pistol. 'Harriet, it's safe,' he called out. She was walking towards him, relief etched on her face. 'Thank you,' he mouthed.

But then she stopped. From the darkness behind him, outside the open front door, Wilde heard a strangely familiar tapping of wood on stone.

He put up a hand to keep Harriet at a distance, then turned away from the helpless form of Quayle, ready to loose another shot as a figure emerged from the gloom. It was Philip Eaton, stick in his right hand – his only hand – and limping as badly as ever.

Wilde ranged his pistol at Eaton's chest.

'Put it away, Wilde. We're on the same side, you fool.'

Wilde didn't move, nor did his gun hand. 'Prove it.'

'Good God, we have been after that man all along.' He nodded towards Quayle. 'You gave us the proof. Now then, Wilde, you're the man I came for. You're to come with me to London. Mr Churchill wishes to see you as soon as he wakes up.'

Wilde lowered his pistol. He'd known Eaton for too many years to think him a threat. 'Are you serious about this?'

'Utterly.'

'And Coburg – will he see him too?'

'Not a cat in hell's chance. But you may well be satisfied with his response.'

'What do we do with Quayle?'

'Oh, he's an embarrassment.'

Wilde hadn't noticed the small handgun that Eaton held alongside his walking stick. Now he saw it, though – and he watched with fascination and dismay as the MI6 man casually brought it to the side of Quayle's head and shot him dead.

Eaton looked up and smiled at Harriet. 'Good evening, Miss Hartwell, I trust you and Herr Coburg are well.'

'We're alive, Mr Eaton.'

'And the bishop?'

'He's in his bedroom.'

'Good. That's good. Well, you're safe now.'

It was then that Wilde noticed that Eaton had not arrived here alone. Outside, in the shadows, stood half a dozen armed men.

Chapter 43

Wilde was shown into a small ante-room on the ground floor of Number 10. He had been driven down to London with Eaton, but the MI6 man left him in Whitehall at the entrance to Downing Street. 'I'm sorry, Wilde, you've got to do this yourself. I have other work.'

The journey had been strange. Wilde had a hundred questions to ask, but Eaton wasn't answering any of them. 'Not my place, old boy. I was just asked to pick you up and bring you down because I know you.'

'But it *was* your place to despatch Quayle, was it?'

Eaton did not reply. Nor did he reply when asked how he knew that Wilde and Harriet had taken Coburg to the former bishop's home or why he had arrived with a squadron of armed officers. Wilde badly wanted answers to these questions, but for the moment the important thing was that he had access to Churchill and that something could be done about Rudi Coburg and his testimony of Nazi atrocities in Poland. All other matters were subordinate and could wait.

Now, though, he had another, rather more trivial need: he badly wanted a coffee or, at the very least, a cup of tea, but no one had offered him anything as he awaited his audience with the great man.

The door opened and the immensely tall figure of Lord Templeman strode in. He smiled at Wilde and instinctively brushed the back of his hand across the port-wine stain on his brow. 'Ah,' he said, 'so very good to see you, Mr Wilde. I can't tell you how pleased I am that you have been granted this audience with the great man.'

'Then you know what it's about?'

'Oh, I have an inkling, but never mind that. You know I was rather worried Mr Eaton would arrive too late at the farmhouse.'

'He did,' Wilde said.

'Really? I rather thought the affair was satisfactorily concluded and that everyone was safely delivered from the threat posed by Quayle.'

'Then you knew about Quayle?'

'Well, not specifically. We were pretty certain there was a Nazi agent in our midst, but identifying him was another matter. At first, we were hoping Cazerove would lead us to the fellow because he too was a traitor, but then he killed himself. After that we rather hoped you or Miss Hartwell would oblige.'

'And you didn't think to tell me any of this? To warn me, as an agent of your principal ally?'

Templeman took a seat at the small table and settled back with his hands clasped behind his head. 'Mr Wilde, forgive me, please. We behaved appallingly, and that is why I'm here – to apologise profusely. We were desperate, you see. We were pretty certain that someone had been feeding information to the enemy for months. We began to suspect Peter Cazerove, but he was too junior to have access to a lot of the secrets being relayed to Berlin, which meant there was someone else and they were working together. We kept tabs on Cazerove and fed him false information, hoping to flush out his confederate.'

'The Dieppe raid, though, that wasn't false information.'

'Actually it was, because Cazerove didn't know it was Dieppe – all he knew was that the target was northern France. The problem was the Germans knew we were up to something already, so they were on extra high alert all along that coast and, sadly for those involved, the raid on Dieppe was a debacle.'

'Are you saying this has all been a case of "hunt the bloody mole", Templeman?'

'Up to a point. There were clearly other matters.'

Wilde wasn't letting him off the hook so easily. 'Such as the rather unpleasant episode of lifting me off the street and drugging me.'

'Yes, that was a rather extreme measure, for which again, I offer wholehearted apologies. In fact, I feel thoroughly ashamed of that. But you see, we had to find Harriet. She was so close to Peter Cazerove that we had doubts about her, too. How could we be certain which side she was on? We needed to keep her under surveillance. Either that or shut her up.'

'Shut her up?'

'We feared she had gone rogue, you see. Apart from anything else, we had to ensure the truth about the Duke of Kent's flight didn't come out. And other things. As a secret servant she has had access to confidential information.'

'She hadn't gone rogue – she was hiding because she thought she was the target. And she was right.'

'Yes, I get that now.'

'God, I could do with a coffee.'

'Haven't you been given anything?' Templeman went to the door and barked an order, then returned.

'You were talking about the Duke's flight . . .'

'Another matter for Winnie. It seems he has agreed to see you at the King's request. Apparently, you visited Her Royal Highness the Princess Marina. Hardly diplomatic protocol, Mr Wilde, but it seems to have paid off. You obviously have a knack for getting your own way.'

The coffee arrived. It was piping hot and Wilde did not wait for it to cool. 'Ah that's better.'

'Good. And I hope I have put your mind at rest on a couple of matters. I am sure you have many other questions and perhaps we could have some supper at my club and talk some more. For the moment, I'm afraid work calls.'

'One thing before you go – what school did you go to, Lord Templeman?'

'The same as you, Mr Wilde – Harrow. I joined the term your mother took you out and shipped you off to America.'

'So Harriet was right, you weren't at Athelstans?'

'Good Lord, no. My father went there and hated every moment of it. He refused point-blank to send me there, despite the urgings of Grandpapa.'

'But you know about the Athels?'

Templeman laughed out loud. 'I suppose you're thinking that both Cazerove and Quayle went there . . .'

'And Coburg – and Harriet's father taught there. Both she and Coburg are terrified of the Athels. They think they run this country and have people everywhere in the Establishment who could harm them. That's who Harriet has been running from.'

Templeman shook his head. 'Oh dear, poor Harriet. I know the Athels have a reputation for plots and conspiracies but it's all nonsense. They couldn't conspire their way into a tea-shop in Tunbridge Wells.'

'But people are scared of them . . .'

'Because of their pathetic secrecy, that's all. Some people at Cambridge feel the same way about the Apostles. Plenty of people in the country feel the world is secretly run by the Freemasons. Bloody Hitler thinks it's all a conspiracy of Jews.'

'What about the link between Cazerove and Quayle?'

'That was something else. It must seem obvious to you now, but for weeks, Quayle was informing against Cazerove, suggesting he and Harriet were the traitors, trying to throw us off the scent. I'm afraid it worked for a while. Anyway, I believe he did the decent thing at the end and shot himself, so that's all settled.'

Wilde finished the coffee and poured himself a second cup. 'But he must have had some sort of hold over Cazerove.'

'Blackmail. I have an old friend from Athelstans, chap named Richard Smoake. As a lad he was chums with Walter Quayle.'

'I think I've heard of him.' He recalled Harriet saying he had bullied the young Cazerove.

'Well, he knew both Cazerove and Quayle from Athelstans days. He's in the FO and I called him last night. He told me all about Quayle and the way he has always worked – he used blackmail to subjugate people. God knows how many – it's probably the way he secured secrets throughout government departments. Anyway, Richard Smoake is certain that Quayle had a homosexual liaison with Cazerove and has held it over him ever since. Quayle never cared a hoot who knew which way his own proclivities lay, but not everyone is so free of convention. Peter Cazerove's family would have been scandalised if they ever discovered what he had done. He would probably have been disowned and disinherited. Anyway, talk to Harriet about it. You'll probably find she either knows or suspects the truth.'

'But the Athels?'

Templeman laughed. 'A bunch of self-satisfied drinking pals, nothing more.'

Churchill was in silk pyjamas beneath silk sheets, his back supported by a bank of white pillows while he dictated a memorandum to a young secretary. As soon as he was finished, she hurried away. Churchill immediately turned his attention to his new visitor, standing alone and rather awkwardly just inside the door. An aide whispered a name in Churchill's ear.

'Ah, so you are the notorious Professor Wilde.' The voice was gruff, measured and deep, the product of a lifetime of smoking and heavy drinking.

'Yes, sir.'

'Well, I must thank you for coming to see me, professor. Are you being looked after? Would you care for a drop of brandy?'

'I have been given coffee, thank you.'

'Good, good, well take that seat by my bed so I can get a good look at you. Dagger Templeman's told me a thing or two about your exploits, of course, but I like to find out about people for myself. Are you sure I can't tempt you to a beverage?'

Wilde found himself laughing at the absurdity of it all. He never drank in the morning. But this wasn't just any morning, and he had not slept. 'Well, sir, I think I could probably manage a small whisky.'

'A small whisky? We don't do small measures here, young man. You'll have a large one or nothing.'

'Then I'll have to have a large one.'

Churchill bellowed. 'Sawyers!'

The butler appeared in seconds. 'Yes, sir.'

'Whisky for this man.' He turned back to Wilde. 'Blend or single malt?'

'Today I think I'll go for the peatiest malt you have.'

The butler bowed. 'Indeed, sir. Perhaps an Islay?'

'Perfect.'

'Now then,' Churchill continued after his man had left the room. 'I believe this has something to do with the Duke of Kent and some damned German fellow. So let's take them in reverse order, shall we? I want to make myself quite clear from the outset: I will not meet your German. That said, I have read your memorandum and I am as appalled as any civilised human being could be.'

'Did you believe it, sir?'

'Every word. I have always known what Hitler's criminal gang is capable of, which is why I spent so long in the wilderness decried as a warmonger and all the while urging the world to take action against him.'

'Why will you not meet Coburg? I don't like him. He has consigned thousands of innocent people to a nightmarish death – but he wants to gain some sort of redemption by broadcasting the truth of what is happening to the world. You are the man who can do this.'

Churchill stuffed a large half-smoked cigar in his mouth and began to relight it. 'I will not treat with Germans, any Germans. I refused to meet Hitler's deputy when he flew to Scotland last year and I will not meet your man. That is the end of the discussion. The question is, what do we do with the fellow and how do we get his testimony heard?'

The butler re-entered and handed Wilde a large Scotch.

'Leave the decanter with us, Sawyers.'

A cloud of cigar smoke drifted Wilde's way.

'So let me tell you,' Churchill continued. 'I have made a decision. Herr Coburg will be interviewed by *The Times* newspaper. I have spoken to Robert Barrington-Ward and he has agreed to put one of his top men on the job. The article will run to no less than 2,000 words and will be accompanied by photographs of

Coburg and pertinent extracts from his documents to give it authenticity. I believe these papers are presently in the possession of the OSS. Is that correct?'

'Yes, Mr Churchill, that is so. And what will happen to Coburg?'

'He will be interned for the duration and will face trial alongside the other Nazi criminals at the end of the war. The fact that he has fled Germany and has told this story will, of course, weigh heavily in favour of clemency. Does this satisfy you, professor?'

He supposed that under the circumstances it was probably the very best that could be hoped for. 'Yes, sir. Of course, it would have added power to the testimony to have your name attached, but I quite understand your reasoning.'

'No, you're wrong, Mr Wilde. My name would merely have allowed Goebbels to sneer at Churchillian propaganda. Let Coburg tell his story in the starkest possible terms and leave it at that.'

'And is there any direct action that might be taken to disrupt the transports? Bombing the railway lines ... even the death camps themselves?'

'It will be looked into, but I confess I am not hopeful. Poland is at the very extremity of our ability to strike at the evil empire. Now then, we come to the second part of your visit: the death of the Duke, which is inevitably linked to the first part. And so I am going to tell you the true facts behind his death and you will never repeat any of what I say outside this room.'

Chapter 44

It was a condition that Wilde could never accept. 'I am sorry, Prime Minister, my allegiance is to America and President Roosevelt, sir. I can't promise to keep secrets from my president.'

Churchill waved his hand dismissively, creating a swirl of smoke around him. 'I wouldn't ask you to keep secrets from your president. Franklin already knows all that I am about to tell you because I told him personally. That is why you were stood down from your investigation when you returned from Scotland.'

Wilde had not seen that coming, but it certainly explained Bill Phillips's sudden change of heart. 'Do Mr Phillips and Mr Winant also know these facts?'

'They certainly do not. You will be one of very few people to know the truth. The King knows, of course, but the Duchess does not, and nor will she, for I have no intention of making her grief and suffering worse than it already is.'

Wilde waited. There was no point in pushing Churchill to go any faster than he was. The Prime Minister seemed to be weighing up his words. Ash from the tip of his cigar spilled across the bedding. At last he judged the moment.

'Professor Wilde, I must tell you that the Duke of Kent was murdered by the Nazis on the express orders of Hitler. The motive was vengeance for the assassination of Reinhard Heydrich.'

'Are you certain of this, sir?'

'Of course I am certain. There is no doubt. A message to the effect that the plane would be brought down was delivered by hand to the British embassy in Stockholm half an hour after the Sunderland took off from a lake near the Palace of Drottningholm. This message was then relayed directly to me. Unfortunately, nothing could be done to warn the crew of the plane because they were observing radio silence.'

Reinhard Heydrich. A name to strike revulsion into the heart of all decent human beings. He was the murderous henchman of Himmler and one of Hitler's most favoured acolytes. The ideal Nazi with a heart of iron. And, as Wilde now knew from the Coburg papers, he was also the leading light at a conference at Wannsee near Berlin in which the fate of Europe's Jews had been sealed.

Two Czechoslovak agents parachuted in by the Special Operations Executive in London had attacked him in Prague on 27 May. They hurled an explosive device at his car, and Heydrich died of his injuries on 4 June. Hitler's reprisals had been characteristically brutal.

A whole village had been razed to the ground, hundreds of men murdered and women despatched to Ravensbrück concentration camp. Even the children had been taken away, some to be brought up as Germans, others murdered.

It now seemed even that had not been enough. Hitler wanted to punish England, too, for sending the assassins into Prague.

'Here, Professor Wilde, read this.' Churchilll tossed a sheet of paper across the bed.

Wilde picked it up. It had a *Sicherheitsdient* heading in Gothic script, with the organisation's Berlin headquarters address: *Prinz-Albrecht-Strasse, 8*. It was written in English and read:

To Mr Winston Churchill. Let it be known that Flight 4026, presently en route to the United Kingdom, will not arrive. Consider this retribution for your *country's part in the murder of SS-Gruppenführer Reinhard Heydrich, acting Reich Protector of Bohemia and Moravia.*

It was unsigned.

'Is that convincing enough for you?'

Wilde nodded. 'It's hard to argue with that, given that it arrived while the plane was in the air.'

'Also,' Churchill continued, 'assassination by plane crash is an established technique of the Nazis. They even used it on their own man Fritz Todt when they wanted to replace him with Speer.'

'How was the Duke's plane brought down, Prime Minister?'

'It is difficult to be certain, but there are three theories. The first is that the oxygen supply was tampered with. It had been planned to fly the plane at ceiling altitude and so, without oxygen, the pilot and other members of the crew would have suffered hypoxia, become drowsy and lost consciousness. The second is that some sort of time bomb was planted to go off soon before arrival in Scotland. Another thought is that a small explosive device might have released a gas into the cockpit to incapacitate the crew, but post-mortem examination has not borne this out. Unfortunately, the wreckage of the plane was so extensive that it has not yet been possible for the investigators to come to a conclusion as to cause. It does, however, seem that the oxygen canisters were empty, which must point to the hypoxia theory. One thing is certain: a Nazi saboteur was to blame.'

'How would he or she have gained access to the Sunderland? Surely it would have been guarded for the whole of the Duke's visit?'

'That is a very good question and one for which I do not have an answer. The obvious thought would be a traitor in our own secret services attached to the Stockholm mission – someone perhaps linked to the egregious Mr Walter Quayle.'

Wilde nodded. It was hard to argue with the Prime Minister's version of events.

'Are you satisfied now, professor? And do you understand why the Duke's mission to Sweden must not be made public?'

'I do, Prime Minister, and I am profoundly grateful to you for receiving me and taking me into your confidence . . .'

'But? You are about to say *but*.'

'But I do feel more should be done to put a stop to the extermination of the Jews. If not, then it is possible European Jewry will be wiped from the face of the earth.'

Churchill's face took on its gravest attitude, the jowls dropped, even the cigar seemed to sag. Wilde was shocked to see tears in the man's eyes.

'I have spoken to your president about this,' Churchill replied slowly, his voice yet deeper and gruffer, almost choking with emotion. 'And we are agreed that for us to bring this to the fore while we are in a position to do precisely nothing would leave us looking desperately weak, and would play right into Hitler's hands. But I have granted you *The Times* piece, and we will leave it at that for the present. Later, perhaps next year, who knows? Good day, professor.'

Coburg tried the bedroom door. It was locked. This space in the bishop's old farmhouse had become a prison cell while he waited. There were half a dozen British guards outside, although he couldn't see them. Harriet was somewhere else in the house with the bishop. Occasionally she came to see him to bring food and refreshment and to talk.

'But what is to happen?' he had pleaded on her last visit.

'That is being decided, Rudi. Be patient. Your physical health is improving and your testimony *will* be broadcast to the world.'

'I'm going mad. My nights are filled with serpents and horror. I can't endure another one.'

She had taken him in her arms to comfort him, but he knew that she was repulsed by the film of cold sweat on his arms, his neck and face. He knew, too, that she was revolted by the knowledge of what he had done. Who wouldn't be? After a few seconds she had pulled gently away. She touched his face with the back of her hand and smiled at him. 'You will unburden yourself and you will be well again.'

'I don't think so,' he had said, head drooping to his chest.

'I'll be back soon. But you must wait here.'

Now here he was alone. It was late afternoon and the gathering clouds told him that night could not be very far away. A chest of drawers stood against the wall by the bed. He looked through them and found various garments. His nostrils were assailed by the pungent smell of camphor. He also found a small pair of nail scissors among other items, probably long forgotten. He took the scissors and placed them on the bedside table, then removed his shoes and curled up on the bed, on top of the counterpane.

The snakes came earlier today. It was only just dark when he saw them. Their hissing was louder, their movements quicker. He could smell their venom. Himmler was there, Hitler and Müller, too, writhing up the wall of the station house to the roof. He hadn't realised they could climb. He had thought he was safe from them all the while he was well above ground. But these three were rising and there was no escape. Eichmann was with them. He hadn't seen Eichmann until then. Where had he come from?

They were all over his body now, writhing as they attached themselves to him with their fangs, their forked tongues flicking and licking at his white flesh.

He couldn't move, could do nothing to stop Eichmann slithering up his chest to his exposed throat, then coiling his cold scales around his neck . . .

Wilde had been at *The Times* all afternoon discussing the interview with the designated reporter. They had agreed that Wilde would bring Coburg down to meet the man in the morning.

He arrived back at Red Farm just five minutes after Harriet found Coburg's dead body. It was obvious that he had used a pair of nail scissors to cut lengths of cord from the sash windows and had then hanged himself from a central beam.

Two members of the guard provided by Eaton were cutting him down and lowering him to the floor.

'Perhaps it was for the best,' Harriet said.

'For him, maybe – but what about the Jews in Poland? They needed his testimony. Now all we have is a batch of documents that will be denounced as meaningless forgeries.'

'He was broken, Tom.'

Chapter 45

It took Heinrich Müller a while, but he finally had his man. Hitler had taken some persuading that Prince Philipp von Hessen was a traitor, but he had got there in the end and it was worth the wait. Oh, the pleasure of seeing the horror on the entitled little lickspittle's face when he arrived under guard at Gestapo headquarters in Berlin.

The prince had been arrested at the Wolfsschanze, the Führer's war base in East Prussia. He and Hitler had dined together and talked as always. But then, in the hours before dawn, when Philipp tried to leave the fortified encampment to return to Berlin, he was taken into custody by an SS general on Hitler's orders.

Müller's drip-drip poison in his master's ear had achieved its aim. He laughed out loud when he heard.

Now, with the usually elegant prince standing shabby and bowed in front of him, Müller allowed himself a little time to simply gaze at the man and enjoy his terror and despair.

'You are not so arrogant now, are you?' he said at last. 'Eh?'

'I always tried to treat you courteously, Herr Gruppenführer Müller.'

'Did you indeed? Well, I don't remember that. So what should I call you now?'

'Forgive me, I don't understand the question.'

'Well, you are no longer a prince or a man of any importance in the Reich. Surely you understand that? You are one misstep from the guillotine or firing squad for your treason.'

'I have never betrayed—'

'Are you accusing the Führer of lying?'

'No, of course not.'

'Well, you are here at his behest. If he says you are guilty of treason, then that is the end of the matter.'

'But . . .'

'But nothing, prisoner. Stand up straight.'

Müller himself was sitting perfectly erect at the desk in his office while the prisoner stood before him in chains. Philipp immediately pulled back his shoulders and raised his chin.

'So, now that you are no longer a prince, what are we to call you? Choose a name, why don't you? Or perhaps you would like me to choose one for you. How about Weinberg? Herr Weinberg has a ring to it, don't you think?'

Philipp seemed to be trying to retain a little pride and dignity. 'If my name is to be changed by decree I would prefer to be called Wildhof, Herr Gruppenführer. It has family connections.'

'Very well, Herr Wildhof it will be. So what are we to do with you? Guillotine or firing squad? Judge Freisler often favours the guillotine, I believe.'

'Am I to be put on trial?'

'That will be for the Führer to decide. For the moment, you are to be taken from here to Flossenburg concentration camp near the mountains of eastern Bavaria.'

'Could I not be kept under house arrest?'

'Sadly not, but I am sure you will find Flossenburg extremely comfortable and pleasant. You will have a chance to mix with the ordinary criminals held there and get used to your new status.'

'Might I at least be allowed to know of what specific crime I am accused? If I am alleged to have committed some treason against Germany, you must produce the evidence and witnesses.'

'Must? Are you telling me what I *must* do, Herr Wildhof?'

'Forgive me, I phrased that wrongly. I am simply entreating you to give me a fair trial before I am condemned to a concentration camp.'

'And now you are compounding the felony by insinuating that the Führer is less than fair in the way he treats you! As for your guilt, you sat at the Führer's table and ate his food and now you doubt his word! Such perfidy! Such treachery! This will be reported to the Wolfsschanze directly, Herr Wildhof.'

'But what is my crime?'

'I am sure you know your crimes far better than I do. But let's start with the affair of Herr Rudolf Coburg, shall we? You helped him defect to our enemies, taking with him secret RSHA documents. I think that's quite enough, don't you?'

Müller slammed the palm of his hand on to a desk bell and two uniformed officers immediately entered the room.

'Take this man away – and have his records changed to show his name as Wildhof.'

The men treated him roughly, dragging him out to his fate. Müller allowed himself a little smile. One day, when Germany stood triumphant in England, he would surely mete out the same treatment to Professor Thomas Wilde. No one snatched a prisoner from under his nose or shot out his tyres before his very eyes and lived to an old age.

The wedding was held in their small parish church. It was organised as quickly as the law and church would allow so that summer would not wholly have given way to autumn, and it was a smaller, more intimate affair than it might have been because so many of their friends were away on war duties.

Wilde's deepest regret was that his mother could not make the journey from Boston, Massachusetts, but she had sent him an affectionate letter telling him it was the right thing to do – as if he hadn't known that for years – even if she would have preferred them to choose a Roman Catholic ceremony. But that aside, the most important thing was that she assured her son that Charlotte would approve.

Lydia had gone down on one knee in the living room to propose marriage. He had laughed at the sight of her and had accepted her offer with the proviso that this time she really meant it and would not leave him at the altar. It was then that she had brought up the subject of Charlotte.

'There is someone else here, Tom, two others. Do you think we have their blessing?'

'I know we do. She would have loved you.'

Charlotte had been his American wife. She had died in child-birth sixteen years earlier. His first son would have been sixteen if he had lived. Wilde knew that he and Charlotte would have become more terrified with each passing year because of the increasing possibility – likelihood – that the boy would be called up to fight in this bloody war.

'I would have loved her,' Lydia said.

'She was warm and kind.'

'I hope I am, too.'

'Sometimes you are. Today you are.'

The ceremony in the little fourteenth-century church was performed by a beaming Oscar Fry, delighted to come out of retirement to do this service for his new friend. They then returned to Cornflowers for a modest reception of tea, beer, cake and a case of whisky, sent by Lord Templeman with a short note wishing them well and suggesting this batch of

Scotch might make up for the ill-effects Wilde had suffered tasting the former sample. Wilde almost found himself forgiving the man.

It was a gentle and low-key reception with gramophone music and a little dancing in the living room, but none the less emotional for that. There was a touch of glitz, provided by a greatly recovered Mimi, who had been accompanied on the train up from London by Tallulah. Both of them were back in harness at the Dada Club, against doctor's orders in Mimi's case.

Despite the air of jollity and romance, Wilde's thoughts kept drifting. One thing nagged and had done ever since his meeting with Churchill. Why, he wondered, had Goebbels not broadcast the message loud and clear to the world that Germany had killed the Duke in retaliation for Heydrich's death?

It made no sense. It was in the very nature of the Nazi regime to enforce their will through terror, and they had gone out of their way to ensure everyone was aware of all the other foul acts of vengeance they had visited on the peoples of the occupied territories, to discourage resistance.

The only possibility that made any sense to Wilde was that the Nazis did not want to reveal that their man had been talking with the British in Stockholm. That, of course, was possible – but was that a feasible reason for not publicising their part in the Duke's death? Surely, they could have claimed responsibility for his murder without mentioning the purpose of his flight.

Which brought another question to mind. If it wasn't the Nazis, who else stood to gain from the plane crash? And why hadn't *they* claimed responsibility? The answer was obvious: Stalin. If he had got wind of the meeting between Britain and Germany, he would have seen it as treachery by an ally – and he would have been ruthless in nipping it in the bud: kill the Duke and blame the Germans. Anything to stop Britain and Germany signing a pact.

From what Churchill had said, the message warning of the plane had come in a couriered message to the British embassy in Stockholm. But how could they be sure who the courier was or who sent him? Perhaps it was from the Soviet embassy, using German headed paper?

And that led on to another unresolved question: who was in a position to sabotage the plane on Stalin's behalf?

Wilde tried to put these thoughts to the back of his mind. This was a day for love and laughter – and Johnny was undoubtedly the star of the show, running around the sitting room and demanding attention. He was a big hit with everyone.

After tea, there were toasts and a speech from Dr Rupert Weir, who indulged in a string of semi-obscene medical jokes and gave an indiscreet potted history of the newlyweds, wondering whether wedded bliss would be as satisfying as their six years of unwedded bliss.

Philip Eaton also proposed a toast, praising Lydia for 'finally making an honest man of Wilde' and apologising to Wilde for any discomfort caused by the 'adulterated whisky' – a reference that meant nothing to most of the guests.

A few days earlier, over dinner in Eaton's club, the MI6 man had confided in Wilde that, since Quayle's murderous attack at the bishop's house, he and Templeman had spoken with Harriet and had reassured themselves that she was no threat, and that the secret of the Duke's trip to Stockholm was safe. He mentioned, too, that they had worried that Harriet might be a traitor right to the very end. 'It was Quayle, after all, who proposed dear Harriet for the service in the first place.

That was a couple of years ago. He told us she was sound and had great attributes for the job – which of course she has. But when we began to worry about Quayle, we had to worry about her, too. That was why we went to such lengths to find her.'

'But she told me she had always loathed Quayle.'

'No reason to doubt it. She wouldn't have known who put her name forward. Anyway, we're happy now. She's proved herself.'

'But what,' Wilde had asked, 'was in it for Quayle? You have told me that his family owned coal mines in the north and farmland in Somerset and that he had untold wealth. Why would he betray the country that gave him all this?'

'Life was a game for Walter Quayle,' Eaton had replied, allowing his brandy to swirl in the glass. 'If the whole world walked one way, he walked the other. If his country was at odds with Germany, why then Germany would be his friend. I'm not sure if he had politics or principles.'

'And his little acolyte, Mortimer?'

'Who knows? Perhaps he was in love with his master.'

Now, at the wedding reception, Wilde took time to sit with Mimi and Tallulah. 'I have to say, you look a great deal better than you did when last I saw you, Miss Lalique.'

'Mimi. My name is Mimi. And I owe you a very big debt of gratitude, Tom, for I doubt I would be here today without you. So my wedding gift to you is a free pass for as many drinks as you like on the house at the Dada.'

'Then you will undoubtedly be seeing a lot of me while I'm in London.'

'We'll keep you to that,' Tallulah said.

She was sitting at Mimi's side on the sofa, with the two Pekingese snuffling around their feet. They had been discovered safe and sound at Battersea Dogs Home. Wilde's eye was once again drawn to the beautiful amber necklace at Tallulah's throat, the piece he had noticed when first he met her. 'Can't take your eyes off it, can you, Mr Wilde? Or are those my non-existent tits you're ogling?'

'I'm a married man now!'

'So's darling Dagger, but that doesn't stop him.'

'Templeman?'

'Didn't you know? He's my secret lover. Not a very big secret, really.'

'And he gave you the amber necklace?'

'He got it on one of his hush-hush missions. He told me it was from the banks of the Baltic and very precious and that I was to give him extra special treatment in return.'

Glenn Miller was playing on the gramophone and Tallulah's hand was claimed for a dance by one of the older college fellows. She blew Wilde a kiss and left him with Mimi.

'I take it Templeman is a bit of a regular at the Dada. Couldn't miss his towering figure in some of your glamorous photos.'

'Isn't he lovely? He adores the high life, which I always thought a little curious. You know, I always wondered if he was a bit of a leftie despite his great wealth, but he loved to come to the Dada and mix with the glamorous and the glitzy. It was so funny to hear him complaining about the decadence of the bourgeoisie . . . even as he quaffed fine Cognac and Dom Perignon. Champagne and socialism – strange how often they mix. I think it was probably like that in Moscow in the early days of the revolution.'

Templeman a leftie? Wilde had always wondered the same about Eaton. He had never been entirely certain about the MI6 man's true allegiances. He looked around the room for him and saw him leaning on his stick, deep in conversation with Harriet Hartwell and Lydia. Yes, something told him that Eaton had always held a torch for the Communists. But Templeman the millionaire?

Suddenly a gale of new questions built up in Wilde's mind. He shook his head. It didn't bear thinking about. Only a paranoiac would imagine that the British secret service was riddled with Communists.

And the likelihood that Templeman had been to one of the Baltic states – probably Sweden – what did that mean? Probably nothing, and it proved nothing. Of course he went on missions to such places; it was his job.

At last Wilde and Lydia found themselves alone together in the kitchen, and hugged. The last of the guests had departed, having bemoaned the fact that they couldn't give the newlyweds a proper send-off because they weren't going away. The honeymoon was two nights at home, then he would be back off to the OSS bureau in Grosvenor Street.

'I liked your beautiful friend,' Lydia said through tears.

'I could tell.'

'I said some horrible things but, you see, I knew you liked her and I was worried. I felt jealous.'

'You shouldn't have. Harriet's OK.' He smiled at her and brushed a tear from her cheek. 'It was very good of you to invite her. I think she was rather surprised and delighted.'

Lydia laughed through her sobs. 'I wanted to know my enemy. Anyway, she's too late – I've got you now.'

'You always had me.'

'I told her how wrong I had been to be jealous and she said no, I was right – because she would have grabbed you given half a chance. But she never had a hope, she said. You were the first steadfast man she had ever met. Oh, these stupid tears . . .'

'You're allowed them today.'

'You know, I shouldn't say it because it might sound mean or disrespectful, but I couldn't help wondering whether she's a little, what's the word, *savant*, perhaps? A little unworldly?'

'Maybe.' He kissed her again, and then the telephone rang.

'I'll get it and say you're out. It's bound to be bloody Phillips cutting short your break. Just like before.'

'No, I'll answer it. Don't worry, he's not getting me this time.'

Wilde sauntered out to the hall, hoping the phone would stop before he reached it, but it didn't. 'Hello,' he said. 'Wilde here.'

'Tom, is that really you?'

He knew the voice instantly, even though he had only heard it for a few hours of his life. 'Jimmy? Jimmy Orde?'

'Aye, it's me, Tom.'

'I thought you were dead. Torpedoed.'

'Aye, that we were. But we were lucky.'

'Well, thank God, thank God you're safe. You don't know how good this day is, Jimmy. I got married today and you've just given me the best present I could have hoped for.'

'Is that so? A married man? Oh, congratulations, feller, and my best wishes to the bride. Jeanie will be pleased as punch.'

'What happened with the attack? Did you lose the trawler?'

'Aye, that we did, but we had an ounce of good fortune. The first torpedo bounced off the hull and failed to explode. It gave us just enough time to get into the lifeboat before the second one hit. All we could do was sit and watch our beautiful trawler sink to the depths. We had no power in the lifeboat, and no oars, and so we drifted for days. But we're all safe home now, picked up by a Royal Navy frigate. Our rations were all gone, so they found us just in time.'

'You've been through a nightmare.'

'Maybe, but others fare a lot worse, so I won't be complaining. I have to say, though, there was something rum about it . . .'

'Go on.'

'I don't like to say it. You'll think I'm crazy.'

'Try me.'

'Well, you see, Tom, I know a bit about subs. My dad served in one in the Great War and I've always been interested in the things – even wanted to join the navy this time and volunteer for the submarine fleet, but I was deemed to be in a reserved occupation.' He paused. 'Anyway, the one that sank us – it had no markings and no flag. Just sitting there on the surface. Visibility was poor but it looked like a T-class boat to me. Couldn't swear to it, though, so I said nothing.'

'T-class? That's a type of U-boat, I take it?'

'No. The T-class is a Royal Navy model. Quite distinctive curve to the prow. In which case, I suppose they must have mistaken us for a German vessel. But it was dusk and, as I said, I couldn't see clearly.'

Wilde went cold. 'Have you said anything to anyone else?'

'No.'

'Well don't, Jimmy. I'll call you in a day or two.' He was about to put down the phone.

There was a click on the line.

He looked across the hallway to Lydia, standing there in her wedding finery, cradling their sleeping son.

He smiled at her, but he realised it was unconvincing. She knew him too well. He had experienced great happiness before, and it had been snatched away from him. Lydia carried the sleeping child towards him and he took them in his arms.

Historical Note

The story of Rudi Coburg is inspired by two men who did their best to alert the world to the horrors of the death camps as early as 1942. They are an SS officer named Kurt Gerstein and a Polish resistance fighter called Jan Karski.

Gerstein, the thirty-seven-year-old son of a judge from Münster, was both a Christian and a Nazi, having joined the party in 1933. But his relationship with the party was difficult. He was once beaten up by a group of Nazis for protesting against their anti-religious policies and was imprisoned twice – once in a concentration camp – for possessing anti-Nazi literature.

Despite this, he had powerful connections and managed to join the Waffen SS in 1941, later testifying that he had wanted to witness their actions from the inside.

In August 1942, when part of the hygiene section of the SS's medical department, he visited several concentration camps. At Belzec in Poland he witnessed the slaughter of a trainload of Jews by carbon monoxide. His recollection of the event is harrowing:

'Forty-five carriages arrived from Lemberg (now Lviv in Ukraine) carrying more than 6,000 people. Two hundred Ukrainians opened the doors and drove the Jews out with whips. A loudspeaker gave instructions: "Strip, even artificial limbs and glasses. Hand all money and jewellery in at the Valuables Window. Women and girls are to have their hair cut in the barber's hut."

Then the march began. Barbed wire on both sides, followed by two dozen Ukrainians with rifles. Christian Wirth (the camp commandant) and I found ourselves in front of the death chambers. Stark naked men, women, children and cripples passed by. A tall SS man in the corner called to the unfortunates in a loud voice: "Nothing is going to hurt you. Just breathe deep and it will strengthen your lungs. It's a way to prevent contagious diseases. It's a good disinfectant." They asked him what was going to happen and he answered: "The men will have to work, build houses and streets. The women won't have to do that. They will be busy with the housework and the kitchen."

The majority knew what was going to really happen; the smell betrayed it. They climbed a little wooden stair and entered the death chamber, most of them silently, pushed by those behind them. A woman of forty with eyes like fire cursed the murderers. She disappeared into the chamber after being struck by Wirth's whip. Many prayed. SS men pushed the men into the chamber. "Fill it up," Wirth ordered. Seven to eight hundred people in ninety-three square metres. The door closed. Heckenholt, the driver of the diesel whose exhaust was to kill these poor unfortunates, tried to start the motor. It wouldn't start. Wirth came up and whipped the Ukrainian who helped Heckenholt. My watch clocked it all. Fifty minutes, seventy minutes and the diesel would not start. You could hear them weeping in the chamber. The diesel engine started after two hours and forty-nine minutes. Twenty-five minutes passed. You could see through the window that many were already dead. All were dead after thirty-two minutes.

Jewish workers on the other side opened the wooden doors. They had been promised their lives for doing this horrible work. The people in the chamber were standing like columns of stone with no room to fall. Even in death you could tell the families, all holding hands. The bodies were tossed out. Two dozen workers were busy checking mouths which they opened with iron hooks. Dentists knocked out gold teeth with hammers. Captain Wirth was in the middle of them, in his element, showing me a big box filled with teeth. "See the weight in gold. Just from yesterday and the day before. You can't imagine what we find every day – dollars, diamonds, gold." Then the bodies were tossed into a big pit.'

The next day, Gerstein travelled on to Treblinka where he saw more gassings. Then on 22 August, he went by train back to Berlin. In the same compartment was a Swedish diplomat named Baron Göran von Otter. Gerstein, deeply distressed and weeping, told von Otter what he had witnessed at Belzec and Treblinka and begged him to alert the Allies so that they might act to stop the killings.

Von Otter had no doubt about the truth of what he had been told and later testified that he passed the story on to the Swedish government. But that was as far as it went. The Allies were not informed. It has since been suggested that this was because the Swedish government did not want to harm trade relations with Germany.

Gerstein spent the rest of the war trying to tell members of the Church in Germany and the Vatican what he had seen, but with little effect. In 1945, he gave himself up to the French but was treated as a Nazi war criminal. He committed suicide in his cell using a strip of blanket to hang himself.

Jan Karski's story is very different. He was a man of immense courage who survived torture by the Gestapo and the deaths of many friends and fellow Polish resistance fighters.

Born in Lodz, he was the youngest son of eight and was extremely gifted, with ambitions to become a diplomat. While at university, he enlisted in the reserve cadets of the Polish Horse Artillery and won the Sword of Honour. He began working in the foreign office but was called up to defend Poland when the

Germans invaded in 1939. After the occupation, he was taken prisoner by the Soviet army and narrowly escaped the Katyn Forest massacre of 30,000 Polish officers by Stalin's NKVD.

Returning home by a circuitous route, he became a vital courier for the Polish underground.

Captured by the Gestapo, his arms and legs were broken by iron bars. Again he survived and escaped and resumed his work for the resistance.

Aged twenty-eight, in the summer of 1942, he accepted an offer from Jewish leaders to witness the terrible conditions in the Warsaw ghetto at a time when the Nazis were taking daily transports of thousands of people from there to the death camps. The Jewish leaders made it clear they were certain that those being 'relocated to the East' were all, in fact, being murdered.

With ridiculous courage, Karski entered Belzec (or perhaps a sub-camp; this is uncertain) disguised as a guard and witnessed the horrors for himself. He then made an incredible journey across Nazi-occupied Europe, via Spain and Gibraltar to London, arriving in November 1942.

Among others, he met Foreign Secretary Anthony Eden, several important MPs and exiled Polish leaders. Eden was disgusted by the Nazi outrages, but lack of photographic or documentary evidence weakened Karski's case. In December, he contributed to a testament on behalf of the Polish government in exile, headed: THE MASS EXTERMINATION OF THE JEWS IN GERMAN OCCUPIED POLAND. This was sent to the twenty-six signatories of the United Nations. Later in the month, the BBC broadcast a speech by Edward Raczynski, Polish foreign minister in exile, in which he referred to the Nazis' 'final solution', based on Karski's testimony.

The BBC broadcast Karski's story again in May 1943, this time read on his behalf by the author Arthur Koestler (because Karski's accent was too strong for a British audience). Part of it said:

'From the ghettos the Jews are "taken East" as the official term goes, that is, to the extermination camps of Belzec, Treblinka and Sobibor. In these camps they are killed in batches of 1,000 to 6,000 by various methods, including gas. In the course of my investigation I succeeded in witnessing a mass-execution in the camp of Belzec. With the help of our underground organisation, I gained access to that camp in the disguise of a Latvian special policeman. I was in fact one of the executioners but I believe that my course of action was justified.'

Sadly, these broadcasts made little impact in the wider world.

From London, Karski went to America where he met President Roosevelt. Like Anthony Eden, the President was appalled, but for him too the lack of photographs was crucial. Also, there were powerful voices in America who did not believe the tales of atrocity, thinking them merely Polish propaganda to gain support in the West.

When Karski asked the President what message he could send back to Poland, Roosevelt said: 'Tell them that we are going to win the war and tell them that they have a friend in the White House.' It wasn't much. Karski then went to the United Nations where he placed his testimony on record before the War Crimes Commission.

Unlike Gerstein, Karski survived and thrived, staying in America and becoming a professor at Georgetown University. He gives extensive testimony in the nine-hour holocaust documentary film *Shoah*. Karski died aged eighty-six in 2000.

What Happened to Them?

Flight Sergeant Andrew Jack
Rear gunner and survivor of Short Sunderland 4026

He never spoke publicly about the actual crash – either because he had no recollection of it, or because he had been silenced by the two officers who visited him in hospital with papers to sign. In his statement to the court of inquiry he recalled being in thick cloud and thought the pilot was trying to get under it. 'I do not remember anything after this,' he said. He added that he did not know who was navigating or who was in the second pilot's seat. He later met the Duke of Kent's widow Princess Marina several times and remained in the RAF after the war, eventually leaving the service and becoming a telephone engineer. He died aged fifty-seven in the 1970s. However, in 2003 his niece Margaret Harris told the BBC that Jack had confided to his family that the Duke himself was piloting the Sunderland and that there was a mysterious extra person aboard the plane.

Prince Philipp von Hessen
Kaiser Wilhelm II's nephew and friend of Adolf Hitler

Philipp survived the war, but when he first fell from grace his future looked bleak. He later recalled his dismay at being interned at Flossenbürg in Bavaria: 'I had always believed that nobody could be put in a concentration camp without good reason, yet I was locked up without any grounds being given.' He was treated better than most prisoners, however, being allowed to remain in civilian clothes and eat the same rations as his SS guards. He had had many enemies in the Nazi hierarchy, including Himmler and Goebbels, and his bisexuality (he had a long affair with the British poet Siegfried Sassoon in the 1920s) did not endear him to the party. In April 1945 he was transferred to Dachau, but on liberation he was held by the Allies, having been ranked in the top hundred on the most-wanted Nazis list. He was tried and in 1947 sentenced to two years' forced labour and loss of thirty per cent of his property, later reduced on appeal. As a free man, he split his time between Germany and Italy, building up his art collection. He died aged eighty-three in 1980 in Rome. His wife Mafalda was the daughter of King Victor Emmanuel III of Italy. She was interned in Buchenwald concentration camp and died in 1944 following an Allied bombing raid on the adjacaent munitions factory.

Heinrich Müller
SS general and chief of the Gestapo

The Gestapo chief was one of the most senior Nazis whose fate was never known. Born in Munich in 1900, his father was a policeman and Müller himself became a police officer in the 1920s. Later, as chief of the Gestapo, he was not only deeply involved in police work but also took a leading role in organising the Holocaust. In the last weeks of the war, he was with Hitler in the bunker in Berlin, only leaving on 1 May 1945 after the Führer's suicide the previous day. Despite an extensive search by both British and American intelligence officers, Müller was never found. In 2013, a German historian, Professor Johannes Tuchel, claimed Müller died in Berlin at the end of the war and was buried in a mass grave, but his only evidence was the testimony of an East German gravedigger who said he recalled burying a man in general's uniform bearing the insignia that Müller would have had.

Hello!

Thank you for picking up *A Prince and a Spy*. It is a thriller that addresses difficult subjects, including the attempted annihilation of Europe's Jews. But it also looks at the theme of class in Hitler's tyranny. One of the alarming things I discovered while researching the book was the way in which the German aristocracy embraced Hitler and Nazism.

I knew that Prince Philipp von Hessen (related to both Kaiser Wilhelm II and the British royal family) was one of Hitler's few close friends until he fell from grace in the middle of the war. But I hadn't realised quite how many other members of the German nobility were paid-up Nazis. Records in the German Federal Archives show that 270 counts, dukes, and princes (and their female counterparts) belonged to the Party, at least two of them joining as early as 1928 – five years before Hitler came to power.

Nor were they the only members of the German elite who decided Hitler was the man for them. More than 40 per cent of medical doctors became Party members – the highest percentage membership of any profession. It is also well known that many top industrialists supported Hitler, including the giant Krupp and I. G. Farben industrial concerns.

Much of this information is to be found in *Royals and the Reich* by the historian Jonathan Petropoulos. It is a book that greatly assisted me in my research.

So, what was it about the Nazis that attracted these privileged people? The obvious answer is that they feared communism and the Soviet Union more than the thugs of the National Socialist Party. Perhaps they thought they could control Hitler and his henchmen and preserve their status, their bank balances and their estates. In the end, of course, they merely assisted in the destruction of their own country and the deaths of millions.

If you would like to hear more about my books, you can visit my website www.roryclements.co.uk where you can join the Rory Clements Readers' Club (www.bit.ly/RoryClementsClub). It only takes a few moments to sign up, there are no catches or costs.

Bonnier Zaffre will keep your data private and confidential, and it will never be passed on to a third party. We won't spam you with loads of emails, just get in touch now and again with news about my books, and you can unsubscribe any time you want.

And if you would like to get involved in a wider conversation about my books, please do review *A Prince and a Spy* on Amazon, on Goodreads, on any other e-store, on your own blog and social media accounts, or talk about it with friends, family or reader groups! Sharing your thoughts helps other readers, and I always enjoy hearing about what people experience from my writing.

Thank you again for reading *A Prince and a Spy*.

All the best,

Rory Clements

Rory Clements was born on the edge of England in Dover. After a career in national newspapers, he now writes full time in a quiet corner of Norfolk, where he lives with his wife, the artist Naomi Clements Wright, and their family. He won the CWA Ellis Peters Historical Award in 2010 for his second novel, *Revenger*, and the CWA Historical Dagger in 2018 for *Nucleus*. Three of his other novels – *Martyr, Prince* and *The Heretics* – have been shortlisted for awards.

To receive exclusive news about Rory's writing, join his Readers' Club at www.bit.ly/RoryClementsClub and to find out more go to www.roryclements.co.uk.